GEOGRAPHIES OF HOME

A Novel

Loida Maritza Pérez

VIKING

VIKING

Published by the Penguin Group
Penguin Books Ltd, 27 Wrights Lane, London W8 5TZ, England
Penguin Putnam Inc., 375 Hudson Street, New York, New York 10014, USA
Penguin Books Australia Ltd, Ringwood, Victoria, Australia
Penguin Books Canada Ltd, 10 Alcorn Avenue, Toronto, Ontario, Canada M4V 3B2
Penguin Books (NZ) Ltd, Private Bag 102902, NSMC, Auckland, New Zealand

Penguin Books Ltd, Registered Offices: Harmondsworth, Middlesex, England

First published in the United States of America by Viking Putnam 1999
First published in Great Britain by Viking 1999
1 3 5 7 9 10 8 6 4 2

Printed in Great Britain by Clays Ltd, St Ives plc

A CIP catalogue record for this book is available from the British Library

ISBN 0–670–86679–2

To my parents, for everything

To Bruce, of course

And to Melody, who would have lived

fiercely had she had the chance

Prologue

❖

Bienvenida's eyes flicked open during the last stanza of the song she had requested be sung to her on her deathbed. Tongue darting out to lick dry lips, she summoned her children nearer: Isidrio, Digna, Benite, Arelis, Eliazer, Obidia, Altagracia, Quintino, Rojelio, and—searching the room—Aurelia. When informed that her youngest daughter was not present, she turned to the chipped saints atop her bedside table. Her face furrowed with concentration. Her lips moved silently. Then, as if exhausted, she fell back against the pillows and closed her eyes.

In the province of Azua, Aurelia bolted upright and pulled the string of a lamp in time to see a large black cat jump from beneath the bedcovers and flee the room. The hairs on her neck bristled. Her heart beat faster.

All black cats in the rural town to which she'd moved were killed at birth.

Not wanting to alarm her husband, she climbed out of bed and went from room to room, searching under the beds of her sleeping children, in closets and on shelves. But the cat was nowhere.

When she returned to her room a bitter scent of freshly cut grass enveloped her. She tasted it on her lips and tongue, familiar as the dirt she had craved since the onset of her pregnancy. With it came an image of her mother turning the soil of the garden behind her childhood home.

"You're too young to speak of dying, Mami," she had said, following her indoors during her last visit. "Besides, I don't believe in spirits." This, in response to her mother's assertion that should any of her children be absent at the moment of her death she would find a way to let them know.

"Everyone dies," Bienvenida had murmured, ignoring her daughter's last remark and squeezing coffee from the cotton sock she used as a filter. "If not now, then later."

A sharp pain contorted Aurelia's body. Though she knew she should relax, she held her breath until the pain subsided.

"Madre mía, ayúdame," she prayed, propelling herself toward the bed.

The cat entered the room and flung itself against walls and chairs in a mad attempt to catch its tail. Aurelia's uterus convulsed—not as if the child inside were moving but as if the uterus itself were shrinking toward its center. Clutching the bedsheets, she tried to wake her husband.

"Papito," she called through clenched teeth. Another contraction doubled her over. "Papito!"

GEOGRAPHIES
OF HOME

CHAPTER

1

The ghostly trace of "NIGGER" on a message board hanging from Iliana's door failed to assault her as it had the first time she returned to her dorm room to find it. Just a few more hours and she'd be home. Already she breathed easier. She locked the door and mounted her suitcases on a cart her parents had let her keep after escorting her to Port Authority eighteen months earlier. Gripping the cart's handle, she dragged it along the corridor and bounced it, one step at a time, down the wide staircase. On another day she would have stepped quietly. But on her departure from the dormitory whose high ceilings and pale arches reminded her of a museum, she took pleasure in letting her steps echo loudly through the morning silence.

Depositing her keys in the Resident Assistant's mail slot, she stepped out into the cold and under the grey and low-slung sky. That sky's color was one of the reasons she was leaving. Its relentlessness put her on edge. She had chosen the university because of its location five hours from New York City—a distance too great for her parents to visit her as often as they had her brother in Albany. The campus was also reputedly one of the prettiest. From glossy photographs of the surrounding lakes and gorges, she had concluded that the university would be the ideal place to escape her parents' watchful eyes. She had not anticipated that, when not collapsing with rain or snow, the sky would nevertheless remain the same threatening shade.

She was also leaving because a voice had been waking her with news of what was taking place at home. The accounts had started several months earlier and, depending on the news, had lasted until dawn. It had gotten so that she rarely slept. As soon as her head touched her pillow the disembodied voice crept close. On hearing it for the first time, her eyes had flashed open, her heart had slammed against her ribs. Hadn't her father warned her?

"Mi'ja," he'd said, drawing her attention as she prepared to board the Greyhound bus and continuing in Spanish, the only language he and Aurelia spoke. "Find a church. There must be one around there. Don't let what happened to your sister Nereida happen to you too."

"I'll keep in touch," was all her mother had said.

Hugging both, Iliana had assured them that she would remain faithful.

"Seven spirits," Papito had added urgently. "Seven evil spirits at your side if you should stray from God. Remember!"

In the single room she had considered herself lucky to obtain, Iliana had remembered. Not only had she neglected waking early to catch the bus to the Seventh-Day Adventist church in town, she had also gone to the local bar and, for the first time ever, to the cinema, where Satan preyed on souls.

"Get thee behind me, Satan," she had commanded the voice, relying, without conviction, on the exhortation she had been taught repelled evil spirits.

"Stop that foolishness, Iliana María!"

The voice was her mother's—authoritative but hinting mischief as when she had taught her to dance merengue on a Sabbath morning while the rest of the family attended church.

Hands trembling, Iliana stumbled out of bed to dial her parents' number.

"Iliana María?" Aurelia asked, instantly identifying her daughter's silence.

Iliana slammed down the receiver.

"Don't be afraid, mi'ja," the voice said, defying the distance Iliana had deliberately placed between herself and her mother. "The devil exists, but it's not me."

Shivers unraveled along Iliana's spine. She willed the voice to go away, but it persisted, hounding her as her mother's had at home. It spoke of her brother Emanuel's visit from Seattle; of the two eldest, Mauricio and Chaco, who, with their families, had moved back to the Dominican Republic; of the dream that had inspired Nereida to be rebaptized after an absence of years from church; of the flowers in their Brooklyn yard; of the vegetables growing so well that the corn reached past Papito's head.

"The Lord is my light and my salvation. Whom shall I fear?" Iliana recited, her voice scraping against her suddenly dry throat so that it sounded barely above a whisper. "The Lord is the strength of my life." Her dilated eyes searched the darkened room. "Of whom shall I be afraid?"

Faintly, so that she strained to hear it, the voice returned.

"Forgive, mi'ja. I didn't think you'd be afraid. You know we can't speak much on the phone. It's too expensive. Your father would be angry."

Cowering beside her bed, Iliana recalled her mother's ears. Those ears, with holes pierced during a past Aurelia rarely spoke of, had both frightened and intrigued her. Raised in a religion which condemned as pagan the piercing of body parts, she had imagined that, were her mother's clogged holes pried open, she would transform into a sorceress dancing, not secretly on a Sabbath when she stayed home by feigning illness, but freely, unleashing impulses Papito's religion had suppressed. This image had sharpened whenever Aurelia had undone the braids wound tightly around her head. At such moments, before Iliana's intruding eyes caused her to braid the cascading locks into submission, she had smiled at her own reflection shifting from an aging matriarch's to that of a young girl's with hoops dangling from her ears.

This memory evoked others to which Iliana had previously attached no significance: Aurelia waking restlessly before dawn to scrub clean floors; Aurelia wringing sheets dry with a strength that defied exhaustion; and Aurelia slicing onions, a sharpened knife blurring dangerously toward her thumb at a speed which would have resulted in the loss of a finger had anyone else attempted it.

This incessant activity, even at moments when she might have opted to relax, now suggested an effort to contain forces struggling to escape.

Initially the visitations had occurred sporadically. But as the racial slurs began appearing on Iliana's door, they increased in frequency. Though unable to explain the phenomenon, she became convinced that the voice was in fact her mother's. When she called home, Aurelia began conversations where the voice had left off the previous night. If asked about events never discussed on the phone, she responded without hesitation.

Everything Iliana had been brought up to believe denounced the voice as evil. Yet her instincts persuaded her it wasn't so. On nights when the radiator in her room gave off little warmth, the voice transported her to a Dominican Republic where summer days were eternal, clouds evaporated in the scorching heat, and palm trees arched along beaches of fiery sand. It spoke of her birth immediately following her grandmother's death; of how she should have been a boy since her sex had been predicted from the shape of Aurelia's pointy stomach and all her siblings had been born to form alternate pairs of the same sex, a sequence only Iliana had disrupted; of how, although Mauricio and Chaco, Rebecca and Zoraida, Caleb and Emanuel, Nereida and Azucena, Vicente and Gabriel, Marina and Beatriz had each been born two years apart, she herself had refused to come until three years after Beatriz and three before Tico, the youngest child.

There, in the attic room of the university whose hilltop location contrived to make her forget the rest of the world and whose courses disclaimed life as she had known it, making her feel invisible, the voice reassured Iliana of her own existence and kept her rooted. She learned that during her absence both her parents had been diagnosed as having alarmingly high blood pressure and that Papito, afraid of dying, had resorted to taking his and his wife's prescribed pills while she refused her own; that Rebecca's accounts of Pasión's abuses had caused Aurelia's heart attack; that Marina, wishing to have her future told, had visited an astrologer to later claim that he had raped her; that Beatriz had left home and not been heard of since; that Vicente had dropped out of graduate school and his wife had packed her things and left him; that Tico rarely left his room; that Laurie had supposedly refused to sleep with Gabriel throughout their first two years of marriage and Gabriel, during one of his frequent, short-lived spurts of religious fervor, had confessed to the pastor and then to Caleb of his adulterous affair with Linda, Caleb's common-law wife; that Caleb had turned his gun in to his parents' custody for fear of killing his own brother; and that Marina had suffered a nervous breakdown.

It was these events, more than her disappointment with the university, which had convinced Iliana to leave school.

She avoided the icy path leading from her dormitory and cut across the lawn. Brittle grass crunched beneath her feet as she headed toward a cluster of buildings on North Campus. Except for a few other students, the campus was desolate. It was at such moments that she enjoyed it most. She was able to walk, unashamed of the stride that had caused her grief since childhood and that she had tried her damnedest to change since then. But, no matter what, her hips thrust forward and swayed as if unhinged. Her friend Ed had described the stride as regal, her sisters as whorish. And it was they whom Iliana tended to believe. Wanting to appear confident, she had taken to walking with her head held high and her eyes staring straight ahead. This, combined with shyness, had gotten her labeled an arrogant bitch. Whenever she had attended parties, even those sponsored by minority organizations, she had never been asked to dance. And when she had attended with Ed, rumors had spread that she dated only white men.

If the rumors hadn't hurt so much, Iliana would have laughed. Not only had no one—black, white, yellow or red—ever asked her out, Ed was Mexican and preferred to sleep with men.

She climbed the steps to his dormitory and called him from the courtesy phone. It seemed to ring interminably before his roommate answered.

"Paul, is Ed there?"

"Holy shit! What time is it?"

"It's almost seven-thirty. We're supposed to catch the bus at eight."

Paul dropped the phone on the other end. "Ed, get up. Iliana's on the phone. Ed, I'm not telling you again!"

Minutes elapsed before he returned to the phone. "I'll let you in on my way out," he said, clicking off before Iliana could respond.

She stamped her feet in an attempt to keep them warm. Just as she was about to redial, Paul flew past her, barely letting her catch the door.

"I can't talk. I have an exam at eight and fell asleep at my desk."

"Well, goodbye to you too," Iliana said.

He whirled around and hurried back to her. Smiling sheepishly, he gave her a hug and kissed her cheek. "I'm sorry. I forgot. You're not coming back, are you?" He released her and ran off, slipping on a patch of ice. "Maybe you'll change your mind," he yelled. "Home is never fun."

Iliana watched him: his limbs flailing awkwardly; his green hair blowing like a tuft of grass. Not long ago, he had asked her to bleach his hair and dye it blue. The peroxide he had insisted she leave on longer than the required time had left his scalp lined with welts and his dark hair a yellow that had turned green with the bright-blue dye.

She would miss him, crazy though he was.

Iliana pulled the cart into the dormitory and stepped into the waiting elevator. From the lounge on the third floor, she saw Ed's door ajar and his body still in bed.

"Shit, Ed. Can't you ever get up on time?"

He peered at her through slitted eyes. "What time is it?"

"There's a clock right beside you."

"Oojale, what's gotten into you this morning?"

"What's gotten into me? You! It's seven-thirty and you're in bed!"

"Will you relax? It'll only take me a few minutes to get ready."

"Whose idea was it to take the early bus? Who insisted I make it here on time?"

"Ay mujer! Ya!"

The authoritativeness of Ed's voice jarred Iliana into silence. Maybe he was right. Maybe she was overreacting. So what if she had spent most of the night packing and had woken early at his insistence? What was the use of clinging to anger because he had accidentally overslept?

She watched him clamber out of bed. As he strolled past her toward the communal baths, he beamed her an impish grin. Its patronizing curve affected her like burrs prickling her skin. It dawned on her then that, should he have been the one to be kept waiting, he would have had a fit. Yet with his "Ay mujer!" he had effectively dismissed her anger. Worse, he knew how she hated those two words, how they reminded her of her father's "Mira, muchacha!"

As clearly as if it had occurred the previous day, she recalled one of the few times she had stood up to Papito. He had just purchased a box of soaps for her mother and had proudly held one out for her to inspect.

"Ummm," she'd said, flattered that he was showing her the gift before presenting it to Aurelia. "It smells like cinnamon."

"Mira, muchacha! Don't you see the strawberries on the wrapper?"

Iliana took the soap from his hand and moved it closer to her nose. "I know, Papi, but it smells like cinnamon."

Papito snatched the soap from her hand and raised it to his own nose. "Strawberries," he insisted. "Strawberries."

"Strawberries aren't spicy."

"What are you saying, that I waste my money buying garbage?"

"Maybe someone mislabeled them," Iliana said. "How were you supposed to know? And the cinnamon isn't bad."

Papito jerked her head closer to the soap. "Strawberries! This is a strawberry-scented soap!"

Iliana again sniffed the soap pressed suffocatingly to her nose. "But to me it smells like cinnamon."

Before she knew what was happening, her father's calloused hand had slapped her face.

"Muchacha de la porra! Admit it! It smells like strawberries!"

"Cinnamon," Iliana mumbled.

"What does it smell like?"

Iliana defiantly braced herself for another blow. "Cinnamon!"

The back of Papito's hand again flew toward her face. Determined not to cry or cringe, Iliana held her ground.

"It smells like cinnamon! Why ask if you don't want to know?"

Her father unhooked his belt and drew it from the loops around his pants. "Sinvergüenza! I'll teach you to disrespect me!"

"Cinnamon—" Iliana had shouted, blocking out the sound of the belt whizzing toward her and glaring at her father with all the contempt that she could muster. "Cinnamon, cinnamon—" she had chanted, her legs stinging and welts rising as the leather strap landed repeatedly on her thighs. "It smells like cinnamon, not strawberries!"

Iliana removed her coat and plopped down onto David's bed. Here it was a year and a half since she'd left home and still certain words triggered self-doubt and left her mute, still she feared the consequences of asserting herself. Her eyes strayed to her suitcases waiting by the door. When packing, she had reluctantly given away the items she dared not take home with her: skirts which, though just above her knees, would have been judged indecent; flat shoes, all except for the boots on her feet, for which she would have been called matronly by sisters who already considered her an old maid; clip-on earrings she had secretly begun to wear; and all her books, including those required for courses and others she had read voraciously without fear of her father's throwing them away.

Only now did she realize the implications of her decision to go home. Throughout all her planning she had mostly thought of taking her family by surprise. She had not stopped to consider that by returning she would be relinquishing her independence. Not only would she have to live according to her father's dictates, she would also have to join him in Bible study, attend church on Saturdays, and listen to his sermons if her face but revealed an expression interpreted as defiant. Should she neglect any of these matters, her name would be brought up for prayer before the congregation.

Even now, remembering the first time its prayers were solicited in her behalf, Iliana's conscience pricked with guilt. She had been only seven and had decided that she did not want to go to school. Knowing that if she postponed being sick until morning her mother would suspect she was faking, she had moaned and tossed in bed during the night. One of her sisters notified their mother. Alarmed when Iliana unwittingly pointed to the location of her appendix as the area where it hurt, Aurelia woke Papito. The two of them knelt beside Iliana and, with hands joined at her side, prayed that God too might place His hand on her to heal her.

The following morning Aurelia insisted on taking her youngest daughter to see a doctor. Terrified that her lie would be discovered and already imagining the sting of her father's belt, Iliana developed a fever. By the time they arrived at the clinic she appeared to be in so much pain and was perspiring so heavily that the doctor, after a cursory examination, decided that she indeed had appendicitis. Fearing that her appendix would burst before an ambulance arrived, he drove mother and daughter to a hospital himself.

As they drove across the Williamsburg Bridge, the sight of Manhattan—a city Papito had often compared to Sodom and Gomorrah—increased Iliana's fear. Although she had not fully understood what he'd meant when he'd said men on that island slept with other men and women with women (hadn't she herself slept with her sisters?), she had concluded that Manhattan too would be destroyed. So real to her was the possibility of being caught in that hell and burning with other sinners that she began to cry.

The doctor, lips stretching into a line more a grimace than a smile, turned to face her from the front seat. "You need to be brave," he said. "You're a big girl now." Then, switching from broken Spanish to English as if confiding a secret he preferred Aurelia not to understand, he added, "It'll be just like a vacation. You won't have to go to school. You'll even get to watch as much TV as you want and eat in bed. That's not so bad, is it?"

His intimate tone convinced Iliana that he knew she had lied and was only taunting her. She mistrusted his eyes, icy blue and dull like metal, which, lacking depth, made him appear to have no soul. Looking at him, his hair shimmering golden in the sunlight slanting through the car window, she believed he was Satan's angel sent to take her off to hell.

"Don't let him take me, Mami," she sobbed. "Please don't let him take me. I'm feeling better. It honestly doesn't hurt anymore."

"Sssh. Don't cry. Everything's going to be okay," Aurelia said, gently squeezing the hand she had held since dragging Iliana, kicking and screaming, into the back seat.

Iliana was hospitalized for four days, throughout which family and church members prayed for her recovery. After the fourth day, the doctors, finding no symptoms of appendicitis, released her to her parents. Convinced that God had performed a miracle in her behalf, Papito donated flowers to the church every Saturday until the one-year anniversary of her recovery. Worse, the pastor forevermore portrayed her as a living example of God's care toward those who believed in Him in a modern, wicked age.

Remembering, Iliana wondered that her lie had never been detected. Either she was a magnificent actress or her parents had been determined to teach her a lesson she would not forget. She tended to believe the former. But if the second were the truth, the lesson learned had not been the one intended. More than realizing the disastrous consequences of lying, she had discovered that authorities, as personified by her parents, the doctors and the pastor, were not as knowledgeable as she'd believed. Furthermore, because throughout the years her father had silenced any questions that challenged life as he perceived it, she had learned to agree with everything he said while secretly composing answers of her own. Only by leaving home had she, on occasion, acquired the confidence to express her opinions, and she feared that by returning she would fall silent once again.

"That didn't take too long, did it?"

Iliana barely turned toward Ed.

"Listen, I have an idea," he said. "Why don't you stay with me before going to your parents' house? They're not expecting you, and I've got Susan's apartment to myself for the entire month."

Iliana shook her head.

"Why not? It'll give you a chance to adjust to being back."

"Ed, I can't. I might run into one of my brothers or sisters on the street."

"I thought you said they all lived in Brooklyn."

"Most of them do, but several work in Manhattan and they'd be quick to jump to conclusions if they caught me out with you."

"Oh, come on. It'd be so much fun. We could go to museums and galleries, then hit the clubs at night. It's a big city. What are the chances of running into them?"

The resentment Iliana had been harboring toward Ed surfaced as she left him to stand before a window. He behaved as if each moment were his to enjoy without guilt or fear of consequence. In contrast, she snatched what little pleasure she could from an ever-watchful God. Each time she allowed music to sway her body, went to the cinema or even had a sip of coffee, she was hounded by the idea that she risked her eternal soul. It didn't matter that she had long since stopped believing in God, or at least in the God her father claimed. The possibility of that God's judgments neverthe-less preyed on her fears. Each night, before drifting into sleep, she reluctantly knelt beside her bed to plead for her soul should He in fact exist.

"You don't understand, Ed. I'd be so paranoid that I wouldn't have any fun. Besides, I'm already nervous enough about going back without setting myself up for trouble."

"You're not having second thoughts, are you?"

Iliana stared glumly out of the window. She trailed a finger along the dusty sill, then rubbed the dirt onto the glass.

"You okay?"

"I just have a premonition, that's all."

"About what?"

"Oh, I don't know. I just think I'm fooling myself. I mean— I've come to hate this place so much that I've convinced myself I should take a year off and help with all the shit going on at home. I've even flattered myself by thinking I'll be welcomed with open arms. But that's pretty funny, considering we were never one big, happy family to begin with."

"Don't go, then," Ed said matter-of-factly.

Iliana whirled around to face him. "Hell is breaking loose at home! How the fuck am I supposed to stay and pretend everything's okay?"

Surprise elongated Ed's already narrow face. "I'm sorry. I only thought—"

His apologetic tone deflated Iliana's anger. Shoulders hunched, she slid under the window and let fall the tears that, years earlier and in defiance of her father's beatings, she had vowed to suppress at whatever cost.

"Are you sure you don't want to stay with me?" Ed asked, attempting to draw her near only to have her raise a hand to stop him. "At least for a couple of days?"

Iliana wiped the tears she hadn't wanted him to see. "Waiting isn't going to make it any easier."

Ed watched her, not knowing what else to do or say.

"I'm okay," Iliana mumbled. "You know I always am."

CHAPTER

❖ 2 ❖

The sound was so faint that Marina thought she had imagined it. But no—if there was one thing she could trust, it was her senses. She had trained herself to use them well. Slipping naked from her bed, she exited her basement room and followed the sound through darkness up the stairs. She then swung open the kitchen door and stepped inside. Again, she heard what sounded like scurrying feet, and so clearly that she wondered why her parents, asleep in an adjoining room, hadn't heard it. That they hadn't convinced her of what she had long suspected: their vigilance was growing weak.

"Be sober, be vigilant: because your adversary the devil walketh about seeking whom he may devour," she reminded herself, reaching for the light switch.

What she saw as her eyes adjusted to the sudden glare chased a shiver up her spine. She seized a towel off a chair and beat the wall near a door leading to the backyard and another to her parents' room. Several of the large, black spiders fell, but more teemed in from under the backyard door to continue weaving a web that already extended toward the ceiling. With an agility surprising for her massive body, she darted to the sink under which her father stored cans of lighter fluid. Careful to spill none on herself, she doused and flung a lit match at the wall. The flames caught the dark wood paneling as if it were kindling and traveled swiftly toward the ceiling.

"Dios mío! The house is burning," her mother screamed.

Marina dashed to the door her father had salvaged from a demolished building. Securing the latch he had installed so that his wife could shut it from the kitchen to prevent cooking smells from seeping into their bedroom, she trapped them in their room.

Aurelia struggled with the door. "Wake up, Papito!"

"It's okay. I've got it under control," Marina reassured, seeing her mother's panicked face distorted by the light of flames and peering through a small window on the door.

"Open the door, Marina Elena!" Papito commanded. "Marina Elena!"

Marina instead fanned the flames to make them spread. "I think I've killed most of them!" she announced, excitement rippling her voice.

Her father's fist smashed through the window. His bloody fingers groped for the latch. When the door flew open, Marina hurled herself against him and knocked him to the floor. She straddled him between her thighs and simultaneously reached out for Aurelia. Papito yanked his daughter down on top of him. His wife rushed past them to the sink. Filling pots with water, she flung them at the flames.

"Are you crazy?" Marina shrieked, attempting to free herself from her father's grip. "Don't you see them? Have you gone blind?"

Smoke swirled through the room as Aurelia splashed water on walls, the ceiling, the furniture, even her husband and daughter struggling on the floor. Gabriel and Laurie rushed into the room. Gabriel, believing that his sister had attacked their father, hauled her off Papito. Laurie, embarrassed by her sister-in-law's abundant breasts, raised a hand to her lips and laughed.

"What the hell's so funny?" Marina yelled.

Aurelia refilled another pot with water and continued to douse the room. Papito got up clumsily from the floor and encircled her in his arms. "Ya, Aurelia. You put the fire out."

She drew away from him and collapsed into a chair. Her body jerked with the adrenaline coursing through her veins. "Maybe the doctors were right," she gasped. "We can't—we can't keep an eye on her all the time."

"Marina set the fire?" Gabriel asked, incredulous.

Laurie sidled up to him. "Look at her. She's not crazy. She's faking it for attention."

"You could've killed us! Do you realize that?" Gabriel shouted.

His sister's eyes flamed like the fire she had set. "All of you are going to burn in hell! Burn! Next time evil comes into this house, it can carry you all off for all I care! Especially you!" she shrieked at Gabriel. "You're the worst of them! Fucking your brother's wife and pretending to be devout!"

"That's enough, Marina Elena!" her father warned.

"You think I don't know the shit all of you have done? I can recount your sins one by one and tell them to your face!"

Gabriel's left eye, smaller than his right since being hit by a stray baseball, narrowed to a slit. "What she needs is a belting. She'd learn some sense real quick."

"Didn't I tell you?" chimed in Laurie. "She knows exactly what she's saying."

"You're damn right I know what I'm saying! Unlike the crazy members of the family you married Gabriel to escape from because nobody else would have you!"

Laurie's green eyes widened. Her face turned a quick red. Unable to think of a response, she glanced at Gabriel, then at his parents, as if expecting them to come to her defense. When no one did, she jerked her head and, whipping her husband with her hair, stormed out of the room.

"Then you wonder why she wants nothing to do with this family," Gabriel exclaimed. "What do you expect if whenever she comes down here someone in this house insults her?"

Aurelia rose from her chair and unfurled to her full height: several inches shorter than any of her children; tall enough to intimidate even the oldest. In a tone that made it clear she expected to be obeyed, she commanded Marina to go downstairs.

"I'll go," Marina said, her eyes brimming malice. "But don't waste your breath praying for me before you go to sleep. Save it for your damned self and your other children."

After Marina left, Aurelia turned to face her son. "How old are you?" she asked.

"Twenty-six," he replied, as if his age were reason enough for her not to address him as a child.

"And how many of those years have you known your sister?"

"Twenty-four."

"And Laurie?"

"What?"

"How long have you known her?" Aurelia repeated.

"What does that have to do with anything?"

"You've known her for five, maybe six years, isn't that right? Yet you have the nerve to stand here in my house and let some stranger—I don't care if she is your wife—tell you who and what your sister is. Do you think Marina would shamelessly expose herself or act the fool if she were in her right mind? Do you think she would purposefully try to hurt us or herself?"

"She should be locked up, then. Look what she just did."

Aurelia watched Gabriel for a long and steady while. Then, as if gathering strength to keep from doing wrong, she ushered him to the door. "When you have children I'll consider taking your advice. Till then I suggest you go upstairs and work on your marriage. It has problems of its own."

Marina immediately made him out: a tall, lean figure absorbing the room's darkness so that he appeared only as a blacker silhouette standing still beside her bed. Her instinct was to run. Yet she could barely breathe, much less move. And she knew that if she screamed her parents would claim that she was crazy, that no one else was there. Eyes adjusting to the dark, she cursed them for not heeding her warnings. They had betrayed her. Having doubted evil, they had welcomed it into their home. Now there it stood: the embodiment of her worst fears. She had known it would arrive. But not so soon, not for her, not as the man who'd raped her. She recognized the shape of his body and its stench—an odor of rotting greens she had been incapable of forgetting.

Paralyzed by fear, she watched him raise his arms. As he reached forward, her will dissolved and her body collapsed onto the floor. A hand clamped onto her mouth. Another held her down.

"You want to know your fate?" he had asked the first time. "Here it is!"

The cold steel of his zipper cut into Marina's hips. His penis found an entry. Shutting her eyes against the searing pain, she attempted to hurl him off.

"Look at me!" he yelled, tightening his mount and jamming into her so that it felt as if he would exit through her mouth. "Look at me, you fucking bitch!"

Marina felt herself fragmenting and her limbs recoiling from her desecrated flesh. She gathered what remained of her strength and sunk her teeth into his palm. Oblivious to the blood seeping from his hand, he continued to pound into her. Her pain was so intense that she expected her body would release its soul. Yet the reserve of energy which had surfaced each time she had slit her wrists or overdosed on pills refused to let her die.

The man grew unexpectedly still inside her. When she dared imagine he had finished, he gripped her hips and thrust himself deeper into her womb. Her stomach convulsed with nausea. Her thoughts scattered. Unable to see his face, she detailed it from memory so as to draw courage from her hate.

No flat-nosed, wide-lipped nigger would claim her soul. No savage with beads dangling from his neck. She would survive all this. There was nothing else to lose. Nothing else to fear.

Marina's thoughts bypassed the blame she had heaped on herself for visiting an astrologer and for remaining despite encountering, not a woman with a turban wrapped around her head, but a man with dreads coiled tight as if to strike: a black man who had divined her loneliness and had predicted the coming of a dark stranger like himself; a seer who became enraged when she said no—surely a white man or at least a light-skinned Hispanic like herself would come into her life.

Her destiny could still be changed. She had realized the dangers of courting evil and of not trusting God to provide answers to her questions. She would beg His forgiveness and survive with her faith intact. She would live to be His instrument and to point out evil wherever it appeared. Her body might be snatched, but not her soul. And her body was merely dust. It did not consist of who she was.

Marina opened her eyes and searched the room. Detecting only darkness, she pushed herself off the floor. She was careful not to let her thighs meet or her arms touch her torso as she went into the bathroom. Behind its closed door and beneath the glare of a fluorescent light, she inspected herself before a full-length mirror. Blood congealed on her lower lip. Bruises swelled throughout her body. Yet she knew that if she informed her parents of what had taken place they would insist that she had dreamed it all, that in the throes of a nightmare she had sunk her teeth into her lips and fallen off the bed. But proof of the events was in her aching body, in its tenacious, rotting smell. Each time she inhaled, nostrils flaring to detect its source, the odor wafted toward her from all directions—her hair, her skin, the roof of her mouth when she raised her tongue to scratch it—confirming that something putrid had been implanted deep inside her and emitted its stench through all her pores.

The longer she watched herself the more repulsed she became. Before, she had been able to manipulate her reflection so as to see only her pale skin shades lighter than any of her sisters' and only slightly darker than Gabriel's wife. That skin color had blinded her to her kinky, dirt-red hair, her sprawling nose, her wide, long lips. Now those features appeared magnified, conveying to her eyes that she was not who she'd believed.

Filled with self-loathing, Marina turned on the hot water in the shower. When its steam obliterated her image in the mirror, she collected a razor, a can of Lysol, several Brillo pads from under the sink, and stepped into the stall. Even in the shower the stench pervaded—sharp—as of vegetables which had remained in a dark, damp place too long. Determined to rid herself of the odor and to reclaim her defiled body, she reached soapy fingers into the folds between her legs. Wincing, she worked the lather into her inner walls, then shaved her pubic hairs as well as those under her arms.

The wiry hairs clung to her thighs and breasts, resisting the scalding water's flow and prickling her skin. She picked them off one by one. When her body was hairless as a baby's, she adjusted the showerhead so that the water burst forth in pelting streams. She meticulously scoured herself with Brillo, lingering behind her knees, under her arms, in the inside of her elbows. When her skin blistered and she could stand the pain no more, she stepped from the stall and sprayed herself with Lysol.

CHAPTER

3

Aurelia hushed the birds pecking insistently on the kitchen window. Opening it just wide enough to fit her hand, she threw fistfuls of leftover rice onto the snow. Despite the cold, her hand lingered on the ledge, outstretched fingers feeling the wind as if to divine from its texture what the day would bring. She had woken later than usual. Already the sun was up, casting a dim, grey light over her backyard. She was able to make out the pigeons scrambling for rice beneath the window and, further back, the now withered leaves of the corn her husband had planted the previous spring. She had been furious when he'd ripped out the sunflowers growing wild, leaving only the roses she had tended carefully so they'd twine about the wire fence. But she had since come to understand. When Papito had turned the soil of the garden with bare hands, had watched his seeds take root, had pulled weeds from around their base, he had been able to forget the problems which, despite his care, had cropped up to choke his own life and his children's. It had not mattered that the garden was small and visible from the windows of neighboring houses or that his children thought him insane for planting vegetables in a Brooklyn yard. The garden had served the same purpose for him as feeding pigeons did for her.

She scraped remains from the bottom of a pot and offered a last handful to the pigeons. As if to show their annoyance at being fed so late, not one hopped onto the ledge to eat from her palm. She let the rice trickle through her fingers and closed the window.

Several of the pigeons glared at her with beady eyes before gathering the grains.

Ungrateful, cocky birds. They behaved as if feeding them were her duty. She had often worried that they were becoming too dependent and would be unable to feed themselves once she died. But the fact that they were resourceful enough to wake her up each morning convinced her otherwise. They were perfectly capable of caring for themselves.

Nostrils assailed by the lingering smell of smoke, Aurelia turned from the window to inspect the damage to the kitchen. Several panels were scorched and smoke-stained. At their base, singed linoleum tiles curled like parchment. She lifted a foot and brought it down on the linoleum edges. When they crumbled, she ground the ashes into the mud-green floor. Just looking at the damage made her want to return to bed and pretend that the previous night's events had never taken place. Yet she did not allow herself the luxury. She had too many chores to do and pretending that life had dished out all the bad it could and was about to let her rest was not one of them.

Five years ago when her husband had purchased the dilapidated, condemned building with the three hundred dollars he had hidden in a woman's purse under their bed, Aurelia had not imagined that one of their children would try to burn it down. Not when it had kept them from the streets. Not when it was the only house in their adopted country which they had been able to call their own. Instead, she had expected each family member to feel secure in the knowledge that never again would they be cramped into a three-room apartment like their first or be evicted as they had from their last. But what Marina had conveyed by setting fire to the kitchen was that the house, like the life she had previously attempted to destroy and which her parents had tried to ensure was better than their own, meant little.

So often Aurelia and Papito had considered returning to the Dominican Republic but had remained in the United States to be near their married children and because their youngest, remembering little of their birthland, considered it a backward, poverty-ridden place. Now she wondered if by emigrating they had unwittingly caused their children to yearn for a wealth generally portrayed as easily accessible to anyone in the States. Of no comfort was the knowledge that she and Papito had tried their best. There had been too many circumstances they had been unable to control, too much they had been unable to provide.

As Aurelia had watched the flames through the window in her bedroom door, she had recalled the dust thick in the air when they'd first moved in; the impenetrable darkness caused by boarded windows and relieved only by flickering candles; the distinct and unforgettable sound of rats scurrying inches from where she'd slept. It was these memories, more than the possibility of being burned alive, which had sparked her terror. Five years of arduous work had transformed the house into a home, and she was incapable of the strength necessary to begin again or to dream of possibilities after she and Papito had invested all they had in the house which was to be the comfort of their old age, the anchor in their children's lives.

Aurelia wearily took a gallon of milk from the refrigerator and poured some into a pan. As the milk simmered on low heat she proceeded to sweep the kitchen. If she didn't know better she would've imagine that the house was gradually disintegrating around her head. Regardless of how many times a day she swept, a pile of dust the size of a large anthill was discarded into the trash bin. And just the previous day Papito had informed her that the ceiling in their bedroom would have to be torn down so that the pipes leaking into the room each time the upstairs toilet was flushed could be replaced. The one thing to be grateful for was that Papito would do the repairs himself. Otherwise they could ill have afforded the expense.

Milk sizzled against the sides of the pan and began to rise. Aurelia quickly turned off the stove and washed her hands in the sink full of dishes Marina had refused to do before going off to bed. She then wiped her hands dry, broke chunks of semisweet chocolate into the pan, and grated nutmeg so that a thin layer floated on the milk's surface.

She missed the ritual of making coffee. Before her conversion to Seventh-Day Adventist and while she still lived with her mother, she and Bienvenida had built a fire behind the house. While darkness lingered and roosters crowed, Bienvenida had roasted coffee beans which Aurelia had ground into a fine powder with a mortar and pestle held snugly between her knees. Then, as the embers faded, they had sat drinking the coffee whose scent had mingled with the green, wet smell of dawn.

More and more Aurelia found herself remembering the distant past. She might be in the middle of a conversation or in church listening to a sermon when she would suddenly recall an event, words spoken, even a scent, a flavor, a texture—each evoked as if she were experiencing it at the moment. It was as if, after years of setting aside memories, the pile had grown too high and had tumbled, obliging her to take an inventory of her life. As she delved into the past she was conscious of something missing in the present—something her mother had possessed and passed along to her but which she had misplaced and failed to pass on to her own children. She could not identify what it was, but its absence was felt as acutely as hunger pangs. And she was determined to discover what had caused the loss and to figure out how she had brought herself to the present moment so that she might guide herself into the future.

It wasn't that she romanticized the past or believed that things had been better long ago. She had been poor even in the Dominican Republic, but something had flourished from within which had enabled her to greet each day rather than cringe from it in dread. With bare feet planted on familiar ground, she had trusted her perceptions. Yet assaulted by the unfamiliar and surrounded by hard concrete and looming buildings, she had become as vulnerable as even the Trujillo regime had failed to make her feel.

Everything had seemed grim and violent: the faces encountered on New York streets; the dirty snow hardened into ice and stained with blood where someone had been wounded; the news read in *El Diario* and heard on Channel 47; the abrasive sound of tires screeching, horns honking, feet trampling above her head. Terrified to step outside and claustrophobic in the three-room apartment shared with Papito and their children, she had deteriorated to a skeletal eighty-one pounds. Only the realization that her children would be left motherless in a country whose language and customs she still barely understood had inched her toward health in defiance of the doctors' prediction that she would die. But although she had recovered, she had emerged from a nine-month hospital stay profoundly changed. Gone were her confidence and self-respect. How could she trust herself when she had willingly brought herself to the brink of death? More important, how could she have expected her children to grow strong and independent after they had witnessed her emotional collapse and increasing deference to Papito who, in turn, placed his burden in the hands of God?

Haunted by these questions, Aurelia stirred the milk until the chocolate melted. When it did, she filled two mugs, placed them on the kitchen table, and went to wake her husband. Even in sleep his forehead remained furrowed and his lids half open, revealing wary eyes.

"What? What's wrong?" he exclaimed when Aurelia shook him.

"Nothing. It's time for you to go to work."

Papito's eyes searched the room as if he were expecting to find some horror. "I feel like I didn't sleep."

"You probably didn't. Your eyes were open when I came in."

Papito rose from bed and stepped into the adjoining bathroom. "I don't know why that surprises me."

A steady stream of his urine splashed into the toilet. As it ended, his wife stood by the bathroom's open door. "I didn't have time to prepare breakfast, but a cup of cocoa is waiting for you in the kitchen."

"That's fine." Papito squeezed toothpaste onto his brush. "I can pick up something to eat on my way to work."

"I forgot to tell you. Leticia called yesterday. She wants you to stop by after work for another payment. Hermana Torres and Hermano Rodríguez are also due."

Papito brushed his teeth, filled his mouth with water, gurgled loudly. "Them I know about," he replied, spitting into the sink. "I'm also visiting several other people the pastor told me might be interested. Who knows?" He winked mischievously at his wife. "I might sell a set of biblical encyclopedias and be able to buy you an authentic rabbit coat like the one the pastor bought his wife."

For the first time that morning, Aurelia laughed. "When I get a fur coat I want it to be mink, not some cheap, old, rodent skin."

Laughing himself, Papito patted her buttocks and nudged her out into the bedroom. "Wait for me wearing no clothes tonight and I just might consider it."

"What's this? One minute you're talking about religious books, the next you're imagining me with no clothes on."

"Are you saying the hots wasn't the reason you followed me into the bathroom?"

"Is that what you think?"

"Admit it, puchungita. You want me."

Aurelia wrapped her arms around her husband's back and trailed her fingers along his spine. Confident that a kiss would follow, Papito closed his eyes.

"Well, you're wrong, viejo," Aurelia announced, laughing triumphantly as she drew away. "You're the reason I got pregnant more times than I can count."

Papito pretended to lunge for her only to then halt and put on the clothes she had set out on a chair for him the previous night. "You think she'll behave today?" he asked, averting his gaze.

His wife sat on the edge of their bed to watch him dress. "That all depends on how long she stays in bed. The less she sleeps, the worse off she seems to be."

"I'm sorry to leave you alone with her when she's like this."

"She's our daughter, Papito. We can't afford to fear her."

"Don't you think I know that?"

Aurelia sighed. "If it makes you feel better, I don't think I'll be alone with her today."

Papito turned to face her. "And what is that supposed to mean?"

Aurelia flashed him an enigmatic smile. "Only that a surprise might be waiting when you get home from work."

Her husband shrugged, indicating that he could not possibly be expected to understand her. "I better have that chocolate now, before I'm late for work."

CHAPTER

 4 ❖

The house looked nothing like what Iliana remembered. It was yellow now—a bright canary-yellow which drew attention to itself, unlike the dull red of the brick facing which had covered its exterior. New too were the white iron fence and gate leading to the stoop. To Iliana, who had been unaware of these changes, the effect was startling. She had expected to find the house cloaked in mourning and somehow, as she approached it, to get a sense of what waited for her inside. Yet, despite the news she had received, the house seemed festive. And compared with neighboring buildings, grey and stooped like the bodies of old men, her parents' residence appeared deceptively new.

She pushed open the front gate and climbed the steps leading to the door. As her fingers moved toward the bell she swallowed her apprehension. This was home: safe and familiar despite its appearance. There was nothing in it she should fear.

Wishing she hadn't packed her keys, Iliana timidly rang the bell.

"Who is it?" a voice asked her from inside.

She dragged her cart closer to the door. "It's me. Iliana."

The door opened wide enough to reveal a face. "What do you want?" it asked, its dull eyes showing no hint of recognition or surprise.

Iliana could only stare. She caught whiffs of Marina's favorite scent and tried to relate the stranger before her to the sister she had known. Yet not even her sister's voice, with its deep and hollow ring, sounded familiar. Marina's face had broadened into a circle, pulling its skin taut across the bridge of her nose, jaws and fore-head; her lips were bruised and scabbed; her brown eyes had re-ceded and darkened to an impenetrable black. As for her skin, it was blotched and pebbly. Her hair was matted in jagged tufts. It was as if each of her features imperceptibly tugged in a different direction, attempting to escape her face. Below it, her neck was stout and solid, so that despite recent weight gain there was no ap-pearance of excess flesh but, rather, of tightness, of skin stretched beyond its limit.

Careful not to betray her shock, Iliana manipulated her lips into a smile. "Aren't you going to let me in?"

Her sister merely stared.

"Who is it?" their mother asked from deep inside the house.

The door was abruptly slammed shut in Iliana's face. She stood motionless, the smile on her lips quivering as she silently denied what had just occurred. Of course she was welcome home. Any minute now, her sister would return and, laughing at her own joke, open the door wide.

"So you're not about to die," Aurelia observed, swinging the door open and drawing her youngest daughter near.

Iliana clung to her as if to a lifeboat. "Of course not. What kind of thing is that to say?"

"You've been on my mind all day, mi'ja. Usually, if I think of someone far away, it means they're breathing their last or are about to visit. But my heart told me you were coming home."

"Titi!"

Two pairs of arms yanked Iliana from her mother.

"Where have you been?" Esperanza asked, in an accusatory tone.

"You haven't come to see us!" Rubén simultaneously declared.

Laughing, Iliana embraced her nephew and niece. "What is this? No kisses? Just complaints?"

"Oooh! Your face is cold!"

"I know. It's a good thing your grandma let me in."

"Are you here to stay?"

"Only if you want me to."

The children's voices pitched to a squeal. "Yes! That way we can come live with you and Grandma!"

"Don't let your mother hear you say that," Aurelia said, dragging her daughter's luggage inside and locking the door behind her. "I don't think it'd make her very happy."

Esperanza, Rebecca's eldest child. shrugged defiantly. "She already knows." Then, as if afraid her words might be confirmed, "But she says you wouldn't want us or even her, that you think we're—"

Anger flashed through Aurelia's eyes. "If I didn't want you, you wouldn't be here now. But enough. Help carry your aunt's things into the living room."

As the children obeyed, Iliana touched her mother's arm. "Rebecca's not about to change. You've said it yourself before. Maybe it's time we tried getting legal cus—"

"Shut your mouth. Children belong with their mother, and Rebecca would be a fine one if we got her to leave Pasión."

"But—"

Aurelia cast Iliana a stern look. "I told you to hold your tongue. The last thing we need is for her to hear us and start arguing in front of the children. You know how she can be."

Iliana set down her backpack and, looking around her, squirmed out of her coat. The living room appeared much smaller than she remembered. Chrome and glass shelves lined a wall against which a couch—now crowded into the center of the room—had leaned. Atop these shelves and others packed tight with Bibles and religious books stood vases of various sizes and shapes; a set of international dolls, porcelain figures of Moses about to hurl the Ten Commandments; David with a sling aimed at Goliath; Eve ever reaching for the forbidden fruit. A crystal chandelier hung awkwardly from the ceiling, low enough for adults to bump their heads on. Pink-veined marble tiles clashed with the oxblood and orange faux–Louis XIV furniture.

To Iliana, eyes opened wide by a year and a half's absence, the room seemed a version of what her parents believed a rich person's house, or at least an American's, might look like. Gone were the hand-carved statuettes and worn but sturdy wooden rocking chairs and tables brought from the Dominican Republic. In their place sat tables with gold-tinted latticed bases and red and gold fringed lamps. Already Iliana felt as if her parents' home were not her own. While she'd been away, her memory had consisted of images imbued with the warmth of a Caribbean sun magically transported to New York and of a house furnished with objects lovingly carved by the inhabitants of an island she had dreamed of. Now she found herself surprised and amused by the house's eclectic contents as well as by the way its lamps and couches had been covered with plastic to preserve their newness.

"Qué, cagona? Think you're too important to say hello?"

Iliana cringed at the use of the nickname she had earned for her childish fear of latrines and sneaky habit of defecating among flowers while in Azua.

"I didn't see you," she said, turning to find her eldest sister seated beside a window with a child settled on her lap.

"Some of the smartest people have never been to school. Don't think going to a fancy one entitles you to an attitude."

Determined not to be baited, Iliana bent to kiss Rebecca's cheek. "This must be Soledad," she said, attempting to lure the child into her arms.

Soledad clung to her mother. Rebecca smiled victoriously and drew her nearer. "She doesn't want to go with you."

"She doesn't remember you," Aurelia countered.

Overwhelmed by the politics of being home, Iliana dropped onto a couch. "The house looks different. I barely recognize it."

Marina, who had watched impassively from the threshold, abruptly stepped into the room.

"Can you smell it?" she demanded, thrusting her face so near her youngest sister's that she instinctively recoiled.

"Smell what?" Iliana asked.

Marina's back arched; her shoulders squared. She rolled a sleeve past her elbow to expose her bruised and discolored arm. Iliana's breath caught in her throat. Needing to touch what her eyes did not believe, she reached her fingers toward the raw flesh on her sister's arm.

"Oh my God."

"Don't tell me you can't smell it! Everyone does!"

"Marina, all I smell is perfume."

"Liar! Why don't you tell the fucking truth?"

Aurelia attempted to calm Marina and was shoved effortlessly back onto the couch.

"Don't touch me, you hypocrite!"

Soledad whimpered in her mother's arms. The other children cowered, as if accustomed to having anger diverted to them.

"I've seen you plotting behind my back and trying to make me believe I'm crazy! What did you think, that I was so stupid I wouldn't notice?"

Iliana searched the faces of those around her for a clue as to what was going on. Hoping that, like a top spurred into a frenzied spin, Marina's fury would topple to a halt, Aurelia held her peace.

"If I'm crazy, then what the fuck is this?"

Marina yanked her skirt above her naked hips. Revulsion contorted her face as she parted the soft, shaved area between her thighs to pull from it what only her eyes could see. Then, enacting a pantomime of something wriggling in her hand, she dangled empty fingers before her mother's eyes.

"Tell me! What the fuck is this?"

Rebecca rose and gathered her children about her like a flustered hen.

"That's it. I'm leaving. I didn't come here to have my babies exposed to such indecency."

Marina's fingers moved as if releasing something. Her feet stomped the floor as if pounding into a pulp whatever it was she'd dropped. Breathing heavily, she approached Aurelia.

"You can't say anything, can you?" she asked, merciless yet sorrowful eyes pinioning her mother. "Not even, 'I'm sorry this has happened'?"

Tears welled in Aurelia's eyes. "Would you believe me?" she asked, braving her daughter's gaze. "Would it help if I told you that I blame myself for your unhappiness and wake each morning trying to figure out where it was that I went wrong?"

Marina's lips curled with contempt. "So I'm supposed to feel sorry for you, the great self-sacrificing mother who left me in the Dominican Republic when you came here?"

At this, Aurelia's eyes shifted from her daughter's. With painful clarity she recalled the February day when not only Marina but also Beatriz and Gabriel arrived in New York wearing wispy cotton clothes and too-tight shoes, their arms hanging thin from sleeves, their feet wrinkled, their toenails a fungus-green because they'd been made to pail water from her sister's repeatedly flooded yard. She also remembered the parasites which had grown snake-size in their intestines to later wriggle free as each child strained to defecate, and her guilty, angry pain at discovering that despite the dollars she and Papito had sent for their children's care—money converted into more pesos than they themselves had ever had in the Dominican Republic—her sister, whom she had trusted to do right, had housed all three children in a chicken coop and barely clothed or fed them.

"Yeah, that's right. Think about it," Marina instructed, seeing her mother's head hung low. "Take all the time you need!"

She stormed out of the room. When her steps resounded on the basement stairs, Iliana turned to Aurelia. Sensing that a show of emotion would only cause the tears brimming in her mother's eyes to fall, she restrained an impulse to go nearer.

"Humph!" Rebecca packed the last of her children into a coat. "The day I asked you or Papi for an apology would've been the day I'd lost my hide. But here I am. Did I go crazy? Did Zoraida, Caleb or Emanuel? All the young ones had it so much easier, and look how they turned out."

Slowly, as if warding off a ghost, Aurelia raised a hand to shield her eyes, then let it fall defeated at her side.

"You don't have to go, mi'ja. The children haven't eaten."

"They can eat at home," Rebecca snapped. "We've already stayed too long."

❖   ❖   ❖

Steam spiralled upward as Aurelia removed lids from pots and heaped food onto a plate. She passed it to Iliana and served herself a smaller portion.

"At least Marina has developed an appetite," she murmured. "For a while there she was letting herself disappear."

"She looks like a bull, Mami. Think what all that weight is doing to her heart."

Aurelia gnawed a bone. "You could do with some yourself."

Exasperated, Iliana watched her wipe off the red sauce trailing down her chin. "My weight is fine, and we're talking about Marina, not me."

"How can you talk on an empty stomach? I'm sure you haven't eaten, and I made your favorite food."

Iliana glanced down at her plate. It was true. Her mother had anticipated the dishes she most craved: fried, sweet plantains and a stew of cow's feet, honeycomb tripe, garbanzos and carrots served over yucca and rice. She had even made sure to scoop some out of the pot in such a way that no bones landed on Iliana's plate. Yet Iliana no longer had an appetite. Nor could she understand how her mother, standing beside the stove licking dripping fingers, could behave as if nothing disturbing had occurred.

Then again, why shouldn't Aurelia eat? Or breathe? Or laugh? Of what good was abstinence?

She watched her mother's head bend toward the bowl held inches from her lips. Each time, after Aurelia's fingers had dipped into the bowl and then into her mouth, moments during which food was chewed and her right hand remained empty, the fingers, ever so slightly, trembled. Selfishly, Iliana wished for Aurelia to meet her gaze, share a secret, speak words which would loop themselves around the two and draw them near. More than anything, she wanted a gesture able to subdue her fears or to persuade her that not everything and everyone had changed beyond recall.

"Mami?"

"What?"

Iliana hesitated. This, despite her pressing need to begin her stay with a clean slate and to be absolved of lies she'd told and pain she'd caused.

"There's something I need to tell you."

Aurelia's eyes narrowed with suspicion.

"It's something I've been meaning to tell you but never had the nerve to say."

"What, mi'ja?"

Iliana dallied with her food. Aurelia set her own plate on the stove.

"It's really no big deal. Just something I've been feeling bad about for a while."

"Tell me," her mother murmured. "You can trust me."

They watched each other, one nervously, the other expectantly. Eventually, a mischievous smile gathered on Aurelia's lips.

"What? That you never had appendicitis?"

Her daughter's mouth gaped open.

"Why—why are you saying that? Is that what you've suspected all along?"

"What, then?" Aurelia asked, her voice betraying her amusement. "What was it you had to tell me?"

"Noth-nothing," Iliana stammered, too bewildered now to confess what her mother already knew. "It wasn't so important that you needed to know."

CHAPTER

 5 ❖

Fetid air from a septic tank momentarily enveloped Iliana as she descended into the basement and groped for the light switch at the bottom of the stairs. To her right, the door to the room she would share with her sister was ajar. Further back, a door had been installed on the side of her youngest brother's room so that he'd no longer have to pass through theirs to reach his own. Assuming Marina to be asleep, Iliana tiptoed into their unlit room. Somewhere, probably in Tico's room, merengue sashayed from a radio. Yet closer and audible above the music's fast-paced notes was the sound of flapping wings.

Disconcerted that a bird had flown undetected into the house, Iliana flicked the light switch by the door. Marina stood in the middle of their room. Her eyes were closed. Her arms were stretched high above her head. Slowly, gracefully, both of them fluttered down, their bell-shaped sleeves flapping through air to graze her sides before they were raised again to repeat the motion. Already she seemed ethereal, as if a part of her had flown into another realm. Watching her, Iliana expected her to defy both weight and mass and to fly magically through walls and ceilings. It seemed possible. Anything seemed possible, or should have been, given the unwavering faith expressed on her sister's face.

Thwarted by gravity, Marina's movements became discordant. Up and down flapped her arms, quickly, despairingly, so that each time they reached her sides the hands balled into fists. Her determination was alarming. It reminded Iliana of a pigeon she had once seen get run over by a car. After the vehicle sped on, the bird had furiously flapped its wings and then expired.

Iliana hesitated before calling out her sister's name. Marina's eyes flicked open. When she saw Iliana, her arms crashed against her hips and her body lurched forward. Iliana attempted to step aside only to be clutched into her sister's arms.

"You look just like a model," Marina murmured.

Iliana's heart pounded against her sister's breasts. She had expected an assault, not a hug. She had been afraid.

"A model of what?" she asked defensively.

Marina withdrew far enough to view her from head to toe, then stepped close to trace the features on her face.

"Like in magazines. Now that you wear contacts you could probably be in *Vogue*."

Iliana waited for the punch line. She was unaccustomed to compliments from her sister who had often called her "four-eyes," "pimple-face" and "doofy" for being tall as well as for possessing broad shoulders and long, thin arms.

Tico banged on the bolted door which had once provided access to his sister's room. "*Vogue!* Huh! Since when has Iliana been anything but ugly?"

Set at ease by her brother's teasing, Iliana kicked her side of the door. "Maybe never, but at least I'm not so ugly that I have to be locked inside my room."

"You tell him, sis."

"So you think you can gang up on me? It'll take more than just the two of you to win!"

"Show your face, then," Iliana challenged.

"Nah, man. I can't waste my time. I've got better things to do."

Iliana winked at Marina before slipping quietly out of their room. Surprising Tico with an unexpected entrance into his, she leapt onto his bed. "Better things to do, huh?"

"Shit!" Her brother grabbed her legs and made as if to shove her off the bed. "A man can't even have privacy in his room!"

Iliana gestured toward the bolted door and the new one installed during her absence. "Is that the reason for those?"

"Sssh!"

"Why?"

Tico clambered out of bed, shut the door his sister had left open, deliberately raised the radio's volume.

"What's wrong?"

"Didn't Mom tell you?"

"Tell me what?"

Tico scrutinized his sister's face. Knowing that the more she pressed him the less he would reveal, Iliana waited.

"Marina said I snuck into her room in the middle of the night."

"So?" Iliana asked, stepping off his bed.

"Are you stupid or something?"

"Tico."

He plumped the pillows on his bed and then burrowed under its sheets. "She claims I tried to rape her. She's also been telling everyone Mom is a dyke and she and Dad abused her."

"What are you whispering about?" Marina yelled from the other room.

Conflicting thoughts and emotions ricocheted through Iliana's brain. Yet she kept herself still, very still, and focused on the heart-shaped mole that throughout the years had traveled the width of her brother's neck to land on the cleft below his Adam's apple.

She would have known if her parents had abused her sister. The apartments they had lived in prior to moving into their current home had been too small to accommodate such activity without the presence of one or more of her thirteen siblings. As for the other accusation, she could not be sure if it was true or not. With only Tico and Marina inhabiting the basement rooms, anything might have happened. Then again, this claim might be taken as additional proof of her sister's precarious mental state.

"I don't know if I can deal, Tico. I really don't."

"I wondered why you came back. I would have stayed away."

The door to the room swung open. "What the fuck is going on here?"

"Get out! I don't go into your room and you don't come into mine!"

"But I feel left out. What do both of you have to talk about that I can't hear?"

Iliana slipped out of her brother's room. "Nothing. Tico was just showing me what he imagines are muscles on his arms."

"He thinks he's a man now," Marina said, following her through the corridor.

Tense, Iliana shrugged. "Maybe he is. He might've done a lot more growing up than we know."

"Talking about men, have you hooked yourself a gorgeous, blue-eyed hunk yet?"

Iliana entered her room and hoisted a suitcase she had dragged into the basement up onto her bed. Afraid that her eyes would betray what her brother had disclosed, she kept her back to her sister.

"Blue-eyed wouldn't be my first choice," she muttered.

"Why? What do you have against white people?"

"I didn't say I had anything against them. And all whites aren't blue-eyed."

Marina snickered. "A big, black stud. That's what you want."

"Yeah," Iliana retorted. "A big-black-man-with-a-great-big-dick. What would be wrong with that if I did?"

"Only that you could do better."

"Better? What the hell is that supposed to mean?"

"You know how black men are."

"No, Marina. Tell me."

"They're lazy as shit and undependable."

"You've been watching too much TV," Iliana snapped.

"TV, my ass. Look at all your brothers."

"Look at yourself. You're suffering from the same thing they are, thinking anything lighter must be better."

"Give me a break, Iliana. How many black people are at your school?"

Iliana whirled around to face her sister. "What are you saying? That blacks are inferior? Is that what you think about yourself?"

"I'm Hispanic, not black."

"What color is your skin?"

"I'm Hispanic!"

Iliana bit down on her tongue. Here it was her first day back and already she was arguing with her sister.

"Let's just drop it."

"Wanna know something else?" Marina persisted. "White people have always been nicer to me than anyone else."

"How many white people do you know?" Iliana asked, unable to restrain herself.

"Enough. My teachers, bosses—"

"Yeah? Well, they're all paid to be nice to you!"

"What the fuck is your problem?" Marina demanded. "You're in school far away from here and can do anything you want! Look at me—I'm stuck at home and can't even fart without asking for permission!"

"You could've done the same thing."

"That's not the point."

"No? Then what is the point, Marina? Why the hell are you throwing everything I've done back in my face?"

"Because you think you're such hot shit! That's why! You always have! Reading stupid books, talking to everyone like you were better, acting like what we had wasn't good enough for you! Well, I've got news for you! We don't need you here!"

CHAPTER

 6

In the photograph—preserved behind dusty glass and contained within a gilded frame hanging between the living room's two windows and just below the only photograph taken of Aurelia and Papito in the Dominican Republic—Marina was seventeen, Beatriz fifteen, Iliana twelve and Tico nine. As in all formal photographs taken of them together, the four were arranged chronologically: Marina first, Tico last. But unlike earlier photos in which their sizes varied in proportion to their ages, this one captured the sisters when they were of equal height, freezing the moment in time before Beatriz surpassed Marina by one and a half inches and Iliana shot up another four.

Marina, her lips seeming to twitch in an effort to maintain a tooth-revealing smile, sat erect with her thighs pressed close and her palms clasped against her knees. Her pale-green jacket gaped open to reveal the ivory lace top of her matching dress, the skirt of which was tucked neatly under her thighs. Her nose sloped gently down her face, widening and flattening above her lips. These, big when closed, now stretched almost to her ears framed by short and reddish-brown hair curled under at the ends.

Beside Marina, Beatriz smiled effortlessly, her glistening lips only slightly parted, her plucked brows arched, her chin raised so that her neck appeared to stretch above the collar of her oxblood dress. Her chest leaned coyly toward the camera. One leg crossed the other under the skirt hitched halfway up her thighs. Long, black hair curled loosely around her face. Its features, angular and severe enough to lend her a calculated look, appeared carved into the ebony darkness of her skin.

Next was Iliana. So ashamed was she of her sprouting breasts thrusting rebelliously against her brassiere that she sat with shoulders hunched, attempting to shrink herself into a former size. Her bony arms were wrapped around her waist and jutted angularly from the short sleeves of her rose-spattered, peplum dress. Her hair, parted at the side and hanging limp, concealed the nut-brown forehead for which she was often taunted with the Dominican idiom "Big forehead, big pussy." Her brows curled every which way and met each other so that it seemed she had not two but one above her horn-rimmed glasses. Her lips, wide as Marina's but the length of Beatriz's, pouted so sullenly that despite chiseled cheeks and a nose her sisters envied as "white" she appeared the ugliest of the three.

Finally, a blue-suited Tico, small for his age, grinned beside Iliana. Like Marina, he too possessed yellowish skin, a wide nose and long, full lips.

Iliana stepped close to inspect the photograph. She tried to detect any previously overlooked traits which might have hinted at Marina's future breakdown. Yet her eyes kept shifting to Tico, Beatriz, even to herself. Whenever she tried to focus on Marina's face, her eyes settled on a single feature rather than on the whole. It was as if a door inside her had willfully slammed shut against a complete view for fear of recognizing something not in her sister but in herself: some shared genetic trait able to hint at her own susceptibility to madness. She involuntarily found herself checking off their differences to persuade herself that although they had been conceived in the same womb it did not follow that she too would lose her mind. No. Her sister's madness had not been diagnosed as schizophrenic. At least not definitely. Her doctors had mentioned it only as a possibility, which meant that Marina might instead have suffered, simply, a nervous breakdown.

This possibility made Iliana angry. It meant that her sister had allowed herself to collapse under life's weight. Life was hard. But so what? One went on. One braced for whatever came and made the best of it. Everyone had to do it.

And this was not all. When Iliana had tried to tell her mother of her conversation with Tico, she had immediately been hushed. Marina meant no harm, Aurelia had insisted. Marina was merely inventing tales which she momentarily imagined to be true. She randomly selected the words to make them up and then flung them like pebbles at whoever was around, quickly forgetting them once they escaped her lips. And Tico should have known enough to dodge and to let the words fall past him into the current of things best left forgotten so that they would inflict no wound.

In the photograph Marina held herself stiffly. Before the camera's flash and for years afterward she rarely caused her parents grief. Her chores were done when asked, and she willingly attended church on Saturday mornings and afternoons, even on Wednesday and Friday evenings when Papito allowed those of his children claiming exhaustion to remain at home. She had also enjoyed buying presents for her younger sisters, especially for Beatriz. Little things: posters, inexpensive perfumes, pencils with carved wooden heads, Magic Markers and watercolor sets, diaries and clear or pale-pink nail polish, hair barrettes and ribbons. Everywhere Beatriz went, Marina had followed close behind. She had doted on this sister like a lover, always wanting to be near her and eternally fascinated by her ability to attract men with cruelty and unabashed flirtation. She had continued to traipse behind her even after Beatriz began to ridicule her in front of others.

Iliana's sight shifted to Beatriz. Looking at her, she decided that theirs was a family of individuals randomly thrown together and unreasonably expected to get along.

Beatriz was beautiful. The problem was that she had known it. Even in the photograph her pose demanded attention as it had done in life. Competitive but indifferent to Iliana, whom she had cursorily dismissed as posing no threat, she had focused her venom on Marina. No one, she had claimed, would ever consider her attractive. Not with her baboon nose and nigger lips. So Marina had better resign herself to becoming an old maid. Then, feeling outdone when Iliana was the first of the three to move out on her own, she had disappeared from home, leaving behind a note in which she disparaged the family she thereafter made no attempt to see.

Iliana inspected her own face in the photograph. Because she continued to think of herself as ugly, she was repeatedly surprised when others described her as beautiful. How that supposed beauty had surfaced struck her as ironic. Resigned to being ugly, she had taken to pulling her hair back into a single braid. It was Ed who, seeing her remove her glasses, suggested that she buy contacts. So desperate had she been to believe her eyes were as pretty as he'd claimed that she had accepted his advice. She had then adopted the habit of plucking and smoothing down her unmanageable brows. This had led her to lipstick—a dark plum which made her decide she liked the fullness of her lips. But beautiful? Interesting, maybe, the contradictory features on her face, but definitely not beautiful.

Remembering the insecure teenager she had been, Iliana wondered what it was that had inspired her to pursue an education when what she had needed most, according to members of her family, was a husband able to provide for all her needs. She suspected her decision had stemmed from an inability to imagine that anyone would ever want her for a wife. But other reasons had existed. Marina had been right to accuse her of dissatisfaction with what her family had to offer. Because her siblings had been paired off by the sequence of their birth and Tico, who should have been her companion, had a nephew his own age, she had spent most of her time observing her family and immersing herself in books. As a result, her perception of what the world could offer had expanded, and she had wanted more than her sisters had obtained. When her brother Vicente left for college, she, despite being female, had claimed similar possibilities for herself. As far back as the sixth grade she had communicated to Aurelia, who in turn conveyed to Papito, her desire to attend a university. With Vicente's help, she had eventually persuaded her parents that it was respectable, even desirable, for a single woman in the United States to abandon home for school.

Iliana's eyes shifted to Tico whom she loved better than her sisters and who, in childhood, had led her into dark rooms she had been afraid of entering on her own. The last son after three daughters and surprisingly kind in a family where entertainment was most often derived from merciless teasing, he was their parents' favorite child. Looking at him grinning beside her on the couch, Iliana remembered other photos of him astride a wooden pony, at the wheel of a fire engine, and atop an emerald tricycle—all toys her parents had been unable to provide for their other children. She also recalled the fateful day in elementary school when she was summoned to the nurse's office because three fifth-graders had pummeled Tico during recess. On seeing him, her stomach heaved up everything she'd eaten. Her baby brother lay unconscious. His eyes were swollen shut, his lips split open, his head wrapped in a bandage red with blood. When the indignant school nurse informed her that—because her mother spoke no English— it would be up to her to call and notify Aurelia of her son's condition, Iliana's body had convulsed with terror at being the bearer of news she believed would surely break Aurelia's heart. Yet she had since learned that her mother was far stronger than she'd supposed and that hearts relentlessly pumped blood even as brains recoiled from whatever horror was presented.

Last of all, Iliana raised her eyes to the enlarged copy of the photo her mother had long ago preserved in one of the family's many albums. The blacks, whites and greys of the copy were so blurred that Aurelia and Papito each appeared to be of indeterminate race and age. They neither smiled nor frowned but gazed unflinchingly at the camera as if prepared to confront whatever challenges life might throw their way. At the center of their impenetrably dark pupils, pinpoints of light—possibly a trick of the camera—receded far back into their heads so that, although their faces appeared to shield emotions, their eyes suggested stories only waiting to be told.

Iliana ached to hear those stories. Knowing little of her parents' lives, she wanted to learn of the past of which they rarely spoke. She also wanted to borrow from both the strength she saw reflected in their eyes.

CHAPTER

 7

Aurelia clicked on the television and made herself comfortable on a couch stretching awkwardly from one end of the living room to another. As if on cue, Marina stood up from where she had been sitting in the dark. She then turned on a lamp, retrieved a Bible from a shelf, positioned herself on a loveseat directly in her mother's view.

"Blessed is the man that walketh not in the counsel of the ungodly, nor standeth in the way of sinners, nor sitteth in the seat of the scornful. But his delight is in the Law of the Lord; and in his Law doeth he meditate day and night."

"If you're so devout, why don't you go downstairs where you can read in peace?" Aurelia asked.

"Why should I hide? I'm not ashamed to praise the Lord."

Aurelia raised the volume on the TV in the hope of drowning out Marina's voice. Except for baseball games and the Spanish news, she rarely watched TV. And she'd be damned if she allowed a daughter of hers to keep her from a brief respite.

"And he shall be like a tree planted by the rivers of water, that bringeth forth his fruit in his season. His leaf also shall not wither; and whatsoever he doeth shall prosper."

Sitting beside her mother, Iliana silently watched her sister. She still hadn't been able to decide if Marina was a religious fanatic or genuinely insane. She had even started wondering if it was possible that Marina actually saw what others couldn't.

"There! You see!" Marina had shrieked earlier that evening.

"What?" Iliana had exclaimed.

Marina cringed against the back post of her bed. "He's beckoning to me!"

Iliana glanced to where her sister's finger pointed.

"Please tell me you see him," Marina sobbed.

"Marina, there's no one there."

"Turn on the closet light! Just turn it on! You'll see!"

Iliana entered the walk-in closet and apprehensively pulled the string of a hanging bulb.

"Maybe it was just a shadow," she said, relieved.

"Then I'm the only one who can see him," Marina whimpered.

"Who?" Iliana asked.

Her sister curled into a fetal position.

"Marina, who do you think you saw?"

"I don't *think* I saw anyone. He was there! He was standing in the closet looking at me like—" She gazed at Iliana. "But you don't believe me, do you? You think I'm crazy, just like everybody else."

Iliana again glanced in the direction of the closet. It was empty. She was sure.

"Everyone sees and hears things. Sometimes it's just because we're tired. But whatever was there has gone."

"He follows me," Marina moaned.

"You've got to get a hold of yourself. Otherwise you'll drive yourself insane." Iliana was careful with her words. "I don't know. Maybe it'd be good if you talked to someone."

"What do you mean?" Marina asked, stiffening instantly. "I'm talking to you, ain't I?"

"You know what I mean. Someone who might help. At school they had people for us to talk to. Everybody went."

"Did you?"

Iliana could not help but recall the voice she had been haunted by at school.

"No," she mumbled. "I didn't."

"Why?" Marina asked, her focus so intense that Iliana felt her eyes boring into her to unearth the truth.

"Because I didn't think I needed to."

"Exactly," her sister had replied. "Exactly."

Marina glanced up from the Bible. On the television, Johnnie Ventura was howling a merengue song as if possessed. His dark skin glistened. His hips shimmied so fluidly that they appeared to contain no bones. Behind him, three women jiggled breasts threatening to spill from their fringed bras.

"The ungodly are not so," Marina proclaimed, leaping to her feet as if the Holy Ghost had moved her, "but are like the chaff which the wind driveth away. Therefore the ungodly shall not stand in the judgment, nor sinners in the congregation of the righteous; for the Lord knoweth the way of—"

"Ay, Marina, please," Aurelia begged.

Marina stood in front of her and leaned in close. "Praised be God's holy name! Mothers shall turn against daughters! Sons against fathers! Sisters against sisters! But the Lord shall conquer evil and the holy shall be redeemed!"

Aurelia slid along the couch only to have her daughter again plant herself in her view.

"You're going to burn in hell!" Marina shrieked.

"I clean, wash and cook all day," Aurelia muttered, "and as if that isn't enough to make me a saint, you expect me to sacrifice this one pleasure?"

"Guess what I have in my hands?" her husband boomed, his voice throbbing with excitement as he barged into the room.

Relieved, Aurelia transferred her attention to Papito. "Aren't you going to greet your daughter?" she asked, gesturing toward their youngest.

Pleasure shot through Papito's eyes as Iliana rose to kiss him. "This is better than I expected." He hugged her briefly before drawing away to hold up a bulging paper bag. "You're educated. You try guessing first."

Remembering the cinnamon-scented soap, Iliana sat herself back down. "I don't know, Papi. You tell us."

Marina flung the Bible to the floor and tried to yank the bag from her father's hand. Laughing, Papito raised it high above her head.

"No peeking. Everyone has to guess."

"Ay, Papito," his wife snapped. "Either tell us what's in the bag or get out of the way. I'm trying to watch TV."

Papito glanced at the TV and stepped forward to turn it off. "This is a Christian home. Such shows aren't welcome here."

Aurelia rolled her eyes in exasperation. "Now I know who she gets it from," she muttered, rising to turn off the television when her husband was struck dumb by the dancers' jiggling breasts.

Papito sheepishly pecked her cheek. "Now that I have everyone's attention"—he slipped one arm, then the other from his coat so as not to release the paper bag—"I'll give you all a clue. It's from Santo Domingo, something one of my co-workers just brought back."

"Dulce de leche!" Marina squealed.

"Que dulce de leche, ni dulce de leche," her father said, flinging his coat onto the couch. "Is this bag greasy? Do you see square edges poking through?"

"So hurry up and tell us," Marina urged.

Papito squeezed the bag so that its contents shifted, taking the shape his fingers gave it. "It's solid, but moves like liquid."

Marina again attempted to snatch the bag out of his hand. Iliana winced. She expected him to slap her sister. Instead, his excitement increased in proportion to Marina's.

"Dear God, my children know nothing. Can no one really guess?"

"Stop messing with us, Papito. Don't you see you're driving Marina nuts?"

Marina feigned indifference. "Who cares. It's probably something stupid."

"Oh, poor baby." Her father held the bag out to her as an offering. "Come here. I'll prove to you how much I love you. Here. Take it. It's all yours." Then, unable to restrain himself, he again pulled the bag out of her reach. "Que va. You're right. It's stupid.

Nothing worth seeing. Definitely not tasting." He smacked his lips exaggeratedly. "I'll just have to keep it for myself. You kids wouldn't know the difference between real sugar and the white dust you swallow in this country!"

"Sugar?" Iliana asked incredulously. "All this and all you have is sugar?"

"Humph! Listen to our 'jucated daughter! Sugar, she says. Only sugar. Well, take a whiff of this!"

Papito opened the bag and held it to her nose. A succulent aroma coaxed saliva from her tongue.

"It smells like sugarcane!"

"No kidding!" Papito grabbed a fistful of the sugar, dark as fertile earth, and let it trickle from his fingers into the bag. "The scent of my childhood! God, does it bring back memories!"

He held the bag up to his nose and inhaled deeply.

"I was only six years old," he began. "My mother had just died. My father was so poor that he couldn't afford to pay anyone to watch me and had to take me to work with him every night. I'd watch him load twenty-five-pound sacks of sugar onto trucks that took them all over the country, even to boats headed for America, India, France—all the places we'd never been to. As he worked, he'd make up stories of faraway places and promise that one day we'd build a boat or grow wings to take us there. When I'd grow sleepy, he'd prop me way up high on sacks of sugar where I'd be safe out of his way. I'd watch him throw a sack of sugar onto his shoulders and stoop to grab another. Sweat would pour down his face as he staggered out of sight. Minutes later, before I became afraid he'd gone to those faraway places without me, he'd come back and start again, working until dawn."

Tears gathered at the corners of Papito's eyes. "I remember watching him every night, then falling asleep while sucking sugar from a ripped sack like from a mother's tit."

He paused, no longer addressing anyone in the room.

"Ay, mi Papi y mi Mami. Cuanta falta me hacen." He wiped tears from his eyes. "No one loves anyone like a parent loves his child."

"He's crying! Papi's crying like a baby!" Marina exclaimed. "Ay, Papi, don't cry," she said, drawing him near. "You have us!"

Papito clung to her for a moment. "You see. This is the only child who loves me, the only one who stayed to take care of me and Aurelia in our old age. And you"—he turned to face his youngest daughter—"you were the one who said you'd stay, and you left as soon as you got the chance."

Aurelia stared intently at her husband. Her lips began to quiver, then gave way to an irrepressible fit of laughter. "You amaze me," she gasped. "You really do. First of all, you were at least ten when your mother died. So if you went to work with your father it was not to fall asleep but to help pay for your keep. And what do you mean you sucked sugar like from a tit? Humph! Filthy old man. Stop telling tales before you give yourself away."

Papito chuckled. "You've got to admit the story was a good one. It even made me cry."

"You had me going too, until I realized you were telling lies."

"Not lies. Just the embellished truth. And that is not a sin."

"Nobody said it was."

"That's right," Marina said, snatching the bag from her father's hand.

"Ay, muchacha," he exclaimed as she poured a mound of sugar on her tongue while keeping him at bay with an outstretched arm. "The pleasure's in tasting a little at a time so that your tongue absorbs the flavor!"

Aurelia sneaked up behind Marina. She pinched a bit of flesh on her arm and twisted it until her daughter surrendered the bag back to Papito.

"Ay, Mami, that hurt!"

Aurelia cackled. "I know. Why else do you think I did it?" Then, tormenting Marina as she would any child who moaned about a minor bruise, she added: "But don't worry. If you die, we'll bury you in a crate at the side of a road so that we can wave to you as we drive by."

"You think that's funny?" Marina asked. "How would you like it if someone pinched you?"

"You wanna try?" Aurelia asked, clamping her fingertips in anticipation. "Come on! See if I don't make you howl."

"Caramba, Aurelia. You look exactly like a witch."

"I am a witch. Didn't you know? Why do you think our children are so strange?"

Iliana smiled in wonder. She had forgotten the humor with which her parents made it through each day.

"So, can I have some sugar or do I have to steal it from you like Marina?"

Papito smiled indulgently as he handed her the bag. "You don't have to steal it. I'll give you as much sugar as you want."

CHAPTER

 8

Multicolored and speckled chickens flocked around Rebecca. A rooster flew into a frenzy, clipped wings lifting its body only inches off the ground. The noise was incredible, the stench worse. But, miraculously, the neighbors did not complain. It was as if the people in that part of East New York had grown accustomed to the discomfort, or maybe the squawking was muffled by constantly blaring stereos and the smell blended with that of a garbage-filled lot across the street. Whatever the case, no one complained. Even if someone thought to do so, the three-story building looked abandoned and its doorbell did not work. Only a determined person pounding mercilessly on the front door could cause Rebecca to poke her head out of a window. Almost nothing ever brought her downstairs.

As for Rebecca, there was little she could do about the chickens. Each morning she fantasized about snapping the neck of every single one—not to eat, but for the sole purpose of seeing their bodies convulse. Pasión would kill her, though. Not long after their marriage she had plucked and cooked one for dinner. Pasión had taken one look at the stuffed bird and punched her in the face. It wasn't even that he planned to sell the chickens—just liked having them around. First thing he did on the rare days he came home was run upstairs to see them. Knew exactly how many there were too. If any died, as many were replaced from a livestock market blocks away.

Rebecca kicked the hens pecking hungrily at her feet. Eight years of waking to the task of feeding them and still she responded with revulsion. On seeing the birds, her eyes signaled her brain, which signaled her nose, which only then registered the stench and formulated an appropriate response. At all other times she was immune to the odor. It was as if, assaulted by information it dared not believe, her brain relied on the eyes to verify its perceptions. The resulting nausea, accompanied by an urge to slaughter the chickens, was a rebellion against her husband's embrace of a farmer's lifestyle idealized in stories told by a father who had himself abandoned it upon arriving in the United States. Having no land, Pasión had converted the top apartment into a coop. In imitation of the American farms he'd seen surrounded by broken plows and tractors, he had cluttered the rest of the house with junk.

Rebecca poured water and grain into cans lined against the walls. As the chickens fought for the rations, scattering feathers that drifted to floors layered with shit, she latched the door, descended to the second floor, and emptied the leftover feed into a bathtub used as a trough. Sidestepping mismatched drawers, torn screen doors, wheels of all sizes, engines, broken machines, other unidentifiable objects Pasión collected from the lot across the street, and magazines and newspapers he had been stockpiling for what seemed like decades, she made her way to the only habitable room in the house.

The children still slept, their bodies huddled together, their open lips smoking from the cold. Already they would be late for school. Better to let them stay. With no heat or hot water in the house, getting them out of bed was torture. Occasionally, Rebecca let them sleep. When she didn't, she rushed them out of the house in the clothes they'd slept in. No need for them to bathe. They might catch cold, and then what would she do?

She climbed into bed beside her children. Yes, they would stay, especially after the sealed note she had received from one of their teachers. Unable to read English, she had asked Esperanza, the eldest child, to translate it:

Dear Mrs. Fernández,

Your son's clothes are filthy and he smells bad. It would be greatly appreciated if in the future you concerned yourself with his hygiene.

With the reluctant child in tow, Rebecca had stormed into the classroom to assault the teacher in Spanish. What did it matter if her children were dirty? At least they were well behaved. And it was true. Outside the house her children were reserved and quiet, though at home they seemed intent on driving her crazy. Like when Pasión came home. They, especially Esperanza, would vie for his attention, leaving her no privacy with her own husband. They also pounded on the bedroom door in the hope of being allowed in to watch TV whenever he made hurried love to her before leaving the house to sleep elsewhere.

Asthma. That's what Pasión claimed prevented him from staying. Rebecca suspected it was a mistress. She had sniffed traces of sex on him and had found scratches on his back. He had also begun to criticize her. Why didn't she comb her hair, change her clothes or bathe? When she explained that she had lost inspiration with so much filth around, he accused her of being too lazy to clean the house.

Pasión was nineteen years Rebecca's senior and handsome in his own way. He measured a giant six feet seven inches, had brown eyes specked with gold, and a hairlessly smooth head. The brows above his eyes arched with humor and cruelty; his lips swelled with reckless sensuality. Combined, these features revealed the spirit of a man who lived life to its fullest but who was confident enough not to boast. He was the opposite of Samuel, the first man Rebecca had ever loved and whose lips had perpetually curved in a self-satisfied smirk. An ugly, boisterous, little man— at least Rebecca's father thought so. During the showing of a video taped at Samuel's house, Papito had paused the film to point to Samuel's bulging stomach and midget-like stature only to recognize, when the figure turned, that he had pointed to himself.

On meeting Pasión, Rebecca had instantly been attracted. His reserve, stature and confidence persuaded her that a relationship with him would be a haven into which she could retreat after Samuel—having broken several of her ribs—rejected her for a woman able to provide him with the residency papers he had assumed Rebecca possessed. Pasión was also an American citizen with what she had perceived as infinite possibilities of wealth.

"Pasión owns a house," she had boasted to those who had called her "spoiled goods" for moving in with Samuel and had then gloated with compassion after he threw her out.

Aurelia had pulled her into a corner of the apartment where the wedding reception was taking place. "Shouldn't you stop bragging, considering you haven't seen it yet?"

"We haven't been married a day and already you're pecking like a hen. Can't you be happy for me?" Rebecca had asked.

Later that evening, on entering her new home, she had stared in disbelief.

"Ignore the garbage," Pasión had said. "I promise to clear it by next week."

Mute with shock, Rebecca had followed him through a corridor lined with stained and gutted mattresses. They climbed a staircase with only inches of cleared space for a person to squeeze through. The second-floor landing was just as cluttered, though an effort had been made to clear the apartment itself. Shabby armchairs were clustered in what was to serve as the living room. In the dining room, mismatched vinyl chairs circled a green Formica table that collapsed when she leaned against it.

"I thought you might like to decorate the place yourself," her husband said, reaching out to steady her and then kneeling to adjust the table's broken leg.

Gradually, Rebecca had depleted the savings from her former job in a garment factory. She bought lace doilies for the tops of peeling dressers, an embroidered tablecloth for the dining room, colorful sheets for the mattress, curtains for the windows, and figurines and plastic flowers for all the rooms. She even attempted to clean the rest of the house, but Pasión continued to haul in junk which eventually filled their apartment too.

"The house is beautiful," she had claimed, trying to keep her voice level and her eyes from tearing when she called her mother several weeks into her marriage. "No, no. I'll visit you instead. Pasión is a private man. He doesn't like people in his home."

She had kept up the ruse even after the gas was cut off and he refused to pay the bill. When the plumbing clogged, she defied him by returning to her former job so as to be able to pay for the repairs, cover bills, buy a few presents she planned to tell her sisters had been purchased for her by Pasión. Days after she was rehired, he appeared at the factory to cause such a scene that the police had to be called in. Still, she had publicly claimed happiness. Only after the birth of her first child had she confessed the state of her marriage to her parents and asked to drop the child off at their house so that she could again go out and seek employment. She had done this covertly throughout her marriage, yet Pasión had eventually found her out each time.

"A little faith," he had said, moments after he'd struck her and she lay weeping. "A little faith that things will soon work out. Is that too much to ask for from my wife?"

He had towered over her, but his shoulders had slumped as if with grief.

"I may not always provide you with everything you need, but God knows I do my best. And how do you repay me? By shaming me and going out to get yourself a job. By letting the world think I'm not man enough to take care of you myself."

Contrite for having caused him to lash out and mindful of the fact that he had helped her escape spinsterhood, Rebecca had apologized.

"For richer or poorer," Pasión often reminded her. "Till death do us part, and only then."

He would step near and tenderly stroke her face. "I could have had my pick. But you're the one I married. You're the only one I've ever loved."

His words would ring with truth, inspiring Rebecca to trust him when she had strength for little else.

Anything was possible, she would persuade herself. *Even the improbable could occur.*

She had been raised on miracles, taught from early childhood to believe. In the Dominican Republic she had walked hand in hand with her maternal grandmother who had pointed out trees that appeared to have rotted from the inside out but had nonetheless branched out to bloom with leaves. She herself had overturned stones to find the life teeming underneath; had knelt to watch Bienvenida pull up brittle stems in order to expose their wholesome bulbs; had watched in awe as it rained and thundered across the road while where she stood, a mere several feet away, the sun above shone bright and the sky remained a turquoise blue.

More miraculous than these occurrences in nature were those manifested in the human realm. During Trujillo's reign of terror, Rebecca had learned of the disappearances of neighbors only to then witness—months later and sometimes years—the return to life of several of these people given up for dead. She had seen others transformed into heroes in the face of danger and, of late, had worked magic herself by scaring up out of nothing meals to satisfy or at least quell her children's hunger.

Compared to these marvels, Pasión's transforming into a better husband, father and provider seemed an easy thing.

Rebecca slid under the bedcovers and stretched her leg until a toe clicked on the television. Cartoon music roused her children. Esperanza, the first to wake, glanced triumphantly at the clock. Though she was only seven, she had the height of a thirteen-year-old and tended to move awkwardly. She now extended a bony arm out of the bed, retrieved a sheet of newspaper, rolled it tightly, stuck it in her sleeping brother's open mouth. Rubén's lips closed around it and immediately spit it out. He lunged forward and wrestled his giggling sister. Their bodies rolled on Rebecca's and Soledad's until the bed was a tangle of arms and legs.

Rebecca grabbed her son by the collar. "If you have so much energy, you can get up and walk to school."

"You see how you are? Why don't you tell Esperanza something too?"

"Because you're a boy and you should know better," his mother retorted.

Esperanza slouched out of the room. Minutes later she returned with a carton of milk, a bag of white bread, a knife, and an almost empty jar of peanut butter and jelly in alternate swirls. Sitting on the bed, she spread the mixture on a slice of bread.

Rebecca snatched the knife from her hand. "Soledad and Rubén need to get some too!"

She wiped peanut butter off Esperanza's bread and spread it so thinly on two other slices that they tore. She then topped them with another slice and handed a sandwich to each child. Despondent, she watched them shove the bread into their mouths and pass the carton from one mouth to another.

Soledad, the four-year-old, bit the white center from her bread and slipped a hand into the crust so that it dangled from her wrist like a bracelet. Rubén ripped it off and shoved it into his own mouth.

"That's enough!" Rebecca yelled.

Sensing his mother's breaking point, Rubén burrowed under the blankets and emerged at the foot of the bed. Rebecca had an urge to slap him, to make him disappear. Despite her knowledge to the contrary, she sometimes imagined that, if not for the untimely births of her children, Pasión might by now have become a better husband or at least not have felt the need to escape into the arms of a mistress. This thought conflicted with her possessive devotion to the children, who resembled only Pasión with their disproportionately long limbs, flat, wide noses and wide-set eyes. As for Rubén, he was a carbon copy of what his father must have been when young, though Pasión insisted he had been cuckolded.

Soledad solemnly watched her mother. She was the youngest child and the most reserved. To Rebecca, she seemed the most disrespectful. Whenever Soledad focused on her—sunken eyes contracting while the rest of her features remained still—Rebecca had the impression that she was being judged. She'd feel claustrophobic and her throat would constrict, as if she were being forced to swallow not only the failure she'd become but also the arrogance of a child reminding her of it.

"I'm going to Abuela's house," she announced, abruptly throwing back the covers.

Her children immediately leapt out of bed. "Can we come too? Please?"

"What do you think I'm made of? Gold? Buses aren't free."

"I don't mind walking," Esperanza asserted.

Rebecca searched her husband's clothes for loose change. "You and Rubén are staying to watch your sister." She shoved nickels and dimes into her pocket, then reached under the bed for her boots. After pulling them on, she grabbed her coat and left the house.

The wind snatched her breath away as she stepped out onto the street. She inhaled deeply and felt the air crystallize in her lungs. It was a refreshing cold, jarring, unlike the numbing cold in the house which made her sleepy. She walked briskly, toes wiggling to keep the blood in her feet circulating. At the corner she stopped beside a group of people waiting for the bus and was surprised when they stepped aside for her. She smiled, unaware that some glared and others covered their mouths and noses. It had been so long since she had bathed that she had become oblivious to her effect on others.

When the bus arrived, she willed it to stop in front of her and climbed in. Passengers moved out of her way as she headed toward the back and took a seat. A man beside her flipped through baseball cards and held conversations with each player, shouting at some, laughing and whispering intimately to others. Rebecca slid away from him, closer to the window. The bus rolled and bumped past blocks of tenement buildings bearing no resemblance to the well-kept brownstones she had imagined herself living in. She remembered how, at the age of twenty-one, she had begged her parents for permission to move to the United States. She had honestly believed that she would be able to pick gold off the streets and send for her parents so they might live as grandly as those who returned to the Dominican Republic claimed was possible. Only after her arrival had she realized that those who moved to the States lived as miserably as most in her own country. One of the few advantages of emigrating was escaping riots and military raids, but even this was often overshadowed by a fear of deportation.

Rebecca got off the bus at the corner of Liberty and Pennsylvania, then made her way toward Bradford, the dreary street where her parents lived.

"Bendición, Mamá," she said when the door to their house swung open.

Aurelia embraced her eldest daughter. "Que Dios te bendiga," she replied, shutting the door and leading her into the kitchen. "Where are the children? In school?"

Rebecca slung her coat over a chair. "Home. Esperanza and Rubén are watching Soledad."

"Aren't they too young for that?"

"Mami, please. I have enough problems without you criticizing me."

Aurelia scrutinized her daughter's face. Although Rebecca attempted to meet her gaze, her eyes kept shifting. The areas around them were sunken and her skin yellowish, making her appear anemic. Wearily, Aurelia sat opposite her.

"Pasión?"

"No. The house, the chickens, the lack of heat. I think I'm going crazy."

"Then why don't you leave?"

"Because it's my home." Rebecca slouched low into her seat. "Pasión and the children are all I have."

"Don't give me that. You know you can always stay here."

"I know, but—"

"Rebecca, Pasión treats you like an animal."

"What do you think? That it would be easy for me to just pick up and leave?"

"How could anything be worse than the situation you're in now?"

"I don't know, Mami! I don't know, okay?"

The words fell heavily on Aurelia. She turned from her daughter and silently smoothed the skirt of her housecoat, her frustration contained between thin lips.

"There's no food in the refrigerator," Rebecca continued. "The house is a mess and Pasión rarely comes home. When he does, it's usually to pick a fight." She sat upright and lifted her sweater to reveal the bruises on her chest. Aurelia flinched. "Sometimes I'm convinced he wants to kill me."

"Dios mío, are you going to wait until he succeeds?"

Rebecca sliced her hand through empty air, ready to lash out verbally. Suddenly noticing her youngest sister watching from the threshold, she raised her hand to her head and tucked strands of knotted hair under her hat.

"Why are you standing there?" she demanded.

Iliana stepped into the room. "I live here," she said, her voice barbed and calculating. "The question is what are *you* doing here?"

Rebecca's brows arched. "What business is it of yours?"

"It's every damn bit my business," Iliana declared. "You come here complaining about broken bones and bruises and have a fit if someone tries to help. If you plan on staying with Pasión until he kills you—"

Aurelia hurled her a warning look.

"—why don't you keep your mouth shut? You've already caused Mom a heart attack."

Rebecca gaped at her mother, then her sister.

"Don't look at me like that. You know exactly what I'm talking about. You're so desperate for a man that you don't even care how your children are affected."

Rebecca lunged from her chair to sneer into her sister's carefully groomed face. "I brought my children into this world, and no one, especially not a rag of a girl like you, is going to tell me how to raise them! Who the fuck do you think you are? You don't know shit about my life!"

"I know enough to know you're a lousy mother. That's why I have every intention of reporting you to Social Services. Maybe then you'll at least learn to take better care of your children since you obviously don't care about yourself."

Rage contorted Aurelia's face as she stepped between her

daughters. "How dare you speak to your sister like that," she scolded her youngest. "I'm her mother, and not even I address her in such a way. And as for you—" She whirled toward her eldest. "I don't care what kind of language you use elsewhere, but in my presence and under my roof I expect you to show some respect. Especially when you know your sister is right. For eight years you and your children have been living in that pigsty. When are you going to stop waiting for miracles and take some responsibility? Pasión isn't about to change!"

Rebecca's mouth shut like the jaws of a trap in which a wounded animal had just been caught. So that was how her mother felt. That was how all the members of her family felt. She understood. They thought she was irresponsible, indifferent to her own fate and that of her children. Having forgotten the past, they compared themselves to her and came up better. But her own memory was longer. Had it not been for her, they would have still been picking mangoes to keep from starving. She was the one who had moved to the United States to work and had saved enough money to send for her parents and eventually her brothers and sisters; she was the one who, though not eligible for residency, had paid for an attorney who succeeded in obtaining green cards for everyone else; she was the one who, until her marriage, had contributed half of her earnings toward her parents' expenses, something none of her siblings had ever considered doing. And where had it gotten her? What thanks had she received?

She snatched her coat from the back of the chair and flung it on. Her hands jerked as she hooked the coat's wooden toggles through frayed loops. Aware that boundaries had been crossed, Iliana and Aurelia watched in fretful silence. When Rebecca finished, she raised steady eyes to theirs.

"If either of you tries to take my children, I'll follow you wherever you go and I'll kill you!"

She stamped out into the hallway and through the front door, letting it slam behind her. The fabric of her pockets tore as she jammed her fists in and turned off Bradford. The laughter of children being released from a half-day at school simultaneously quickened her steps toward her own children waiting for her at home. She had borne the burden of carrying each child inside her for nine hellish months, and if she had not relinquished them then, she would definitely not do so now.

CHAPTER

 9

Aurelia stared at the chair Rebecca had abandoned, as if to will her to reappear. Iliana too remained still, attempting to read from her mother's face which words might justify the argument she'd begun.

"You're going over there, aren't you?" she finally asked.

"What would you prefer I do? Give up on Rebecca?"

Iliana knew what she was supposed to say: *That's not what I meant, Mami. We can convince her to leave Pasión. This time she will stay. She will forget him and be grateful for the opportunity to begin again.* It would be so very easy for her to say these words. She had said them often enough. Yet, this time, she could not bring herself to speak them.

"Mami, she has given up on herself."

Aurelia raised her eyes to her daughter standing tall.

"It's not Rebecca I worry about anymore. It's her children and it's you." Iliana groped for words. "I saw her face. I watched her as she spoke. It was almost as if she enjoyed talking about how Pasión beats her. As if— As if she grew stronger the more her descriptions caused you pain. That doing so only helped her to go back."

Aurelia's head shifted so imperceptibly that Iliana was not sure whether she had nodded or shaken her head in disbelief.

"I know it sounds crazy, Mami, but I saw it. That's why I got so angry. And it's not like I don't care what happens to Rebecca. Of course I do. But there's nothing we can do. Not until she's willing to help herself."

"Did you read that in a textbook?"

Iliana felt the air knocked out of her. Like a balloon spiralling from its height, she struggled to stay aloft.

"There are statistics about battered women, yes. And there are studies of how they stay with their husbands no matter how badly they're treated. But that's not why I'm saying what I'm saying. How many times have we tried to get her to leave Pasión? How many times have we moved her here only to have her go back to him? And that's exactly what she'll keep doing until things get so bad that she decides to leave him on her own."

Disdain tightened the muscles on Aurelia's face as Iliana spoke, barely pausing to catch her breath.

"I know she's your daughter, Mami. She's my sister too. Before I went away, I was always the one who went with you and Papi to move her out. I was always—"

"And not anymore?"

"Mami, it's a waste of time."

"Rebecca's a waste of time?"

"That's not—"

"And here I thought they'd taught you nothing in that school. But you've obviously learned a lot. You can even predict your sister's future. Tell me," she continued, her eyes locking onto her youngest daughter's. "What else did you learn, besides how to turn your back on your own family?"

Iliana had rarely heard her mother use that tone—razor-sharp and able to shred to insignificance any argument she might choose.

"Never mind," she backtracked.

"Never mind? No, no. Let's talk," Aurelia insisted. "It seems you've wanted to ever since you came home. I'm sure you have a lot to say, and I'm interested to hear. Tell me, have you suffered so much that you know what it's like to be your sister or to be so afraid of the future that you hold on to the only thing you have for fear of losing even that? Eh?" Aurelia waited. "Why so silent now? I'm giving you the chance to talk, to teach your mother who knows nothing."

"Just forget it," Iliana mumbled. "Forget I said anything at all."

Aurelia watched her. Then, so slowly that it seemed her head had inexplicably grown heavy, she released its weight onto her hand resting on the table. Without deigning to glance back at her daughter, she waved her other hand in a gesture of dismissal.

"Go," she muttered. "I know you're itching to get out of the house."

Iliana hesitated. She wanted to be kind, to feel herself opening wide enough to apologize for all she'd said. She wanted to forgive her sister for what she'd become and to accept her as she was. But she found that she could not.

It was not as if Rebecca had no options. All of her children were American-born. As such, she could divorce her husband and qualify for state assistance or move in with her parents until she found a job and an apartment of her own. Either way, she'd be better off than she was now.

The longer Iliana thought about it, the less she was able to justify her sister's apathy. She was sure that in her place she would handle matters differently. She was so afraid of being beaten down, physically or mentally, that, if unable to fight with fists and feet, she at least plotted silently to escape. Look at how she had managed to get away to a university—this though she had been told she was not smart enough and several of her guidance counselors had advised her against applying.

"You'll be terribly hurt when the rejections come. Save yourself the disappointment," they had said, smiling kindly. "Besides, people outside the city are not like us. Even just upstate they're—well—you know—racist. They won't want you there."

Then there was the way she had handled the student who had stalked her everywhere she went during her first semester. The one time he had forced himself on her she had been so terrified and incensed that her adrenaline had surged and she had managed to shove his muscular body off her own. So obvious had it been to him that she would be willing and able to kill him with her bare hands that he had instantly backed off.

What Rebecca needed, Iliana decided then and there, was psychiatric help. Not because she allowed Pasión to beat her, but because he was not the only one who had. Before marrying Pasión, she had been involved with Samuel, who, in addition to beating her, had supposedly molested his teenage daughter from a previous marriage. That Rebecca had nonetheless stayed with him until he threw her out was inexcusable. She should have left him of her own free will.

At a loss for apologetic or reassuring words, Iliana left the room. As she did, she heard her mother murmur to herself.

"God forbid that Papito or I should die today. This family would fall apart."

"I heard," Marina said.

"Heard what?"

"The argument you had with Mami and Rebecca."

"So?"

"So why bother?"

Iliana rummaged through a purse for the money she had saved from her part-time jobs at school. Her sister propped herself up on an elbow but made no move to rise although it was way past noon.

"It's been going on for years. Your coming home ain't gonna change things."

"Please don't start with me. I'm not in the mood."

Marina picked lint off her blanket. "You're never in the mood." With her shoulders bared, she appeared vulnerable, like an over-sized child waiting to be embraced.

"I've gotta go," Iliana told her, unwilling to absorb the loneliness emanating from her like a scent. "I'm meeting a friend and I'll be late if I don't leave right now."

"I wish I had someone to go out with."

Iliana did not reply.

"Wanna do something later?"

"I don't know. We'll see when I get back."

Iliana rushed out of the room. Aurelia joined her in the upstairs hallway as she paused to put her coat on.

"Another date with your rooster?"

"He's not my boyfriend, Mami."

"A butterfly, then?"

It might have been a joke, but Iliana nevertheless wondered how her mother had guessed that Ed was gay.

"Why don't you invite him here one afternoon. I'll make you both some lunch."

"You wouldn't mind?"

"Of course not. It would be nice to meet one of your friends from school."

Iliana was again amazed. She would not even have bothered telling her mother anything about Ed had she not answered the phone when he'd called the previous day.

"I think he'd like that," she replied.

Aurelia smiled. Then, as if embarrassed by her efforts at reconciliation, she gruffly nudged her daughter out the door. "Now go," she commanded. "Just make sure you return before your father does."

Iliana stepped outside. As she headed toward the train station it dawned on her that, except for Rebecca, who had openly defied her parents by moving in with Samuel, she was the first of her parents' daughters allowed to meet unescorted with a man. Even while engaged, her other married sisters had been made to take along a sibling on all dates. Each had stolen private moments by bribing whoever was sent along, but neither parent had ever been the wiser.

She purchased a token, pushed herself through a turnstile, and climbed a set of stairs to the outdoor platform rather than huddle by a radiator in the waiting room reeking of urine. At the platform's edge, she squinted in the direction from which the train would be arriving. A pinpoint of light in the distance revealed that she had a wait of at least ten minutes. To save herself some time at Chambers, she walked to where she'd be able to get off by the stairs leading to the 6. Restless, she peered over the platform's rail.

In a lot below, large boxes, insulated with rags and cardboard, served as shelter for the homeless. Beside these, a man lay curled inside a gutted refrigerator. A bit of newspaper, swept along by the wind, perched itself on his chin. Twitching and tossing in the midst of sleep, he instinctively reached out to flick it off.

A woman and child emerged from one of the larger boxes. Both of them were bundled from head to toe in clothes soiled to shades of grey. Yet the ends of a diaphanous fuchsia scarf billowed like a sail from around the woman's neck. This jolt of color drew Iliana's attention. She wanted to see the woman's face. She wanted to know why, in light of her dire circumstances, she would wear such a festive thing.

The woman led the child to the rear of the lot where barren shrubs separated it from the fenced-in playground of an elementary school. She squeezed herself between the fence and branches not dense enough to hide her. Turning and crouching so that Iliana for the first time saw the sharp features of her face, she gestured for the child to do the same. The child, whose sex was indistinguishable, appeared to be no more than five. Iliana watched it turn—apprehensively, or so it seemed—to search the area. She had the impression not only that the child was unaccustomed to urinating or defecating in a lot, but also that it was shamed by having to witness the woman doing publicly what should have been a private act. Glimpsing Iliana, the child frantically yanked the woman's arm and pointed to the platform. The woman immediately crouched still. Iliana too, inexplicably, found herself held in place. They gazed at each other for what were only moments but for Iliana seemed a lifetime during which she remembered more than she would willingly have allowed.

Ever since her return to New York she had rushed past homeless people asking for money on corners and on trains. Not wanting to be reminded of the nights she had gone to bed hungry only to sleepwalk to the refrigerator to gnaw a piece of cheese or guzzle the remains of a gallon of milk her mother had been rationing out to last the week, she had learned to look away. Now she found herself remembering the summers when she, Tico, Beatriz and Marina had waited on line for the free meals distributed by the city and had then hurried into other neighborhoods to stand on other lines, as many as four a day, until they had collected enough to feed their entire family. With a shudder, she also recalled the unheated apartment where she had slept weighted by blankets beside her sisters and had nonetheless felt the relentless cold seep into her bones. She remembered as well the morning she had attempted to warm her bath with pots of boiling water and, half asleep, lifted one off the stove with her bare hands, scorching her fingers against the pot and clumsily releasing it so that the scalding water spilled on her midriff and peeled off layers of her skin.

These memories made her wonder where she and her family would have been had her father not managed to save, throughout years of scrimping, the three hundred dollars with which he had purchased their current home. They also made her wonder if her married siblings would have welcomed them into theirs. Not knowing for sure lent meaning to her mother's words: "God forbid that Papito or I should die today. This family would fall apart."

Fourteen thousand dollars. Fourteen thousand dollars and a fistful of change—the sum of Papito's annual earnings but thousands less than the yearly tuition at Iliana's school. Only now did she understand why her mother had reused every bit of oil; had beaten egg whites before mixing in their yolks to make omelettes which, swollen large with air, had fed more mouths; had mended and remended their clothes until the fabric could not withstand the prick or pull of needle and thread. She understood as well why, unlike others who had been able to donate out of their own pockets the thirty-five dollars Seventh-Day Adventists were required to raise during Collection Month, she and her family had instead dressed in their best, sported buttons identifying them as Adventists, armed themselves with pamphlets explaining that the funds would be used to feed the hungry, and, with cans shamefully held in hands and hearts praying that they not be mistaken for beggars intending to use the money for themselves, had solicited the public's help.

Still, the woman did not move. Held accountable by her unflinching stare, Iliana felt like a Peeping Tom who had derived, if not pleasure, then a certain measure of self-worth by comparison. She was also struck by the absurdity of having considered herself superior, as if, unlike the woman, she would forever be in control of her destiny and would never suffer a misfortune for which she might need the help of others.

The woman abruptly pulled the child down onto the ground beside her. Standing on the platform and buffeted by a wind fiercer at that height, Iliana too turned away.

For a year and a half she had lived in a town whose pristine appearance had deceived her into believing, because she had wanted desperately to believe, that, having entered into the company of the elite, she would never again suffer hunger or abuse. She had clung to this belief despite hearing the word "NIGGER" erupt from the lips of strangers; seeing swastikas scrawled on the walls of synagogues; and witnessing women, marching to "take back the night," attacked for calling public attention to the town's hidden violence. When classmates had presumed to know the inner workings of those of her race and class—inferring their inherent laziness, lack of motivation, welfare dependency and intellectual deficiency—she had stopped up her ears and gradually trained her eyes not to see. Yet rage had turned her body against itself, transforming her stomach into an acidic mass that heaved bitterness into her mouth.

A train clambered into the station. Iliana gratefully stepped into its heated cars and let her eyes glide across the faces of the people around her. These—belonging to Italian, Polish and Asian Americans who boarded the train in Queens and deeper inside Brooklyn, then to African, Caribbean, Latin Americans and, finally, Hasidic Jews—she had missed during her absence from New York. She liked the homeboys whose arrogant faces challenged the assumption they had no business cutting school with Christmas vacation just around the bend and whose pants slid tantalizingly from their hips and made them appear to sway even as they stood still. As for the girls with hands fluttering like birds aching to fly free, they reminded her of herself at the same age and of the friends she had since lost track of. Her eyes strayed to the swollen belly of one who could have been no more than thirteen and to the swaddled baby in a carriage another gently pushed and pulled. Their voices—high and shrill as the sound of a metal spoon scraping remainders from the bottom of a pot—put her in mind of the saddest blues she'd heard. As she had listened, the notes had struck a chord and her soul had responded, swaying her body against its will and despite the teachings that attributed such songs to the devil and the damned. An elderly woman beside the girls shook her head in blatant disapproval. Watching her, it was easy for Iliana to imagine her clucking her tongue and storing under it words of advice for grandchildren who would have no idea what had inspired the undeserved harangue.

Iliana turned toward a window on the door she leaned against. As a child she had feared the train would veer off its tracks and plunge into the river's murky waters. It was possible, what with the Williamsburg Bridge in need of repairs and the train speeding so close to the edge. As this thought crossed her mind, a metallic shriek sent her heart leaping toward her mouth. She instantly gripped a pole beside her and turned to find a man at the center of the aisle clutching and blowing into—for it could not be described as playing—the most dented and bent-out-of-shape saxophone she had ever seen. This relic of an instrument was what had produced the sound and now offered what was intended as a rendition of "The Saints Go Marching In." But even with a stretch of her imagination, Iliana could not believe that the man—his cheeks alternately puffing out and then collapsing—considered himself a musician and expected contributions from the passengers he had disturbed.

As if he had read her thoughts, the man let fall the clump of metal. He smiled broadly and, reaching inside his ragged coat, pulled out a paper cup.

"Now I know y'all don't like my playing," he said, his voice a deep rumble that traveled the car's length and made itself heard above the train's own roar. "But if y'all want me to stop, y'all are gonna have to make it worth my while."

Amused and guilty laughter erupted from the lips of several passengers. For a brief moment, as many reached into pockets and purses for loose change, they were transformed from strangers into individuals bound by an event which would lose its appeal upon the telling of it to others.

A man beside Iliana dropped a bill into the outstretched cup. "I hope I never have the misfortune of hearing you play again," he said good-naturedly.

"That all depends," replied the trickster, his proximity revealing the dirt embedded deep in the furrows of his aged face. "If I collect enough, I'll buy myself a new horn and you can come hear me play at the Savoy."

"Didn't that place close years ago?"

"Now why you wanna blow on an old man's dream? I don't know if it has closed or not, but if it has, it'll open just for me."

CHAPTER

❖ 10 ❖

Ed waved from a corner of the dimly lit café. "I thought you'd never get here."

Iliana slid into a chair beside him. "Ed, look at me," she instructed, leaning close. "Do I look like a drag queen to you?"

He looked at her as if she had lost her mind.

"I'm not kidding!"

"Give me a chance. I'm trying to decide."

"You're supposed to be able to tell immediately!"

"Why? Did one of your sisters accuse you of looking like a drag queen?"

"You still haven't answered my question. Do I look like one or not?"

"Of course not! That's absurd!"

"Then why the fuck did those guys act like I was one?"

"What guys?"

Iliana unbuttoned her coat and shrugged it off. "I was waiting for the light to change at Astor Place and noticed these two men, good-looking too, staring at me from across the street. When the light changed and I walked past them, they shouted, 'Drag queen in style! And look at her walk!' "

Ed broke into peals of laughter. "Nah!"

"They did!"

"Are you sure they were talking about you?"

"Who else could they have been talking about? They were looking straight at me."

"Then you should be flattered. They probably meant it as a compliment."

"A compliment? How the hell would you like it if someone told you you looked like a goddamn drag queen?"

Ed attempted to wipe the laughter from his voice. "Actually, you do look the way most drag queens wish they could. Those guys were probably fags and just thought you look as dramatic as Diana Ross, Patti Labelle, Sade or any of the black divas. Then there's the way you walk."

"What about the way I walk?"

"You know—it's a—it's a runway walk. The kind drag queens usually adopt."

"Oh, great," Iliana said.

"You should count yourself lucky. At least you have it naturally. Even models have to work hard to glide the way you do. And if nothing else, it gets you attention as you're walking down the street."

"I'd rather do without."

Ed gestured to a waitress. "You'll have to get used to it, Iliana. You're attractive, and I don't think you have any idea of how you appear to others."

"Yeah?" the waitress asked.

"I'll have a cappuccino."

"Hot chocolate," Iliana muttered, picking up a salt shaker and toying with it until the waitress left. "If I'm so damn attractive, why do I have such a hard time getting dates?"

"Because straight men are terrified of you. You're so convinced you're ugly that you behave in ways that make you seem arrogant and warn people to stay away."

"That's bullshit." If they were attracted to me, they'd find some way to let me know."

"Not if they thought they'd be rejected."

"So either I change my attitude or I'll be stuck with men like you?"

"And what is that supposed to mean?"

Iliana sprinkled a layer of salt on the table and drew a tic-tac-toe pattern into the crystals. From the outset, she'd had a crush on Ed. There was something about his narrow hips, graceful hands, shoulder-length hair and lashes longer than most women's that had set her sexually at ease. Nights at school, after her mother's voice had faded, she had lain awake aching to be held and to be reminded that she was more than spirit and possessed a beating heart and flesh needing to be touched. Ed would be gentle, she had thought. He would ease her into womanhood and rouse her without shame.

She wiped the salt off the table onto her palm. When the waitress brought her order, she flung the salt over her left shoulder to blind Satan, should he exist. She then darted a sideways glance at Ed as she recalled the first time they had discussed his being gay. Something she'd said had made him lean back against the vinyl upholstery of a diner's booth.

"You don't know me as well as you think you do," he'd said, smiling smugly.

"No?"

"No, you don't. There's quite a bit about me that might surprise you."

Iliana had watched him, a smile of her own playing on her lips.

"I know enough," she had asserted, "to know about you and Steve."

The grin on Ed's face had immediately disappeared. "Steve?"

"Yes. Your friend in San Francisco."

"What about him?"

"Oh, Ed," Iliana had replied, not relishing his alarm. "You know a lot more about him than I could possibly ever tell."

"Well," he'd said after an uncomfortable silence. "How'd you know?"

"I have no idea," she had conceded. "Somehow, I just knew."

Ed reached a hand across the table and waved it in front of Iliana's face. "So where'd you go?"he asked, drawing her back into the present. "I know you weren't here."

"I'm sorry." Iliana sipped her cocoa. "I drifted, but at least I was thinking about you."

"Yeah? What about?"

"The first time we spoke about you being gay."

Ed rolled his eyes back to hide their pupils. "Iliana the psychic. Knower of all things."

Iliana giggled as he held up an imaginary crystal ball and went into a trance.

"Oops," he said, pretending he'd dropped the ball and it had shattered on the floor. "So much for psychic powers."

"Magic balls don't break that easily." Iliana lifted the ball into her own hands. "See?"

"I'm still convinced Steve's name slipped my lips. Otherwise there's no way you could have known."

"Yeah. Uh-huh. Whatever," was all Iliana said.

CHAPTER

❖ 11 ❖

Rebecca tore the cardboard off a second-floor window in time to see her mother step back against a streetlamp to peer up at her.

"Hurry and open the door," Aurelia shouted. "It's freezing out here."

"What the hell do you want?"

The door on the driver's side of Papito's Buick opened. "What? Do we need an invitation to come see you?"

Aurelia looked thin and frail beside him. Her expression suggested she had been crying. As for Papito, though he attempted to appear nonchalant, his shoulders were squared in anticipation of a dispute.

"If you're here to try and make me leave, you're wasting your time!"

"We just want to talk."

"There's nothing to talk about!"

"Rebecca, please. We're your parents."

"Parents? My parents died the day I married!"

Aurelia hooked an arm through her husband's, her face averted so as not to see the pain reflected in his eyes. Esperanza and Rubén crept up behind their mother and squealed with delight at a glimpse of their grandparents. Rebecca shoved them out of sight.

"Mi'ja, think of the children. They can't spend another winter in that house. Move in with us. If you don't like it, you can return when it gets warm."

Rebecca's brows arched with scorn. So her mother thought she was a fool and would snatch the offered crumbs. In the Dominican Republic she had felt honored when chosen to eat the last spoonful from her father's plate. She had even competed for the privilege. But she was an adult now and would not be satisfied by small gestures. If her parents were genuinely concerned, they could pool their resources and set her up in an apartment instead of offering what they knew she could not accept. They could sacrifice as she had done for them.

"Both of you are such pendejos! You think I'd move in to have you be in my business all the time? I'd rather live with the devil himself!"

"That man is twice your age," Papito reminded her. "And look at the way he has you living. How can you bear to stay with him?"

Rebecca leaned farther out the window and gestured obscenely. "Because he fucks me like this," she shouted to the amusement of passersby. "And he licks me where I like!" She stuck out her tongue and flicked it. "Like this!"

"What's wrong?" she asked, when her parents did not respond. "Can't you fuck anymore? Is that why you don't understand?"

"May God forgive you," her father said, so low that she barely heard.

The snowflakes which had begun to fall gathered on his shoulders and whitened his dyed black hair. Remorse momentarily flickered behind Rebecca's eyes as he raised an ungloved hand to wipe his nose.

"Rebecca, you're our eldest daughter. We would do anything for you. You're young. You could find another husband. We would help you. There are plenty of eligible men in church."

A spasm of fury unfurled along Rebecca's spine. "Where the hell do you think I found Pasión? You think people are perfect just because they go to church? All anyone there knows how to do is be self-righteous! They talk about charity and kindness, but what have they ever done for me? What has God ever done for me?"

Papito gaped at her, then abruptly nudged his wife into the car and climbed in after her. "Maldita!" he shouted from a rolled-down window. "This is the last time we try to help!"

"Go to hell! You and the whole fucking congregation,"
Rebecca yelled. "I can do just fine on my own!"

Aurelia's heart lurched irregularly. A sharp pain—as of pins piercing the valves of her heart and extending outward—throbbed inside her chest. She tried to alleviate the pain with a tentative breath
and felt it lodge inside her lungs, forcing her to pause until the pain
subsided and her breath eased out.

Papito jammed his key into the ignition. Aurelia heard his angry breaths and saw them condense against the windshield. She
leaned forward to wipe the glass. A gash between buildings revealed a night sky tinged with the pinkish-purple haze that usually
preceded snow. To Aurelia it appeared as if the sky had recently
been bruised and was hurting too. She wanted to distract her husband from his anger and to point out to him that patch of sky. But
familiar with the intricacies of his moods, she knew that to speak
would only be to make things worse.

The car pulled away from the curb and sped toward the corner.
Papito slammed a foot on the brake just as the traffic light turned
red. A man on the sidewalk to Aurelia's right yelled something that
she did not quite hear. She began to roll down her window and
then fearfully closed it when she saw the man approach. He might
only want directions, but she was unwilling to take a chance.

As if to indicate that he understood her caution, the man
formed a peace sign and pointed to the car.

"Papito, the headlights. Do you have the headlights on?"

Papito turned to her and scowled. Then, seeing the man himself, he switched the headlights on. In the brilliance of their glare
Aurelia saw snow falling in drifts that would blanket the streets by
morning. She would have to remember to wake her husband earlier. Surely the trains would run late with the winter's first big
snow.

The traffic light switched to green. Papito swerved the Buick
around the corner so quickly that Aurelia had to grab the dash-
board to keep from being thrown against the door.

"Getting us killed won't make her leave Pasión!"

"Bestia! Perra!" Papito spit. "How dare she speak to us like that!"

His wife braced for what was coming.

"An animal! That's what she is! The itch in her crotch keeps her from thinking straight!"

"And what are we if we speak about her in such a way?"

"We're pendejos, exactly like she said! Pendejos for wasting our time worrying about how she lives! And then those people standing around laughing at us like we were fools! Never again! You hear me! Never again!"

Aurelia reached for his hand clenched around the steering wheel, but Papito flung hers off.

"What kind of language was that to use on us? Eh? Did we ever speak to her that way? Did we raise our children to have such filthy mouths or to hang around with dogs? We did our best, Aurelia. We did our best and all our children think that it was easy, that it was all just fun and games. Here we are old people and we still can't rest in peace. I come home from a long, hard day at work and for what? To be dragged out into the street and be insulted! To be insulted by my own daughter and to have her insult God too! And why? Because we try to help! But she's a grown woman! She can live any way she wants—I no longer care! May she rot in that house and may her soul regret the day!"

His wife again wiped condensation from the glass. "That's a strong curse, Papito. Are you willing to live with yourself if it comes true?"

"You heard me, Aurelia. I don't ever want her in our house. She'll have to learn what it means to truly have no parents."

"And what about the children? Is it their fault that their mother has no sense?"

Papito's face set into determined lines even as his voice wavered. "They're her responsibility, not ours."

"They're our grandchildren, Papito. If they were to come to harm, we'd be more at fault because we should have known better than to let it happen."

"What? Are we supposed to take them from her by force? Are we supposed to bring them home to live with us?"

Aurelia turned from her husband to gaze out of a window. The heat in the car was on, but only slightly. Whenever it was on full-blast, she had difficulty breathing. She understood the need for artificial heat, yet despite all her winters in New York, she was still unaccustomed to the idea of hot air spewed from vents or radiated from hot metal. She preferred to be warmed by blue-tipped flames that she could see or by a brilliant sun whose heat absorbed into her skin.

"If that's what it takes, then, yes."

"You'd be willing to raise three more children after bringing up fourteen of your own?" Papito asked, incredulous.

"What choice would I have?"

"Why can't Zoraida, Nereida or Azucena take them in?"

"It's not a matter of taking them in, Papito. It's a matter of dealing with Rebecca if they did. And none of them would have the patience."

Papito parked the car around the corner from their house, pulled the key from the ignition, then remained seated, too exhausted, suddenly, to move.

"Not only do we have Marina to worry about, but again and again we have Rebecca. When will it ever stop?"

Aurelia opened the passenger door to step out. "Ay, Papito. Not until we're in our graves. Not until we're buried in our graves."

CHAPTER

❖ 12 ❖

Marina tried to summon sleep, but darkness pushed against her, stifling her breaths. Not far from where she lay, her sister slept on the bed they had once shared. Marina resented the persistence of Iliana's breathing and the ease with which it flowed. Its sound was oppressive, luring her own to meet its rhythm. When young, she had repeatedly disturbed Iliana's sleep to ask that she breathe quietly or please take smaller breaths. Iliana had agreed but had slipped back into the same rhythm. On other occasions and still in the midst of sleep, she had responded by rolling over on the narrow bed where they lay head to foot and gently rocking her hips against Marina's leg. Fascinated by her sister's rippling motion, Marina had remained still. Only after Iliana's body had collapsed contentedly against her own had she again roused her to insist that she move to her side of the bed.

Ever since her sister's return home, Marina had been finding their basement room increasingly claustrophobic. Each night and even with her eyes open, she felt the walls, with their damp, cold stones embedded deep in granite, heave as they nudged the room's furniture toward its center. Unlike her sister who slept peacefully, she knew, with frightening conviction, that—if not on that night, then on another—their bodies would be crushed by these shifting walls. This awareness of the instability of their home was what caused her to attempt to control her own death by dictating the time and manner of its occurrence.

Marina rolled to the edge of her bed, then rose cautiously to a stand. The concrete floor exuded cold as she dragged her feet along its surface. So indistinguishable was she from darkness that, as she pulled the string of a light fixture in the walk-in closet, she prayed that she too would not dissolve with light. Relieved to find herself intact, she slipped on a pair of sandals and tucked her naked body into a floor-length coat.

It was earlier than she'd believed. Outside, streetlamps were still lit and the grayish blue of night revealed no hint of dawn. A lone car rolled through snow which must have fallen as she lay in bed. Veiled and glistening, everything appeared pristine: the neighborhood's neglected buildings, the cars lined along the street, even the cans heaped with trash.

She descended from the stoop and closed the gate behind her. Excited at the prospect of wandering the streets, which, for a while, would be hers alone, she turned north on Bradford and walked toward Sunnyside. There she paused and, turning to see her footprints trailing close behind, smiled at what she imagined were the prints of an angel guarding her as she walked.

Her feet sunk into the snow. Its wet seeped into her sandals. This sensation too added to her joy. For the moment she was alive and free and could breathe with ease, walk to where she pleased, sing her praises to the night.

Along Sunnyside—just south of Highland, a park she had stumbled on by chance during a longer walk away from her tenement-ridden neighborhood—turreted and angular houses, unlike the standard one in which Marina lived, lined the sidewalk. Several of these houses, relics of the middle-class families who'd fled the neighborhood shortly after black and Hispanic families moved in, had fenced-in lawns, shrubs, even a tree or two separating them from other homes. It was one of these houses Marina had grown to love. Standing at the corner and apart from its neighbor, it had the luxury of possessing windows on all sides. In front of it, an iron fence teased passersby with a glimpse of a densely foliated area. A wooden fence guarded its backyard. Behind this fence and extending gnarled, icy limbs toward heaven stood a weathered oak. So wide was its girth that only upon first seeing it had Marina finally believed Brooklyn had once been mostly farmland.

Indifferent to the cold, she paused in front of the house to imagine herself looking out of one of its windows rather than trying to see in. A loving husband approached her from behind. He wrapped his arms around her and sprinkled kisses on her neck. Turning to face him, she returned his kisses with her own.

She then saw herself climb a flight of stairs to the top floor she assumed must be an attic. Beneath its slanted ceiling, she browsed through leather trunks and cedar chests. The faces and words of those who'd built the house and bequeathed it to their descendants blurred from sepia photographs and faded letters. She felt their collective past reach like tendrils through the walls and floors. Her own history twined with theirs, forming an extensive web of roots that assured her she too belonged as surely as did the oak outside.

Marina reached into the largest of the trunks and unfolded yellowed sheets of paper. From their midst, she withdrew antique lace, silk, brocades and linens. Her hands caressed the tattered fabrics. Her mind evoked elegantly dressed women wielding parasols against the sun. She stood before an oval mirror and held one of the dresses to her breast. Gone were the ninety-two pounds which had bloated her body to its massive two hundred and seventeen. Not only had her weight decreased: her hair had grown straight enough to billow with the slightest breeze. She raised a tentative hand to touch a strand. As her fingers tangled in knots of kinky hair, a car behind her skidded out of control. Startled, she leapt away from the curb's edge. The car crashed into another parked beside her and, with a grating, high-pitched sound, scraped paint off its side before shrieking to a halt.

At a glimpse of the driver's face clenched as tightly as a fist, Marina's eyes darted in search of pedestrians to whom she might run for help. But although the murky light of dawn had begun to rise, there was no one else around.

A well-dressed black man climbed out of the car. As he stepped toward the damage, the fear smoldering at the base of Marina's uterus caught flame. Its heat extended through her veins, thawing her feet which had numbed unnoticed and lending her the impetus to flee. She raced toward Fulton in hopes of finding an open store. Hearing a train approach, she hurled herself up the stairs of an elevated station, past the booth of a clerk screaming for her to pay her fare, through the doors reserved for exits, up another set of stairs and, finally, through the doors of a waiting train.

"Please, dear God! Please let the doors close!" she prayed.

As if God had for once heard her plea and answered, the train doors closed behind her. Gasping, she leaned against them and tried to quiet her pounding heart.

She had escaped. Not once had she looked back, though had she dared she would have glimpsed the man's own shock at witnessing her flight.

Marina collapsed onto an empty seat beside the doors. Her body was sweating profusely, but her feet were cold and wet. She lifted them onto the seat to remove her sandals. Barbs of pain shot first through one foot, then the other, as she tenderly massaged each. When both began to warm, she leaned back to rest her head against a window. Only then did she notice the black woman across the aisle. As soon as their eyes met, the woman lowered hers and pretended that she hadn't been caught staring. Three other people in the car did the same when Marina looked their way.

Her hands began to shake, imperceptibly at first, then so violently that the tips of her fingers drummed her thighs.

Disgust. That's what she had glimpsed in the eyes of each. Sheer, unadulterated disgust.

She glanced down at her ashy thighs, at her feet filthy from her habit of walking barefoot, at her coat gaping open at her crotch. She clutched the coat against her naked body and lowered her feet back onto the floor. Not once before sneaking out of her parents' house had she given a thought to her appearance. Now she became conscious of her uncombed hair and unbrushed teeth. She also felt the itch and prick of hair growing back in the areas she had shaved and smelled the stench oozing from her pores.

The black woman fumbled through her purse. When she blew her nose into a Kleenex, Marina understood that she had caught whiffs of and been offended by the smell. When a Hasidic man boarded the train on Marcy and quickly headed into the next car, she realized that he had smelled her from afar. When the train swayed precariously across the Williamsburg Bridge and a Puerto Rican woman at the end of the aisle coughed and then darted out at Delancey, followed by the black woman, no more doubts remained.

Marina slumped into her seat. She wished the Williamsburg Bridge had collapsed. She wished the river had swallowed the train and all its passengers so that not one had survived to recount the details of her appearance or of the nauseating smell. Her humiliation was complete. The knowledge gathered from the eyes of others had carved a path into her brain to become a part of her very being, unreconcilable as the color of her skin and the texture of her hair.

At Broad Street, the J train's final Manhattan destination, the conductor instructed everyone to disembark. Marina remained seated. She would not willingly walk through the labyrinthine station to reach the Brooklyn-bound J. Not if it meant submitting herself to other gawking eyes. Unless she were forcefully expelled, she would wait until the train swerved back to Brooklyn. And if luck would have it, no other passengers would board the train to see her shame.

CHAPTER

❖ 13 ❖

Iliana lingered outside the kitchen. Moments earlier she had dragged her body, weighted with the remains of sleep, up the basement stairs and toward her mother's voice. But she knew that if she entered the kitchen Aurelia would cease to sing. Each morning of her childhood days and until she grew impudent enough to demand an interpretation of the wordless lyrics, Aurelia had woken her with similar songs. Yet only now did Iliana fully appreciate their beauty.

Her mother's voice swooped. When it was able to descend no lower, it leveled and resounded like a palm against a drum. Quivering, it began its long ascent—a wail like the chants of women who mourn their dead. At each scale it grew sweeter and more frail, admitting sadness but reaching for joy until it remained defiantly afloat.

Listening to those sounds, Iliana believed in magic. She glimpsed its shimmerings at the extreme of her peripheral sight— too potent to be viewed directly. She even felt it flickering within her, awakening a knowledge of things she'd never seen and lives she'd never lived. Her spirit soared toward her mother's. Gratefully, she embraced her with the strength of all the affection she had grown too embarrassed to express.

When she and Tico were children and their elder siblings were at school, Aurelia had taught both to speak a wordless language. Re-creating and inventing sounds, they had tapped into their emotions and conveyed them purely, unhindered by words that limited or defined. Yet Iliana's tongue had since lost that magic. It rested heavy, burdened by a need to speak like others, trapped by an education which had early on impressed upon her the need for clarity. As if life itself were clear. As if anything in this world were delineated and easily discernible.

Iliana reluctantly recalled her sixth birthday. To her consternation, it had fallen on an overcast day. Worse, rain pelted and slithered down her bedroom's single window, leaving behind ugly trails of dirt. She pressed her forehead against the cold glass and gazed out onto the street below. On any other day she would have relished tramping through puddles on her way to school. But on that day she had hoped for sun.

She trudged into the kitchen. Her three-year-old brother grinned happily as she pulled out a chair and sat beside him. Iliana paid him little mind. She was too intent on Aurelia ladling oatmeal into a bowl. Weeks earlier a classmate's mother had celebrated her daughter's birthday with the entire kindergarten class. But judging from the soiled housecoat hanging loosely on Aurelia and the braids unraveling sloppily against her shoulders, Iliana knew that her mother had no intention of leaving the house, much less of entering the classroom with a cake held aloft in one hand and a shopping bag full of presents and party favors in the other.

> *Un feliz cumpleaños te deseo yo*
> *y otro. . . .*

Aurelia smiled and set the bowl in front of Iliana. "Happy birthday," she announced, brushing her lips against her daughter's cheek.

A sudden rage invaded Iliana. She reached out and flung the bowl across the table. Aurelia tried to catch it, but the bowl smashed to the floor and the oatmeal spread into a lumpy puddle.

"Oooh," exclaimed Tico, glancing from his sister to his mother. "Oooh . . ."

Aurelia silently scooped up the oatmeal with two pieces of broken china. She emptied her hands into the trash, gathered the remaining shards, dragged a rag across the floor. Iliana waited. Her younger brother, sensible enough to remain silent, clutched the edge of the table and swayed nervously. But Aurelia ignored them both. She washed the remaining dishes, pulled a towel from a drawer, and proceeded to wipe everything dry—a rare activity since the dishes were usually allowed to drip-dry on a rack beside the sink. Only when everything had been stacked neatly on a shelf and she had wiped her hands did she turn to face her daughter.

"So what's wrong?" she asked, her tone so even that it seemed nothing out of the ordinary had occurred. And that was the very problem. To Iliana that calm voice and patient, steady gaze meant Aurelia was indifferent to her misery. Here she was, finally a year older, and her father had left the apartment without wishing her a happy birthday; her older brothers and sisters had ignored her as they prepared for work and school; and her mother had served oatmeal as if the day were just like any other. Yes, she had sere-naded her with "Un Feliz Cumpleaños," but Iliana had expected to receive at least one gift-wrapped box with which to make her brother jealous.

"Nothing," she yelled. "Nothing's wrong!"

"Then why are you shouting?"

Iliana bit into her lower lip. When angry with her father, she usually felt strong enough to withstand a beating tearlessly. Yet when angry with her mother, she felt childish and absolutely helpless.

Aurelia extended a hand as if offering a truce. "Come, or you'll be late for school."

"I'm not going," Iliana blurted out.

Her mother watched her. "Fine. You don't have to go," she said, exiting the room.

Tico clambered out of his chair and followed. Minutes later he returned bearing his favorite toy—a red fire engine complete with hose, unfolding ladder and a hard-hatted fireman tucked behind the steering wheel. Plopping the truck onto his sister's lap, he wrapped one arm around her and, with the other, patted her head as their mother often did to him when he felt sad.

"We can play," he offered, his childish voice serving only to remind Iliana that she was now a year older and should not be distracted by silly games.

Beyond the kitchen, Aurelia ushered Beatriz and Marina to the door. Iliana heard her inform them that their youngest sister would remain at home.

"Here," she said, returning her brother's truck. "You play. I don't want to now."

When the door closed, she trudged behind Aurelia. Yet her mother did not pay her any mind. Instead, she spread sheets onto the children's beds and tucked their edges tight under each mattress, leveling all ripples.

"You don't even care," Iliana accused. "It's my birthday, and you don't even care!"

Aurelia slowly stood erect. Chest heaving as if to store oxygen before diving under, she turned to face her daughter. "I know it's your birthday, mi'ja. And I wish you many more."

A dam collapsed behind Iliana's eyes. Aurelia knelt beside her and drew her near.

"Ay, mi'ja," she murmured, rocking her slowly.

Iliana's body convulsed. Her sobs grew louder. She pressed her face against her mother's neck, soaking its collar with her tears. She wanted Aurelia to explain the absence of gifts and to apologize for sending her to a school where her child's mind had early on grasped that she was poorer than the other students. Only now, thirteen years later, did she finally understand why Aurelia had allowed her to remain at home, had left the kitchen, had then consoled her in her arms. What words could Aurelia have spoken, what theories could she have formulated which would have made sense to a six-year-old girl beginning to question the world and her own existence?

Aurelia's voice penetrated to the depths of Iliana's soul. It conjured images of Papito sitting beside a sewing machine in a previous apartment, his eyes momentarily closing from exhaustion after a long, hard day at work, then flashing open as the fabric beneath his fingers sped toward a needle darting up and down;

Aurelia meticulously unraveling the seams her husband had sewn improperly; their children stuffing cotton and synthetic fabric into the dolls their father pieced together; and the hundreds of Snoopy dolls themselves piled throughout the room. The voice guided Iliana through memories of when her mother was sick and she was not allowed to visit her in the hospital; of her fear of homelessness before her father purchased their current home; and of the first time she saw her mother cry. But the voice's magic was that it rendered fear harmless, transformed despair into a well of strength, and mitigated painful memories with images of the entire family— their faces crinkled with joy and laughter—piling into a train on their way to Coney Island or proudly gathered in church as Aurelia received a bouquet of flowers and a brooch inscribed "Mother of the Year."

At a lull in her mother's singing, Iliana opened the kitchen door. She found Aurelia squeezing water out of a mop.

"Bendición, Mamá," she murmured, meaning, for the first time in her nineteen years, the words that asked her mother's blessing.

Aurelia looked at her and smiled. "Que Dios te bendiga, mi'ja."

Iliana stared at her mother's face. So accustomed was she to seeing it that she rarely took notice of its features. Yet they were as startling and disparate as the song she had just heard. Aurelia's hair, several strands of which were plastered to her forehead, was an unblemished silver-white. Iliana had assumed that its color was the result of age. But now, noting the jet-black brows and equally dark lashes curling above Aurelia's eyes, she realized that her mother was not yet old enough at sixty-one to possess such hair. Vaguely it came to her—a memory of two black braids wrapped around Aurelia's head, then an incalculable period during which she was hospitalized only to return as if from the dead with a halo of ghostly white. Iliana continued to inspect her mother's face: the milky-white layered throughout her eyes and clotting her pupils so that they appeared blue and seemed to look out blindly; her narrow, purple lips; her olive skin which gave the impression of being sunkissed even in the midst of winter.

"Had your fill of looking at an old woman?"

Iliana did not reply. She entered the kitchen and, trying to leave no prints on the freshly mopped floor, tiptoed to the refrigerator.

"How about plantains?" her mother asked, leaning the mop against a wall. "If you peel them, I'll prepare some codfish."

"Why don't you sit. I can prepare everything myself."

"Sit and do what?" Aurelia asked, nudging her aside. "You know I can't bear to sit around doing nothing."

"You have no problem doing exactly that in church."

Aurelia chuckled. "That's only because I have to. If I could get away with knitting—"

"Mami!"

"Oh please. You mean to tell me you went to church every Saturday and listened to boring sermons in whatever that town was called?"

"I went," Iliana replied evasively, "whenever I had the chance."

"And how often was that?" Aurelia challenged.

Noting the mischief in her mother's eyes, Iliana laughed. "I went. That's all that matters. Now—do you want me to make us breakfast or don't you?"

"Humph. Nobody salts an egg without a reason. What do you want? For me to iron your clothes or something?"

"Ay, Mami, since when are you so suspicious?"

"Since my prodigal daughter offered to make me breakfast."

"That's because I'm grateful for all you've done," Iliana replied, self-consciously leaning to kiss her mother's cheek.

Even more embarrassed, Aurelia drew away. Suddenly faltering, she clutched her breast with one hand and with the other groped for Iliana. Too stupefied to move, her youngest daughter merely stared.

Aurelia's eyes glazed over. Her pupils dilated as if in horror of something they had seen. Slowly, soundlessly, her lids slid shut and she collapsed onto the floor.

"Mami?" Iliana asked. "Mami!"

A strand of saliva dribbled from Aurelia's lips. Iliana dropped to her knees to shake her. "Mami, wake up!" she demanded.

"Mami!" She grabbed her mother's wrist and attempted to take its pulse, but her own heart pounded so loudly that she detected only her own pulse. "OhmyGodOhmyGodOhmyGod!" She released her mother's hand and peeled back one of her lids. The white of Aurelia's eye stared blindly.

An ambulance! I need to call an ambulance, Iliana thought, her hysteria rising.

She lunged for the telephone on the kitchen table. Hands trembling, she dialed 411, hung up and frantically dialed again, this time 911. "Oh please, please," she begged. "Please!" But no one answered. And as the phone rang shrill against her ear, she heard a gagging sound erupt from her mother's lips. "They'll be here any minute," she assured, her voice splintering into sobs. "Please, Mami, just hang—"

The words she had been about to speak caught in her throat. The phone slipped from her hand. Coughs and—but, no, it couldn't be—though there it was again—originating from somewhere deep inside her mother and rolling forth in waves.

"Hello? Hello?" crackled a voice from the phone at Iliana's feet. "Is anyone there?"

By now her mother had sat up on the floor. Maniacal laughter rocked her body. "Ay, ay," she gasped. "Your face! You should see your face!"

Mute with shock, Iliana retrieved the phone and placed it on its cradle. Aurelia struggled to catch her breath.

"You look like—like you've just seen a ghost!"

Iliana stared. Just stared. Rage, slow and crippling, held her still. Watching her, Aurelia again broke into laughter.

"Are you crazy?" Iliana asked, restraining, with all her might, an impulse to slap the mirth off her mother's face. "What the hell was that supposed to be? Your sick idea of a joke?"

Her mother pushed herself to a stand and made an effort to control her laughter. "God, I needed that." She lifted the hem of her housecoat and wiped saliva off her chin.

"You won't think it's funny when I watch you die one day, thinking it's another joke."

Aurelia grinned as she leaned for support against the stove. "Life is short, mi'jita. Have a sense of humor. Besides, the way you responded, I would have been dead by now." Then, taking pity, she added, "Ay, mi'ja. You shouldn't be so afraid of death. Not of mine, yours, or anybody else's. It's just a matter of time before it takes us all."

Iliana stared at her mother as if to identify the madness she was beginning to suspect had infected all the members of their family. "You're crazy," she finally muttered, resigned. "You know that, don't you?"

"Of course I'm crazy," Aurelia admitted, smiling. "But not so crazy that I forgot your offer to make me breakfast. Just make sure to throw in a plantain for your sister. She'll be hungry when she wakes up."

Nerves fragile as a thread stretched taut, Iliana brushed past Aurelia and stepped toward the fridge. "Marina's not in bed," she said, pulling out two plantains and placing them on the table. "I don't even remember hearing her get up."

Aurelia immediately swung Iliana around to face her. "What do you mean, she's not in bed?"

"I—I don't know," Iliana said, alarmed. "Her bed was empty when I—"

Aurelia was already on the phone. "Check if she's upstairs. I'll call Zoraida and Azucena. Sometimes that's where she goes."

"What's the—"

"Just go!" Aurelia yelled.

CHAPTER
❖ 14 ❖

Marina looked out of a window on the train to see patches of ice forming tiny islands in the river's brackish water. She counted as many as she could, but her view of the river was soon obstructed by the factories lining its edge. Already their lights were on. Through their windows she saw women and children busily at work. In that part of Brooklyn, where immigrants eked out a sort of life and employers sought cheap labor, the existence of underage workers was quite common.

As a child Marina too had worked in one of those factories. Owned by a church elder who had allowed Rebecca to work overtime on Sundays and her younger siblings to work part-time, the factory had produced women's clothes sold in nearby shops. While Rebecca and other women sewed, Marina had climbed onto a stool to lower what resembled a giant lid onto a metal table on which Beatriz, also perched atop a stool, laid out individual garments. When steam seeped from the table's edges, Marina had hoisted the lid back up so that Beatriz could remove the freshly pressed, hot clothes and pass them to Iliana, who then draped them on hangers.

Glimpsing the activity inside those factories, Marina was relieved that she no longer worked. On weekday mornings, after graduating from high school she had joined the thousands crowded into trains and had daydreamed of one day attracting an attorney who would support her so that she'd never again have to suffer the humiliation of being pressed against strangers and of smelling their rancid breath. For this reason she had invested her salary in clothes purchased not on Pitkin or Knickerbocker Avenue where her elder sisters shopped but in boutiques along Madison and Fifth Avenues. Yet, in all her years of working in law firms, not one person had proposed. She had instead attracted men who recognized her desperation and pawed her under tables when they invited her to lunch.

On one of these occasions she summoned the courage to remove the clammy hand slithering up her thigh. "When you place a wedding band here," she said, tapping the ring finger on her left hand and smiling nervously, "you can touch anything you want."

The man—a second-year associate working seventy-hour weeks in the hopes of someday becoming a partner—stared at her as if she had lost her mind. Then, signaling a waiter, he tossed a credit card on the table.

"I have to meet a client," he announced. "You'd better get back to work."

Later that afternoon he handed her a stack of documents. "I need twelve sets of each reduced by five percent and darkened at least two levels so that my comments in the margins are legible. Understand?"

Marina nodded. As she walked away, he called her back into his office.

"And don't let the copy machine do the stapling. I want each set paper-clipped by hand."

Marina wasn't even assigned to that attorney. There were three others for whom she worked. But firm policy stipulated that secretaries were required to assist any attorney in need of help.

She diligently headed for the copy room. On her way there she ran into the attorney's secretary, a pretty blonde with lipstick bleeding from the edges of her lips. Marina ignored her greeting and rushed past her. The whizzing of laser printers, the loud hum of a soda machine, and the clicking of nails on keyboards converged to give her a sudden headache. She placed the documents on one of the copiers and massaged her temples. Behind the blood red of her closed lids she again saw the scorn on the attorney's face. She also remembered his secretary. And for some reason it was the memory of her green eyes and smiling lips which sent the bitter taste of bile rushing toward her mouth.

Marina opened her eyes and seized the documents off the copier. As if from a distance, she watched her hand fling the documents into a recycling bin and reach into a pocket of her silk blouse for the matches she had slipped into it as a souvenir during lunch. The fluorescent glare of lights stung her eyes. The drab white of ceilings and walls began to pulse. Without pausing to think, she removed one of the matches and flicked it along a side of its cardboard box. The match flared into a blue-based flame that quivered delicately as it traveled toward her fingers, consuming the wood and licking her thumb with heat. Mesmerized by the beauty and destructive power of that flame, she flung the tip of the match into the bin and stood back to watch as the papers caught fire.

The flames leapt into the air and spoke to her with their forked and incandescent tongues. She was free, they murmured, free of the conventions which had kept her wobbling on a tightrope for fear of plummeting into the abyss she now reached in the quickest blink of an eye. That one could survive the fall was the ancient secret. That she had discovered the realm reserved for the few brave enough to dream was reason enough to rejoice. But what the flames, quickly expiring into smoke, failed to convey was that her sorrow would not cease because she had allowed herself the free fall, nor would others cease to mock her from above.

Intoxicated by her newfound freedom, Marina began to laugh. At first her joy was contained by the tight-lipped chuckle she had adopted so as to sound demure, but as a smoke detector shrieked and her co-workers rushed into the room, her mouth opened wide to let her laughter rumble forth.

She had been sure that her life would change dramatically because her hand had wielded fire. She had taken for granted that her future would rise from ashes to reward her with new possibilities of existence even as her boss fired her on the spot.

Colora—that was the nickname her sisters had given her for her yellowish skin and the faint trace of red in her dark hair. She had been so proud of these features that, after being fired, she had relaxed and dyed her hair a brighter orange in the hopes of further embodying that name. Against the advice of her sisters and to the consternation of her parents, she spent the last of her savings on a professional photo shoot. She then carried the portfolio from one modeling agency to another. Yet, despite her perseverance, she was not ushered past any of the receptionists, nor were any of her calls returned.

Marina continued to gaze out of one of the windows on the train. She lifted her legs onto her seat and, gathering the skirt of her coat around them, wrapped her arms around her knees.

As teenagers, she, Beatriz and Iliana had often stood outdoors waiting for their parents to emerge from church. On one memorable afternoon a flock of pigeons flew over their heads and let fall a stream of feces which landed on Marina. This, she now concluded, had been the true indicator of what her life would be. It had not mattered that she and her sisters were gathered in a tight circle reading a letter an admirer had slipped to Beatriz during the sermon. Nor had it mattered that their heads were pressed so close that the shit should have splattered onto all three. No. Like a sign from God Himself, the shit had dropped from the sky to land steaming on her head alone.

"Why, mi'ja, why?"

Marina tramped into the hallway. When Aurelia reached for her, Marina targeted her with such a menacing look that her hand instantly fell away.

Laurie stepped out of her second-floor apartment. Her Siberian husky darted out from behind her. "Where have you been? Your mother was worried sick!" she scolded, seizing the dog by his wagging tail when he tried to barrel down the stairs.

The dog yelped as Laurie dragged him back upstairs and then came down herself in the hopes of witnessing a scene. Yet she was not allowed the satisfaction. Upon entering the kitchen, Marina slammed the door shut behind her mother so that her sister-in-law wouldn't follow.

"Fine! See if I ever waste my time worrying again," Laurie yelled.

Ignoring her, Marina went about the kitchen collecting a mixing bowl, a spoon, an unopened box of Cap'n Crunch and, last of all, a gallon of milk from the refrigerator. She plopped down onto a chair opposite Iliana and straddled it so that her coat gaped open. Her sister's face remained bare of emotion even as their eyes met across the table. Marina had expected her to turn away in disgust, but Iliana's eyes held steady. Marina felt them boring into her, picking her apart like the spiders whose legs Iliana had once plucked off in order to figure out why they twitched long after their bodies died. She also sensed her mother formulating thoughts before daring to speak a word. Their silence was offensive. Had she been any other person, neither would have hesitated before expressing their anger or relief. Their refusal to hold her accountable confirmed her suspicion that they considered her insane. Otherwise they would have treated her as an adult.

She tore the cereal box open and emptied half its contents into the bowl. She then poured in enough milk so that the cereal floated to just below the bowl's rim. Later she would bathe. She would scrape grime off her body and watch dead cells clump grey against the bleached tub in her parents' bathroom. But for now she wanted both her mother and sister to see her as she was and to acknowledge the odor they kept insisting did not exist.

Marina lowered her head toward the bowl and voraciously spooned cereal into her mouth. She wanted to stuff full the emptiness inside and to numb her awareness of all that was missing from her life. As far back as the Dominican Republic she had sucked mangoes until their hairs had stuck between her teeth and their pits had been stripped bald. In the United States she had chewed grapes and swallowed their seeds, all the time ravenous for the sweetness she continued to believe existed in the lives of others. Her mouth had opened wide for any food within her reach.

Her body had ripened to a shape the envy of her sisters, then past the plumpness she had been told Hispanic men preferred and, finally, to the obesity which had drawn down on her the ridicule of others. Yet still her life had remained as empty as before.

Resentment seeped into Marina's soul. She glanced at her youngest sister who had fled home only to return and be embraced as she herself, who had remained, had never been. The possibility existed that she too would have been missed or that her parents and siblings would've mourned her loss had she ridden the J train to the end of its line in Queens and then walked as far as her feet could carry her, never to return. It was more likely that they would've been relieved.

Aurelia's hand tentatively grazed Marina's shoulder. "There are vicious people in the world, mi'ja. You know that more than me. In your condition, you shouldn't have—"

"And what condition might that be?"

"This condition." Aurelia reached down to button her daughter's coat. "Running around naked in the streets."

"What are you saying? That it was my fault I was raped?"

Her mother sighed. "Anyone could've tried to hurt you."

"So what was I supposed to do? Stay indoors? Be afraid? Wait until someone was nice enough to take me out? And who exactly would that have been? You? Papi? Definitely not Iliana! She's much too proud to be seen with me or to introduce me to her friends!"

"I didn't know you wanted to go out," Iliana lied in self-defense.

"You never asked!"

"You never showed any interest!"

"What was I supposed to do? Beg?"

"Ever since I came home, you've made it clear you resented having me around!"

"You go away for more than a year, come back, and don't even ask me how I've been!"

"Marina, all my life it was you and Beatriz! I was too young, too ugly, too stupid for the two of you! Why should I have thought that—"

"You're not even listening to me!" Marina shrieked. "You're not even listening!"

Iliana slammed her fist on the kitchen table. "What do you want? You want me to introduce you to my friends? You want us to go out?"

"Yes! That's exactly what I want!"

"Fine! I'll take you out! I'll even introduce you to my friends!"

Marina watched her sister, unsure whether to be pleased or not. "We're the only two girls left," she finally murmured. "It's not good for us to fight."

Iliana slumped back into her chair. Aurelia seemed about to speak when her youngest daughter unexpectedly began to cry.

"Don't," Marina begged, stepping past her mother to comfort her sister. "Please don't. We just need a little time."

CHAPTER

❖ 15 ❖

The Greater Brooklyn Seventh-Day Adventist Church stood tall and wide in the middle of a block of stores with racks of clothes and bins of wares lined along the sidewalk. On Saturday mornings and afternoons hundreds of people, regardless of the weather, crowded the avenue to shop in stores selling everything from $4.99 acrylic sweaters, $2.99 sneakers, and $1.19 five-pound boxes of detergent to colorful plastic tubs of all sizes, aluminum pots and pans, and twelve-for-a-dollar hangers. In markets with crates of produce randomly stacked without thought to neatness or appearance, women reached for dusty Idaho potatoes, twenty-pound sacks of rice, large tomatoes cheaper for being green, and five-for-a-dollar plantains whose price was made even more reasonable if one was lucky enough to find Siamese twins which still counted as one. Not in this neighborhood the luxury of shopping as a leisurely activity. Fear of not finding what was needed at affordable prices hurried people into stores and kept fingers rifling through merchandise. On the street itself frustrated drivers—caught in a jam of slowly moving cars or intercepted by pedestrians anxious to return to the warmth of their homes—pressed angrily on horns whose blare, though loud, only added to the cacophony of managers hawking their wares through bullhorns, shoppers arguing for a lower price, merengue and hip-hop blasting from music stores competing for attention. Amidst this commotion the Greater Brooklyn church silently vied for potential converts, only occasionally drawing strangers who stumbled in—too drunk or high to notice that what had formerly been a movie theater and a dwelling place for Satan was now the house of God.

The marquee that had once listed the names of films now announced upcoming sermons. A series of glass doors—shielded by a metal gate when the church was closed to prevent bored youths from breaking in, and requiring the strength of two men to push it up—led to a lobby with mirrors hung in peeling, gold-painted frames. Beyond these, a foyer with carpets the color of sacrificial blood and bearing the scars of cigarettes crushed beneath heels, plagued the recently converted with memories of the chatter and bustle of crowds prepared for nights of fun. These carpets, regardless of how often cleaned, emitted a faint scent of tobacco which hinted at the pleasures of the forbidden. In the church itself or, rather, in the auditorium, rows of balding, velvet-cushioned seats led to a stage on which a pulpit stood and behind which navy curtains hid the rarely used baptismal font. Because of an Adventist belief that images were tributes to a pagan past, no crucifixes, saints or paintings concealed any part of the crumbling walls.

In this cavernous interior with twenty-five-foot ceilings and seats at most a quarter occupied even after evangelical tent meetings on rented lots drew curious visitors to the church itself, Sabbath School was divided into ten groups of about twenty members each. So big was the space that even with six classes seated on two side aisles and four in the middle, each separated by rows of empty seats, teachers could make themselves heard above other voices. As for the more disruptive infant and toddler classes, these were held in the second-floor lobby which had doors leading to the balcony where those aged six to seventeen were taught.

It was on this balcony that Iliana usually sat after Sabbath School ended and the pastor began to preach. Bored by the sermon, she would peer at those below to see who read, dozed, gossiped or scrawled notes on the backs of programs a deacon handed all as they went into the church. If not sufficiently amused, she would glance behind her to discover which teenage children of which avidly religious parents had slumped low in their seats to make out in the dimly lit back rows.

However, on this particular Sabbath, Iliana remained attentive. Curious about how others were responding to the sermon, she leaned forward to peer over the rail. Heads nodded as if in agreement with the pastor's words. Marina, seated beside Aurelia in a center aisle, shouted an Amen. Yet though several people turned to glare, Iliana suspected it was not because they too were dismayed that her sister agreed with what was being said but, rather, because they believed that when in church one sat humbly, never uttering a word.

Pastor Rivera pressed the microphone to his lips. Taking a moment, he wiped his brow with a handkerchief ceremoniously pulled out of a pocket.

"Many men," he stated, "many men enter the sanctity of marriage. They fall in love and promise their chosen one their lives. This is as it should be."

Again Marina shouted, this time "Hallelujah!" Aurelia gestured for her to be still.

"But tell me. Can the sanctity of marriage be upheld when men are mercilessly tricked by women?"

Iliana reached for her program.

"Let me give you an example. A man meets a woman. She has the smoothest skin, the reddest lips. And her hair, Lord, is the softest he's ever touched. It frames her face and makes her look prettier than any painting he's laid eyes on in his entire life. Then there are her lashes, fluttering like the wings of birds whenever he comes near and making him feel like he's soaring toward heaven. She is beautiful, more beautiful than he had imagined a woman could ever be."

Bristling, Iliana looked up the sermon's title.

"But wait," Pastor Rivera commanded, as if someone had attempted to interrupt him. "On his wedding night the man is anxious to be with her alone. He paces impatiently. He fluffs the pillows on their bed and smooths its sheets, all the time waiting for her to emerge from the bathroom into which she has locked herself to prepare for bed. The bathroom door finally opens slowly. So excited is he that he can barely breathe. He lifts his arms, ready to draw her near. But something is wrong. Something is definitely wrong."

The pastor paused. In the church everyone sat still. Even the children, who usually whined or struggled in their mothers' arms, seemed mesmerized by the story he told so well.

"Who is this creature daring to impersonate his wife? Who is this being with a helmet of green and blue plastic things around which strands of its hair are wrapped? And its face! Mercy me! It is pockmarked and creviced like the moon!"

Raucous laughter erupted from the lips of several men in the congregation. Iliana again glanced at her program to make sure that she had read it right.

"The Virtues of Marriage," my ass, she thought.

"But that's not all," the pastor continued, enjoying his own tale. "There's more. The woman's lashes are now gone. And she's bigger. Can you imagine? Rolls of flesh jiggle on her belly, so that her husband suddenly realizes she'd used a girdle to cinch her waist."

Why the hell doesn't he talk about why women feel the need to do this? Iliana wondered. Why the fuck doesn't he criticize men for falling in love with hair, lips and perky tits? And what place did this tirade have in church? What did any of it have to do with God?

"Ah! The vanity of women. It's been so since the time of Eve. That is why so many marriages fail. How can they succeed when they have not been founded on honesty and truth?"

Eve. So that was to be the biblical connection, Iliana concluded. Same old shit about how Eve had ushered sin into the world and was responsible for everything that had ever gone wrong since. Damn man's wife had probably caught him having an affair, and he was attempting to justify his position from the pulpit.

Iliana leaned back against her seat. She had already been angry before stepping into church. And now this, as if she had not heard that sermon a million times and again needed to be warned that as a woman she was inferior to all men.

"You know," Gabriel had said earlier that morning when he and his wife went downstairs to hitch a ride in Papito's car and ran into Iliana who was still not ready, "if you weren't my sister I wouldn't know if you were a man trying to look like a woman or a woman trying to be a man."

"What the fuck—" Iliana had said, taken by surprise as she secured a towel around her body.

Gabriel had ignored her and instead turned to his wife. "Laurie, look at her. Doesn't she look masculine with her hair pushed back like that?"

Clutching with one hand the stockings she had gone upstairs to borrow from her mother, Iliana had self-consciously reached with the other to touch the hair wet against her scalp.

"Be honest. With no makeup and her thick brows, who could tell the difference?"

Just remembering Gabriel's laughter ignited Iliana's anger. Then too, there had been Laurie joining in. Laurie, whom she disliked. Laurie, who had married Gabriel because he'd been the most sought-after male in the high school they'd attended, a school where she'd been in the minority and the few white boys had preferred the Puerto Rican girls. Laurie, who had forbidden Gabriel to kiss her throughout their first three years of dating, a refusal he had interpreted as modesty and which had fueled his passion until he'd recklessly proposed only to have her recoil from intimacy for another two years after they married.

But Gabriel had deserved it all, Iliana thought. Deserved it after years of craving a white woman and accusing black women of being the ugliest, loudest and most demanding—like in the joke he loved to tell of a Latina cooing in the midst of sex, "Ay Papito! Ay Papito!"; a black woman shouting, "Give it to me, motherfucker! Give it to me now!" and a white woman whispering some nonsense.

Other memories rushed forth, not only of her brother but also of his wife. Like the time she and Laurie rode a bus to East New York and Laurie, tucked in a seat between two women, gathered her hair to one side and began to brush it, brush it, brush it, so that it was repeatedly flung at the face of the woman to her right. Horrified, Iliana had watched from across the aisle. The woman had waited patiently for Laurie to be done, but when Laurie had prolonged brushing her hair, the woman had snatched the brush out of her hand and flung it to the floor. Laurie had turned as if to attack. Then, seeing the woman trembling with a fury ready to be unleashed, she had instead stooped to retrieve the brush.

"Damned kinky-headed bitch!" she'd cursed, only after she and Iliana had safely gotten off the bus. "Probably jealous of my hair!"

Iliana glanced at Gabriel sitting beside Laurie in one of the front rows. Everyone in church liked him. His manner was so easy and he was so visibly Adventist, what with his involvement in several of the church's philanthropic groups. Yet he was not so good a Christian that he had abstained from sleeping with his brother's wife or, after being caught, making a show of confessing to the pastor—an unnecessary act since Adventists believed that God's forgiveness could be had without the intercession of others. Gabriel had done this knowing that his wife's and brother's rancor would be condemned while his own behavior would be extolled as proof of his repentance.

An unexpected silence jarred Iliana from her thoughts. Something had changed in the atmosphere around her. The tension was palpable.

She looked at the pastor and found him staring at a center aisle. She then saw her brother turn and search behind him as others in the congregation did the same. But, following their stares, she detected nothing wrong. Then her attention too was caught by a commotion in her mother's row.

Marina's arms twitched spasmodically. Her head, hanging as if from a broken neck, rolled listlessly each time what appeared to be an invisible, outside force yanked her forward, then shoved her back against her seat. Her arms fell to her thighs. Her elbows banged painfully against the armrests, echoing loudly in the surrounding silence. No one moved. It was as if the force powerful enough to jerk Marina's body like a yo-yo in a child's hand also held the congregation still.

All of a sudden and with the strength of a mother determined not to see a daughter harmed, Aurelia took hold of Marina's shoulders and shook her massive frame. Shivers extended through Marina, growing into convulsions that made her body flail. Horrified, Aurelia released her. As she had never done in all her life, she raised a hand and fiercely slapped her daughter.

Marina immediately grew still. Words, barely audible, trickled from her lips.

"Hallelujah, hallelujah, hallelujah."

Her body began to sway, the incantation spilling forth, faster now—a gravelly, gurgling sound like that of pebbles carried downstream by a brook.

"Hallelujahhallelujahamenhallelujahhallelujahhallelujah-amen!"

Aurelia looked on, stunned.

"Que Dios nos libre del mal," someone, Iliana did not know who, prayed.

"Hallelujah, hallelujah, haaaaaleeeluuuuujaah!" Marina screamed.

Papito, sitting with other deacons behind the pulpit, frantically gestured for his daughter to shut her mouth. Marina instead sprang from her seat. Dazed and wobbling, she looked around her as if to establish where she was.

"I have seen God's face," she proclaimed. "He has revealed Himself to me!"

A rumble of anger and dismay erupted from the congregation.

"Blasphemy! Blasphemer!"

"The devil has possessed her soul!"

Those in seats nearest to Marina edged away. Iliana saw their faces contort with hatred. It was as if at any moment they would rise and fall upon her sister with stones they had waited all their lives to throw. And then it struck her, the absurdity of it all—how in a Baptist or Pentecostal church Marina's behavior might've been attributed not to the devil but to the Holy Ghost.

"Get her out! Someone get her out of here," the pastor commanded, his own face a grimace as he struggled to regain control.

Aurelia tugged on her daughter's arm in the hope that she would sit. Marina weakly clutched the seat in front of her in order to remain upright.

"He—" Her arms began to quake. The tremors extended toward her shoulders, causing them to twitch and jerk. "He held me close," she exclaimed, her voice tremulous with wonder. "He saw me as I am and held me close! Me!"

Two ushers rushed toward her up the aisle.

"What? You're going to throw her out?" Iliana demanded, astounded to find herself on her feet shouting down at the congregation. "I thought anyone was welcome in this church!"

Papito too leapt to his feet. "Don't you dare," he warned. "Don't you dare make a fool of yourself too!"

Aurelia bowed her head. Marina stumbled past her, toward the aisle.

"No one has to throw me out," she said, her voice ebbing as her strength drained with her effort to make her body do as she willed. "I'm going home where I belong. My Redeemer Himself will deal with all of you."

Iliana ran up the stairs of the balcony, out into the second-floor lobby, then down another flight of stairs where she caught up with her sister.

Marina's eyes glowed brilliantly. Her face was a vision of ecstasy, raw and pure. Only once had Iliana glimpsed such passion, and even then it had been a mere glimmer of what was now visible on her sister's face—an inner light briefly refracted through Rebecca's eyes as the pastor had uttered the final marriage vows and her veil had been lifted by Pasión.

"I'm going home," Marina stated, glancing at Iliana before searching for her coat on a rack by the lobby doors. "I am going home."

Unable to bear her sister's countenance, Iliana turned away to search for her own coat on the tightly packed, sagging rack.

"Don't," Marina said, recoiling when Iliana's elbow accidentally brushed hers. "I have seen God's face, and my body is still not completely here."

"I'm going with you," Iliana said, refraining from responding to her sister's words. "Just let me find my coat."

"What? You don't think I can get there on my own?"

"I'm not doing you any favor," Iliana said warily. "I just don't feel like staying here myself."

Marina threw her coat on and started toward the door. Still not having found her own, Iliana darted after her.

"Please don't follow me," Marina warned. "I need to be alone."

Against her better judgment, Iliana stopped.

"I'm tired, okay?" her sister claimed. "I just want to sleep. And don't worry. I'll take the train. I only pretended to put my money on the offering plate."

"You promise, Marina? You promise me you'll go straight home?"

"Where else do you think I'd go?"

CHAPTER
❖ 16 ❖

A gust of wind slapped Marina. Momentarily confused, she paused beneath the marquee. Pedestrians rushed past her, their breaths weaving into clouds exhaled by others, their voices loud and shrill. She thrust her shoulders forward and joined the crowd. Amidst all the scurrying, she felt earthbound, heavy, burdened once again. Gone was her ecstasy at having floated into the arms of God as lightly as the dandelions she used to blow on as a child to make a wish. Oppressing her was a memory of the congregation's doubt. She recalled the faithful who, in times of old, had been stoned, cast into a lions' den or burned alive for acknowledging God's influence in their lives. She would have thought that among Adventists—prepared to be martyred for their beliefs—she'd be safe from persecution and the incredulity of others. Yet this Sabbath had made her painfully aware that she was an outcast even among those who claimed to believe in God.

Disheartened, Marina made her way along Knickerbocker Avenue toward Myrtle. The train station there was as crowded as the street. She waited to buy her token behind a baby peering at her over its mother's shoulders. Each time the child inhaled, a trail of snot was drawn into its nose to be blown out again as bubbles. When its mother carried it through a turnstile, the child flashed Marina a toothless grin. There was something about its innocence that she instantly despised. She had an impulse to wrap her hands around its throat and to squeeze until its body slackened and the mucus quivering outside its nostrils stilled. She felt a need to see the light of its eyes snuffed out.

So shocked was she by the intensity of the urge that she immediately turned away. Her hands shook as she slipped her money
through the slot of a glassed-in booth and toward a clerk. Satan,
she realized, would increasingly tempt her because of the proof she
had received of God's existence. This thought made her barely able
to draw breath. She snatched her token, pushed herself through a
turnstile, and rushed up the stairs to the elevated platform. Her
heart pounded inside its cage. She prayed for it to burst and to release her soul. She did not think herself able to endure another day
or to keep up a vigil against the temptations which had been as-
saulting her of late. She feared that she would one day look down
to find her hands drenched with blood. Her impulse toward
violence was daily growing stronger, as if stealing into life from
the recurring dream she had of slicing into bodies and of reaching
her fingers in to extract the organs responsible for motivating the
evil that almost a quarter-century of living had failed to help her
understand.

Her body swooned with dizziness and despair. She gripped the
platform rail and waited to be struck dead. When minutes passed
and God did not punish her for the evil she had thought to do,
something shifted in her mind, causing a door to creak open and
exposing alternate paths her thoughts might take. She remembered how, throughout the Bible, God had demanded the shedding of blood as sacrifice. She recalled as well how Cain's sacrifice
of his crops had been spurned and how he had eventually gone
mad. That God was also requiring blood from her filled her with
righteous indignation. She suspected that, were she to obey, she
would succumb to madness and possibly hurt a loved one as Cain
had inadvertently slain his brother Abel.

The longer she considered how God had introduced violence
into the world by demanding sacrifices from those who had previously not conceived of shedding blood, the more she questioned
His wisdom in other things. God, she realized, had more than
once been wrong. He had been wrong to conceive of evil when
He might instead have created a perfect world, wrong to have required blood, wrong to demand this of her now. Her thoughts
went further along their newfound path. Loving God, she would

instead offer Him her soul. She would whisper in His ear. She would be His personal adviser, revealing to Him the error of His ways and providing Him with solutions to the problems of a modern world.

Iliana fidgeted in her seat. If she waited long enough, the receiving line at the bottom of the lobby stairs would disperse and she'd be able to avoid shaking the pastor's or her father's hand. He was the one whom she blamed most. Had he, as deacon, reminded the congregation of her sister's mental state, they might have been moved to pity rather than to fear.

The congregation spilled out into the aisles. Iliana trailed behind other stragglers leaving the balcony. From the top of the second flight of stairs she saw her mother standing beside two of her sisters. She wove her way toward them through the crowded lobby. Just as she thought she would reach them without having to stop and chat, she felt someone sling an arm around her shoulders. She turned to find Pastor Rivera beaming her a smile. When he extended a hand for her to shake, she antagonistically let it hang.

"Welcome," he said. "It's nice to have you back."

"Is it?"

"Sure it is. You've been gone for quite a while. That's why your behavior is excusable."

Iliana clutched her Bible to her breasts.

"I understand your concern for your sister, but the devil works in mysterious ways." The pastor rocked on his heels as if the very words excited him. "In these matters it's better to trust those who know best."

There were a million things Iliana might have said. Yet she opted for the simplest. "My sister has had a nervous breakdown. How could that have anything to do with Satan?"

"Appearing as God is one of the devil's most cunning tricks. God Himself has better things to do then to appear to those needing proof that He exists."

A sigh of frustration escaped Iliana's lips. Just then a woman, ancient enough to have everyone respectfully address her as Abuela, stepped forward to greet the pastor. Iliana took advantage of the moment to slip away.

"We'll continue this conversation during lunch," Pastor Rivera called after her.

Iliana did not pause to reply. She had forgotten the Christmas luncheon scheduled for that day and also the covered bowl her mother had carried into church. She hurried to Aurelia's side. Papito was already there when she arrived.

"Only half an hour," he insisted. "That way people can't say we left with our tails tucked between our legs."

"In that time anything could happen."

"We're staying," Papito said, belligerently. "I won't have people talking about us too just because Marina stormed out of here on a whim."

"They were going to throw her out!" Iliana said.

Her father turned to face her. "Iliana María, I'll deal with you when we get home."

"Fine! Then let's go now!"

Zoraida mercifully stepped forward to intercede. "Papi," she said, although she had long ago started calling him Papá. "Benny and I are going home. If you want, we'll stop by the house to make sure everything's okay."

Papito's eyes remained fixed on his youngest daughter. "That would be good," he said.

"And what if she's not there?" asked his wife.

"If she's not, then there's nothing we can do."

The specks of white clotting Aurelia's pupils coalesced; her mouth tightened as if she were about to spit. Ever so slowly, she undid the buttons on her coat. When she spoke again, she measured out her words precisely enough for Papito to understand.

"If anything happens to Marina," she said, pinioning him with her eyes, "I will forever, and I mean forever, hold you responsible."

Her husband winced but managed to force a smile. "God is with us. Nothing bad will happen to Marina. Trust me. I feel it in my bones."

CHAPTER

❖ 17 ❖

Marina teetered on her heels past a neighbor attempting to pry loose a garbage can frozen in place outside his home.

"Cold, isn't it?" he asked. "I predict it'll be one of the worst winters we've had in years."

"Yeah, but at least it's sunny," Marina contended. "We should enjoy it while it lasts."

The man, so stooped that his chin nestled against his collarbone, wrapped his coat tighter around his body and squinted disapprovingly at the sky. "Sun or no sun," he muttered, "this weather will get you down. Make you feel old as I am."

No sirree, Marina answered silently, almost jovially. I don't plan to be around that long.

She opened the gate to her parents' house. Cautious despite the salt her father had sprinkled on the stoop, she clung to the rail and heaved herself up the steps. Blue, Gabriel and Laurie's Siberian husky, barked ferociously.

"It's only me," Marina yelled upon entering.

The dog ceased barking but began to paw the apartment door. "I know. I know. It's a terrible thing to be cooped up."

Marina kicked off her shoes, flung her coat onto a couch and headed into her parents' room. Flicking a light on, she sat on the edge of their bed and opened the top drawer of her mother's bureau. Heaped inside the drawer were countless vials of pills for arthritis, high blood pressure and heart problems; wooden spools of thread; Valentines, birthday, Christmas and Mother's Day cards;

combs and brushes matted with hair; utility bills; empty bottles of Enjoli, Charlie, Tigress and other cheap perfumes; hundreds of bobby pins; brooches shaped like birds and insects, several with rhinestones missing, others dented and with gold or silver paint chipping off; glossy, wallet-sized funeral cards; and stockings in various shades of brown whose runs Aurelia had tried to stop by dotting them with clear nail polish.

Garbage, all of it, Marina concluded. Not a single item had been worth saving.

Her eyes shifted to inspect the room cramped with the swan-shaped bedroom set her father had bought for her mother on their fortieth wedding anniversary. What, she wondered, could her parents possibly bequeath to their children? Their garish furniture? Their house in a slum she had hoped to escape? Old photographs of family and friends who had lived equally dismal lives? It was unimaginable that anyone would want these things. It was more unimaginable still that, during their lifetime, either of her parents would acquire anything worth the value of ink or paper for a will.

Marina continued to rifle through the drawer. The funeral cards commemorating the Adventist dead portrayed Christ with staff in one hand, lamb in the other. Those for Catholics showed the Virgin Mary or the deceased's patron saint. At the bottom of all cards was printed: "Yea, though I walk through the valley of the shadow of death, I shall fear no evil. . . ." On the back of each card was inscribed the name, the dates of birth and death, and the funeral home where the deceased had lain. Nothing of their lives. Nothing to make them linger in the memory of their survivors.

She set the cards aside. With the rounded edge of a bobby pin, she scooped wax first from one ear, then the other. Her free hand collected vials from the drawer and meticulously arranged them by size atop the bureau. She had no idea how to go about selecting which of the vials' contents to ingest. In the past she had slit her wrists or swallowed aspirins. But this time she wanted something potent enough to leave her dead, not merely weak or retching.

Holding each of the amber vials toward the light, she settled for the one that appeared most full. She then stepped into the dining room and withdrew a wineglass from a cabinet with china reserved for guests. In the kitchen she let the water run until clear and cold before filling the glass almost to the rim. Careful not to spill a drop, she went out into the hallway and down the basement stairs.

Her bed had been left unmade. Strewn across its crumpled covers were the clothes she had opted not to wear. She placed the glass on a night table, gathered the clothes into her arms, and chucked them into the walk-in closet. Because she wanted everything to be just so, she carefully made her bed. She then reverently reached for the glass with stem slender enough to snap at the slightest pressure from her thumb. Cupping her palms so that only the glass bowl was held, she raised it to her lips. Through the red crystal, the water appeared dark as the wine she had yearned to taste. She remembered how, on the occasion of her first communion, she had reached for a thimble-sized cup from a passing tray only to discover that what filled it was Welch's grape juice. Her tongue traced the glass's edge and curves. Here too the crystal was thin and fragile. She was tempted to sink her teeth in, snap a piece off, feel it slice into her tongue as her lips simultaneously pressed against the jagged edges, turning the water truly red. Instead, she took a sip and carefully swished it around her mouth, against its walls, under her tongue, all the time imagining that the liquid tasted salty and felt as viscous as surely blood must be, all the time imagining that what slid toward her throat and down into her stomach was the blood of Christ Himself and the power of the Holy Ghost entering to set her free.

Thrilled by the prospect of her own death, Marina set the glass aside and impatiently pried off the vial's child-proof cap. She reached in to extract one pill, then another and another, which she piled onto her tongue. When they began to dissolve, she poured out the remaining pills and swallowed the lot with water.

Her skirt felt tight around her waist. She reached behind her to undo its zipper. The skirt slid and caught around her hips. She forced it down, stepped out of it, threw it on the bed, yanked her sweater off. She then took hold of the bands of her panty and

stockings and rolled both off her belly, past the pubic hairs growing rough as the stubble on a man's face, down her thighs which
rubbed together when she walked and, finally, off her callused
feet. Last of all, she unhooked the bra ordered from a catalogue because stores did not carry size 48DD.

Naked, she edged toward her bed. She expected to experience
dizziness and to feel her limbs begin to numb. Yet she was aware
only of her heart beating powerfully inside her chest.

She cupped her hands under her breasts heavy enough to tug
her bra straps deep into her shoulders. Had she given birth, surely
her breasts would have sagged to her knees like those of a woman
in Azua who had suckled twenty children and in old age had supposedly rolled and tied the flat appendages with a cloth to make
them appear erect. Her own were as ugly as that woman's must
have been. Their nipples were large and black, their areolae speckled with little bumps.

Remembering the teeth marks that had lingered on her breasts
after she was raped, Marina shamefully slid under the bedcovers. A
doorbell rang shrill throughout the house. Startled, she immediately sat upright. It couldn't be her parents. They had keys and
would never have rung the bell. She considered rising to see who
was at the door. But she was so comfortable there in bed, and the
floor would chill her feet.

She settled back against her pillows. Suddenly, she felt weary
and could barely move.

Again the doorbell rang—or was the insistent ringing in her
head?

Marina closed her eyes. She wondered if her exhaustion was a
symptom of the pills or the result of a restless night. Regardless of
the cause, the effect felt good, what with her heart beating so
slowly now and so nearly inaudibly that it might have been the
echo of a drum serenading her from afar. She smiled contentedly
and imagined that what she lay on was a snowbank where no one
had yet stepped. In her fantasy her arms fluttered high above her
head to glide down against the snow so white, pure and miraculously warm. Electrical currents darted through her body, sending

tremors along her limbs. Her spirit gathered itself into her heart. Simultaneously, her heart lurched violently. Yet she felt no pain. Rather, she had the sensation that her spirit had burst free through an open wound to soar higher than the angel she had formed against the snow.

Aurelia pushed away the plate Nereida had placed before her. "I refuse to eat food prepared by those who've wronged us."

Rosita came up behind Nereida and, nudging her aside, set a different plate in front of Aurelia. "Well, then," she said, "here's some of your own salad and the eggplant I made myself."

"Please, Rosita. My stomach is in a knot."

"Exactly. That's why you need to eat."

Rosita, a woman with hawkish eyes and the broad features of a Peruvian Indian, pulled out a chair Papito had abandoned. Resting an arm on her friend's shoulders so that anyone watching would see she cared little about their opinion, she plopped down beside Aurelia. Their heads were a perfect contrast—what with Rosita's black hair draped defiantly down her back despite her fifty-something years and Aurelia's white hair braided and wrapped into a crown.

"How could they?" Aurelia moaned.

"If I hadn't been so shocked, I would've gotten up myself." Rosita reached across the table to pat Iliana's hand. "I'm proud of you, mi'ja," she said. "You did right. Don't let anyone tell you different."

Iliana smiled in spite of herself. She tried to imagine Rosita— shorter and so much stockier than Aurelia that she appeared rooted to whatever ground she stood on—admonishing Pastor Rivera with her birdlike, screechy voice. Chances were that she would've been thrown out too for never having been baptized and for appearing in church sporadically for fifteen years to taunt, with her presence, any pastor who attempted to convert her.

"Besides, what did you expect?" Rosita pointed to the pastor stuffing his mouth across the room. "He's a fool. And look at his wife. She wears more makeup than the whore of Babylon and is trapped in a marriage to a man any woman would despise."

"Not one person came to our defense."

Rosita sucked her teeth. "Most people in this church are such hypocrites that they would've watched Christ Himself be crucified. Take that one," she said, targeting one of the ushers who had risen to throw Marina out. "My husband saw him a couple of weeks ago in a bar. And I can tell you one thing. He wasn't sipping no Holy Ghost." She settled back against her chair. "As for Papito—" Her voice broke off when Aurelia silenced her with a look.

Iliana watched as her father served the old woman who had earlier approached the pastor. Abuela flashed him a toothless grin. Papito conversed with her briefly before darting between tables to greet others. It was his responsibility as a deacon to ensure that guests and members felt at home. Nonetheless, he was being particularly obsequious. What surprised Iliana most was that everyone was responding to him as if nothing out of the ordinary had occurred. Even when she had descended into the basement, no one, other than the pastor, had mentioned a thing about Marina's or her own behavior. Their silence on the subject had bewildered her into returning their smiles and accepting their kisses on her cheek. Yet she suspected that they would later heap condemnation not only on Marina and herself but also on her parents for having failed to raise them right.

She turned her attention to a table of people her own age. Several were students at Adventist universities. The rest were those who had married shortly after high school. Her friendship with them, predicated on shared beliefs, had begun to unravel when she announced her decision to attend a secular university. Any remaining knots had come undone when she'd leapt from her seat to defend her sister.

Her eyes focused specifically on Esther. She wanted to force Esther to meet her gaze and to scream every one of Esther's secrets to her face. Like the time Esther fucked the pastor's son in the balcony and for an agonizing month feared that she was pregnant.

Then there was the time she sneaked into the basement to smoke a joint. The two of them had been confidantes for years. And to think that now, having married a man to whom she had lied about her virginity, Esther had self-righteously turned away.

Bitterness curved Iliana's lips. She let it linger there, savoring it for fear of tasting instead the hurt of lost friendships and the uncertainty of what might be found when she and her family returned home.

"You know," Nereida said to her, "I never did thank you."

"For what?" Iliana asked, surprised.

"For keeping Juan and Manny overnight and for bringing them to church with you every Saturday before you went away."

Nereida paused. She was as light-skinned as Tico, Marina and Rebecca but with the chiseled features and high cheekbones of her darker siblings. She was also as tall as her brothers and towered above her sisters at five feet ten inches.

"If you hadn't saved their souls, I would never have made it back to church."

Iliana shrugged. She'd had no intention of saving souls and had taken her nephews only to provide their working mother with some free time.

"It was no big deal."

"It was for me," Nereida countered. "When my sons kept begging me to bring them to church and I repeatedly refused, when God appeared to me in a dream and showed me that if I didn't bring them, Juan would become a drug dealer and Manny a—a—" She blinked to hold back tears. "Anyway, I'm grateful. You have no idea how much coming back has helped me."

Embarrassed, Iliana did not reply. She had not been aware that Nereida needed help. Instead, she had considered Nereida to be the strongest of her sisters and had held her up as a role model for herself. One of her earliest memories was of Nereida standing with her hands outstretched as Papito poured a bowl of steaming oatmeal onto her palms for having fed a spoonful of it to Marina. Nereida had not even snitched on her sister who had begged despite repeated warnings that she might scald her tongue, nor had she cried about the oatmeal she later claimed miraculously cooled before it reached her hands.

No. Iliana could not imagine how church or God had helped her sister. But she could conceive of how faith might have distracted her preadolescent nephews from the temptations in their neighborhood caught smack between a junior-high and a high school outside of which drug dealers employed children as their runners: a neighborhood in which ten-year-olds could make in one day what their parents dreamed of earning in one week; where the concrete walls of a playground sported murals honoring those shot down in youth; and where it was advantageous to smile at dealers so as not to be harassed. But God having helped Nereida? It was in the name of God that she had been ostracized by church members for marrying a non-Adventist. It was also in the name of God that she'd been erased from the church's records until she agreed to suffer the humiliation of being baptized a second time.

Iliana was knocked out of her thoughts by Zoraida rushing into the room.

"I rang and got no answer! But she's there! The old man next door saw her going in!"

"Get your brothers," Aurelia instructed, already throwing on her coat. "Tell them we're going home."

Iliana hurried to find her brothers.

"I'm staying," Tico said when she informed him of what was going on. "I've had it with her crap."

Chilled by his indifference, Iliana turned to go. She was about to search for Gabriel and Laurie but realized that doing so would be a waste of time.

"They're not coming," she told her parents waiting for her in their car.

She climbed into the back seat of the Buick. Her teeth began to chatter. Although she tried to keep them still, they continued to rattle noisily inside her mouth.

Marina will be fine, she assured herself. *She was calm when she left church. She couldn't have meant to do herself any harm.*

She glanced at her father's face in the rearview mirror. It

seemed as if his thoughts had already reached home to find the worst. Her mother's face she could not see, but her posture was that of a person struggling with fear.

Traffic stretched bumper to bumper along Knickerbocker Avenue. Papito swerved onto a residential street with fewer motorists, then sped toward Bradford where he screeched to a halt behind Zoraida's car parked outside his home.

"She still hasn't opened the door," Zoraida wailed as Aurelia leapt out onto the sidewalk.

Iliana watched her mother unlock the front door of their house and dash inside. She watched her sister and brother-in-law rush in too. Yet only when her father reluctantly did the same did she summon the courage to climb out of the car and step into the hallway.

A howl, shrill enough to penetrate walls and ceilings, erupted from the basement. Iliana felt it pierce her body. She felt it alter the very rhythm of her heart. With hellish fury, the sound reverberated throughout the house and trailed off into a wail. A hiss, like that of a punctured balloon, seeped from her father's lips. Her own mouth opened, snapped shut, opened once again.

"We need to call an ambulance," she heard Zoraida say.

"An ambulance will never make it here on time!"

Iliana stumbled back out onto the stoop. Her body shivered fitfully. Her brain refused to absorb its shock. She gripped the rail and felt her palm freeze against metal slick with ice. Moments later she turned to see her father fling himself onto Marina being carried in Aurelia, Benny and Zoraida's arms.

"Her blood is on your hands!" Aurelia shrieked, pushing past Papito.

"Ay, mi hija," he cried. "Mi hija!"

Marina's arms slipped from the blanket into which she had been rolled; her fingers scraped the floor. Aurelia tried to hoist her higher.

"Help me!" she yelled at her youngest daughter.

Yet Iliana did not, could not move, not to touch her sister.

Aurelia, Benny and Zoraida staggered past her. It was then that she caught sight of Marina's face. Her eyes were closed, her lips curved into what appeared more than anything like a smile.

"Iliana, please! The car door!"

Iliana moved as if submerged to open the back door of Benny's car. As her sister was maneuvered into the car's back seat and their father's sobs spilled from inside the house, she turned away, certain of her complicity for not having followed Marina home.

CHAPTER

❖ 18 ❖

Iliana found her father slumped in an armchair he had pulled into the darkest corner of the living room. His sobs had subsided. Yet his silence belied a greater grief. She wanted to seize and shake him. "Marina will be fine," she wanted to shout. "The doctors will pull her through! You'll see! They can work miracles! They can even bring the dead right back to life!"

She could not, would not grieve. She believed that to do so would be to cause her sister's death. Each time she considered the possibility that Marina might not recover, each time she confronted the fact that Marina had again attempted suicide, the panic that had been pursuing her since her first day home caught up with her and invaded her body. She repeatedly told herself that her sister would regain consciousness, that as long as family members kept their thoughts from death it would lack the power to intrude into their lives. Surely her sister's recovery depended on everyone's having faith. And their father, who had brought them up to believe in God, should have been exercising his.

Iliana pulled back the living-room curtains to disperse the gloom. Her father slumped lower into his chair. She had a childish urge to sit at his feet. Ironically, at that moment, she would have accepted as wisdom anything he said and have willingly swallowed for heartache the cod-liver oil he had once credited with being the cure for anything that ailed.

Every night throughout her childhood her father had reached into a cabinet for the panacea whose taste Marina, Tico, Beatriz and she had hidden all over their apartment to avoid. On occasion his steps had passed her by and she had heard her siblings squeal as he drew them from their hiding places to tickle them until their mouths opened wide enough for the spoon. With dread and anticipation, she had hoped to be overlooked. Yet her father had always found her, and she had afterward slept comforted despite the bitterness on her tongue.

Hide and seek. Seek and find. With faith, anything you ask for shall be yours.

"Look at everything around us," her father used to say. "This roof over our heads. The food on the table. These clothes we're wearing on our backs. All of them are gifts from God."

Believing him in the depths of her soul, Iliana had learned to pray. She prayed for a bigger house and for a bed she wouldn't have to share; for more food so as not to wake hungry in the night; and for better-fitting clothes, not the hand-me-downs her sisters had outgrown. Already at the age of seven and eight she had known enough not to ask for toys. By nine, then ten, she prayed for longer days so that her father might get some rest; prayed that the factory where Rebecca worked would employ her, Marina and Beatriz so that they could help pay for their keep; prayed for their mother to stop complaining about the price of milk and bread. At eleven she bartered her soul to God and pleased her father by being the youngest in their church to be baptized. She had continued to pray until her faith inevitably dissipated and she resorted to reading secular books instead.

The Hobbit, Lord of the Rings, The Little Prince, The Chronicles of Narnia—books whose content was alien to her reality had been best. She learned to make up stories of her own. In time these stories evolved from fantasy into plans. Excelling in classes became her immediate goal, school her venue for escape. Yet throughout her absence home had been a place whose permanence she had believed in, her parents and siblings people whom she had expected to find unaltered when she returned.

Iliana pulled back the last of the curtains and turned to leave the room. Her father startled her by rising from the couch and falling to his knees as she passed him.

"Our Father who art in heaven," he began. "Hallowed be Thy name."

Iliana respectfully dropped to her knees beside him.

"I come to you not because I deserve an audience, but because of your kindness to the undeserving such as I."

As when young, Iliana shut her eyes for fear of glimpsing an angel with sword upraised to slay her for having attempted to see God's face.

"You, who know all secrets in men's hearts, must know the grief I bear today."

She impulsively reached for her father's hand.

"My daughter—one of my daughters—"

Papito began to cry. Iliana held herself still beside him. She expected that at any moment his voice would grow strong enough to reach God. If anyone's could, surely it was his.

"My daughter Marina—she—she may—"

His voice again splintered into sobs. Realizing that he would be unable to go on, Iliana self-consciously picked up where he'd left off.

"I don't know what words to speak," she mumbled. "To tell the truth, I—I don't even know if You exist."

Iliana hesitated. This was the first time she had confessed her doubts out loud.

"But my sister believes you do, and she's the one I'm here to speak to you about."

Beside her, her father made an effort to subdue his grief.

"All I know is that I'm scared and have nowhere else to turn."

Papito reached for her other hand.

"My sister is in the hospital. We found her unconscious this afternoon."

Behind closed lids, Iliana again saw Marina carried out in their mother's arms. She also recalled her smile. And it was that smile, more than Marina's body slumped as if it possessed no bones, which made her fear that her sister would not return.

"She looked—she looked like—like she was already— Dear God, please! I know I have no right to ask, but just let her be okay and come back home. I couldn't bear it if she died. Not this way. Not when . . ."

Iliana's voice strained toward God. She prayed for her sister, her parents and herself. With the last tenets of her faith, she persuaded herself that God really did exist and was actually listening to her words. She spoke to Him of all that she had been unwilling to admit even to herself: of her bewilderment since her first day home; her lack of compassion for her sister; her fear and shame of madness; her current anxiety that what she and her family had to offer might not be enough to compel her sister to remain alive. She spoke until her voice grew hoarse and her knees numbed against the living room's marble floors. She spoke until she forgot her father's presence and wore out her tongue speaking of what lurked in the recesses of her mind. When she finally opened her eyes, she recalled little of what she'd said. Yet, inexplicably, her soul had calmed.

She rose awkwardly to her feet and attempted to help her father stand. He insisted on remaining where he was.

"Papi, please. You can't stay on your knees all day."

"But Marina," he whimpered.

"Marina will be okay," Iliana told him. And although she had said those words only to reassure him, she instantly sensed that they were true. Her sister, her parents and she herself had been granted a reprieve. She had no idea how she knew. Somehow she just did.

She employed brute strength to haul her father up.

"Come. You need to get some rest."

Papito docilely allowed her to lead him to his room. She sat him on his bed, removed his shoes and socks, lifted his legs onto the mattress. When he made no move to take off his coat or suit jacket, she removed both and persuaded him to lie down.

"She'll—she'll never forgive me, will she?" her father asked.

Iliana reluctantly met his gaze. "Marina?"

Papito nodded. "Your mother too."

"I don't know about Mami, but Marina will probably blame each of us in turn."

Papito pushed himself up on an elbow. His face transformed into a mask of unexpected rage. "Well, she—she shouldn't have—"

His voice broke off into silence. The shoulders Iliana had instinctively tensed simultaneously relaxed.

"What I remember most about my youngest daughter as a child," her mother often said, "is that she liked too much to tell the truth."

Iliana was familiar with the anecdote. Supposedly, at the age of four, she overheard her mother complaining about the woman whose children she watched during the week. The next day, to Aurelia's dismay, she greeted Bertrudis at the door:

"My mother doesn't have to take care of your brats, so you better pick them up on time."

"Humph!" was all Bertrudis had replied.

"Que ni humph, ni humph, ni humph! Humph is that you pay my mother pennies to do your dirty work!"

"I know it's the truth," Aurelia had later scolded. "But you don't always have to say it."

Prompted by a memory of those words, Iliana stood to go. "I'll be downstairs," she told her father.

CHAPTER

❖ 19 ❖

"I have some things to give you," Aurelia recalled hearing her mother say on the fateful day of her last visit to her childhood home.

"And will I have to return them if you don't die?" she had retorted, wanting to be as cruel as her mother had just been by announcing her own death.

Bienvenida had smiled benignly. "You may not want them to begin with."

She entered the part of the one-room shack that served as bedroom and pulled a quilt out of a drawer.

"Do you recognize this?" she asked, sitting beside her youngest daughter and draping the quilt between their laps.

Aurelia trailed a finger along the patch Bienvenida had pointed to. "Should I?"

Her mother sighed. "You should. If you haven't allowed forgetfulness to kill Virgilio a second time."

Aurelia's hand froze on the faded patch of green. It had been years since she had allowed herself to think about that brother, equally long since anyone had voiced his name. Yes. She recognized the fabric. Recognized it although it had once been a deeper shade of green. Recognized it although the shirt it had been stripped from must have been washed and scrubbed and bleached to remove the red that had soaked it through—a red bright enough to stain her sight so that for weeks after her brother's suicide everything her eyes had seen had been filtered through their memory of blood.

Bienvenida led her daughter's hand to a crocheted triangle sewn onto burlap and stitched into the quilt. "This was your sister's who died before your birth. And this"—she guided Aurelia's hand to another patch, forcing the fingers to feel what the eyes had turned from—"was your father's. This was my mother's. This her sister's and your great-aunt's."

Aurelia's face paled as if the dead her mother spoke of had one by one stepped into the room.

"Stitched into this quilt are all family members who have—"

"Why? Why are you doing this?" Aurelia moaned.

Bienvenida's fingers grazed the quilt; her eyes stared at nothing as if to decipher events to come.

"Because the future can hurt if you deny the past. Because I want you never to forget. Because, as the youngest of my children, it is for you to sew me in."

Aurelia thrust the quilt aside and stepped toward the front door left ajar despite the midday heat. Outside, the town's one road gleamed with bits of glass. A lone hen mistook their reflections for pools of water and hopped from one to another, disturbing dust that hovered momentarily before slowly settling back down. Alongside this road—as if proximity might motivate the town's inhabitants to follow it to lives they dreamed of—stood the weathered houses into which most residents had retreated from the sun.

This remote town of old women saddened by the deaths of husbands and by the abandonment of children; of men stooped by labor that donkeys, had they possessed them, would have had to be beaten into doing; of girls yearning for marriage; and of boys aching to escape to Santo Domingo, had been Aurelia's home for the first twenty years of her life. In it her mother commanded more respect than the migrant priest who visited once a month. She was the one who, as midwife, presided over births and deaths. She was also the one who initiated rituals to appease the prematurely dead and give hope to their survivors. On most days her house creaked with the traffic of those seeking her advice. At night, it heaved with the forlorn sigh of spirits.

Back turned purposefully toward her mother, Aurelia remained standing just outside the door. Several hours remained before she'd have to walk to the town's edge to meet the bus that would take her home, and she was restless for her departure, for the demanding presence of her children able to prevent her thoughts from straying to where it was best that they not go.

She gazed up at the clear and turquoise sky. Had she been with her husband, he would have evoked for her the God he claimed could reach down from His height to calm all troubled hearts. That God was the one spirit she wanted to believe in, not the spirits her mother claimed lingered after death to resolve the problems of former lives. It did not matter that she herself felt their presence as tangibly as she did the breezes which in summer arrived at sunset and lasted only until dawn or that throughout her visit she had lain awake at night listening to their voices and hearing her mother's respond. She preferred to believe in a death that laid spirits out to rest and in a God Who would one day reward those who had suffered. She did not want to consider that after dying she too might continue yearning or seeking answers to what she did not understand.

Aurelia stepped back inside the house. She saw her mother silhouetted against darkness and appearing to float toward her.

"A strip of this would do just fine," Bienvenida murmured.

She unwrapped an embroidered shawl from around her shoulders and ceremoniously placed it on her daughter's. In the dim interior light she appeared to have begun her withdrawal into another realm. Spooked, Aurelia snatched off the shawl and flung it at her.

"You're not even ill! How can you talk to me of dying?"

Bienvenida stooped to pick up the rumpled shawl. "Mi'ja, my soul is tired and senses what my body will soon begin to feel."

"For Christ's sake, Mamá! That's nonsense and you know it!"

Bienvenida watched her with such intensity that Aurelia was sure her gaze penetrated to her very core. Unwilling to withstand such scrutiny, she stepped outside to lie on a hammock strung between two beams. When her mother followed, she shut her eyes against her.

"I have other things to give you," Bienvenida continued.

Aurelia considered what her mother had already bequeathed to her: an ability to perceive the invisible that only she and Virgilio, from among their siblings, had inherited. This ability was what had driven her brother mad and had tormented her into seeing and hearing what others couldn't. She wanted no more of such a legacy. Having witnessed Virgilio's end, she had vowed not to follow in his path or even in her mother's. For this reason she had converted to her husband's religion and had shared with him little of her past. She wanted simply to live her life and, upon dying, to stand before God as one of the meek and not as one of the rebellious led astray by abilities she dared not trust.

Bienvenida dropped a sack onto the hammock and again directed her daughter's fingers toward what she was determined that she should see. Aurelia allowed her hand to be guided but made no effort to identify the objects pulled out of the sack. She heard her mother's voice but did not listen to the words. The heat lulled her into a restless dream. In it she found herself standing at the edge of impenetrably dark waters. With every crash of waves against the shore, she heard her name called clearly and echoed by her blood. An unbearable loneliness washed over her. Drawn by the sea offering the comfort of its touch, she stepped forward into water. The shock of its cold drew a gasp from between her lips. She tried to wade back toward shore, but waves hauled her deeper in. Realizing then that it was useless to fight the sea of which she too was a part, she forced herself to submit. Her body instantly floated to the water's surface. Waves which had dragged her into their depths subdued to ripples and gently rocked her.

So this is what I have feared, she thought.

Later, having left her mother's house and paused to inspect the gifts, she wondered if Bienvenida had induced that dream. For, strange as it was, her brain had retained what her mother had intended that she remember.

A fistful of the earth to which we return to nourish those who follow, she heard Bienvenida say.

Settled in the dirt was an earthen jug corked to contain water. *To remind you that in our blood we carry the power of the sea.* Also in the sack was a clear piece of glass reflecting rainbow colors. *Because beauty exists in the most unlikely places.* Deeper still lay a stone with features resembling Bienvenida's face and mysteriously radiating heat; a wishbone, clean and smooth; a scroll of bark; an owl's feather. *To quell your fear of darkness and teach your spirit that it can soar.*

Sitting in the hospital emergency room, Aurelia for the first time regretted having discarded her mother's gifts, including the quilt and shawl, at the base of a palm tree beside the road. She regretted as well the many years she had spent running from her heritage as if the past had the power to transform her into a pillar of salt as it had Lot's wife.

So many lessons she had refused to learn because they had been taught to her by her mother. She recalled Bienvenida's claim that the devil was one's own fears called forth by self-doubt. Only now did she accept those words as truth. For too long she had relied on God to grant her peace, reluctant to believe that He, in His wisdom, had endowed the world and its creatures with the powers each needed to survive. It was these powers which she had spurned so many years before and which her soul had ached for with a constancy that prayers had not soothed.

Aurelia took a long, hard look at the way she had lived her life and at the point to which that life had brought her. She turned critical eyes on herself and picked apart each of her deepest fears. Thankful for the heart propelling her blood in currents that evoked the power of the sea, she summoned the strength she had inherited from her mother and cast her fears out one by one.

"Mami, are you sure you don't want Benny to drive you home? He can pick you up as soon as we hear —"

Aurelia cut Zoraida off with a scowl and rose from the chair into which she had collapsed after hospital attendants prevented her from following Marina through doors beyond which family members were not allowed to go. With a determined stride, she approached the admissions counter. A Puerto Rican nurse who had helped complete Marina's forms braced herself for trouble.

"Doña, please. The doctors will let you know about your daughter."

"It's been hours since she went in. How long does it take them to determine if she's going to live or die?"

The nurse gestured toward the crowded room. "Your daughter isn't their only patient. It's been this busy since last night, and nobody has gotten any sleep, including me. So do me a favor and sit down."

Aurelia made an effort to appear calm. "I'm sorry, but it's not every day a child of mine decides she wants to die. Can't you send someone to find out how she's doing?" She pointed to an aide filing papers into a cabinet behind the counter. In a tone the nurse's own mother might have used, she added: "Mi'ja, please. It'll set an old woman's soul at ease."

The nurse eyed her warily. "Look," she compromised, "just take a seat and I'll see what I can do, okay?"

Aurelia wove her way back to Benny and Zoraida. As she did, she noticed a woman convulsing against a wall. She was about to ask if she might help her to a seat when the woman spewed up globules of blood. Aurelia instantly stepped back. Red dribbled from the woman's lips. Red dark as the blood on Virgilio's clothes when she found him in a field. Red thick as the blood which had spurted from Marina's wrists after one of her suicide attempts.

It took all of Aurelia's willpower to approach the woman a second time. She reached into a coat pocket for a handful of the Kleenex she carried whenever it was cold. Placing them directly into the woman's hand, she led her to a chair. She then looked at others in the room. A woman with bruised eyes swollen shut comforted a man sobbing into her lap and promising, "Never again . . . never again"; a youth beside them struggled to regulate his breaths; an infant tucked into its mother's arms gradually turned blue. Victims of all types of diseases, disorders and infirmities; several who appeared to have overdosed on drugs; a few sporting gun and knife wounds, sprawled and slumped throughout the room. Aurelia gazed unflinchingly at each.

Never again would she avert her eyes. Never again would she recoil in fear.

In the presence of strangers like those she had sheltered herself from since her arrival in the United States and in a hospital worlds removed from the New York depicted on postcards her eldest daughter had mailed to the Dominican Republic, Aurelia for the first time granted herself permission to sprout roots past concrete into soil. Throughout more than fifteen years of moving from apartment to apartment, she had dreamed, not of returning, but of going home. Of going home to a place not located on any map but nonetheless preventing her from settling in any other. Only now did she understand that her soul had yearned not for a geographical site but for a frame of mind able to accommodate any place as home.

Aurelia inhaled deeply. She felt her soul expand to accommodate her grief for Marina who had tried to end the life she had barely begun to live. She accepted full responsibility for this daughter's choice prompted by her own negligence as well as by her hope that the next day, if not the next or the next, all problems would miraculously resolve themselves. Exhaling, she expelled the resentment she had harbored toward her husband. From that day on she would hold only herself accountable. She would no longer depend on anyone else to do for her or her children what she should have taken it upon herself to do.

CHAPTER

❖ 20 ❖

The nurse handed Aurelia a slip of paper. "She's been moved up-stairs. Here's the ward and room number. But before you go, one of the doctors needs to see you." She turned to Benny and Zo-raida. "Do either of you speak English?" When both nodded, she pointed to a set of swinging doors. "It'll be the third room to your left."

The room they were sent to was an office reserved for the tem-porary use of doctors. Everything about it was impersonal: its white, bare walls; a metal-topped desk devoid of knickknacks which might have served as comforting reminders of the clutter of human life; two hard-backed chairs; another on which the waiting doctor sat drinking coffee. He had a kind face, but his bloodshot eyes revealed exhaustion, and the agitated manner in which he swiveled in his chair suggested his barely suppressed frustration.

"Dr. Rosenberg." He stood to extend a hand and dropped the file that had rested on his lap. Placing the cup of coffee on his desk, he stooped behind it to collect the papers. "Which of you is the parent?" he asked, not bothering to offer his hand again.

"She is." Zoraida carefully enunciated the English she had learned while working as a nanny. "But she no spea-ke Inglish."

"And who are you?"

"The sissssterrrr of Marina." Zoraida then pointed to Benny. "My husssbannn."

"He can wait outside."

Benny complied without an argument. After he left, Dr.

Rosenberg invited mother and daughter to sit in the two chairs facing his.

"So," he said, speaking as if Zoraida's slow English had been an admission that she was deaf, "who in your family suffers from heart disease?"

Baffled, Zoraida only stared.

"You are aware that what your sister ingested appears to have been pills prescribed specifically for that?"

Aurelia watched her daughter. Upon hearing the translation, her eyes exposed the storm thundering in her soul. "Las mías. Entonces fueron las mías que se tomó."

"Listen," the doctor instructed, noting her distress. "Tell her it doesn't matter what her daughter took. The point is that she survived. She has an incredible constitution and one hell of a guardian angel." He waited for a translation before shooting off more words. "I doubt she was being selective or knew what the pills were for. In her state, anything would have done, and physically she's going to be fine. We're keeping her to determine the damage her heart sustained, but chances are it won't give her problems until she's old."

Zoraida translated the minimum she had understood. When Aurelia remained silent, Dr. Rosenberg stepped around the desk.

"Ask her how she feels."

Zoraida did as she was told. It was minutes before Aurelia answered.

"Como si se fuera a partir mi corazón. Como el doctor si su hija hubiera hecho lo mismo. Dile!" she commanded when Zoraida hesitated.

"Like—like her heart breaks. Like yours if your daughter do the same."

"I see." The doctor returned to his chair and sat back down. "As I was saying, physically your sister's going to be fine. But that's not what I wanted to discuss."

Again, Zoraida translated.

"We gathered from her wrists that this wasn't her first—"

"Dile que queremos verla," Aurelia interrupted.

Her daughter diplomatically rephrased the demand into a question. "Can we go to see her now?"

Dr. Rosenberg very deliberately opened the file before him. "Marina. Is that your sister's name?" When Zoraida nodded, he thumbed through the pages in the file. "According to this, Marina has attempted suicide at least three times."

Translating the word "suicide" for herself and anticipating the suggestions the doctor was sure to make, Aurelia stood from her chair and nudged Zoraida to do the same. Taken aback, bewildered, the doctor also rose.

"I'm not finished—"

Aurelia was already heading for the door. "Dile que gracias, pero que mi hija me espera y no tengo tiempo que perder."

"Mami, por favor—"

"What if your sister tries to kill herself again? What will your mother do then?"

Aurelia let herself out of the office. Dr. Rosenberg tried to reason with Zoraida.

"I wasn't suggesting that your sister be institutionalized, but she needs help, much more than your family can provide!"

Zoraida mumbled an apology, then followed her mother out of the room.

"Well?" asked Benny, who had been waiting just outside the door.

Aurelia thrust the slip of paper with Marina's room number into his hand. "There's the room number. Call everyone. Tell them Marina will be okay and they can visit her as early as tonight."

The room Marina had been moved to was shared by three other patients and partitioned by movable, accordion-pleated walls. What served as her private space consisted of a few feet cramped by a narrow bed, a night table and two chairs. A swiveling tray for meals had been pushed aside to accommodate an intravenous stand. A telephone, lamp, plastic pitcher and stack of cups were grouped on the night table. Everything else was white or a pale green intended to be soothing. Yet these dull colors lent the room a morbid air compounded by an underlying smell of sweat and of gradually decaying flesh insidious enough to arouse feelings of depression.

It was this odor which Aurelia first noticed upon entering. It affected her viscerally, reminding her of her own mortality and evoking memories of her daughter extending a Brillo-scarred arm as proof of her body's putrefaction. Only now, confronted by this daughter's deathlike state, did she realize that it had been whiffs of this underlying odor which Marina, in a state of heightened awareness, had detected on herself—an odor which had convinced her of the futility of life.

Fighting an urge to weep, Aurelia sat on one of the two chairs beside the bed. The smile that had curved Marina's lips had flattened into a line. Her lids fluttered restlessly, as if behind them her soul were deciding whether to stay or go.

Aurelia wanted to tell this daughter truths. She wanted to sift through sixty-one years of living to find the words to persuade her to remain. She wanted to guide her out of despair and offer her foolproof ways to achieve happiness in this world. Yet she had grown wise enough to know that the lessons she herself had learned could not be applied to another's life.

"Do you remember?" she asked, her voice solemn as the rustling of dry leaves. "I almost lost you twice before you were born."

Aurelia paused. Although an eternity had elapsed since her body had miscarried five fetuses, each of whom she had previously felt moving in her womb, the names she had prematurely given each lingered on her tongue, and her arms still ached with the disappointment of never having held them.

"I was so scared to lose you that I spent the summer with my legs propped up in bed so that you wouldn't slip out ahead of time.

"Do you remember?" she asked again, hoping to lure her daughter toward her voice. "When the midwife placed you in my arms, you clutched my pinky and would not let it go. When I kissed you, you blessed me with a smile. I was so grateful to have you alive and well that I spent the day watching you and inhaling the scent that only newborn babies have."

Aurelia wiped beads of perspiration from Marina's brow. Zoraida wept silently beside the bed.

"You used to have a smile for everyone. It scared me, how trusting you seemed to be. I worried that once you'd had a closer look at life you wouldn't want to stay. Superstitiously, I kept your given name secret. I didn't want death to hear it or to remember that he had lost you twice and try again. So until you turned three and strong, I called you ugly names to ward him off—not 'Marina,' a name I prayed would keep you floating above harm.

"As you grew older, almost anything made you cry. Your brothers and sisters leaving you out of a game, your father scolding you for some mischief, a stranger throwing you an unkind glance, even a chained-up dog barking as you passed. You rarely played alone. You were so dependent on others for happiness that I thought someone had given you the evil eye to make you so—"

A sigh seeped from between Aurelia's lips. For a moment she appeared to drift.

"Now I think the person who did might have been me, that by fearing the worst I called it down on you."

She clasped her daughter's hand. Caressing it, she attempted to convey the love she feared she had not sufficiently expressed.

"I remember how, once, as a teenager, you told me a dream you'd had. In it you wandered into a store to look at clothes you could not afford. A stranger offered to buy you everything you wanted, not just there but anywhere else as well. You spent the rest of the afternoon going from one store to another and stocking up on everything you thought you'd need throughout your life.

"The day you told me that dream was the first time you saw me cry, and I was so ashamed that I couldn't say a single word."

Aurelia hesitated.

"Maybe I should've told you then and there how much I cared. Maybe I should have assured you of how much I wanted to be able to provide you with everything you'd need. Or maybe it would have been best had I explained that your longing would not have ceased had I and your father been rich enough to buy you all you wanted. But the truth is that I had not discovered this even for myself, and that I too believed that if we lived in a bigger house, in a better neighborhood or at least wore better clothes, we would think better of ourselves and the world would too."

The hand which held Marina's began to shake.

"What I'm trying to say, mi'ja, is that I don't think Papito or I will ever be able to provide you with everything you need. I don't even know if you'll be able to obtain it all yourself. But if you hang on long enough, you'll discover that there are other things that make staying alive worthwhile, things that have nothing to do with money, not even with anybody else. I wish I could tell you what these things might be, but I only know what they are for me and not what they will eventually be for you."

Aurelia's voice quivered like the limbs of trees in autumn which would bloom again in spring. She gathered the loose threads of her daughter's life and wove them into tales. She spoke of the first time Marina rode a horse at a Seventh-Day Adventist camp and straddled it again after being thrown; of her determination to swim at Coney Island despite the ferocity of the waves; and of her talent for music which had inspired her to learn to play the church piano on her own. She reminded Marina of her delight with wet grass under her toes and of her love for the stars that occasionally peeked through the Brooklyn sky. She evoked the cold of snow and the heat of sun, the intensity of colors able to dazzle eyes, the diversity of tunes and sounds that engaged the ears. She spoke of both the magic and the mundane, and of life with all its contradictions and surprises. She tried to convey that although pain and sadness existed in the world there was also beauty and even joy.

And as Aurelia spoke, Marina felt herself spiraling into a void. She flailed and kicked, but still she did not wake. Frantically, she groped for something to cling to, but there was nothing and she was nowhere. So much darkness pushing against her chest; so much darkness that she could barely breathe; so much darkness that she could not breathe at all. Where was the light? Where was the tunnel and God waiting with open arms? She was dying. She was dying and on her way to hell. It must be hell—her body was burning so. She did not want to die. She did not want to go anywhere but home. She fought the sinking feeling and found herself plummeting deep and deeper still—no—she was floating weightless now. Floating, then ascending ever so slowly out of the void. She dared open her eyes. To her amazement, she saw shimmering strands unravelling from her pores to spin an incandescent web that kept her cocooned and safe. She did not move. She did not move for fear the web would tear, it was so frail. Mesmerized, she watched luminous hands swoop through darkness to draw the web and her gently out of the void. She released herself into those Godly hands. Her mouth opened wide to take in air. To her relief, she discovered that she could breathe. She could breathe and did. As she took in all the oxygen her lungs could hold, she saw what appeared to be fireflies flickering in the dark. Yes, fireflies, fireflies and many more. In their light, she recognized herself and her mother too. Her mother cradling her like when she was young. Her mother whispering in her ears so that she would know she was not alone. Her mother drawing her nearer still and enveloping her in arms strong enough to lift her high—

CHAPTER
❖ 21 ❖

The sun had long since set and the Sabbath ended when Aurelia entered her house and slammed its door behind her. Lying in their bed, Papito woke startled by the room's darkness. To his body it seemed as if only moments had elapsed since his youngest daughter had tucked him in, moments since he'd watched the afternoon's winter light filtering in through a curtained window across the room. Disoriented, he turned to a bedside clock. Its glowing digital numbers revealed that it was half past nine. He drew himself up to sit. Leaning for support against an outstretched wing of the swan-shaped headboard, he recalled that the day had already begun to fade by the time his son-in-law called with the news that Marina would survive. Relief had sunk him into sleep. Yet neither his limbs nor his soul had benefited from the rest.

He felt the weight of each of his sixty-five years heavy as rocks at the base of his skull and along his spine. They pained his joints, pinched his muscles and collided inside his aching head. He could not imagine himself shouldering the burden of another day. That Sabbath had robbed him of his strength. The hours of waiting to hear if his daughter would live or die had snapped his endurance after years of its being stretched too taut.

Bits of conversation reached Papito from the living room. He isolated his wife's voice and tried to detect her mood. Moments later he heard Iliana retreat into the basement and Aurelia approach their room. Halfway through the kitchen her steps came to an unexpected halt. For several minutes no sound at all was heard: not the swinging of the refrigerator door, the opening of cupboards, or the clatter of silverware and dishes. No sound able to persuade him that she had paused for any reason other than to avoid him.

His heart skipped a beat and contracted. He wanted to beg his wife's forgiveness. He wanted to explain that he had attempted to do right and had not foreseen that their daughter would attempt to end her life. Had he been able to muster the strength to rise, he would have loosed his tongue to confess the fear which had left him prone. But the prospect of his wife's blame drained him of any courage he might have roused.

A chair scraped the kitchen floor. Defeated, Papito slunk back under the bedcovers. So great was his need for solace that he was unable to see beyond it to Aurelia's own self-blame and need for solitude in which to sort through her emotions before sharing them with him. In the past, whenever misfortune had crept into their lives, she had leaned on him for support. She had relied on the strength he'd feigned even when he too had been exhausted and overwhelmed. Should one of their children have required discipline, she had waited for him to administer it when he came home from work. When it became obvious that their children needed a rock to stand on in this world, she had left it to him to introduce them to his God. Had they been about to be evicted, had a daughter chosen an inappropriate spouse or a son gotten himself into trouble, she had depended on him for solutions.

It was he who had sought employment in the New York they both feared. He who had guarded their family against the city's violence and denied himself the luxury of turning away from horror to grant his soul a much-needed respite. Wary lest his daughters wind up whores and his sons in jail, he had wielded religion as sword and shield in their defense. Not once had he expected those methods to cause them harm.

To him, God was more than an invisible entity to Whom he prayed. God was real as the remote sky which nevertheless rained, thundered, brightened and darkened to affect his days. Had it not been for God, he would have long been dead. It wasn't only because faith prevented him from giving up. God, in His mercy, had performed miracles that had literally saved his life. One which had made him vow never to renounce God occurred shortly after he and Aurelia had moved out of her mother's house. In defiance of the dictatorship responsible for the death of family and friends, he refused to hang a portrait of Trujillo in his home. When news spread of soldiers inspecting homes and executing or carting off to jail those daring to disregard the law, he had dropped to his knees to pray that his house be overlooked. Yet God had had greater things in store. Even as he'd knelt, soldiers had pounded on his door. He had risen to let them in. The soldiers had stormed past him to halt before a portrait of him and his wife on their wedding day. One of them had smiled approvingly while pointing under the portrait to a shelf on which stood the unlit candles reserved for blackouts.

"Excellent," he had exclaimed, although Trujillo was nowhere in the portrait and there were no burning candles anywhere in sight. "I'm glad to see candles lit in honor of El Capitán!"

There had also been occasions when Papito's prayers had resulted in unexpected visits from friends who'd brought bushels of whatever they'd harvested on their land—offerings which had staved off his family's hunger during trying times; others when God had reached down from His height to deliver his wife of a breech birth, to place a hand on the brow of a sick child, to protect their home from storms which had razed the houses of their neighbors. It was also God Who had provided visas for him and his entire family at a time when throngs of Dominicans had been denied exit from their country; God Who had then led him to employers interested in his skills; God Who had provided his family with a home of their own on the eve of their eviction.

Papito had also witnessed phenomena which had verified that Satan too was real. In his mother-in-law's house invisible forces had clawed at his arms in retaliation for his attempts to exorcise the demons posing as spirits of the dead. On evangelical rounds throughout the province of Azua he had watched horrified as the faces of the possessed distorted with hatred and then reconfigured into features not their own. He had heard sacrilege spewed in voices that could only have originated from Lucifer himself. He had seen bodies, endowed with supernatural strength, fly across rooms to attack those wishing to share God's word. He had observed the ecstasy of the possessed as they moved unharmed through flames, tore at their flesh, and offended their bodies in ways which would have been inconceivable to them had they truly been themselves.

His terror during these events had been similar to what he had experienced in church that day. One moment he'd been listening to the sermon, the next it had been disrupted by Satan's host. Yes, it had been his daughter's voice he'd heard. Yet its primal throb had convinced him that she had become a medium for something else. He had suddenly been thrust back to the Dominican Republic where he had too often heard drums bewitching enough to alter the rhythm of his heart and unnerving enough to chase shivers up his spine. Without needing to trail the drumming to its source, he had known that in those very hills and valleys where he had chosen to take an evening stroll, pagan rituals were transpiring and bodies swaying to achieve the delirium necessary for demons to possess souls. It was this delirium which his daughter had exhibited, this delirium which had made him forget her mental state and persuaded him that all he'd done to protect his family from evil had been to no avail.

As he'd watched Marina's body being wrenched and pushed by the hands of one he could not see, he had believed, without a doubt, that the susceptibility to demons his mother-in-law had possessed had been passed on to one of his own children. This belief was what had sparked his rage toward his youngest daughter. Unlike Iliana, he knew that Satan preferred those very guises insidious enough to be attributed to the Holy Ghost. He knew as well that God was gentle and would not have tormented Marina so. Had seizures not accompanied her vision, he might have recognized it as merely a symptom of her emotional collapse. Moreover, had she not swung like a pendulum between depression and false euphoria during the previous months, he might have been predisposed to believe her vision had been from God.

All this his wife should have known. Having shared his life for forty-five years and witnessed much of what his eyes had seen, she should have understood the terror which had led him to attribute to their daughter what he could not now in darkness utter even to himself.

Papito no longer had any idea what it was he was supposed to do. He was weary of struggling daily. For once, he wanted to admit defeat and have someone else be strong for him. That he had so grossly miscalculated the consequences of his actions confronted him with the possibility that he had failed in other ways. Look at how the lives of so many of his children had turned out.

He thought back to his conversion from the Catholicism of his youth. What had appealed to him about Adventist doctrine was its specificity in distinguishing right from wrong. In a country where both had shifted according to a tyrant's whims and little had offered relief or hope, religion had granted him salvation, unmediated access to the divine, and steadfast rules by which to live. These he had offered to his children as buffer against poverty and pain. He had hoped, with the promise of heaven, to shield them from disappointment in this world. Yet in a United States where the fulfillment of dreams was considered possible and the young demanded satisfaction in the here and now, he, who had long ago given up on dreams, had been unable to discourage his children from theirs or to fathom what, other than faith, he might in old age offer to help them endure their lives.

Papito drew the blankets up under his chin. He recalled the dreams of his youth which had since been ravaged by the strain of trying to make it through each day. He remembered the people whose collapse he'd witnessed, not once able to make them stay after they decided to give up even their own ghosts. Pressing fingertips to his lids, he attempted to push back the flood of memories, but they rushed forth in waves that he was powerless to stop.

Six decades, five years, a fistful of months, another of days, and from among all these his thoughts returned him to the few hours he had tried hardest to forget. On that afternoon clouds had darkened the sky to make it appear like night. By evening heaven had collapsed and the wind incited what threatened to be one of the worst hurricanes in years. Along the beaches of Barahona the swollen Caribbean Sea stood erect and stormed toward the shore, stooping only to snatch into its foamy hands and swallow greedily anything lying in its path.

Papito was nineteen. As the favorite son born to his father in old age he had inherited three acres and a shack situated a quarter-mile from the sea's edge. He lived in it alone, his siblings having shrugged off responsibility for their father so beaten by a lifetime of heavy labor that his body had bowed toward the earth as if longing for its grave. For eighteen months during which he'd learned more about sorrow than any youth needed to know, Papito had listened to his embittered father rail against God, country, the wife who had willed herself to die, the children who had drained his strength. He had watched him shrink to a skeleton racked by arthritic pain and pneumonically spewing blood. He had bathed and clothed him. He had held a baby's bottle to his lips and mashed his food, his father's teeth having rotted from a diet supplemented by sugar stolen from the warehouse where he'd worked. Papito had done all of this and more only to come home one day to find his father's body convulsing with its last breath and his eyes brightening at the realization that he was finally about to die. Papito had seen him buried six feet deep and had not known, even then, if his father had confused the unlabeled bottles by his bed or had purposefully poisoned himself by ingesting the ointment for arthritis rather than the medicine to relieve his hacking cough.

A bolt of lightning slashed the sky. Papito emerged from what had once been his father's room. Ears attuned to the wind rattling his walls and to the rain pummeling his roof, he ignited the wick of a candle a draft instantly blew out. Already most of his neighbors had sought refuge in a cathedral built on higher ground. Yet he kept postponing the moment when he would join them there.

Fumbling through darkness, he stuffed rags into cracked windows leaking water onto dirt floors. He shoved furniture away from where he discovered other leaks by touch. Determined to safeguard all he could against the storm, he draped oilcloths over perishable objects and also over those he was unable to move alone. As he stepped blindly from room to room, he muttered prayers for his home not to flood or be hauled into the sea. He vowed that if it remained intact he would rebuild it strong enough to withstand both wind and rain; he would add additional rooms; he would furnish them well enough to lure a bride able to disperse the gloom which had lingered since his father's death.

Both of the shack's two rooms were miserably small and forlorn. Few things in either provided comfort. Their meager furniture—a table, several chairs, a stack of crates, a woman's dresser with an empty frame where a mirror should have been, an iron bed, a rolled-up mat—all showed the wear of time. The exterior of the house, with its splintering walls and corroding roof, lent it the appearance of one which had stood uninhabited for years.

Ever since his father's death Papito had been finding unbearable his solitude in those rooms. He longed for companionship but not for that of male friends or of the women who welcomed him into their arms in exchange for a few pesos, a pound of sugar, a bushel of one thing or another. He yearned for someone to whom he could earnestly give himself, someone who'd be waiting when he came home each day and whose warm body beside his would remind him that he too was alive.

He had already decided who that bride would be. The first time he saw her she had been sitting on the beach in a white cotton shift hiked to just below her hips and with her plump legs extended to receive the sea rolling like her lover onto shore. In the tropical noon glare her bronzed skin had seemed to radiate light and heat. Her woolly hair—whipped by a breeze and highlighted with strands of gold—had stirred as if alive. Although she had appeared to be about fifteen, possibly as old as seventeen, it had been clear, from the presence of the younger sisters who traditionally served as chaperones for marriageable daughters, that she had not yet been claimed by any man. Nonetheless, her face—with its features drawn tight across its bones and chiseled precisely in contrast to the cushy roundness of her body—had made her seem not like someone still in the midst of a protected childhood but, rather, like someone who had lived far beyond her years.

"Anabelle, you coming in?"

Her name rang in Papito's ears as her sisters beckoned for her to join them in the waves.

"Anabelle!"

One hand letting sand trickle slowly through its fingers, the other planted flat behind her, Anabelle remained focused on something at the horizon's edge. And although she had not said a word, Papito imagined that her voice would be as enchanting as her name, her character as strong as her sculpted face, her passion as untamed as the hair curtaining her eyes. Watching her from a distance of a few feet, he felt his blood pulse riotously through his veins.

His father had been wrong. Life could not possibly be all bad if it had resulted in beauty such as Anabelle's.

Right then and there and without having planned to, Papito yanked off his shirt and dived into the sea. He lay on his back and licked the taste of salt from his lips, content for the moment to have Anabelle within his sight and to release himself to the waves whose motion matched the rhythm of his heart.

Having never encountered Anabelle before, he assumed that she had recently moved to Barahona. But after inquiring among friends, he discovered that she had lived there all her life.

"Stay away from her," they warned, "or her father will come after you with a machete."

He learned that her mother had died young and that she and her sisters lived in the countryside with their father. Rumor also had it that he controlled them with an iron will and was especially possessive of his eldest.

"Didn't you hear what he did to Juan for just looking at Anabelle? And what about his falling-out with Don Lucas and Manolo?"

Whenever Papito had thereafter glimpsed Anabelle sitting in church with her head bent low, buying staples at the market or washing clothes at the river's edge, she had invariably been accompanied by her sisters. Yet although he and she had not been introduced, she visited him in dreams.

Silently, stealthily, she'd slip into his room to join him in his bed. From between her naked breasts she would magically produce a mango whose green skin fading into pink hinted at the ripe perfection of the fruit inside. Her fingers would gently knead the fruit, transforming its pulp into a nectar that moved tantalizingly beneath its skin. Then, lips scarcely opening, she'd puncture the mango's tip. The bit of flesh her teeth had torn would drift onto her lap. Her lips would bloom into a bud against the fruit's small wound, and her hands would massage its flesh, cajoling its nectar into her mouth. Any drops that rolled onto her chin she'd offer to Papito on a fingertip. Hungrily, shamelessly, he would lick them off. Only when he had begged for more would she recklessly strip off the mango's skin and offer the fruit to him in the hollow of her palm. Rivulets of its juice would ooze onto her fingers. Papito would reach his tongue between them. One by one he would take her fingers into his mouth and lingeringly suck each. When unable to postpone any longer savoring the fruit itself against his lips and tongue and teeth, he would twine his hands through his love's dark hair and draw her near so that she too might partake.

In anticipation of the fulfillment of this dream, Papito had begun to oil his ashy skin and to slick his hair back with pomade. The shoes he had not once bothered to polish prior to his encounter with Anabelle were now buffed daily despite the countryside's perpetual dust. Clothes he had been indifferent to wearing torn were mended with seams he sewed surprisingly straight.

He began to take notice of other things as well: the windows dirty enough to prevent the sun's rays from shining into his home; the chairs perched on wobbly legs; the warped, wooden table slick with grease; the ants perpetually marching across his floors; the cobwebs strung across beams and draped from corners; the weeds sprouting leaves through the crevices in his walls.

The desire to prepare a home for his intended bride served as an impetus for what he had previously ignored. He set aside time to dust, sweep, scour and polish. He even learned to repair furniture, cork holes, spread dung on floors until they acquired a glossy sheen.

Once he had replaced the leaky roof, he intended to ask Anabelle's father for permission to visit her at home. To prove his intentions were honorable, he would assure them that he was employed and owned a home able to accommodate her and the many children he hoped they'd have. These and other details had been carefully worked out in his mind. Should his offer be refused the first time, he would try again and then again. He would remain patient until their resistance had worn down. He would comply with any demands either of them might make. More important, he would not, as he suspected others before him had, disrespect the father or the daughter by attempting to meet with her alone.

Papito paused between the two rooms of his home. He made a mental list to check if he had left anything undone. Between bursts of thunder, the wind vehemently shook the house and threatened to lift its roof right off. Hesitant to leave it but unwilling to endanger himself by remaining any longer, he pushed open the shack's front door. A gust of wind snatched him from the threshold and flung him back inside the house. Sheets of rain simultaneously slanted in. The water which had begun to seep in under his walls streamed freely through the open door, hauling in sand, twigs, pebbles, a host of palmetto bugs, the sea grapes for which Barahona was well known, anything else the rain had amassed on its way downhill.

Drenched, Papito struggled to his feet. A tarantula hopped onto his hand and scampered up his arm. He swiped it off and dipped the same hand into the inch or so of water covering his floors. From the weight of what had been hauled into the house, he calculated that the storm was quickly gathering force. Worried that he had lingered far too long, he kicked off both his shoes. On bare feet better able to grip the earth and detect changes in the terrain, he cast himself into the storm.

The wind howled evilly as he bent his body forward to push against it. It snatched leaves and fruit and limbs off trees, flinging them weightlessly through air. It snapped the trunks of slender palms. Gleefully, rolls of thunder joined the merriment of destruction with a frightful noise seeming to originate from massive drums. Bolts of lightning slashed the sky cloaked in funereal greys.

It was as if the devil himself had taken possession of the world, as if during the preceding weeks of sweltering days and nights— weeks during which the sun and moon had slithered lethargically across the sky and everything in nature had succumbed to a list- less stupor, remaining inert or moving sullenly on water, soil or air had it been necessary to move at all—the devil had busied himself sowing seeds of restlessness and instigating violence which the ele- ments, out of boredom, had decided to unleash.

In the midst of this torrential storm through which he could see no further than several feet ahead and at the bottom of a hill made treacherous by the waters rushing down its side, Papito found himself thrust back into the recurrent nightmare which, upon waking screaming, he had barely been able to recall. Each step he took nonetheless persuaded him that he had taken the ex- act same step in dreams. Every clap of thunder, bolt of lightning, drop of rain that slapped his face was one he was sure he had expe- rienced innumerable times before. Although awake, he discov- ered, as in his dreams, that nature had turned against him. With an uncanny sense of premonition which he was unable to shake off, he also understood that everything he had worked for during the previous weeks would on that very night be undone. It would not matter that he had exerted himself trying to safeguard his home against the storm and might actually survive the night. Nothing he had planned for himself and Anabelle would ever come to pass.

This premonition shook Papito to his core. Yet, unwilling to accept it as prophetic, he tucked it away from conscious thought and concentrated on reaching higher ground.

His feet slid on mud and tangled in roots unearthed specifically to trip him. Shivering fitfully, he avoided the cover of trees and tried to orient himself in the dark. But the footpath which had zigzagged up the hillside to meet the road to town had been en- tirely washed away.

He managed to climb the hill on his hands and knees. The

storm was far more treacherous on the open road. It ripped planks from the sides of houses and tossed them with the fury of a child grown restless with his toys. It ripped out two poles strung with a clothesline and twined these around the branches of a tree where the garments flapped like ghosts aching to take flight.

Papito shielded his eyes from the debris and pelting rain. For every few steps he took forward the wind shoved him back another and threatened to lift him off his feet. Offended by the un-provoked assault, he summoned the strength of rage to keep him-self upright. He had almost reached the town when he detected, through sheets of rain rent by lightning, someone walking from the opposite direction. So disconcerting was the sight that he came to an immediate halt. The apparition—for no person of this world would have moved so carelessly in a storm—drifted toward him with its back against the wind, its white dress transparent against its skin, its feet barely touching ground. When it moved past him, its body reeling from the force of the wind pushing it along, Papito believed that fatigue and the terrors of the storm had made him see what could not possibly be there.

Heart pounding with alarm, he turned to follow with his eyes the apparition posing as Anabelle. Unaware of his presence, she stumbled toward the sea. Her tangled hair whipped her face. Her mud-smeared dress gaped with a rip from her shoulders to just above her waist. This strip of fabric fluttered behind her, lending her the appearance of one who had lost a wing and was attempting to make do with the remaining appendage too water-logged to propel her off the ground.

Leaves and twigs spun at a dizzying speed around her. A plank flew inches above her head. Yet she made no effort to protect her-self at all. It was as if she were the eye of the storm and the sur-rounding violence lacked the power to provoke her fear, as if her thoughts were focused on a private realm impervious to whatever affected the body she inhabited like a shell.

Papito watched her halt in the middle of the road. Her arms flew up and her torso bent forward at a precarious angle. In defi-ance of gravity, she sustained this position and offered herself to the wind. When moments passed and her offering was spurned, her arms plummeted back down. It then appeared that her body grew heavy and her height diminished, as if she were being sucked into soil. She jerked her head around to inspect the landscape. Sighting a squat palm with wide, long leaves whipped into a frenzy, she veered abruptly off the road. Dismayed, Papito watched her drop at the base of the tree's gnarled trunk. Even as a child he had learned not to do this in a storm. And Anabelle was not a child. She was a woman witnessing a storm powerful enough to level trees, a woman placing herself directly in harm's way.

Anabelle slumped against the tree and brought her knees up to her chin. She wrapped her arms around both legs and tucked her head between them.

Papito battled the elements to reach her. Pelting rain stung his eyes; his feet slipped repeatedly on mud; the wind propelled him at an angle from the path he urgently needed to take. When he at last reached Anabelle, he found himself absurdly held back by the impropriety of approaching a lone maiden in the dark. It made no difference that he was doing so to save her life. His upbringing prevented him from seizing her against her will.

"Anabelle?" he called out, only to have a burst of thunder obliterate her name.

He stepped nearer the tree scarcely tall enough for an adult to stand under its leaves. His hands shook as he reached for Anabelle. On contact, she instantly leapt to her feet. Papito himself stumbled back. In the glare of lighting he detected the terror in her eyes. He also saw the body he thought he had grown familiar with in dreams. His own suddenly convulsed. Facts, details and hearsay burst in quick succession to the forefront of his thoughts. He recalled that neither Anabelle nor her sisters had ever been glimpsed alone. He also heard the hushed voices of friends speaking of how her father, like a jealous rooster, chased off potential suitors; of how he had forced Anabelle to take on the role of her deceased mother; of the town's many widows who would have gladly helped him raise his family; of his refusal to rewed and estrangement from the in-laws who had snooped around his house out of concern for the three girls.

Papito's thoughts scurried forward, sidestepped, then retreated only to again masochistically advance toward the idea taking shape like the blurred image of a ghost which, once it has appeared, forever destroys any preconceived notions one might have held of life.

Barahona was a small town. Rumors spread quickly. Unless the gossip of the moment pertained to an act so abhorrent that its mere mention inspired dread, it was spoken of unabashedly and with glee. Otherwise, the words chosen flitted around edges, only hinting at, never naming the horrid thing itself.

Only now, confronted with the evidence of Anabelle's belly protruding against the soaked fabric of her dress, did Papito understand why his friends had warned him to find himself another girl. Only now did he understand as well why she had hidden in shapeless garments throughout the previous months.

Had the culprit responsible for her condition been one of her admirers, the townspeople would have forced them to marry. Such things had occurred before. Desire, a lack of restraint among the young, foolishness and mischief were for the most part acknowledged and occasionally condoned. Moreover, in such a case, the girl's own father would have hunted down the man. Yet no such effort had been made in Anabelle's behalf.

Something inside Papito snapped. He approached his beloved, his heart attempting to leap out of his mouth to offer itself to the hand she held up in self-defense. Her lips emitted a sound which held no words, a sound like that of a rabbit caught in the claws of its prey and swooped into the air. At the utterance of that sound Papito irrevocably understood that it had not been foolishness but a determination to encounter death which had sent her out during one of the the fiercest storms.

Flinging caution to the wind, he seized Anabelle by her thickened waist. Her body stiffened against his; her fists struck him anywhere they could reach. Yet he did not loosen his grip. To release her would mean that he too had relinquished hope and believed that life was not worth the trouble of drawing breath.

He lurched onto the road with Anabelle struggling in his arms. Again, he recognized bits and pieces of his recurrent nightmare. For some inexplicable reason he also recalled a story his father had loved to tell. In it an old man walked home with his donkey and his dog. He led them across a field and beat the donkey beginning to trail behind. After this had gone on for some time, the donkey squatted on its hind legs and refused to budge. When the old man raised his cane, the beast of burden opened its jaws to speak.

"I am tired and will lay myself down to die. Your beating me has no power to change my mind."

The old man was so taken aback that he dropped his cane and ran from the donkey as fast as his legs could carry him. His faithful dog followed close behind. When they collapsed at the edge of another field, the dog cocked its head toward its master.

"Imagine that!" it exclaimed. "A donkey speaking!"

Papito's father had told the story in the mischievous voice he'd often employed before his sense of humor was strangulated by discontent. As a child Papito had watched him succumb to a fit of mirth, not understanding the humor of the tale and filled with dread at the possibility that animals might speak. That this story should now return to haunt him unnerved him almost as much as everything else he had experienced throughout that night. Despite proof to the contrary, he needed to believe in a world where man and beast both had their specific roles and where wrongs were redressed and good deeds repaid in kind. He could not accept that what he perceived as reality might shift.

Papito tightened his grip on Anabelle. He dodged sheets of tin ripped from roofs and tried to avoid as well the limbs of trees and fist-sized rocks hurtling through the air. When Anabelle slumped against him, he settled into his resolve of the previous weeks. He would remove her from her home. He would marry her and help her raise her child so that she'd never again have to hang her head in shame. He would deliver her from the unnamable misery she had endured until that day.

Rain pummeled them both as he stumbled on the road transformed into a river of rushing mud. He ran a palm along the base of Anabelle's spine where her dress had torn. The memory of her flesh glistening in his dreams quickened his steps and lent him strength. He reached the cathedral and kicked its doors barricaded against the storm. When they creaked open, he thrust both himself and Anabelle inside.

It took a moment for his eyes to adjust to the hundreds of candles flickering in exchange for divine protection. Already most of the townspeople had settled themselves inside to wait for the storm's end. They lay on pews with their possessions, leaned exhausted against walls, huddled in family groups along the back and up front, near the altar of an impaled Christ. Their lips murmured silent prayers. The heat of their breaths and of their crowded bodies gave the cathedral a claustrophobic air.

Papito searched for a spot where he and Anabelle might rest. So intent was he on his task that he did not hear the sharp intake of breath as he passed by the old priest. Nor did he notice the silence that overtook the townspeople closest to the doors as he patted Anabelle's backside to let her know they had arrived.

When she did not respond, he lowered her onto the floor and ever so gently leaned her against the cathedral's hindmost pew. Her head rolled listlessly to one side. He cupped and settled it at a more comfortable angle. As he withdrew his hand, he noticed the red smearing his palm. He stared at it, wondering from what wound the blood had spilled. His emotions grew strangely numb. He wiped the blood off on his rain-soaked pants. Flipping his palm back up, he observed that it was neither cut nor scratched. Still unwilling to understand, he directed his gaze toward Anabelle.

Her eyes remained closed, their lashes damp and glistening, every other feature peacefully at rest.

Papito grew as still as she. He discovered that he was unable to stretch out his arms to touch her, unable to shift his gaze from her face, unable to lift his tongue to call her name. Kneeling there before her—the space in his soul where his hopes had resided vaulting shut, his heart decelerating of its own accord—he was presented with the conclusion of his recurrent nightmare. He saw each of its details clearly, as if, like Anabelle's, his own ghost had flown from his body to become omniscient. Yet although he had reached the events from which he'd woken screaming in his bed, he was unable to utter a single sound or shed a single tear.

His eyes and mouth were as parched as if his body had passed through flames. His soul was as barren as a grave.

CHAPTER
❖ 22 ❖

On bad days Papito believed that Anabelle had willed herself to die. On worse days he knew it was he who'd killed her, he who had seized her against her will to place her directly in death's path. On good days he did not think of her at all.

The pain of remembering pulsed behind his lids—a secret pain that had proliferated like cancerous cells to infect every aspect of his being; a pain that conjured up his other imperfections to make him believe he was far less than he ever was; a pain that induced him to live penitently in order to redeem himself before God, the sole witness to all that had occurred on that night so long ago.

Papito tucked his arms under the blanket. He hid the hands that had seized Anabelle and, years later, embraced Aurelia, carried their children, changed their diapers, tickled their bellies until laughter sputtered from their lips. Those hands had enjoyed flinging his infant children into the air. They had held forth a promise that he would catch them, that his arms were strong enough to lift them up and to bear their weight should they trip over their own feet. Yet, one by one, his children had fallen so far beyond his reach that he had come to doubt his ability to protect them.

The evil spirits which had clambered onto Papito's back whispered sacrilege in his ears. They claimed that his dependence on God had been the ruin of his family; that the meek inherited nothing, neither a place in heaven nor better lives on earth; that for his fate to change he'd have to resign himself to the values of this world. They insisted that had he been worthy God would have granted him the means to provide his children with fruitful lives. As if imparting secrets, they lowered their voices to breathe that a compassionate God would have created a sinless world, would have spared Marina from being raped and driven mad, would have revealed what it was Papito should have done to prevent her from attempting to end her life.

Anguished, Papito tossed in bed. He tried to hush the voices and to fling the evil spirits off his back. Like a drowning man clutching at waves, he clung to his faith and refused to let it go. He begged God to pardon him for his sins and to grant him another chance to prove himself worthy of the family with which he had been blessed. He vowed to rise at dawn and to start each day with prayers. In the name of Jesus Christ, crucified to save sinners like himself, he promised that if his daughter regained consciousness he would forever place God above all else.

There, in the solitude of his room, Papito felt utterly alone. He suspected that God had turned away. He doubted that his prayers had been heard.

A sound reached him from the kitchen. He rolled over to feign sleep as his wife stepped into their room. She flicked on the light switch by the door. The sudden glare tinged the darkness behind Papito's lids a dark and pulsing red.

Aurelia silently undressed. Despite her many winters in New York, she continued to sleep nude. Nights were the only times her body breathed freely, she had often claimed, unwilling to admit what her husband already knew—that, like her mother, she too believed that garments confined her dreams.

Papito waited for her to climb into bed beside him. He waited for her to slip into her habit of waking him with what she had not found the words to say during the day or had not wanted to voice in the presence of their children. Her silence was unbearable. He wished she'd unleash her fury and once and for all lash out at him with the accusations he had seen dart across her eyes in church. When unable to endure his anxiety for a moment longer, he opened his lids to find her.

His wife stood still and naked before a mirror. Surreptitiously,

Papito watched her. The anger he had expected to find on her face had been replaced by something formidable but which he was unable to identify. He was certain that the turmoils of the day had sparked the change, but he suspected that it had been fueled by something else as well. Her expression projected an array of contradictions, so that when he thought he had glimpsed an emotion he was simultaneously confronted by its reverse. She appeared younger and older too, as if the prospect of her daughter's death had thrust her outside of time.

Aurelia drew pins out of her hair and loosed the braids wrapped like a crown around her head. She ran her fingers through each until the white locks sprang free to cascade midway down her back. As a young woman in the Dominican Republic she had sauntered along the roads of her hometown with her mane rippling or with strands slipping from her braids to cling seductively to her face. Either way, young men had transformed into fools to attract her attention, and old men had found comfort in the belief that, had they still possessed their youth, they might have succeeded in doing with dignity what the young men of the day could not.

Upon first meeting Papito, Aurelia had told him all she remembered of the father from whom she had inherited that hair. In contrast, she had barely mentioned Bienvenida. The few times she had, it had been to convince Papito that she had little in common with her mother, whose reputation had reached him long before he'd visited their town. As an Adventist eager to save souls and traveling the countryside for that purpose, Papito had been warned of Bienvenida's powers and of her youngest daughter's sullen disposition. This, although he'd had no intention of approaching either. Despite his religious fervor, he had, at that early stage of his conversion, been too afraid to tangle with Satan or to meddle in Bienvenida's business. As for her daughter, her beauty alone had been enough to keep him from her after his experience with Anabelle.

It was Aurelia who had eventually requested Bible lessons; she who had invited Papito home in the hope that her mother might convert; she who had proposed they marry before he'd ever thought to ask. Their love was supposed to have been enough to ensure their happiness. It was supposed to have kept their children safe. Neither he nor she had counted on the circumstances which would wreak havoc in their lives.

Aurelia turned from the mirror and flicked off the overhead light. When she climbed into bed, Papito noticed how careful she was not to allow any part of her body to touch his.

"Did you know it was my pills she took?"

Papito remained absolutely still. Aurelia placed a hand on his shoulder. It lingered there for a moment. When he did not respond, she slid closer and, throwing off the bedcovers, rolled him over until he faced her in the dark. She did not bother to ask why he had his church clothes on in bed. Instead, she reached out to loosen and extricate his tie. Then, one by one, she undid the buttons on his shirt and pulled its hem out of his belted pants. Holding him as if he were a child, she removed his shirt and undershirt. She flung both aside and slithered down toward his legs. Her hair draped his chest, then thighs and calves as she undid his belt to pull off his pants and boxer shorts. When he lay naked, she covered him with the blanket and settled herself beside him.

Her flesh was unexpectedly warm as she wrapped her arms around him and twined her legs through his. The tenderness of that gesture unleashed tremors along his spine. He shut his eyes to steel himself. Yet, as she pillowed his head between her breasts, his tears burst forth in streams whose flow he was powerless to stop.

For the first time ever he cried for Anabelle who had died with her despair intact. He cried for Marina whom he did not know how to help. He cried for Aurelia whom he thought he might lose. With remorse and shame, he cried as he had never done throughout his life.

His tears splattered onto his wife and rolled off to soak the sheets. They threatened to spill over the sides of the bed, to leak onto the floor, to inundate them both in grief.

Aurelia drew him nearer. Although her embrace elicited more tears, she did not try to stop them, nor did she suggest that he be strong. When he attempted to pull away, she placed her palm at the base of his skull and shifted his head so that it came to rest directly over her heart. Papito heard its insistent beats. He heard it murmur that she forgave and loved him still.

His body heaved against hers. Years of pent-up grief drained with his tears. Consoled and grateful, he reached out to caress her breasts whose elasticity had early on been sacrificed to the hunger of infant mouths. He traced as well the stretch marks that mapped the nineteen pregnancies through which she'd labored, the arms that had carried the fourteen children who had survived, the shoulders against which each of them had slept. His fingers traveled lower and lingered on delicate folds as if to discover the softness of her flesh, the hardness of the bones beneath, the secrets of the soul within. He explored every inch of her familiar body which nevertheless offered up surprises to his touch.

Aurelia's body arched. Her hips rose to meet his hand. She rocked against it ever so slowly, her body quivering, the softest of moans escaping from her lips. When her breath began to veer out of control, she forced herself to pull away so as to lay him flat beside her.

His body became malleable in her hands. She massaged his muscles and shaped his flesh. She rid his limbs of aches and pains. When he thought she could do no more, she wiped devastation from his soul and returned to him his strength.

Papito rolled onto Aurelia as though on waves. He parted her to dive in, expanding, submerging, trusting their motions to buoy him back. Welcoming and unafraid, his wife floated toward him. She accepted his embrace, the passion of it, the gentleness of each caress. Their bodies eased into a rhythm, undulating and melding into one. Their spirits soared briefly beyond pain and grief and horror. This, despite the secrets they could not reveal, the emotions they could not shape into words, the things neither of them understood.

CHAPTER

❖ 23 ❖

A torrent of cold water woke Rebecca. A hand reached out and slapped her. Confused, she tried to adjust her eyes to the dim light of the black-and-white television.

"Couldn't you turn off the goddamn thing before you went to sleep?"

Pasión stood beside the bed, his face in shadow, his tall figure daunting as an apparition. Rebecca glanced at the TV whose programs had long since gone off air, leaving behind a flickering screen and an electric hum. Beside her, Esperanza and Rubén— clothes drenched, teeth chattering, eyes wide with fear—cowered in the bed. Their younger sister whimpered.

"And haven't I told you to keep your children quiet in my presence?" Pasión roared, lifting the empty ten-gallon can at his feet and hurling it at them.

Rebecca leapt from bed like a wildcat. "My children? My children? How many times have I begged you to wear a rubber? But no! You want me giving birth in this house like some kind of bitch!"

Pasión seized her by her hair. He hauled her across the room and slammed her face against a wall. Blood spurted from her nose, splattering the wall and trickling onto the floor. He twisted her arm behind her back. Her hands clenched into ineffectual fists. He forced one of them to unfurl and systematically bent its fingers until their bones were heard to snap. Rebecca shrieked. Her shock was so intense that it postponed her pain as she struggled to break free. Further incited by her helplessness, Pasión swung her around to face him. A malicious smile settled on his lips as he jammed a fist into her mouth.

"I didn't hear you," he taunted, yanking her tongue out as far as it would go. "What did you say?"

Rebecca choked on her tongue and on her husband's hand. Rubén darted up behind them to pummel his father with tiny fists. Pasión released Rebecca and effortlessly flung him back onto the bed. Rubén crumpled beside his sisters. His expression conveyed that he would kill his father if he could.

"I shit on the mother who gave birth to you," Pasión cursed, turning on his wife as if she were responsible for their son's hatred.

Blood and bile trickled from Rebecca's mouth. Her tongue clumsily formed words.

"Maricón! Next time you come into this house you'll find me and the children gone!"

Pasión lunged at her as if to silence her once and for all. Then, repulsed by her appearance, he released her and turned to go.

"You'll never leave," he yelled from the hallway. "Who's going to be interested in your stinking, flaking cunt?"

Moments later the sounds of objects crashing down the stairs and of the front door slamming ascended to the bedroom. Rebecca employed her one able hand to gather her sobbing children near.

"Ya, ya," she crooned. "Ya, ya."

Rebecca lay awake long after she and her children had collapsed on mounds of dirty laundry dumped on the bed as protection against the wet mattress. Each time she blinked, darts of pain pierced her scalp. If she closed her eyes for more than several minutes, terror wrenched them open. The room was so dark that she could barely see the children bundled inside their winter coats. Her own was buttoned to her neck, but still the cold crept in beneath the layers to rouse her discontent.

In the past Pasión had always followed up his abuse by making tearful love to her. His tremors had conveyed remorse and aroused forgiveness. The urgency of his thrusts had seemed an effort to convey all the emotions he could not utter, restoring her faith that in time he would transform into the husband she had hoped for. Now, deprived of his tears, she found herself replaying his parting words. These few words violated her peace of mind more than the blows Pasión had dealt or other criticisms he'd often voiced. Unlike those, these had been pointed enough to leave her with no doubt that he had lost his appetite for the very thing she had depended on to entice him.

Masochistically, she went over the many indignities she had endured in the hope of keeping her husband at her side. As early as a few months after their marriage, he had strapped her into a chair so that she'd be present as he had his way with a girl no older than in her teens.

"Whore! You cock-sucking, filthy whore!" Rebecca had shrieked, convinced that the girl had begged Pasión to bring her into his home as shamelessly as she was begging him to enter her again.

The words had leapt from her tongue to be muffled by the cloth tied around her mouth. Determined to do the girl some harm, she had propelled the chair toward the bed. It was then that the girl had turned to face her. It was then that she had slapped Pasión's thigh so that he too would witness his wife's humiliation. His laughter, when it spilled forth, was contemptuous in its calm release. Rebecca felt it more than heard it. She felt it whirl around her and submerge her with its undertone of glee.

Something inside her rebelled against the rising wave of shame. She thrashed against the ropes. The violence of her movements knocked the chair sideways onto the floor.

The girl leaned forward to peer over the bed's edge. Her eyes expressed neither loathing nor even triumph, just an indifference which conveyed that Rebecca's existence was as crude and meaningless as her own. Gazing into those somber eyes, Rebecca felt suddenly obscene. She felt implicated for witnessing her husband's infidelity and for not turning away. It made little difference that

Pasión had bound her against her will. Having done so, he had effectively stripped her of virtuous conceits. He had obliterated her self-esteem and convinced her that she was deserving of his scorn.

As her limbs numbed against the ropes, as the springs on her bed continued to creak and morning came and went, Rebecca held herself responsible for all that had occurred. Had she submitted to each of her husband's sexual demands, he would not have found it necessary to prove to her that other women were willing to comply. His actions confirmed how sexually naïve she'd been. A virgin until the age of thirty, she had disdained alternate forms of sex. Moreover, previously involved with a man who she suspected had preferred the youthful body of his daughter, she blamed herself for having lacked the sexual skills to distract him from the girl.

Her moral ground shifted with her belief that it had been no coincidence that the two men in her life had sought sexual satisfaction elsewhere. By the time her husband undid the ropes that bound her, she had sunk into a mire of depravity and vowed to indulge his every whim. When he began to spend his nights away, she had swallowed her anger whole and derived comfort from the fact that it was she whom he had needed enough to marry. On the rare occasions when he came home, she had indulged in believing that he had returned to stay. Now, having adapted herself to fit his life, she had seen him turn in disgust from the thing she had become.

Rebecca rolled out of bed. She groped for the string of a hanging bulb. Its light illuminated the cluttered room. A cracked mirror above the bureau revealed exactly what it was she had become.

She stepped forward to inspect her lids bruised purple, her dry skin flaking off, the dirt embedded deep in the furrow of her prematurely wrinkled face. She touched the nose bent beyond recognition and peeled off a scab that caused her nostrils to bleed again. She slid her swollen tongue along her split lips and cavity-rotted teeth. Last of all, she fingered a strand of her greying hair.

So all of this was what Pasión had seen; what others regularly saw whenever she stepped outside; what her mother and sister had noticed too.

Rebecca slipped off her coat and let it fall in a heap around her feet. She winced as she raised the arm her husband had twisted behind her back. Employing the hand whose fingers he had left intact, she pulled the pilling fabric of her sweater away from her skin and sniffed under her arm. The odor of perspiration was unmistakable even to her nose accustomed to offensive smells. She lowered her arm and unzipped her shrunken woolen pants. Hooking a thumb inside the waistbands of her pants and panties, she awkwardly drew both down around her knees.

Eight years of living with Pasión had whitened her pubic hairs. She parted those matted over her vaginal crease. Bending forward, she drew several sharp breaths. An acrid odor confirmed his claim about her stinking cunt.

She straightened to her five-foot height and, drawing her pants back up, turned to inspect the room. Amidst all the filth she felt even less desirable than the trash her husband hauled into the house. That he had succeeded in bringing her so low pervaded her with a sudden rage. Here she was forty years old and she had spent most of those years waiting to be wed. She had wasted others waiting for Samuel to change and then for Pasión as well. Not having learned her lesson, she had wasted still other years waiting for kinder days and, when none arrived, waiting for night to lull her into a forgetful sleep. So many years of waiting and all she had to show for them was her battered face, her bruised body whose flesh daily sagged further from her repeatedly broken bones, and three children whom Pasión should have provided for better than he had done for her.

Rebecca snatched her coat off the floor and flung it on. She reached for her boots and shoved a foot in each. This done, she shook her nearest child awake. When Esperanza woke, she reached for Rubén and Soledad.

"Get up out of bed!" she shrieked, her words slurring and her voice tripping over her swollen tongue.

The children stared at her, their terror magnified for having sprung from an unexpected source.

"I told you to get up!"

"What's wrong?" Soledad whimpered.

Rebecca employed her one able hand to haul her out of bed. "I'm sick of this stinking place! That's what's wrong!"

The children struggled out of bed. Rebecca seized a handful of garbage bags from a pile and flung one at each child. "Now start packing! And you'd better be done before I set foot back inside this house!"

The children scurried around the room and randomly stuffed clothes into the bags. Their mother went out into the hallway and made her way down the flight of stairs.

"Hijo de la gran puta! Sinvergüenza! He's got another thing coming if he thinks I'll wait around for the day he decides to throw me out!"

Two men warmed their hands by a flaming garbage can just outside Rebecca's door. She hurried past them, daring them to speak or look at her askance. As if sensing her mood, neither man said a word.

At the corner Rebecca dialed zero and her parents' number.

"Collect from Rebecca," she said, annoyed by the operator's friendly voice she associated with her husband's whore.

"Can you repeat that?"

"Collect from Rebecca!"

"Rabeca?"

"Rebecca!"

Aurelia's pebbly, sleepy voice came on line.

"Collect from Rabeca," the operator mispronounced. "Do you accept?"

"Sí!"

"I'm leaving him. Will you come get me?"

"I can barely hear you, mi'ja. Is he there now? Are you okay? Do you have the children with you?"

"I'm leaving him! Isn't this what you've been waiting for? What else do you need to know?"

Silence stretched between them as Aurelia came fully awake. "We'll be there in fifteen minutes. Listen for us."

CHAPTER

❖ 24 ❖

Tico wouldn't go. Not if his mother begged. Not even if his father stormed into his basement room to insist.

He listened as Aurelia repeated that Rebecca was about to leave Pasión. He then heard Iliana agree to go help move her out. This although she could not possibly believe that their eldest sister would actually leave her husband for more than a week or two. *But good,* he thought. By agreeing to go, Iliana had saved him the trouble of having to refuse. Besides, she had been away long enough to have forgotten what living at home was like, and it was high time that she realized exactly what it was that she had missed. He had already had his fill, what with Marina trying to choke him as he slept and later claiming that it was he who had assaulted her. And as if her stunts at home were not enough, there was the one she had pulled in church. So she had later swallowed pills. He didn't give a damn. If dying was what Marina had intended, then she should've just gone ahead and killed herself once and for all instead of her many half-assed suicide attempts meant to elicit pity as well as pardon for the trouble she repeatedly caused others. God knows, he and his parents had already shed enough tears to compensate for her dying five times over. It made little difference to him that this time she had come quite close. She had given him so many opportunities to adjust to the possibility of her death that the prospect no longer provoked his tears.

The sounds of his youngest sister stumbling out of bed reached Tico in his room. He continued to eavesdrop as she questioned their mother about what Rebecca had told her on the phone. Iliana's voice was raspy with the remains of sleep. It was also brittle, as if she were on the verge of giving in to tears as she had done earlier that night.

"You should've seen her, Tico," she had sputtered when he entered her room on his way to the bathroom and found her crying on Marina's bed. "She looked like—like she was already dead."

He had listened politely until she had started babbling about how people did not just go crazy overnight. Someone in their family should've recognized the signs, she'd said. Someone should've done something, anything, before things ever got so bad.

"Who the fuck do you think you are?" Tico had asked, offended. "What? You think we let everything go to hell while you were gone and now that you're back you can make everything all right?"

Iliana's eyes had widened in bewilderment. "That's—that's not what I meant, Tico."

"No? Then you should've kept your big mouth shut!"

Remembering, Tico had an urge to scream at Iliana the many ways in which he had tried to help only to wake one night to Marina's hands tightening around his throat. Until then it was he who had reassured her when she woke screaming; he who had first noticed her depression and had mentioned it to their parents; he who had resisted making fun of her when she started prophesying and predicting everyone's future as catastrophic except her own. He was also the one who, despite anxiety and shock, had remained levelheaded enough to call an ambulance the first time she swallowed a bottle full of aspirin and then again when she slit her wrists.

So Iliana had no right to judge him. She had no business telling him what he should or should not have done. Especially not when she had been hundreds of miles away throughout the worst of it and had not once bothered to call or visit the sister she now vociferously expressed concern for.

All the anger that Tico had been accumulating since Marina had accused him of trying to rape her peaked at the prospect of

Rebecca and her three children moving in. He knew from experience that they would be lodged in the space outside his room. He knew as well that he would not have the nerve to ask her to bathe or to keep her children quiet no matter how disruptively they behaved. His eldest sister had the habit of defending her children tooth and nail against everyone but her husband. She also had the foulest mouth and was quick to take offense. Tico could easily imagine the arguments that would ensue after she moved in. He could also picture the filth that would accumulate throughout the basement and already smell the odors that would creep in under his bedroom door once she and her children had been around for a few days.

He settled back against his pillows. As Iliana and Aurelia went up the basement stairs, he wondered if what went on in his family went on in others. It wasn't normal that one of his sisters lived with hens and another kept trying to kill herself. Then there was the way his father prayed about everything and his mother insisted that everyone be patient, as if things would eventually work out on their own. He would have thought that, as responsible parents, they would have dragged Marina to a psychiatrist and adopted Rebecca's children until she came to her senses and permanently left Pasión. That they had done neither and persisted in keeping Marina at home although she had endangered the lives of their other children had convinced him that he needed to move out on his own.

His fantasy was to one day climb into a brand-new car and speed away from the house whose refurbished aluminum siding failed to disguise its ramshackle condition or to detract from its location on a neglected street lined with potholes that tripped feet, punched holes into tires, pooled with rain and melted snow and, on sunny days, glittered with broken glass and stank with the shit of dogs and the piss of drunken men. Not once would he look back at the two-story house his father was so grateful to have purchased. Nor would he glance sideways at the neighborhood's upturned garbage cans spilling rotten food, threadbare rags, bloody napkins, condoms, crack vials and hypodermic needles onto the sidewalk. He would not even bid farewell to the people whom he considered a sorry excuse for a family.

As far back as he remembered, his brothers and sisters had behaved like strangers. They shied away from and were barely civil to each other. They also exchanged no presents, not on birthdays, Christmas or any other holidays, not unless the obligatory envelopes with cash tucked inside a card and slipped into their parents' hands were to be considered gifts. He could not even recall ever having seen his parents kiss, hold hands or hug. And he had no memory of being embraced himself or of hearing tender words. All his family ever seemed to do was argue and accuse, preach and pray. So he was able to think of no good reason why he should stay.

He had already started squirreling money away so as to move. Every weekday, after school let out, he hopped on a Manhattan-bound train and then walked to the luggage factory where two of his brothers worked full-time and he worked part-time from 4:00 P.M. until 9:00. As an apprentice to his brothers who had the tedious but high-paying job of cutting fine leathers, he made fifteen dollars an hour—a grand total of three hundred dollars a week of nontaxable income due to his status as a full-time student. Half of this money went straight into a bank account. Out of the other half he gave his parents fifty bucks to help them out. With over five thousand dollars in the bank, he was only biding his time until he finished high school. As soon as he did, he had every intention of disappearing from his parents' house.

CHAPTER

❖ 25 ❖

Papito was already in the car, having spent the last ten minutes warming its engine so that it wouldn't give out somewhere en route to Rebecca's house. Iliana climbed into the back seat. She suspected that it was sometime around 3:00 or 4:00 A.M. In retaliation for being hauled out of bed at such an ungodly hour, her body refused the warmth of the clothes she had hurriedly thrown on. She reached inside her coat pockets and discovered that she had left her gloves at home. She had also left the hat with which she had meant to hide her uncombed hair, and her eyes felt gritty, her mouth sour.

Barely awake, she gazed out of a window. This was the one time of the year when the neighborhood was somewhat pretty. Tenants dug out their Christmas decorations, strung them around windows and hung them on trees placed where they'd be visible to pedestrians. These colorful lights remained on throughout the night, lending the neighborhood a festive appearance able to persuade passersby that the following year would bring them better luck, better lives, or at least less crime so that they might find some peace of mind. Even the weathered pairs of sneakers strung over lampposts and power lines acquired a decorative rather than a sinister appearance. Iliana had often wondered if they were the sneakers of victims forced to walk home barefoot, of teenagers hoping their parents would buy them a more expensive pair or merely of neighborhood residents who had outgrown them. Whatever the reason, she had no idea why they were displayed so prominently or how anyone had managed to climb high enough to place them there.

A few days remained until the 25th and only now did it dawn on her that her mother had not yet brought out the artificial tree she had purchased during their first Christmas in New York. Most years, Aurelia dragged it out right after Thanksgiving and then left it up until way past Three Kings' Day. This year she seemed to have forgotten. She had not even mentioned the family dinner she usually held at the end of each year or sometimes at the beginning of the next. Nor had she started scoping supermarket sales or stocking up on the vast amounts of food she traditionally served to her children and their families as a substitute for the gifts she and Papito could not afford to buy.

The years they had splurged on Christmas presents were so few that Iliana had a clear memory of what she had received each time. At the age of five, a long-haired, lifelike, three-foot doll to be shared with Marina and Beatriz. At eight, Hi Dottie, a popular blond doll who spoke into a phone. At eleven, a black, mod, miniskirted, Afro-wearing doll who sang "I'd Like to Teach the World to Sing" in eight different languages. Shortly after the Christmas holidays she and her sisters had also been escorted to Pitkin Avenue, to Delancey Street on Manhattan's Lower East Side or, when a bit more money was available, to Alexander's in downtown Brooklyn where their father had purchased on sale the winter clothes they would each wear until the garments were threadbare or outgrown. Rarely had they been allowed to choose clothes they liked over those which were sure to last. Quality, in Papito's opinion, had meant somber colors, itchy fabrics, long sleeves, ankle-grazing skirts and loosely constructed garments able to shroud the bodies of his daughters and to compel them to behave as maturely as they had appeared when wearing the clothes.

"Papi, can you turn on the heat?" Iliana asked, leaning forward. "I'm freezing."

Her father glanced at her mother who tended to get claustrophobic whenever the heat was on. Aurelia nodded. As Papito cranked up the heat, Iliana settled back against her seat.

They drove along Pennsylvania Avenue and past a lot where a building they'd lived in had long since been demolished. Their apartment there, the length of the second floor, had been the largest they had lived in before purchasing their current home. It had also been the one they had occupied for the longest—approximately six years during which Iliana had been seven through twelve years old. That apartment was where she had run screaming from a murdered child which had turned out to be her first doll, by then limbless and tucked away on a closet shelf; made friends whose apartments she had been allowed to visit because their parents were Seventh-Day Adventists and lived upstairs or down the block; bartered her soul to God; menstruated and was horrified to think she'd shit her panties; lost the greater part of her faith.

Catching sight of that rubble-filled lot, Iliana recalled the pre-Christmas evening when she was eight and her mother, tired and dressed in a housecoat, went upstairs to fetch her from the apartment where she had been playing with a friend. Myra, Lily's youthfully jeaned mom, detained Aurelia in the hallway. Intent on postponing the moment when she would return to her own apartment, Iliana planted herself beside them to listen in on the conversation.

Myra asked Aurelia about her family's Christmas plans and then commenced to speak about her own. So childishly excited did she become that, forgetting Iliana's presence, she unwittingly described each of the presents she had purchased, wrapped and hidden for Lily and Pepe, her two children who believed in Santa and had bedrooms full of toys. She even mentioned the pine wreath and genuine Christmas tree her husband, who worked as a car salesman in the suburbs, would be bringing home that night.

Something about Myra's excitement and the tension in Aurelia's voice as she gave the briefest of replies alerted Iliana. Accustomed to family members who spoke, for lack of privacy, in coded language about what they hoped she would not understand, she had early on learned to delve behind words and to intuit their intent. She now watched Myra's lips curve with the joy of one who had believed in Santa and had passed that faith along to her children. It was not that Myra was being intentionally cruel. However, her enthusiasm for the holidays made her oblivious to the discomfort of Aurelia, who lacked the means to celebrate as she too would have liked.

Iliana stepped closer to her mother. Wanting to lend emotional support and to convey through touch that she cared little about the presents she already knew neither she nor her siblings would receive, she reached for her mother's hand and held it tight. She simultaneously glared at Myra. With childish scorn, she willed Myra's perfectly pink lips to shrivel like the potted roses Aurelia grew on the fire escape each summer but whose petals dropped off after a few short weeks. She was so intent on wishing this evil on her friend's mother for making her own feel bad that she missed the end of their conversation and was roused only by Aurelia dragging her downstairs. When they reached their apartment, Aurelia raised a hand and fiercely struck Iliana's face.

"Take that," she spit, as her youngest daughter reeled from the impact of the single blow. "Listening in on people's conversations! Embarrassing me and staring at our mouths like I raised you with no sense!"

Iliana's head jerked back. Eyes wide with shock but tearless with indignation, she focused on her mother.

"I should slap you again for good measure!"

Iliana braced for another blow. She glared at her mother with an intensity which left no doubt that she knew the real reason why she'd been struck. She continued to glare even as her mother, who had never hit her before and never would again, looked away in shame. Despising the small body which made her vulnerable to adult whims, she glared until her mother retreated into the bathroom and shut herself behind its doors.

The next afternoon, when Lily invited her to play upstairs, Iliana suggested that they do so in the hallway. Although she usually preferred for the two of them to play alone, she insisted that Lily bring Pepe, six years old, to join them.

"I have a secret to tell you," she confided. "And Pepe should know it too."

She had to threaten not to reveal the secret to Lily who wanted to exclude her brother. Afterward, the three of them sat at the bottom of the first flight of stairs well beyond the reach of their mothers' ears. Iliana's voice thrilled with malicious intent and the eyes of her friends widened, then teared with disillusionment as she explained to them that adults lied about many things, one of which was Santa.

"I know, I know," she crooned, although she had never been privileged enough to believe in Santa Claus herself. "I cried too when I found out he wasn't real. And I was angry that Mami and Papi lied."

"But how do you know?" Lily whimpered.

"Think about it," Iliana instructed. "We don't have chimneys. How else would Santa Claus get in?"

"Through the window!" exclaimed Pepe.

"We all have gates and keep the windows locked."

"But we seen him!"

"Where'd you see him?"

"On the street! And Mommy took us to Macy's and we sat on his—"

"I seen him too," Iliana interrupted. "I seen him asking for money on the street, and then I seen him again at another corner."

"So he's real!"

"Those are just men like your father dressing up. If you get real close you can see their beards are fake. And most of those men are mean. They keep all the money to themselves. I asked one for a dollar and he told me to go to hell."

"But what about the presents?"

Iliana rolled her eyes.

"They're from your mother, stupid!"

That very evening Myra pounded on her neighbors' door.

"Your daughter," she fumed, huffing into their apartment, "your daughter had the nerve to tell my children . . ."

Minutes later Papito hauled Iliana out of bed. Iliana snapped awake as soon as she saw Myra.

"Did you tell Lily and Pepe that Santa isn't real?" Papito demanded.

Iliana's features settled into a defiant scowl.

"Well?"

"He isn't!"

"Why, you insolent—"

Papito moved as if to knock some sense into his daughter's head. Aurelia quickly stepped between them. Her own face contorted with rage as she bent toward Iliana.

"Tomorrow you're going to go upstairs to tell Lily and Pepe that you take back everything you said!"

"I'm not gonna lie to them!"

"Not only are you going to take back everything you said," Aurelia continued. "But you're going to convince them that Santa exists and leave them with no doubts! You're going to apologize for making them cry and for intruding where you had no business! You hear? Do you hear me?" she repeated.

"Yesssssss!" Iliana hissed. "I hear!"

She had not yet eaten lunch when Aurelia sent her upstairs the following afternoon. Lily answered her knock and, seeing her, slammed the door shut on her face. When Myra let her in, Iliana saw her friend run from the room. The same friend who had daily sought her out. The one whom she had holed up with after school, sat beside at church, told her secrets to. The one friend who had neither hesitated to share her dolls nor insisted on the preferred roles of princess, teacher or mother during pretend. Playing in the hallway or in Lily's room, lying on her bed and flipping through the pages of her children's encyclopedia for inspiration, the two of them had made up worlds, traveled to distant lands, flown up to the stars, plunged to the bottom of the sea.

"I—I—"

Myra left Iliana in the living room and went after her daughter. Pepe waddled in a moment later. A pudgy boy with hair that appeared to have been cut around the edges of a bowl, he wielded a hero sandwich in his stubby hands.

"Liar!" he said, spewing out a chunk of masticated bologna and retrieving it from the floor as if the oversized sandwich in his hand were not enough to fill him up.

Iliana resisted the urge to punch his bulging and perpetually blushing cheeks.

"I was only joking," she muttered. "Everybody jokes. I didn't expect you and Lily to believe me."

"Mom says you're jealous because you know Santa won't be bringing you any toys."

"Your mother—your mother doesn't know how Santa feels about me."

"You're bad. You'll see. He ain't gonna bring you nothing and we ain't gonna let you play with what we get!"

Iliana cut her eyes at Pepe as he sunk his teeth into his sandwich. It crossed her mind that on any other day his mother would immediately have asked her to join them at their meal or, if they hadn't been eating, at least have offered her a treat. Her stomach grumbled as she watched the contents of Pepe's hero poke out with each bite. She forced herself to look away and fortified herself with the idea that she had been right to tell the truth, her parents wrong in commanding her to lie.

"Lily's never gonna be your friend again," Pepe taunted between bites.

"Sticks and stones," Iliana muttered under her breath. "Sticks and stones can break my bones, but words will never hurt me."

She sat at the far end of the couch and silently chanted these words as Pepe stuffed his mouth and sporadically pelted her with abuse. Unlike the couch in her own apartment, the one in Lily's was soft and bare of the thick plastic that creaked and stuck to her legs if she sat on it for long. The room also smelled nice, like the rose-scented air fresheners Myra tucked in corners. On the center table were Archie and Veronica and Jughead comic books. Strategically placed on a shelf by the television to encourage Pepe and Lily to read instead of watch TV were several Dr. Seuss books, *Where the Wild Things Are, James and the Giant Peach, Mother Goose, Curious George, The Little Engine That Could* and *Charlotte's Web*. In her room Lily also had a shelf with what seemed to Iliana like a hundred other books, including a stack of fairy tales from which she claimed her mother read to her out loud.

Although Lily's parents were Puerto Rican, both spoke English with no trace of a Spanish accent. The first time Iliana had visited them she had been shocked to discover that English was the language they spoke at home. Accustomed to addressing adults as "usted"—the same as "you" but implying respect as opposed to the familiar "tu" reserved for peers—she had been unnerved by the ease with which Lily and Pepe conversed with their parents as if they were friends. The more she had visited the more impressed she had been by the dynamics of their relationship. Lily and Pepe spoke to their parents about whatever was on their mind. They asked Myra questions. They even challenged their father and demanded an apology if they thought he'd been wrong.

Iliana had noticed other things as well. Each child slept in a separate room: Lily's with Minnie Moused sheets and matching curtains, Pepe's Donald Ducked and blue. They also owned countless toys: Barbies, GI Joes, stuffed animals, trucks, Play-Doh, coloring books, Magic Markers and Crayola crayons—the kind that came in a box equipped with a sharpener—drawing pads, even a fully equipped dollhouse and a railroad set. Because it was just the two of them, neither Lily nor Pepe wore hand-me-downs. Their refrigerator was kept full, and a drawer in their kitchen was stocked with Now & Then, Mary Jane's, Hershey bars, licorice sticks, boxes of cupcakes, donuts, cookies. If one of their teeth loosened, their mother slipped a dollar under their pillows while they slept. She dyed and hid Easter eggs and rewarded them for those they found. She dressed them up and allowed them to trick-or-treat. She celebrated Christmas and never Three Kings' Day.

Whenever Iliana went upstairs, she was conscious of how vastly different Lily and Pepe's lives were from her own. She had initially attributed this difference to her parents' being poor. But now, prompted by a memory of her mother's slap, she decided that her parents had more than enough money and just didn't want to spend any of it on her. She recalled that, unlike her, Tico received presents on his birthday and on Christmas; that if they went grocery shopping and he had a tantrum over some item he desired—a water gun, a box of hunter-green plastic soldiers; a Pez candy dispenser, bubble gum from a vending machine—Aurelia usually purchased it for him. She went on to make a mental list of all of her brother's toys, including the rocking horse for which her parents had bought him a cowboy hat, fringed shirt, matching pants and a pair of spurs to be slipped onto his shoes. She also listed his emerald-green tricycle, the Batmobile big enough for him to ride, the miniature piano for him to bang on.

Aurelia maintained that she humored Tico because he was the youngest and did not understand when she told him no. Iliana only partially believed her. It was true that her brother was a sensitive child whose feelings were easily hurt. She herself coddled him and could rarely bear his disappointment. Yet her mother's reason did not explain why Beatriz, born in the Dominican Republic three years before Iliana, had also been on the receiving end. Iliana had heard all about the joy that had accompanied this sister's birth, stories which Beatriz often begged their mother to repeat and which were confirmed by older siblings who jealously described the intricately carved wooden rocking cradle Papito had ordered custom-made especially for her. Iliana had also heard more than enough about her sister's rattles, chimes, teething toys, dolls and the brand new, store-bought walker for when she began to crawl. She had heard even more about the beautiful child Beatriz had been with her dark, dark skin and head full of soft and blue-black curls.

Caught between a brother and sister who had received more of everything than she, Iliana tried to come up with a good enough reason to forgive her parents for their preferential treatment of Tico and Beatriz. But regardless of how she tried to justify the disparity, she found little she had done to deserve being treated worse. The one explanation she kept coming up with was that her parents valued her less for not being as pretty as Beatriz as well as for not being born a boy—an act which had defied their expectations and disrupted the pattern of two boys, two girls, two boys and so forth.

Iliana waited for Lily and Myra to return. Each passing minute increased her sense of injustice for what her parents were forcing her to do. Right then and there she began to hate them for their favoritism, their hypocrisy in commanding her to lie, the beatings they administered for any infraction ranging from accidentally shattering a glass to speaking with a defiant tone. She hated them for not speaking a word of English and for embarrassing her by being older than the parents of the children who were her age. She hated them for making her wear hand-me-downs and for not providing her with most of the things she believed she needed and deserved. More than anything, she hated them for quoting the Bible to justify their disciplinary acts and for insisting that she consider herself blessed.

The longer these thoughts circulated in her brain the more she persuaded herself that she should not apologize at all. Maybe she would just go downstairs and tell her mother that she had. That single lie would be no worse than the many she was expected to tell in order to convince Lily and Pepe of Santa's existence. Besides, if Myra told on her, the worst she would receive would be a beating, something she had learned to steel herself against.

Iliana pushed herself to a stand. She was about to leave when Lily entered the room and sat down at the opposite end of the couch. Her expression stopped Iliana in her tracks. There was no resentment at all on her friend's face: just sorrow for the trust that had been betrayed. Meeting that mournful gaze, Iliana felt a wave of regret powerful enough to sink her back onto the couch.

"I'm—I'm sorry," she sputtered as an apology to Lily and Pepe for the pain she had caused them; as an apology to Myra who, until the previous day, had treated her with kindness; but also as an apology to her parents because it must be her fault that they loved her less. "I'm so—sorry," she blurted out again.

Pepe inched forward and shyly sat beside her. Lily too went near. Yet neither embraced Iliana or said a word, as if sensing, as only other children could, that any pity would make their friend feel worse. Myra peeked into the room. When she saw Iliana crying and Lily and Pepe sitting silently beside her, she wisely stayed away.

Later, without needing to be prompted, Iliana explained magic to her friends. She spoke of the invisible which faith sometimes enabled one to see. She conjured Santa for them with her words and breathed life into him with her descriptions. Determined to restore the fantasy which circumstances made it impossible for her to share, she told Lily and Pepe of how Santa traveled at the speed of light and how, if one listened quietly on Christmas Eve, one could hear the tinkle of sleigh bells ringing faintly through the night. She explained that, like Jeannie in *I Dream of Jeannie* on TV, Santa could transform into mist and seep into apartments through chinks and cracks. She spoke as well of the Santas encountered on street corners and in department stores. She explained that these were men imitating Santa for those who lacked imagination, but that the real Santa often appeared to children like themselves in the same way that Jesus appeared in visions to the faithful. From deep within a part of her that wanted desperately to believe, she provided previously unknown details of Santa's life, mesmerizing her friends and briefly convincing herself that he was real.

A week later, on Christmas Day, Iliana, Beatriz, Marina and Tico were each handed a gift carefully wrapped in paper saved from the presents their parents had received on Mother's and Father's Day. Iliana held hers and shut her eyes to postpone discovering if she had received at least one of the things that she had asked for from Santa as she had prayed to him each night in the manner in which she also prayed to God.

Maybe, she told herself, just maybe, Santa really did exist. Maybe with such short notice he had not had sufficient time to get her all she'd asked for but had managed to get her what she had wanted most.

Her hands trembled with anticipation as she removed strips of tape and gently peeled the wrapping paper off the oblong box. She immediately recognized the doll. It was one of the ones she had seen advertised on TV. She withdrew it from its box. Aware that Aurelia was watching, she smoothed Hi Dottie's long blond hair and adjusted her yellow and orange dress. She then withdrew the doll's telephone from the box. Pressing a button on Hi Dottie's wrist, she listened to her greet an imaginary friend.

The doll had the rubbery smell that only new toys have. Iliana fingered the hem of its orange skirt and the plastic of its matching shoes. Any other year she would have been delighted with the gift. But that doll was not one of the ones she'd asked for. The doll she had wanted most was able to do back flips and somersaults like those she had learned to do on a mat in her school's gymnasium. The one she had wanted had hair tied back in a ponytail and wore a gymsuit instead of a polka-dotted dress.

That evening, as her family celebrated Christmas by playing dominoes, stuffing food into their mouths and raucously telling tales, Iliana slipped into the walk-in closet that ran along the length of the apartment. With the overhead lights off to ensure that no one found her, she hid behind a rack of clothes and yanked her new doll from its box. Her rage at discovering that faith lacked the power to make her dreams come true and her resentment toward the parents who had taught her to believe, if not in Santa, then at least in God, lent her the strength to tear out every strand of Hi Dottie's blond and silken hair. She then snatched off the doll's clothes and ripped them between her teeth. Still not satisfied, she smashed its skull against a wall and did the same thing with its phone. Last of all, she shredded the box the doll had come in.

The memory of her mother slapping her mocked her for having cared about the effect of Myra's words. So what if they had made her mother feel bad. There had been a million times when her own feelings had been hurt and no one had come to her defense. There had been a thousand others when it was Aurelia who had made her feel bad by scolding her for something she would not have scolded Tico for.

Iliana crumpled onto the closet floor. She refused to forgive her mother for having expected the offering of a single doll to compensate for the slap or for having purchased gifts for Marina, Tico and Beatriz who had not suffered the same fate. For once Aurelia should have known enough to treat her special. If a few toys were all she had been able to afford, then she should have given them all to Iliana or at least have made sure that the one she bought her was the one she wanted.

Breath ragged, energy spent, Iliana reached through the darkness for the doll she had destroyed. She fingered its bald and caved-in skull, its bruised and naked flesh. Only then was she struck by the magnitude of what she'd done. The violence of it stunned her.

It stunned her because she had not expected it from herself, because she had not known that lurking under her skin was a rage like her mother's when she'd slapped her; like her father's whenever he lost his patience; and like Tico's when he unexpectedly knocked his head against a wall and, if Aurelia tried to calm him, pummeled her with blows. This same monster which Iliana had often glimpsed through the eyes of those whose souls it had possessed now made its presence known within her own.

Her hands began to shake. Her mind deviously excavated and offered for inspection every mischievous thing she'd ever done. It magnified and distorted each, shaping them into evil and convincing her that hers was a wicked soul. Although she was only eight years old, she became terrified of her impulses.

From that day on she kept her emotions tightly lidded and attempted to be fair in all she did. If, while playing with Lily, she sensed that Pepe felt excluded, she made it a point to include him in their games. If Tico demanded her attention, she interrupted whatever she was doing to spend her time with him. If a sibling verbally abused another, she immediately leapt to the victim's defense. If Marina asked, she gave her a portion of her food and wound up sleepwalking to the refrigerator to appease the hunger she had carried along to bed.

She developed a myriad of neuroses and began ascribing emotions to things which had none. When preparing breakfast, she spread butter evenly on both sides of her toast and also along its crust so that no crumb would feel neglected. She nibbled around sandwiches to distribute the pain she was sure they suffered while being chewed. Whenever possible, she chopped her food into equal-sized pieces and measured out every forkful and spoonful before placing it in her mouth. She rotated any glass she drank from so that her lips kissed its circumference and no part of the glass experienced jealousy.

This need to be fair carried over into how she went about her chores. When doing dishes, she alternated the order of the articles she washed first. One day she would begin with plates, then glasses, cups, forks, knives, spoons, serving utensils, pots and pans.

The next day she would begin with glasses and so forth. She behaved similarly when sweeping, not only alternating the order of
the rooms she swept first but also determining at which corner to
begin, going as far as to start at the center of a room and sweeping
dust into piles that others present had to step over or around. Her
brain became so cluttered with lists of the order in which to do
things that she acquired the habit of muttering to herself.

It was this preoccupation with details which enabled her to
do well in school and called her attention to what others often did
not see. She noticed that her siblings had radar for what made others feel bad and that their favorite form of entertainment was merciless teasing. They wielded language like a weapon, employing it
to alienate and assault. Because Marina had an enviable body, she
was made fun of for her long, wide lips and kinky hair. Beatriz,
who was beautiful, was ridiculed for her flat nose. Tico was teased
for being small. She herself was offered pity because that, and not
insults, was one of the few things able to make her cry.

Iliana remembered as well how, during her years in that apartment on Pennsylvania Avenue and in that neighborhood where
few other Dominicans had resided, she had yearned to look like
the Puerto Rican or black American girls so that she could be
easily identified as belonging to either group. She would have
traded her soul to have the long, straight hair and olive skin of her
Spanish-speaking friends or to wear her hair in cornrows and have
no trace of a Spanish accent like the Johnson girls down the street.
She used to hate the question "Where you from?" because few of
her classmates knew of the Dominican Republic and several of her
black friends assumed that she claimed to be Hispanic in order to
put on airs.

"What you talking about, girl?" they'd ask. "We don't care
where you come from! You be black just like us!"

"Nah, you speak Spanish. You one of us," her Puerto Rican
friends would say.

She used to feel like a rope in a game of tug-of-war. Throughout elementary, junior-high and high school she had frequently
been harassed by black friends for hanging out with greasy spics

who in turn questioned why she wanted to be in the company of loud-mouthed spooks. With her skin color identifying her as a member of one group and her accent and immigrant status placing her in another, she had fit comfortably in neither and even less in the circles she had found herself in when she finally went away to school.

Iliana shifted in her parents' car. She wondered if the bewilderment she had felt thoughout most of her life had been shared by her sisters and was what had triggered Marina's breakdown. She would have given almost anything to discuss the particulars of what had led this sister to swallow a bottle full of pills. She would also have liked to discuss each of that day's events so as to determine if all she had witnessed had actually taken place. Yet theirs was a family in which such things were not discussed. This tradition of silence was the reason why she had failed to grasp the extent of her sister's depression until that day. Whenever she had received long-distance news, the accounts had been brief enough to reassure her that her sister would soon get well. It had not mattered if the bearer of the news had been Aurelia, Papito, Tico or Gabriel. Their self-protective tones--tinged at moments with patience, faith, humor, anger or indifference—had obscured the truth about Marina's mental state.

CHAPTER

❖ 26 ❖

In most other neighborhoods Papito would have had a hard time finding parking. But in Rebecca's, where few residents owned cars and those who did parked several blocks away for fear of being vandalized, he had his pick of spaces and slid the Buick right in front of his daughter's house.

"You don't have to go in," Aurelia offered, turning to face him as he shut off the engine and prepared to climb out of the car.

Papito shrugged. "I'm here. I may as well be useful."

The brownstone Rebecca lived in was three stories high and had a storefront with windows boarded up against intruders. Above the entrance all that remained of the "3" in "1307" was its dirty imprint. The "7" dangled by its tail, threatening to fall off.

Iliana stepped toward the metal door similar to the one her father had salvaged and installed at the entrance to his and Aurelia's room. Kicking aside a soiled sheet of newspaper the wind kept trying to wrap around her legs, she pounded on the door. In the silence of the predawn hour the noise resonated along the street. She waited a couple of minutes before backing toward the curb. The cardboard on one of the second-floor windows flapped open and whipped the broken panes.

Papito warily eyed two men huddled by a fire lit inside a garbage can. The elder, a man with grey brows that appeared white against his dark skin, sullenly stared back. The younger, a tall man Iliana imagined might have been handsome were it not for the ashiness lending him a spectral shade, watched her with brazen interest. As their eyes met, his hand dispersed the smoke spiraling toward his face and his lips cracked a smile that instantly disappeared when she did not return it.

"Rebecca!" she yelled out. "Rebecca!"

"Soledad! Rubén!" her mother chorused.

"Rebecca! Open the door!"

A window on the third floor of a neighboring building scraped open and a woman, bracing herself against the winter air, leaned out.

"Shut the fuck up! Decent people are trying to get some sleep!"

"Ansorry," Papito murmured, gesturing with a hand meant to convey, *Okay, okay, take it easy, we'll stop.*

"Don't tell *me* to shut up!" the woman snapped. "You the one making all the noise!"

"He was trying to apologize!" Iliana shouted.

"You wake my baby and I'm gonna run down and rip your face!" the woman warned, slamming her window shut before Iliana was able to respond.

"What *you* looking at?" she asked, turning on the old man sneering at her like he was the one who had scored a point.

"I'm looking at you," he said, his voice clawing out of a throat obviously accustomed to the fiery wet of cheap liquor. "What you gonna do?"

Iliana decided that he'd be best ignored and so turned to kick her sister's door.

"That's enough," Aurelia told her. "And wipe away that expression so we don't start off on the wrong foot with your sister."

"It's the middle of the night. You think she expects to find us grinning like fools?"

"I told you to watch yourself," Aurelia said.

Iliana backed away from the house. Like several others on the block, her sister's retained traces of its former grandeur. The sculpted heads of lions gazed regally from their perch between the windows. These windows were about six feet tall, the ceilings behind them twice as high. Prior to the influx of blacks, then Latinos to the neighborhood, these houses had been middle-class, single-family homes like those nearer to Prospect Park. Now the few occupied houses on the block showed the wear of poverty and negligence. Stoops crumbled and gates leaned precariously, their wrought-iron details twisted out of shape. The garbage sanitation workers rarely bothered to collect overflowed from cans and jutted out from ice and snow.

"Maybe she changed her mind."

"Shut your mouth," Aurelia snapped.

Just then the front door to the house opened wide enough for a person to squeeze through. Rubén and his sisters popped out one by one.

"Bendición, Tía! Bendición, Abuela y Abuelo!" they greeted.

"We're coming to live with you!"

"Yeah! And Mami says this time is for real!"

Iliana embraced each child and tried to ignore the stale odor emanating from their clothes.

"Where's your mother?" Aurelia asked.

"She's hiding behind the door," Esperanza answered.

"Papi hit her," Rubén chimed in.

"Yeah, and he threw water on the bed," Esperanza added, her voice thrilling as if her memory had already transformed into a game the horror she and her siblings had endured.

"Why, you—" Rebecca rushed out of the house and indiscriminately lashed out at her children. The attack was so unexpected that for a moment each child remained rooted as she struck blows anywhere her hands could reach. Recovering from their shock, the girls scattered behind their aunt and grandmother. Their brother dashed out into the street and froze, crippled by the unknown dangers of escape.

Rebecca lunged for Esperanza, hiding behind her grandmother.

"Don't you dare!" Aurelia yelled.

"Ya, Mami! Please, Mami! Mami, please!" Esperanza begged.

Papito tried to drag his grandson off the street. Convinced that he intended to beat him too, Rubén resisted him with all his might.

"Sinvergüenza! I'll teach you to talk about what goes on inside our house!" Rebecca again reached for her eldest daughter.

"I'm sorry, Mami! Please!"

"You're sorry? That's all, you're sorry? You shame me and all you can say is 'sorry'?"

Rebecca snagged a hand in her daughter's hair, then clawed at Aurelia trying to move the child out of harm's way.

"Make her stop," Esperanza wailed. "We'll be good! We didn't mean it!"

Iliana darted into the fray. Yet, with Soledad clinging to her and Rebecca furiously striking out, all she managed was to get herself a busted lip.

"Whooooooiiiiiiii!" the old man hooted.

"Help me, Papito!"

Papito had hauled his grandson off the street, but Rubén was now terrified to let him go.

"Ay, ay!" Aurelia cried.

Papito broke free from Rubén and managed to pry Rebecca off his wife. His grandson flung himself onto the Buick and beat his head against it. Dragging his sisters with her, Iliana seized and held him still in the circle of her arms.

"You fucking bitch!" she screamed at Rebecca. "You stupid fucking bitch!"

"We're sorry!" Esperanza howled as her grandmother prevented her from rushing to her mother's side.

Spit flew from Rebecca's mouth. "All of you are the reason why my life is crap! If I hadn't had any of you, I could've made something of myself!" She stilled long enough for all of them to see her face. "Look at me! You don't think I look like this because of you?"

Only then did Iliana notice her sister's eyes partially swollen shut and the mangled hand with which she had managed to lash out.

"That's no reason for you to take it out on them!"

"Where do you think your father is?" Rebecca continued. "Why do you think he spends most of his time away?"

"That's enough," Papito warned.

"I'll tell you why! Because of you! That's why! Not because of me! If none of you had been born, he would've never left my side!"

"If you don't shut your mouth right now," Papito said, "I'm going to shut it for you even if I have to do it out here on the street!"

Rebecca flailed in her father's arms. Her mother comforted the granddaughter who, at seven, was almost as tall as she.

"Sssssssshhh," she murmured. "Ssshhhh."

One of her hands stroked Esperanza's hair as the other inspected the injuries she herself had sustained. She traced a scratch extending from her brow toward her jaw. She then fingered another throbbing painfully on her chin. Profanity spewed from her eldest daughter's mouth. Her youngest simultaneously hurried to Papito's side.

"Give me the car keys. I'm going to put the children in."

Her father handed her the keys. Iliana immediately led her nephew and nieces to the car.

"It's okay," she assured them. "You're coming home with us."

She opened the back door to let them in, then slid into the driver's seat to turn on the ignition and the heat. At that moment she wanted nothing more than to flee with the children and to leave behind the madness pitting the members of her family against each other and themselves. Yet she knew from experience that no place would be far enough and that familial ties would inevitably draw her back.

"I'm going to go help get your things," she said, turning to the children huddled in the back seat. "Lock the doors and don't let anyone in unless its me, abuelo or Abuela, okay?"

When they nodded, she climbed out of the car and waited for them to lock its doors. An eerie silence had descended on the block. She noticed that the old man who had hooted his encouragement throughout Rebecca's onslaught now soberly watched her and Aurelia. The younger man watched them too. As for the woman who had complained about the noise and later threatened to dial for the police, she leaned attentively out of her window as if she had lost all interest in getting back to sleep.

Iliana looked at her father's face twitching as if it did not quite know whether to submit to fear or awe. She then glanced at Rebecca's. There too she detected an anxiety so palpable that it infiltrated her own soul. She stepped toward her mother. When she caught sight of Aurelia's profile, her brain conveyed that the information her eyes were transmitting defied all reason. For right there—on a Brooklyn street lit by a few dim lamps—her mother stood shape-shifting as surely only apparitions could.

Aurelia's eyes had narrowed to mere slits and darkened to an impenetrable black that hypnotized its prey. She swooped toward her eldest daughter, her legs appearing to glide rather than to walk, her neck stretching forward from shoulders broad with strength. Conflicting emotions tugged at her sharpening features, lending them a hawkish edge. The scratches clawed into her face faded even as her lips—thinned by years of biting down on them to force their silence—appeared to beak, then exhaled steam that evaporated in cold air suddenly smelling of rain-washed grass although there was not a speck of green anywhere in sight.

Iliana could only stare. She wanted to jar her mother out of her trance. She wanted to verify with her own hands what her eyes were seeing.

Held motionless by awe, she recalled having once glimpsed Aurelia watching herself in a mirror which had inexplicably portrayed her as the fierce woman she must have been when young. Improbable though it was, she found herself wanting to believe that her mother possessed supernatural powers and had actually been the one whose voice she had heard at school just as she was now seeing her transform. She even persuaded herself that with such powers her mother might somehow right the wrongs in each of her children's lives and conjure happiness into their futures.

"Rebecca." Aurelia spoke so softly that those around her were forced to lean forward to hear her words. "You talk about my grandchildren ruining your life, but have you given a thought to all you've put them through?"

Rebecca seemed taken aback by her mother's unexpectedly subdued tone. Then, recovering her nerve, she jerked free from her father. Papito instantly moved to restrain her. Aurelia raised a hand to stop him.

"What I do with my children," Rebecca said, leaning menacingly close, "is none of your goddamn business."

Aurelia remained unearthly calm. "Either I raised you a fool or your husband has beat you so often that you've grown hard of hearing. But you seem not to have understood my question. Do you need me to repeat it, or should I try another?"

Rebecca stared as if Aurelia were someone other than the mother she had known throughout her life.

"Tell me, what've you done besides raise your children in squalor and let yourself be abused?"

Aurelia waited. Rarely held accountable for her misery, Rebecca took her time in answering.

"You have some nerve calling attention to how I raise my kids. You think you did such a great job raising me? Why the hell do you think I was so desperate to get married? To get you out of my fucking hair! That's why! Every day of my adult life I had to listen to you rattle off the assets of every available prick as if I wasn't working hard enough to reel one in. You think I didn't notice you never worried about Zoraida or Nereida turning into old maids? Long before either of them married, you'd already given up on me! So I took the first man who came my way! I took him to shut your mouth!"

"I've got news for you," Aurelia replied, not missing a single beat. "Ever since you sprouted tits, you started eyeing every man who crossed your path. I don't know what bug bit you at the time, but I know it wasn't one I sent your way. If memory serves me right, I never encouraged you into the arms of any man. Instead I tried to dissuade you of the notion that your life would bloom into a thing of wonder just because someone offered you his hand. When that didn't work, I pointed out the men I hoped would at least be kind. But no, like a fool, you waited for two men you didn't know a thing about."

Rebecca tried to interrupt, but her mother cut her off.

"I've had enough of being blamed for your bad choices. It was you who stayed with Samuel although he'd broken half your bones. It was also you who took up with Pasión and stayed with him although he's had you living in filth since the first day. And since you have conveniently forgotten, he had already set about trying to kill you before any of your children were even born. So don't you dare blame your life on them. You are responsible for it, Rebecca. Not your children, and definitely not me. I may have made mistakes, but I refuse to take responsibility for yours."

Hatred settled on her daughter's face.

"That's right. It was my choice to move into this house, and it is now my choice to stay. Take a good look at it because, as bad as it is, I'd rather live here any day than put up with your shit!"

Mesmerized, Iliana could only watch. Pinpoints of light appeared in her mother's eyes. Pinpoints like those in the only photograph taken of Aurelia and Papito in the Dominican Republic. Pinpoints of light which burst into tiny flames and flickered at the center of Aurelia's pupils.

What Iliana would never have expected then took place. Her mother began to laugh. Her mother laughed a sonorous laugh which left no doubt that it ascended from the depths of a soul which had discovered there was nothing at all to fear. This laughter rolled off Aurelia's tongue, shattering the surrounding silence and fading as abruptly as it began.

"'Ay, mi'ja, mi'ja, mi'ja. Do you expect me to beg you to move in with us like I've done every other time?"

Rebecca appeared as astonished by the question as Iliana and Papito.

"No, mi'ja. I've laid myself down for you to walk on once too many times. You want to wait until Pasión kills you? You want to rot inside his house? Go right ahead. You won't hear a peep from me. Your life is yours, and I don't plan to spend the rest of mine worrying about you."

Rebecca's jaws fell slack. She glanced at her father standing speechless, then at her sister who would not have ventured to speak even if she had been able to conceive of words to match her thoughts.

"So the truth comes out," she replied, speaking as quietly, as coolly as her mother had. "After all these years you've finally worked up the nerve to tell me how you've felt all along. Like I didn't know it before now. Like I ever thought you gave a damn about my life."

Perhaps it was that night was fading and that the illusions cast by the meager light of streetlamps had dispersed. Whatever the case, Aurelia suddenly appeared old, weary, battered, even frail.

"That's right, Rebecca. I never gave a damn about your life and neither did your father. That's why we dropped everything to come get you every time you called and even when you didn't. That's why, whenever you needed money, we gave you what we had and sometimes what we didn't by borrowing it from someone. That's why we bit down on our tongues each time you insulted us and went as far as to wish us dead."

Her voice ebbed into a murmur.

"As for the truth, Rebecca, the truth is that you don't know the smallest part of how I feel. And if you did, you wouldn't understand it because you'd be too busy twisting it to fit your needs."

Aurelia turned from her eldest daughter. She turned to look at nothing in particular, as if the sight of Rebecca's bruised face might rob her of the courage to say the remainder of what needed to be said.

"You claim we never do a thing for you, but you snatch up everything we give. You console yourself with the thought that if we cared we'd set you up in a better place, but when we offer you our home, you refuse it time and time again."

Her chest heaved visibly.

"Well, mi'ja, if what we offer isn't good enough, you'll have to make do with what you have. I won't worry anymore. You're a grown woman, and if staying with Pasión is what you want, then we'll abide by your decision. But there's one thing you should know."

As difficult as it was for her to do, Aurelia again focused on her eldest daughter.

"When we leave, we'll be taking the children with us."

All color drained from Rebecca's face.

"You'll have to kill me first!"

Aurelia gazed at her long and hard.

"You'd like that, wouldn't you? You'd like me to kill you so you can continue blaming me from the grave—"

Curses stumbled from Rebecca's lips. She took a determined step toward her father's car. When he darted past her to stand guard beside the Buick, her children reclined against the back seat as if relieved.

"Well—" Aurelia's voice broke off, yet she forced herself to go on. "I have no intention of spending the rest of my days in jail. But mark my words, Rebecca. You cross me one more time and I won't hesitate to report you to Social Services for what your children have had to put up with all these years. God help me. I should have taken them long ago, and I'll be damned if I stand by and let another minute pass before I do."

CHAPTER
❖ 27 ❖

Almost three days, Rebecca thought. Every single one of her husband's beloved chickens was probably dead by now. Or maybe not. Maybe the rooster and a few of the hens were surviving by eating their own kind. It had happened once before. After several weeks at her parents' house she had returned to her own to find a mess of plucked feathers, rotting carcasses and layers of shit in the midst of which the surviving birds had all turned wild. On another occasion she had left out extra food and water to last the birds until her husband came home to check up on them and find her gone. But this too had backfired. Many of the birds had gorged themselves and died. Pasión had then avenged each of their deaths on her. A broken rib for the rooster that had cost him more than any of the hens; kicks for the one whose chicks had most often hatched and grown full-sized; blows to her pelvis for the combined loss of the others.

This time, defiant, Rebecca had made no provision for the birds.

She leaned against a wall in the basement of her parents' house. Bricks scraped her back through the flannel nightgown her mother had slipped over her head after making her strip off the clothes she'd worn for weeks and helping her into one of two cots her father had set up for her and her children outside of Tico's room. Too exhausted to argue during the early-morning hour of their arrival, she had sunk right into sleep. When she woke, it had taken her several minutes to recognize where she was and longer to recollect the events of the previous night. She had then inspected her hand bound in a cast as well as the stitched lip she had sunk her teeth into upon realizing she had no choice but to climb into her parents' car or risk losing her children.

Rebecca again flicked her tongue along the four stitches she had received. She wondered if her mother had paused long enough to reflect on the significance of having two daughters with self-inflicted wounds rushed to the same hospital within hours. Surely Aurelia, who had once starved herself to a point near death, could not deny that her daughters had taken after her.

Every fifteen minutes, or so it seemed to Rebecca, Aurelia descended into the basement to complain and nag. Rebecca no longer paid her any mind. She behaved similarly with her children who, now that they bathed daily and brushed their teeth with the toothbrushes their grandmother had immediately bought each, held their noses whenever they came down to bed. At such moments Rebecca would brim with resentment toward them. It disturbed her, how impudent they had grown. Had it been in her power, she would have kept them small enough to fit in the cradle of her arms, so sheltered that they would have lacked comparisons, so dependent that they might've continued to express gratitude for the few things that circumstances had made it possible for her to give.

So little had turned out the way she had expected. As the eldest daughter she should have been the first to marry, to bear children, to be sufficiently settled to provide her sisters with words of wisdom and advice. Instead, she had suffered the humiliation of watching two of them marry before she herself had any prospects. She had primped in anticipation of the day when she too would leave her parents' house with her head held high. Yet here she was, disgraced and dependent on them once again.

Rebecca gazed from her cot out of one of the half-windows beyond which she was able to see no further than to the backyard's frozen earth. Listening to the sound of her children's feet on the floor above her, she recalled how she had prayed for a child only to have her husband beat her in the hopes of forcing her to abort. She recalled as well her relief at learning that her body was strong enough to withstand beatings and defiant enough to reward her with children whose existence had established her as mother when her role as wife had been unclear. Each of her three children had been her solace, distracting her from the misery of her life. As their mouths had enclosed her nipples and their hands had reached up to caress her face, she had reveled in the knowledge that it was she who had willed them into the world, she who satisfied their hunger and was sensitive to their needs. Enthralled, she had watched their eyes gradually begin to clear, their hair to grow, their limbs to straighten and acquire strength. Her satisfaction had been so great that she had concealed it from her husband for fear he would hurt the children and deprive her of the good their marriage had produced. For her children's sake and for her own, she had pretended that they were a nuisance whenever their father was around. She had done this in order to convince him that each child was another chain he had strung around her life. Yet as the children had matured into more than just mouths for her to feed and bodies for her to cuddle against on the nights when her husband slipped out of the house and did not return for days, as they began to make demands and to condemn her with their eyes, she had secretly begun to despise them for their needs as much as she did herself for her dependence on Pasión.

She shifted her gaze from the window partially webbed with ice to the plastic bags spilling clothes throughout the basement. Her soul felt strangely numb. With no need to feed hens, send her children off to school, worry about how to provide for them and herself, or count the hours until six o'clock when Pasión might surprise her with an unexpected visit, her days merged into an undifferentiated stretch of time which she whiled away waiting for a revelation to inspire her to go on with her life.

As a girl in the Dominican Republic she had taken for granted that her future would unfold as effortlessly and satisfyingly as it often had in dreams. Raised by her grandmother from the age of two until she was eight and able to help care for her younger siblings, she had spent the greater part of her childhood convinced that she was as special as Bienvenida had led her to believe and resentful of her parents for seeming to be ignorant of that fact. Dissatisfied with how they treated her, she had habitually sneaked out of their house to trek to an isolated spot. Perspiration had dampened her skin and caused her clothes to cling. She had flung these off to sprawl naked on the earth cooled by midday rains. Blades of grass had caressed her back and teased the underside of her limbs. Sunlight filtered by the low-hanging leaves of papaya trees had summoned blood to the nipples on her ripening breasts and aroused desires unsettling to her conscience yet thrilling to her imagination. There, away from the demands of her parents and the distracting cry of siblings, she had dipped her fingers past the pubic hair she had sprouted at the age of twelve. The movement of her hands massaging the tender flesh between her thighs; the bitter taste of a blade of grass tucked between her teeth; the heady warmth of the Caribbean sun; and the musty scent of cracked papayas spilling black, gelatinous seeds and baring their pinkish-orange pulp had sent her senses reeling and evoked the dreams which had kept her tossing in bed each night.

It was these fantasies which had never been fulfilled, this yearning to share with another the tenderness she had conjured on her own which no amount of abuse had managed to subdue. Despite two failed relationships and a haggard body which she doubted any prospective husband could desire, she breathed solely for the possibility of fulfillment the future might someday bring.

CHAPTER

❖ 28 ❖

Aurelia took hold of a broom and began to sweep the kitchen floor. With her eldest daughter and grandchildren living in the house, it was unbelievable how quickly everything dirtied. She'd wash the dishes and, no more than an hour later, the sink would be full again. The dining room was as chaotic: its table streaked with fingerprints and littered with crumbs and flakes, its floor sticky with spilt milk and whatever else the children dropped. In the living room, furniture was moved closer to the TV, cushions were scattered, knickknacks it had taken her years to collect were toyed with, broken, placed where they did not belong.

Not that she minded much. It was a relief to have Rebecca and her children there. And although she would not have admitted it out loud, it was actually nice to have a full house once again. She had not adjusted to cooking for fewer than a dozen mouths. Regardless of how she'd measured, she had inevitably prepared more food than those at home could eat and had wound up with a refrigerator full of leftovers only she and Marina ever ate. With her grandchildren there, however, pots and pans were empty by the end of every meal. It mattered little what she prepared. The children seemed to have bottomless pits into which vast amounts of food quickly disappeared.

"Okay, everybody on the couch," she said, entering the living room and nudging the children off the floor where they had sprawled to watch TV. "This will only take a minute."

Their eyes remained focused on the TV screen even as they

scampered onto the couch. Aurelia swept near the windows and then edged the broom behind the radiator where dustballs formed because neither Marina nor Iliana ever swept there. Time and time again she had told each to sweep under furniture and behind appliances. But Marina tended to forget, and Iliana claimed that it was useless to clean where no one saw.

"You want me to develop allergies and die before my time?" Aurelia had once asked her, slipping the broom under the couch to expose the dust that had accumulated there.

"You're too hearty to let a little thing like dust kill you," Iliana had replied. "And if it did, you'd be spiteful enough to rise from the dead to clean it."

Aurelia reached a hand behind the tepid radiator to feel whatever the broom had snagged on. To her amazement, she pulled out a quarter-loaf of Italian bread. She stared at it for a moment, trying to figure out how it could have come to be there. A disturbing thought led her to check between the radiator's columns. This time her fingers extricated a wilted carrot, a stalk of celery, several crumbling bread sticks. She placed the food in a pocket of her housecoat. Her expression was a mask of calm as she addressed her grandchildren.

"I'm sorry, but now you have to get back on the floor."

They barely paid attention to her as they obeyed. She slipped a hand under the couch's cushions. Sure enough, she found several individually wrapped slices of American cheese. She proceeded to search elsewhere. Tucked behind a row of books, she found stale cookies, a banana, a colony of roaches. She reached into a basket of dried flowers and withdrew an apple with a few bites taken out. Her fingers curled into fists around it as she attempted to steady her trembling hands. Only when her body had absorbed the shock and she thought she was ready to take in more did she again turn to her grandchildren seated quietly in front of the TV.

She studied their slender necks, their shoulder blades outlined sharply against badly fitting clothes, their bony wrists and hands. She noticed the curve of their spines and for the first time acknowledged that Soledad was too small for her age and that Rubén had not grown during the previous year. She gazed at Esperanza's bowed legs and recoiled from a memory of how she had once slapped her hand for grabbing morsels off the floor.

Yes. She too had experienced hunger. But never such hunger that she had hidden food for fear that its sources would permanently run dry. In the Dominican Republic there had been orchards to steal from and neighbors who had shared the little they had during trying times. In New York she and Papito had slipped in and out of poverty but had nonetheless managed to scrape up at least two meals a day. Her children might have craved delicacies or yearned for more food. But, to her knowledge, not one had experienced the hunger exhibited by her grandchildren.

Aurelia returned to the kitchen and emptied her pockets into the trash. She recalled seeing Esperanza shield her food as if she were afraid someone would snatch it from her hand. She was haunted by a memory of Rubén avidly licking his lips during commercials advertising food and could not help wondering at the shame or fear that had prevented him and his sisters from demanding second helpings when she had failed to refill their plates after noticing that they had been licked clean.

Tears formed in her eyes. Tears of sorrow as well as of rage for her willful blindness; for her eldest daughter's lunacy in remaining with Pasión; for his cruelty in denying her the few dollars a week she would have needed to feed their children and herself.

A wave of hatred surged in the wake of Aurelia's tears. She had an urge to unearth the gun her son Caleb had placed in his father's care for fear of killing his ex-wife and Gabriel. She wanted to point that gun at Pasión so as to elicit a terror greater than that which he had instilled in his children and his wife. She wanted to riddle him with bullets and to spit on him even as he breathed his last. Yet she feared that to kill him would be to add to the misery his children had endured.

Choking back her rage and hate, Aurelia bent over the kitchen sink and washed away all traces of her tears. She then wiped her face dry and returned to the living room where she deliberately turned off the TV.

"Abuela!" cried her grandchildren.

"Don't Abuela me," she said, adopting what she hoped was a playful tone. "You've been watching TV since you got up."

"But this show's almost over," Esperanza said. "All we need is five more minutes."

"That's what you say every single time."

"But this time it's really true!"

"Please, Abuela," Rubén piped up.

Aurelia pointed to the digital clock at the base of the TV. "How can it be five more minutes when it's only a quarter to?"

"Fifteen minutes, then," Esperanza begged. "Please!"

Soledad, the youngest, glared resentfully at her grandmother. Aurelia scooped her up into her arms and sat down on the couch with the four-year-old squirming on her lap.

"Come," she told the others, patting the couch. "You can watch as much TV as you want after I get through with what I have to say. Only right now you have to listen." She smiled to soften the edge sharpening her voice. "How's that for a good deal? You listen, then TV until you go to bed."

The children reluctantly approached. Soledad climbed off her grandmother's lap but remained quietly beside her. Aurelia wrapped an arm around her and drew the others near.

"So, are you hungry? Are you about ready to eat again?"

Her grandchildren nodded although it was only approaching two o'clock and they had eaten their fill at lunch.

"Well, then, I'm about to start dinner."

Aurelia fingered the cornrows Iliana had braided into Esperanza's hair. The child dodged her hand, then looked away, embarrassed.

"Do you like living here?" Aurelia asked, suddenly needing their reassurance.

The children eyed her warily. Their silence conveyed that they knew she hadn't called them to say that dinner would be prepared or to ask them how they felt.

Aurelia changed tactics. "I want to show you something," she said, rising from the couch and leading her grandchildren into the kitchen.

She opened the refrigerator to allow them to take a look inside and also pointed to where boxes of cereal, tins of crackers, loaves of bread and bags of chips were kept. She then went about the kitchen opening the cupboards where other foods were stored.

Her grandchildren's interest was absolute.

"Anytime you're hungry, you can reach inside and take out anything you want."

She turned to see if each child had understood.

"That means you don't have to ask. You can just go right ahead and take whatever it is you want."

"Anything?" Esperanza asked in disbelief.

"Anything."

"Orange juice?"

"Or milk, cookies, a peanut-butter-and-jelly sandwich, even bologna and cheese without bread if that's the way you like it."

"Me too?" asked Soledad.

"Of course," her grandmother replied.

Rubén directed a furtive look toward the dining room. "What about . . . ?"

Aurelia followed his gaze to the heaping bowl of fruit centered on the table. "Yes, bananas, apples and oranges too. You want one now? Go ahead and get it."

Esperanza nudged her brother, daring him to try. Rubén entered the dining room and hesitated before snatching a Granny Smith apple. He nervously eyed his grandmother as he sunk his teeth into the fruit. When his sisters realized that he would not be punished, they hurried toward the bowl. Aurelia pretended not to notice as Esperanza seized a banana and tucked another inside the waistband of her pants.

"You see," she said, "you can have anything you want, anytime you want. You just have to promise me one thing."

The children glanced at her, prepared to agree to anything she said.

"You have to promise me that you'll stop hiding food."

Esperanza's eyes grew as wide as bowls; her brother edged guiltily away from the table.

"Not because it makes me or anybody angry. But because it attracts roaches and goes bad if not eaten right away."

The children's anxiety was palpable. Sensing that they expected her to lash out, Aurelia resisted a desire to embrace them.

"Old food can make you sick," she explained. "Besides, now that you know you can have some anytime you want, there's no need for you to save it to eat later."

She waited for the children to respond. When they remained silent, she followed them into the dining room and knelt before them so as to be level with their eyes.

"Look," she said. "How about this? If you promise not to hide food, I'll promise to replace whatever you tell me is running out. That way, you don't have to worry about someone else eating whatever's left. Do we have ourselves a deal?"

Esperanza was the first to nod. "But Rubén has to promise too."

Her brother shot her an evil look.

"Well?" Aurelia asked.

Rubén sucked his teeth before muttering a reply. "Yeah."

"Yeah, what?"

"I promise to tell if I see Esperanza hiding food or if what we got is getting low."

His grandmother smiled, amused. "That's good enough for now."

Aurelia carried a tray in one hand and with the other felt her way down the basement stairs. The makeshift bedroom from which her eldest daughter had not once bothered to emerge was cluttered with boxes, stuffed bags, scattered clothes and shoes. Also littering the floor were wads of Kleenex, candy wrappers, dirty dishes and the peelings of fruit her grandchildren must have eaten while in bed. She stepped cautiously and placed the tray of food on a night table beside her daughter's cot. Flicking on an overhead light, she gathered clothes off the floor and dumped them into the washing machine Papito had managed to buy for her only after most of their children had moved away. She then collected and arranged shoes by pairs along a wall, emptied a brimming bedpan her grandchildren pissed in for fear of going alone to the bathroom in the middle of the night, returned upstairs to fetch a broom, descended again to sweep.

Although neater, the basement continued to reek of what Aurelia imagined despair would smell like if it possessed a scent. This odor of sweat and human waste oozed from Rebecca's pores and saturated her clothes, the sheets, blankets and mattress on her cot. Whenever Aurelia stepped near, this odor threatened to lull her into a depression of her own.

"Wake up," she murmured, leaning over her daughter. "I know you hear me."

Aurelia waited.

"Come on, mi'ja. You have to eat."

Rebecca pretended to be asleep.

"Do you know what I found today?" Aurelia asked. "Food. Food your children have been hiding."

Her eldest daughter did not answer. Confronted with her apathy, Aurelia snatched the blankets off the bed. Rebecca merely rolled over onto her side.

"Food your children hid because you allowed them to go hungry! You did that to them, Rebecca! You! As their mother, it was your duty to make sure they got fed! It was your duty to leave Pasión before things ever got so bad!"

The words tumbled from Aurelia's lips—bitter, judgmental words which she was powerless to stop. She seized her daughter to rouse her conscience by sheer force. Rebecca pulled away and curled up like a child. This position was one she had adopted throughout her youth. If either of her parents had resisted her adolescent whims, if she'd overheard Papito whispering news of Trujillo's dictatorial madness or had stumbled on Aurelia burying a stillborn child in the field behind their house, she had withdrawn to lie in bed. Only after her memory had dulled had she risen to sneak out of the house and pretend that what had caused her to retreat had never taken place.

On one of these occasions, Aurelia followed her to see what it was that she went off to do. Her horror was not so much in seeing her remove her clothes to lie naked on the ground as in realizing that desire made her heedless of the dangers existing for a girl her age. Alarmed but unwilling to intrude on what had been intended as a private act, she averted her eyes and remained near until moments before her daughter headed home. She then took a different path to beat her there. Once home, she made no mention of what she'd seen. She was familiar enough with this daughter's traits to know that she would disregard all warnings. What she did do, however, was to watch her like a hawk from that day on. If Rebecca wanted to go out, she was given time-consuming tasks to keep her in. If she insisted, she was made to take along a sister. In this manner, Aurelia had prevented Rebecca from coming to any physical harm. Yet at a time in the Dominican Republic during which people daily disappeared and the horrors of nightmares appeared full-blown in life, a time during which she herself had felt as if life were a state from which she could not wake, she had lacked the wherewithal to prevent her eldest daughter from mentally drifting off.

"Be patient with her," Bienvenida had warned shortly after Rebecca's birth. "This child has a very rough road ahead."

Aurelia assumed that it was for this reason that her mother, claiming to want to allow her sufficient time to recover after the birth of her second child, took the first and insisted on keeping her until she was old enough to help raise her younger siblings. Now, seeing her curled up like a child, she wondered if Rebecca's life had been destined to unfold as Bienvenida had predicted or if they had unwittingly caused it to be so with their overprotectiveness and fears.

"You think if you stay in bed long enough Pasión will come beg you to stay alive? Is that what you're waiting for? Is that what it would take to make your life worthwhile?"

Rebecca rolled further from Aurelia's voice.

"Damn it, Rebecca! Answer me!"

This time Rebecca cupped her palms around her ears. At her wits' end, Aurelia sat beside her. She was at a loss as to what to do. Since helping to move Rebecca in, she had tried everything ranging from patience to harassment. She had even feigned indifference in the hope that Rebecca would rise from bed of her own free will.

Resisting an urge to weep, Aurelia fingered her daughter's hair. Lint and dirt were clumped along the matted strands. Dandruff showed at the edges of her scalp and flaked off the hair she had once habitually straightened with a hot comb so that prospective husbands would believe it was naturally that way. Only after each man had resorted to beating her had she given up the ruse to pick it up again if she planned a reconciliation.

"No, I fell," she had claimed whenever her mother had commented on her battered face.

"Papi, please! He'd never hit me!"

"Of course not. I accidentally slammed a car door on my hand."

"He didn't mean to. Honestly! He just lost his temper."

The idea of one of her daughters' suffering such abuse had been so horrifying that Aurelia had willfully gone blind. Yet as Rebecca's excuses grew more outlandish and she began to sport black eyes and bald patches where her hair had been ripped out, as she hid other bruises under long-sleeved and high-necked garments even on the hottest days, Aurelia had had no choice but to confront the truth.

She remembered this and more: Rebecca's long-lasting relationship with Samuel despite his brutal treatment of her; Rebecca's unwillingness to believe that someone she had fallen in love with might possibly prey on his daughter; her insistence that he would eventually transform into a better man; her despair when he finally kicked her out. Remembering, Aurelia was forced to admit that if none of this had been enough to motivate Rebecca to leave Samuel, then it was doubtful that she would now find it in herself to leave Pasión.

Any compassion Aurelia might have felt for her eldest daughter dissipated as she thought of the food she had found hidden throughout the house. Seething, she stood up from the bed and stepped into the basement bathroom. Locating what she needed in a cabinet, she returned to her daughter's side, hauled her up by the hair, reached into a pocket for the pair of scissors she had gone to fetch. She then fiercely snipped off a clump of the hair this daughter would have made sure to wash and straighten in anticipation of returning to Pasión.

Rebecca's hand instantly shot up.

"You want me to cut off your hand too?"

Rebecca tried to swing out of her mother's reach, but Aurelia yanked her back.

"Are you crazy?" Rebecca shrieked, speaking for the first time since she'd moved in.

"You have the nerve to open your mouth now? After turning a deaf ear to your children and pretending to be mute each time I dragged myself down the basement stairs?"

Aurelia lopped off another clump of hair.

"Take that!" she said, flinging the matted strands at her daughter. "Let's see how much your husband likes you now!"

Rebecca silently began to weep. Aurelia randomly snipped more hair.

"Hussy! Maybe now you'll face your shame and cry for more than just your hair!"

Rebecca leapt abruptly off the bed. "Shame? Shame? What the fuck do you know about shame or how I feel?"

Aurelia stooped to retrieve the scissors her daughter had seized and flung across the room. "I know a lot more about it than you think."

Rebecca looked at her with contempt. "On the day you live inside my skin, you can tell me all about what goes on inside my head! Till then you can keep your opinions to yourself!"

Aurelia straightened to her full height. "You think I owe you, don't you? You think the whole world owes you because you've suffered. Well, I've got news for you," she said. "You will shrivel up and die waiting for the world to care when you don't have the sense to care about yourself."

"Oh, but you care, don't you?"

Aurelia expelled a weary sigh.

"You care so goddamn, fucking much. You who are so worldly and no one can teach a thing to because you've learned all you'll ever need to know living inside four walls. Well, let me tell you something. You don't know a goddamn thing! You—you don't know—" Rebecca's voice gave way to sobs as she fell back onto her cot. "How could you? You have everything and have—have never lost—"

She hid her face behind her palms.

"I did everything. I tried—" Her hands balled into fists and pummeled her own lap. "I tried to—to—make him happy!"

She turned inconsolably toward her mother.

"Wasn't that supposed to be enough?"

CHAPTER

❖ 29 ❖

Ed's eyes strayed from Iliana to two men seated at a nearby table. Iliana gave up on trying to command his attention. Each time she'd tried, he had drifted or purposefully changed the conversation. This, despite having learned over the phone bits of all that had occurred since she'd been home.

She gazed dejectedly out of one of the café's floor-to-ceiling windows. Slow-moving cars sloshed through days-old snow as pedestrians skidded on sidewalks patched with ice. The drab light filtering down on them through dull grey clouds lent the hour an appearance of dusk although it was only half past two.

"You see that guy?" Ed whispered. "The one with the ponytail and goatee? He tried to pick me up last night."

Iliana turned to him instead of to the man he'd specified. "So?"

"So," Ed replied, "that's probably his lover."

"Oh." Iliana shrugged and resumed looking out of the window. "We should have gone to Central Park."

"There's still time."

"No. I have to get home before dark."

"Damn, I've barely had a chance to see you."

Iliana focused hostile eyes on him.

"What?" he asked, defensively.

"You astound me," she muttered. "You really do. I've been trying to talk to you all day, and now, when I'm about to leave, you have the nerve to act like you're interested in spending time."

"What are you talking about? I'm the one who called."

"Yeah, to ask if I could join you at something you'd already planned to do, not to talk about any of the things I told you I needed to discuss."

Ed shook his head in disbelief. "I can never do right by you, can I? You want us to talk? Let's talk."

"Why, thank you. You're too kind."

"You see how you are? One minute you want to talk and the next you don't. What the hell's your problem?"

"What the hell's my problem? You wanna know what my problem is? My problem's that my sister tried to kill herself, that my nephew and nieces have been hiding food, that Rebecca will probably go back to her husband, and that I can't think straight and have been needing to talk to you for days! That shouldn't have been so hard for me to do!"

"Ay, mujer, I didn't want to pry into anything painful or embarrassing."

"You didn't want to pry? How could it have been prying when I was trying to talk about it openly? Besides, you have no qualms about prying when it has something to do with you!"

"And another thing," Iliana spewed. "What the hell do you mean by embarrassing? Is that what you consider all of this to be? Embarrassing? As for painful, the more reason for me to want to talk! Or would you prefer it if I spoke only of what's happy? Is that what you want? You want me to tell you about all the fun I've been having lately? None! Zilch! Zero! Is that interesting enough for you, or should I shut my mouth since I have nothing nice to say?"

Ed looked at her with a pained expression. His emotional support was the one thing she had hoped to take for granted. She had expected it because he was the one who had chosen her as a friend and had defined as limitless the parameters of their friendship.

"I'd also appreciate it if you stopped calling me Mujer! My name is Iliana, spelled I-L-I-A-N-A, not Y-L-Y-A-N-A, as you insist I spell it because you think it's exotic spelled that way!"

Ed slumped against his chair. Iliana turned from him to stare out of the window. She had an impulse to slam her fist through glass, to kick the table over onto its side.

"So," Ed asked after a while, "are you going to talk about it or what?"

Iliana did not deign to glance his way. "Don't do me any favors, Ed."

At this, he rose from his chair and walked away. Only then did Iliana turn to watch him maneuver his way toward the bathroom. She waved the waitress over and asked her for the check. It was brought just as Ed returned.

"I'll get that." He handed several bills to the waitress and then folded back into his chair. "Look," he mumbled. "You're right. I haven't made myself available. I know it's not a good excuse, but I just couldn't bear to hear about your family. I've been lucky. No one in mine has ever had a breakdown or attempted suicide. I didn't know how to respond."

"I needed you, Ed, and I wouldn't have come to you had you not led me to believe I could."

Ed reached for a cigarette, then put it down again. "I'm sorry. I really am. There's nothing I can say to justify how I behaved. But I'm willing to listen now."

Iliana met his gaze. Now that she had the opportunity to speak, she was at a loss as to how to organize into words the chaos of that week. Just the previous day she had accompanied her mother to the hospital and been informed that her sister was bipolar manic-depressive and exhibited symptoms of schizophrenia.

"She'll have to stay on lithium, Dapakote, Mellaril, and Cogentin after she's released," the doctor had explained. "Once her body adjusts, the drugs' narcotic side effects will wear off."

"How long?" Iliana had asked.

"How long what?"

"How long will she have to be on drugs?"

The doctor had glanced from her to her mother. "Indefinitely for now."

Iliana wanted to tell Ed of all that had occurred. She wanted to exorcise the grief and fear and rage that had taken possession of her soul. Instead, she related bits and pieces that bore little resemblance to the whole. She informed him that Marina had regained consciousness but failed to mention that she had then attacked a nurse. She told him of how her sister had gazed through heavy-lidded eyes but was unable to describe her appearance as she was carried into her brother-in-law's car. She gave a brief account of accompanying her parents to Rebecca's house but refrained from mentioning that her eldest sister had lashed out at her children. She admitted that her mother had chopped off Rebecca's hair but could not convey her own dismay at discovering that this sister looked prettier and would probably be returning to Pasión.

"And you?" Ed asked when she paused for breath. "Are you still planning on staying home?"

His question took Iliana entirely by surprise. "Were you even listening?"

"That's exactly why I'm asking. I think you forgot you can return to school."

"Ed, I made the decision to come home and I intend to stay."

"But why? It's not like there's any way for you to help."

"I can be there if they need me, all right?"

"I'm not trying to work your nerves, Iliana. I just don't understand what you think you'll be able to accomplish. Besides, you should be taking care of yourself."

"I *am*."

"Oh please. You've lost weight and look like you haven't been getting any sleep."

"Well what the fuck did you expect?"

"Don't give me that crap. You've been home, what? A little over a week and already you're a wreck. What'll you do a month from now when you have no choice but to stay?"

"I'll get a job."

"Yeah, and go to church every Saturday, but what else?"

"This isn't about me. It's about my family."

"Have you even started looking for a job?"

"Just drop it, Ed."

"What about that letter?"

"What letter?"

"The letter requesting a leave from school."

"I can call the registrar's office when school begins."

"Well, thank God. At least you still have the option to change your mind."

"I'm not changing my mind, Ed. I intend to take the full year off."

"Wouldn't a semester be enough?"

"It's my decision."

"Yeah, and it's your life. Have you thought about that? Have you thought about what a hell it's going to be, or have you forgotten how nervous you were about coming home?"

"A year is little in context of my life."

Ed rolled his eyes in exasperation. "You're not thinking rationally."

"No, Ed. Maybe not."

"What are you trying to be, a martyr or something?"

"Yeah," Iliana retorted, matching his sarcasm. "A martyr. That's pretty ironic considering I left home and never bothered returning until now."

"For God's sake, is that why you're staying? Out of guilt?"

"This isn't about guilt. It's about obligation."

"Are you sure about that?" Ed asked. "Are you quite sure?"

Iliana turned away from him. "I have to go," she said, rising from her chair.

Ed reached across the table for her hand. "I'm worried about you, Iliana. I don't think you have any idea what you're leaving yourself open to."

"I'm a big girl, Ed. I'm perfectly capable of taking care of myself."

CHAPTER

❖ 30 ❖

"Uh-uhh." Aurelia shook her hair free of Soledad's and Esperanza's hands. "When I'm dead, both of you can comb my hair. Till then, only one of you at a time."

"Mami, please," Iliana said, glancing up from the yucca she was grating. "You'll scare them."

Aurelia reached for Esperanza's wrists. "You," she said. "You see that big pan in the kitchen? Bring it here, then go back in and wash your hands."

"Just let me finish this one braid."

"I told you I'm not dead yet, or are you trying to rush me there?"

Esperanza giggled. "Getting your hair combed isn't gonna kill you."

"No, but having it pulled will, and then I'll have no choice but to let all of you do with me as you please."

"But, Abuela," Esperanza said, "nobody's gonna wanna touch you when you're dead."

"Maybe not. But they'll have to."

"Why? You can't make them."

"Now, how do you know that? How do you know I can't come back as a ghost and make everyone do anything I want?"

"Because," Rubén chimed in, "Mami says ghosts aren't for real."

"He's got you there," Iliana said.

Aurelia sucked her teeth. "Oh, I see. So your mother knows everything, does she? Well, young man, let me tell you something. I'm a lot older and I know more."

"You ever seen a ghost?" Esperanza asked.

"Would you believe me if I said that I had?"

Esperanza shrugged, unsure.

"Yeah!" This from Soledad.

"You so stupid," her brother blurted out.

"Okay, that's it," Aurelia said. "Since you know so much, you can tell me why it's bad luck to have more than one person comb your hair."

"I don't know."

"I don't know," Aurelia mimicked. "I don't know." She nudged Esperanza into the kitchen. "Go get me that pan like I told you. Rubén, you go with her and bring two bowls. While you're at it, bring me that pot sitting on the stove. I know it's dirty, but that doesn't matter. When you get back, I'll teach you both a thing or two."

Both children scampered into the kitchen. Aurelia watched them from the dining room. Maybe it was wishful thinking, but she imagined that each had finally gained a bit of weight.

"Okay," she said, when they'd done as they'd been told. "Go back and wash your hands. I'm putting you to work."

"What about—"

"I didn't forget. Now go. And make sure you clean under your nails. I don't want you touching food with dirty hands."

Water splashed onto the floor as the children crowded around the kitchen sink. Minutes later, they returned.

"You," Aurelia told Rubén. "Since you think you're such a man, you can squeeze in behind Iliana and sit at the head of the table on that side. Esperanza, pull out that chair and sit beside him on his left."

She handed a bowl to each and placed the pan of soaking beans between them. "You'll be peeling them like this." She demonstrated by snapping a garbanzo between her thumb and index finger until its skin slipped off. "But be gentle. I don't want you squishing them. Then, when you're done, throw the peeled garbanzo into your bowl and the skin into that pot."

"Show us again—"

"Like this. You'll get the hang of it after a while."

"This is girls' work."

"Is eating girls' work too?"

"No, but—"

"Well, then, you'd better peel the beans exactly like I showed you."

"Can I help too?" Soledad asked.

"Oh, bless you." Aurelia scooped her up into her arms and carried her into the kitchen. "Here. Let me help you wash your hands, then I'll give you a special job."

Soledad squirmed out of her grandmother's arms. "I can do it by myself." She dragged a chair up against the sink and clambered onto it to reach the faucet.

"I knew you could," Aurelia said.

Already she had discovered that the youngest of Rebecca's children had the coordination of someone twice her age and the uncanny ability to absorb lessons as if through her pores.

"Now use that towel over there. Your hands need to be completely dry."

Aurelia reached for the loaves of half-priced Italian bread she had purposefully bought stale. She handed them to Soledad, then rummaged in a cupboard for a bowl.

"Hurry up, Abuela," Esperanza urged.

"Don't you rush me."

Aurelia took her sweet time looking for a mixing bowl. To further exasperate her grandchildren, she inched into the dining room as slowly as she could.

"Oh, oh. You've really done it now," Iliana said. "You'll soon learn it's not good to provoke Abuela."

"Nooowwwwww," Aurelia continued to move in slow motion even as she plopped Soledad onto her lap. "IIIIIII waaaaant yoooooou toooooooo take theessssssse loavvvvvvves aaaand—"

"Abuela!"

"See?" Iliana said. "What did I tell you?"

Aurelia let out what even she recognized as a cackle.

"You break the loaves into as many pieces as you want," she instructed Soledad. "Then you crush those until all that's left is crumbs."

"That's wasting food," claimed her youngest grandchild.

"Not if we're making bread pudding."

"Yippeeeeee! Bread pudding!"

"What you so happy about?" Esperanza asked Rubén. "You don't even know what bread pudding is."

"It's like cake, only not as sweet," Iliana said.

Rubén immediately smacked his lips.

"Why you making cake?" Esperanza asked.

"Because Marina will be home in time for Christmas and a party would be nice."

"We're really gonna have a party?"

"What did I just say?"

"But we don't even have a Christmas tree."

"Yes we do. It's up to Iliana to put it up."

"Can we put it up today?"

Iliana furrowed her brow with mock concern. "I don't think so. I have a lot to do."

"We'll help!"

"Naaaah," Iliana shook her head. "I don't think you can be trusted. You're not doing too good with those beans."

Esperanza immediately began to peel the garbanzos she had not touched.

"Is everybody gonna come?" asked Rubén.

"They better," Aurelia said.

"Abuela—"

"What now?"

Esperanza dipped a hand into the pan and peeled a garbanzo perfectly. "Why's Titi in the hospital?"

"Ah, shit." Iliana inspected the knuckle she had scraped against the grater.

"She was sick," Aurelia answered. "But she's much better now."

"Sick how?"

"Ay, mi'jita. Sometimes a person's thoughts just get all confused."

"So she's crazy?"

Aurelia sighed. "I guess so. But when you think about it, we're all a little crazy too."

"Abuela," Soledad said, turning around to face her, "why me and Esperanza couldn't comb your hair?"

Had Soledad been older, Aurelia would have assumed that she had sensed her sadness and purposefully changed the subject.

"You mean I never did get around to telling you?"

Soledad solemnly shook her head.

"Well, then. I guess I better tell you now. In the Dominican Republic—"

"That's where Mami and you were born, right?" asked Esperanza.

"Yes, and your grandfather, aunts and uncles too."

"Mami says it's pretty," Rubén volunteered. "But she also says people there are stupersti—supersi—are stupid, and that's the reason why she left."

Iliana snorted.

"I didn't say it! Mami did!"

"She did, did she?"

"I ain't lying!"

"What else has she told you?" Aurelia asked.

"She says you didn't have a toilet and—and had to—"

"Yeah?"

"You had to shit in a disgusting hole."

"A latrine," Aurelia corrected. "A latrine."

"Yeah, that's what I said! A hole!"

This time Iliana laughed out loud.

"Okay," Aurelia admitted. "It was a hole, but not inside the house. It was way out in the yard."

"Couldn't you fall in?"

"No, it wasn't quite that big."

"Let me tell you," Iliana piped up. "It looked gigantic to a kid."

"Now, how would you know?" Aurelia asked. "If memory serves me right—"

"Mami, don't!"

"What was it we used to call you?" Aurelia asked, grinning with all teeth bared.

"Titi had a nickname?"

"She had a lovely nickname."

"You wouldn't, Mami!"

"Abuela," Soledad whined.

"That's right, sweetie. Make her stick to the story she meant to tell."

Aurelia kissed the back of the child's head. "Okay, okay. I was telling you about—"

"—about Titi's nickname!" Rubén said.

"Why, you little brat! You're lucky you're sitting way down over there!"

Aurelia winked mischievously at her grandson. "Don't worry. I'll tell you that story some other time."

"In the Dominican Republic—" Soledad prompted.

"Yes. In the Dominican Republic people are not stupid." Aurelia darted another sly look at Rubén. "They're like those in any other place. The town I lived in was way out in the country. I remember I used to have to walk several miles just to—"

"Is that far?"

"So far that if it were here you'd have to take a bus. Anyway, the town didn't have a funeral home or church. That meant that when a person died—"

"But where did people go to pray?"

Aurelia chuckled. "People can pray anywhere they want."

"Yeah, but God don't listen unless you pray in church."

"Who told you that?"

Esperanza shrugged. "Nobody. I just know."

"Look at me, Esperanza."

Rebecca's eldest child resumed her task of skinning beans.

"He listens, mi'ja," Aurelia murmured. "Sometimes it just takes Him a while to answer."

"I pray every day."

"And?"

Again, Esperanza shrugged. "Nothing. Nothing happens."

Aurelia took a loaf of bread in hand. "I see." She snapped the loaf in half and handed it to Soledad to crumble. "Maybe things will change now that you're living here with us."

"We ain't staying," Rubén mumbled. "We never do."

"I think this time you will."

"No," Rubén replied. "He's too big."

"God?"

Rubén silently shook his head.

"Who's too big, mi'jo?"

"You know."

"Mi'jo?"

"My father, okay? He's too big! I can't—" He bit his bottom lip to keep from crying. When no one pressed him to say more, he leapt to his feet and tried squeezing past his aunt.

"Let him go," Aurelia said.

"But he—"

"I told you to let him go."

Rubén darted from the room. His aunt stood from her chair to follow.

"Iliana—"

"What?" she yelled. "Are you just going to sit there and do nothing?"

"He needs to—" Aurelia's voice broke off at the sound of Rebecca's in the hallway.

"Just go downstairs," Rebecca said again. "I'll be back sometime soon."

Aurelia nudged Soledad off her lap. "Stay here with the girls," she instructed Iliana. She then rushed out to find Rubén crying in the hallway and his mother preparing to leave the house.

"It's okay, mi'jo," Aurelia told her grandson. "Go on downstairs. Your mother's not going out."

Rebecca whipped around to face her. "Don't start with me, Mamá."

Aurelia stepped past her to stand guard beside the door.

"If I have to shove you out of the way," Rebecca said, "I will."

Aurelia waited until her grandson's steps sounded on the basement stairs. "Nice shoes," she said, glancing at the sling-backed high heels Rebecca was wearing, then back up at her carefully made-up face. "But won't your feet be cold?"

"That's none of your goddamn business."

"I also like your hair," Aurelia continued. "I like the way it curls all on its own. You don't even have to comb it."

"I'm warning you, Mamá."

Aurelia smiled. "Come here. Let me see what you're wearing under that coat."

Rebecca jerked away as her mother reached for her lapels.

"I only wanted to see if you had on one of the things I washed." Aurelia leaned closer. "Ummm. Perfume. Did you just douse yourself or also take the time to bathe?"

Determined, Rebecca seized the doorknob. Aurelia's voice remained as cool as steel.

"You probably did. You probably showered and put on your nicest clothes. That's good. You need to practice looking respectable so that when I tell the judge what kind of mother you've been he'll maybe think of giving you back your kids."

"You think I don't know that's an empty threat?"

Aurelia stepped away to hold the door open for her eldest daughter. "You want to go give Pasión some ass? Go ahead, I won't stop you. I'll just make sure to tell the judge you had no problem walking out that door."

Rebecca took several steps outside only to slip on the ice-patched stoop.

"You haven't had enough of broken bones? You have to go out and try to break one on your own?"

Rebecca regained her balance by clinging to the rail. She then descended from the stoop and swung open the creaking gate. What appeared like melancholy settled on her face.

"He's my husband, Mami," she said in a tone that sought approval.

"I know, mi'ja. He's your husband, and you have every right to see him. It shouldn't matter how he treats you or your kids."

Rebecca had the decency to avert her gaze. Aurelia shivered in her housecoat and slippered feet.

"You can pray all you want," her friend Rosita had told her. "But you've got to lend God a helping hand. This world is crawling with Pasións, and God's got a full-time job taking care of everything else to keep saving the likes of your daughter all the time."

"I've already done everything I can."

"I've known you for a long time, comadre," Rosita had replied. "You may have fooled your husband and children but not me."

"And what is that supposed to mean?"

"You know very well what I mean. Take matters into your own hands. Keep on praying if it makes you feel better, but you know you've got a lot more than prayers on your side."

"You should hurry," Aurelia advised her daughter. "You don't want to miss Pasión if he bothers coming home at all."

Rebecca hesitated.

"What? You don't think he'll be there? Or are you afraid he'll be there with someone else?"

Rebecca's mouth fell open as if she'd been struck. Aurelia simultaneously had a vision of her bound and thrashing in a chair.

"Oh, mi'ja." She stepped out into the cold. "I didn't know. I really didn't."

Defeated, Rebecca released the gate. Aurelia closed it and took her hand to lead her back inside.

"It's cold, mi'ja. It looks like it might snow."

CHAPTER
❖ 31 ❖

Papito finally gave up. Enough people were pressed against him that he figured he wouldn't fall no matter how violently the train lurched. He let go of the pole he'd been holding on to and drew his arm back from where it had been tucked out of sight between the bodies of other commuters. His arms and fingers ached. His eyes did too. And the overheated train had him sweating under his clothes.

He'd had a particularly hard day at work. More than once his thoughts had strayed, causing his foot to slam on the pedal of his sewing machine and his hands to still of their own accord. The leather he'd been piecing into luggage had gathered into a wad and been haphazardly sewn with pleats and folds. Each time, he had jarred himself from his thoughts to untangle and rethread the sewing machine. He had wasted still more time ripping apart knotted seams and trying to conceal the holes the needle had punctured into the leather. He had then been dismayed to discover that each piece had been cut so stingily that sewing wider seams rendered them too small.

"We may be from the same town, but don't think I'm going to risk my ass just so I can save yours," his foreman, a Dominican like himself, had yelled. "You're lucky you have a job. You know how many people need one? If I fired you, there'd be a line around the block."

"Ya, ya, hermano. It won't happen again. I've got a lot on my mind. That's all."

"We all do, so watch your step. This is the last time I'm gonna tell you."

Papito had swallowed his pride and thanked the man for not firing him on the spot. He was fully aware that at his age with his lack of English he'd be hard-pressed to find another job. He also knew that the main reason he'd been employed was because his foreman preferred hiring Dominicans. If not for this, he would have been forced to sell religious books full-time instead of part-time. The supplementary income enabled him to make ends meet, especially now that he was supporting Rebecca and her children. Yet he despised going from door to door like a common peddler. It left a bad taste in his mouth to speak of God as his hands reached out for money. It also bothered him to recognize that his best clients were widows and neglected wives who invested in his most expensive books and paid in installments so that he'd find it necessary to return. On occasion they waited for him wearing only negligees. Unwilling to commit adultery, he'd back out of their doors and promise to return another day. He would then purposefully bring his wife along. Many were the women who had darted back into their bedrooms to change their clothes upon encountering Aurelia. It was these same women who then tended to submit to Bible studies and to convert to Seventh-Day Adventist.

Pastor Rivera repeatedly told him that what mattered most was the comfort religion provided for these women. Papito often said the same thing to himself, but his conscience nevertheless plagued him.

For some time now he had been trying to work up the courage to ask his foreman for a few of the overtime hours usually allotted to younger employees. His life would be so much easier if he didn't have to run home from the factory to change into a suit before rushing out again to persuade strangers to trust him enough to open up their doors. He had postponed making the request because his foreman had already done him the favor of allowing him to leave work early on Fridays so that he could welcome the Sabbath at home and on his knees. Now he worried that his mistakes had cost him whatever chance he'd had of getting the foreman to agree.

Papito was sixty-five years old and tired. As he rode the subway he was distressed at having to continue working for someone else. It had been his intention to gain independence with the profits from a business he had hoped to start. This plan was what had served him as an incentive to peddle religious books after work. By juggling both jobs, he had hoped to earn the capital to purchase an industrial sewing machine and any other equipment needed to set up a shoe-repair shop. All the details for this enterprise had been carefully worked out. His many years of working with leather goods had provided him with the expertise to repair and make from scratch anything ranging from shoes to luggage. The area outside of Tico's room would have served as a temporary commercial space. His congregation's patronage would have ensured the business' success. Yet each time he had saved a bit of money and had set aside a date to buy the first of the equipment, an emergency had cropped up to consume his funds.

The train lurched out of a Manhattan tunnel and across the Williamsburg Bridge. Already the city was veiled in darkness. Papito hated the way winter nights overtook his days. When he left home each morning the sky was as dark as when he returned. This, and the many hours he spent cooped up inside a factory, made him feel as if he were living like a mole.

His current fantasy was to quit his job, rent his house and have the checks forwarded to the Dominican Republic where he could conceivably buy a piece of land and live comfortably off what he farmed. He had mentioned this as a possibility to his wife who had admitted to fancying the same thing. They had then spent several late-night hours planning how they would move their family back to the Dominican Republic and into a house they'd make sure possessed indoor plumbing and enough guest rooms to accommodate their married children. Papito had also expressed interest in designing the house himself. Aurelia had agreed on the condition that he build it on a coast and with windows looking out over the sea. They had discussed all of this at length, but Aurelia had then concluded that neither Marina nor Tico would agree to go and that they themselves would hate living so far from their children.

"It's true Marina wouldn't want to go," Papito had replied.

"But we could make her. It'd be better for her if we did. She'd have suitors and could find herself a husband. You know people there are crazy for anyone who's lived in the United States. Besides, once she married and had children, she'd have no choice but to keep her head on straight."

"What about Iliana and Tico? What would we do about them?"

"We don't need to worry about Iliana until she's through with school, and Tico is a boy. He'd be fine moving in with one of his brothers or alone."

"So it'd be you, me, Marina, Rebecca and her children?"

"You'd want us to take them, wouldn't you?"

Aurelia nodded.

"Well, then, it'd be perfect. Since Rebecca doesn't have a green card, she'd be forced to make a choice. Either go and stay permanently with her children or choose Pasión."

"She's the one who brought us here, Papito. It wouldn't be right to—"

"Yes, and she's drilled that into our heads a million times."

"We at least owe her—"

"We don't owe her nothing. The only ones we owe anything to are her children."

"Why are we even discussing this? Have you set aside money I don't know a thing about?"

"No, but—"

"Then let's stop talking about how we're gonna move. It was fun for a while, but we're stuck here, and no amount of wishing is going to change that fact."

The two of them slumped back against their bed. An eternity seemed to pass before Aurelia reached for Papito's hand.

"I'm sorry," she said. "It's just that I can't go on wishing or looking ahead to some other time and place. I've been doing that way too long." She massaged his hand and tried to will him to understand. "I know we're tired. Me as much as you. That's why I want to focus on how we're going to live right here and now. This is home, Papito. We've worked hard for it, and I don't have the energy to start over one more time. I really don't. I'd like to think I do, but I just can't see myself moving. Not at this point in my life."

Papito maintained his silence.

"I'm not saying moving back is a bad idea. I dream about it all the time, about walking on soil I know is mine, swimming in the warm waters of the Caribbean, visiting my parents' grave and paying them the respect I didn't when I was there. But we have children, Papito, and grandchildren too. Rebecca's aren't the only ones, and I can't do without them no matter how hard living here might be. It wouldn't make a difference if we had the money to leave right now. I couldn't go unless all of them went too."

Papito withdrew his hand from hers. "Just listen to me, Aurelia. Please. It's true we don't have the money to buy a house there. But Mauricio or Chaco could find a cheap one for us to rent, and our children could visit us as often as they wished. We always said once they were grown we'd consider moving back. Well, they're grown, Aurelia, and we're getting older every day. It's time we started thinking about us."

"You didn't understand a word I said."

"I understood every single word and would miss our children too. But look at Marina. We should've figured out a long time ago that New York wasn't doing her any good. We've already lost Beatriz. We can't have Marina run off too. As for Rebecca, we should've done something about her children long before things got so bad. But it's not just them, Aurelia. It's us too. We need to get out from under while we still can. I've been doing a lot of thinking and have decided that I don't want to spend the rest of my days worrying about how we're going to get by after I'm too old to work."

"We have the house," Aurelia reminded him. "And with your Social Security—"

"I've never earned much. If I retired, Social Security would give us a couple of hundred dollars a month and not much more."

"I'm not saying it would be easy, but we could manage. We've managed on less before."

"Is that what you want to do, just manage?"

"What I want has little to do with it. I've wanted a lot I'm never gonna get. All I'm saying is that I can't leave our children just because I think we'd be happier somewhere else. This is more about what I need than what I want. And what I need is to be with them."

"But what about Marina? We have to think about her and Rebecca's children too."

"Oh, please," Aurelia said. "You really think Marina would get better if we dragged her to a place she didn't want to go to or that she'd marry some campesino just because he'd want her?"

"Okay, okay," Papito conceded. "I agree about Marina. But Rebecca's another thing. As long as she's got legs, she's gonna walk or crawl back to Pasión."

"She won't go back to him. Not this time. And if she does, I guarantee she'll turn around and come back here to stay."

Aurelia had ended the conversation by rising from bed to pee. Papito had watched her from their room. He had known before, as he had then, that it was foolish to argue about returning to the Dominican Republic when he lacked even the money to purchase plane tickets. But he had wanted to believe that if he'd had the resources his wife would have agreed to go. He had wanted to believe that she trusted him and took for granted that he would make everything turn out right.

The J train swerved onto the express track and sped from Marcy to Myrtle Avenue. Papito mumbled an apology as he was tossed against other passengers. At Myrtle and again at Eastern Parkway he edged closer to the doors to be one of the first to get off at Van Siclen. Cold air stung his face as he stepped out onto the platform. He took its stairs two by two, hurried through a turnstile, down another flight of stairs, then out onto the street. Fulton appeared menacing with its busted streetlamps and gutted buildings. Papito veered toward the light and relative safety of Atlantic Avenue, then impulsively into a corner store.

He had recently developed an insatiable sweet tooth. His desire for sugar was so compulsive that if he purchased a pack of gum he immediately popped all five sticks into his mouth. At work he'd hide and surreptitiously rip open packs of cupcakes, cookies, rock candy and licorice to suck or nibble on throughout the day. On his way home he'd boost his energy with chocolate. Aurelia, who had overcome her addiction to sweets at about the same time he'd acquired his, made an effort to limit his sugar intake. Papito took pleasure in reminding her that her own desire had been so strong that she had habitually woken him in the middle of the night to demand that he go out and buy her whatever it was she'd craved. If stores were closed, she had clambered out of bed to search for the ingredients to whip up a quick dessert. She had then carried a bowl of it into bed to slurp at as he tried to sleep.

"I never did such a thing," she had countered just the previous night. "The children would've heard me in the kitchen and I would've had to prepare something for the entire brood."

"Uh-huh, and you never begged me to bring you whole Valencia cakes."

"At least I was younger then. I didn't need to worry about my health. You're an old man. You should know better."

"You think you were young at fifty-nine?"

"Younger than you are now."

"The ladies don't think I'm old," Papito had said, grinning wickedly. "Besides, if sugar's bad for me, I have years of indulging before it does me the harm it's already done to you. Look at you. You look about ready to be rolled into a grave."

"If that's the case," she'd said, grinning back, "then you must like the way my old bones taste. Yep, you must think I'm like a perfectly ripe cheese you can't go a day without."

Papito went up and down the bodega's aisles. He handled a box of Oreos before deciding he'd be better off purchasing it in the morning. He also made a mental note to buy a bag of the sour balls he'd been meaning to try out and the licorice sticks of which he was running out at work. As he browsed he was amused by the fact that he used to abhor sweets. He assumed his repugnance had been the result of his years of hauling sacks of sugar onto trucks. Yet he now considered that job as preferable to the one he had sitting on his behind and would have given almost anything to uproot a stalk of sugarcane and to sink his teeth into its sweet and stringy flesh.

Empty-handed, he ambled toward the counter to greet the

Puerto Rican man who had owned the store for years. "I'll take four of those," he said, pointing to a box of Snickers bars behind the counter.

The old man winked conspiratorially. "Are you sure four's enough?"

"No, but my wife would kill me if I brought more into the house."

"Mine's the same with beer. She gives me a hard time if I take a can home and then complains if I go somewhere else to drink." He smiled as if to prove he wouldn't have it any other way. "You'd think at our age they'd let us have a bit of fun."

Papito returned the smile although he disapproved of anyone who drank. Outside he hid three of the Snickers bars in his coat pockets before proceeding to eat the fourth. The others were for his grandchildren. Ever since his eldest daughter had moved in he had taken to bringing home treats her children greeted him at the door to find. He was of the opinion that they could use some spoiling. He was also painfully aware that it would be a while before sweets or anything else diminished their boundless appetite.

The red light on Atlantic flicked to green. Papito crossed the avenue, made his way toward Bradford, and rounded the corner onto his block. To his amazement, he saw his son-in-law step off the curb on the opposite side of the street and stride purposefully toward his house.

"Don't you dare open that gate!" he bellowed as Pasión reached out to do just that.

"Compadre," Pasión said, amiably, "with Christmas so near I thought I'd come visit my wife and kids. It wasn't nice of them to run off like they did. You'd think—"

Papito's hand tightened into a fist around one of the candy bars hidden in his coat pockets. "You have no idea what I think!"

"Now, now. Let's not argue. I only want to see them."

Papito took a threatening step forward. Not intimidated by someone older and shorter than himself, his son-in-law stood his ground. His sardonic grin stopped Papito in his tracks. He became suddenly aware of his little more than five-foot height. Hoping to appear bold, if not broad, he squared his shoulders and made to draw his hand out of his pocket, but his fist locked around the candy bar and caught against the pocket's flap. The abrupt motion wiped the smile off Pasión's face.

"Her-hermano, I meant no disrespect."

Papito stared incomprehensibly at Pasión.

"We can—I'm sure we can work this out. There's no need to—"

An exhilaration like none he'd ever known possessed Papito as it dawned on him that his son-in-law believed he'd been about to draw a gun. He thrust the Snickers bar farther against his coat pocket. The mere gesture made him feel taller, stronger, fiercer.

"You spineless piece of shit," he snarled, relishing the novelty of curse words on his tongue. "You beat up on women but don't have the guts to stand up to a man."

His son-in-law glanced anxiously toward the house. "There's no need to get upset. I—"

"There's no need to get upset?" Papito asked, genuinely incensed. "You starve my grandchildren, smash my daughter's face, and have the nerve to tell me there's no need to get upset?"

"I—I only wanted to see my wife. Really. But I can—I can go now. I wouldn't have come if I'd thought . . ."

Pasión's voice trailed off into a wheeze. Unmoved, Papito stepped up behind him and pointed the candy bar at his back.

"Let's go," he said, unwilling to have a family member step outside and catch him at his bluff. "We're going for a walk."

His son-in-law made to reach into a pocket.

"Put your hands up in the air!" Papito yelled.

Pasión instantly obeyed. "Please. I'm hav-having trouble breathing. I can't—I don't think I can—"

Wary lest he possess a gun, Papito rifled with one hand through his son-in-law's pockets and pulled out an inhaler, a set of keys, a wallet stuffed with twenty-dollar bills. The sight of all that money affected him like a match applied to an already smoldering heap.

"You fucking bastard," he cursed, shoving Pasión away from the house and off the curb. "All this money and you give your wife and children none!"

Pasión stumbled, but managed to keep his hands up in the air. "My medicine," he wheezed. "I need my—"

Papito watched him, sure that he was faking an attack of asthma. "Just walk. I'll give these back to you when we're through."

Pasión crossed the street and faltered halfway up the block. "Please—"

Governed by a violence needing quick release, Papito shoved him headlong into an abandoned lot. Pasión tried to stand, but was forced down once again.

"Hermano, please. I need—"

"Yeah, I know," Papito said, surprised by his own sudden and eerie calm. "You need your medicine. You think you're about to die."

Pasión rolled over onto his back and gasped for air. Papito watched him with a detachment that exempted him from guilt.

"I could kill you," he said. "I could stand here and watch you breathe your last. And you know what? I'd get pleasure out of watching you die. I'd feel like justice had finally been done."

His son-in-law's breaths fragmented into coughs. "You're— you're a religious man. You wouldn't—"

These words sent Papito into an unexpected rage. He leaned forward to smash his fist into Pasión's mouth. Not satisfied, he kicked him until his own legs ached. Pasión tried to protect himself as best he could. Spurred on by a memory of the many times he had failed to stop the abuse his eldest daughter and grandchildren had endured, Papito kicked him again and then again.

"You don't know a thing about me! Otherwise you wouldn't have shown your face! You wouldn't have maimed my daughter or starved her kids!"

Papito's breath stumbled out in quick, short spurts. Yet neither this nor his dangerously racing heart kept him from disputing what he had long suspected about himself.

"Did you think I was such a coward that I'd let you go on doing as you pleased? Did you think I'd tuck my tail between my legs and let you set foot inside my house?"

Pasión raised his head and for the first time met his father-in-law's gaze. Papito's loathing mounted. He watched Pasión struggle for each breath. Not once had Pasión apologized for any of the misery he'd caused. Not once had he acknowledged that he had done anything able to be perceived as wrong. It was as if he not only recognized but had also submitted to the ruthlessness with which Papito had begun to act, as if, in his narrow world of victors and losers, he had discovered that his father-in-law was not the man he had taken him to be.

A pernicious thought formed in Papito's mind. It would be so easy to kill Pasión, so very easy to wrap both hands around his throat until breath flowed neither in nor out. It would be even simpler merely to walk away and leave him writhing among heaps of trash. Such a crime would involve no blood and would leave no trace. It might not even constitute a crime since death would result from asthma and there would be no witnesses to the role he'd played.

Persuaded of the justice of such a death, Papito watched Pasión claw desperately at his throat. He continued to watch as Pasión's features warped with an agony equal to what Rebecca must have felt each time her face had been smashed against a wall, her body pummeled with whatever was at hand, her backside kicked until she lay in a senseless heap. These unforgivable acts were what resolved Papito's will and made him turn toward home.

As he walked out of the lot, Papito soothed his prickling conscience by telling himself that he had rightfully avenged his eldest daughter and that his grandchildren would be better off with their father dead. He then tried to shift his thoughts to his wife waiting anxiously for him to drive her to the hospital from which Marina was scheduled to be released and to Marina herself about whom he still had to worry. Yet as he prepared to cross the street, as he risked a backward glance and saw his son-in-law feebly stand and then collapse, his thoughts tripped past Marina's mental illness, back to Pasión's abuses and those of Samuel, then, unexpectedly, further back to those of another man whose daughter he had tried to save only to inadvertently place her directly in harm's way.

Perhaps it was his decades-old realization that attempting to alter another's fate could result in unexpected twists which made him abruptly turn around. Or perhaps it was a fear that his eldest daughter would curse him for her freedom or an irrational hope that she would leave her husband on her own which made him re-trace his steps. Whatever the reason, he found himself thrusting the inhaler into his son-in-law's hand and returning as well the wallet stuffed with bills. Only when Pasión had raised his head to suck despairingly at the inhaler, only when his breath began to ease and it became clear that he would be able to get back on his feet, did Papito leave his side.

CHAPTER
 32

Marina watched as her father inserted his keys into their front door. She felt her mother clasp her elbow with the same hand that had gently nudged her forward each time her feet had hesitated and had helped her dress because her own hands had fumbled with the hooks on her bra, the zipper on her pants, the laces on her boots. She concentrated on the grip of that hand to keep her eyes from sliding shut and her body from crumpling right there on the stoop. Her head felt so heavy that she could barely hold it up, her lips so dry that her tongue kept worming out to lick them.

"Rebecca's children have been asking for you," she heard her mother say in a voice that sounded strangely muted. "Everyone has. They couldn't wait for you to get back home."

Marina let herself be guided into the house. Her father opened the door to the living room and grandly stepped aside.

"Look who I brought home," he announced.

A tangle of arms immediately enclosed Marina. She swatted them away. Her nephew and nieces mistook her gestures for a game and pressed their bodies closer. Their laughter was oppressive. It spiraled around Marina, shattering the composure she had been trying to maintain.

It was happening again: the body crushing hers, the arms forcing her to submit. She reached through her narcotic haze and feebly lashed out with hands whose nails she had chewed back to the quick. Hysteria clogged her throat as she opened her mouth to scream. The body that had retained a memory of its degradation simultaneously stiffened to absorb the pain that shot between her thighs and extended upward, exploding behind the lids she'd shut to block out the face that daily haunted her in dreams and insidiously materialized in life.

"Okay, that's enough," Aurelia exclaimed, prying the children from Marina and attempting to quiet them as she herded them into the living room. "Your aunt's not feeling well. We have to give her room to breathe."

The children's voices and a dog's persistent barking assailed Marina. She clapped her palms around her ears. Her legs, weakened by drugs and by days of immobility, folded under and landed her in a heap. She scrambled toward the door, her body cringing in anticipation of the blows that tended to follow each assault, her mind conjuring the details of the first.

"Mi'ja," Papito said. "The children were only trying to welcome you back home."

Marina opened her eyes to find him extending a hand to help her up. Behind him and past the open door leading into the living room, she made out Aurelia and Iliana comforting the children whom she now vaguely recognized as Rebecca's. Colored lights flickered distractingly around them, casting shadows throughout the room so that its furniture appeared to heave and lurch. She glanced back at the faces of those she had rashly assumed were members of her family. Only then did she notice the shadows that played on their faces too. She focused again on the man she had mistaken for her father. His scowl deepened as she lunged past him for the door.

"I've had it with your nonsense," Papito said, seizing her just as she was about to bolt outside.

Marina broke free from his grip. She needed to find an alternate route out of that house, needed to locate the family she would easily recognize as hers. The individuals inhabiting those rooms were all impostors. She identified them as such by the cagey manner in which they watched her as if she were someone they had met just then. Their contrived expressions also betrayed a hostility similar to that of the strangers among whom she had found herself confined. Like them, these people were in on the plot to break her will and to persuade her that what her senses conveyed as real was unreliable. But she was smart and far too vigilant to be deceived. Not only had God marked her as special by resurrecting her from among the dead, He had also seen fit to equip her with a sight that enabled her to see into the hearts of those who wished her ill.

Papito again made the mistake of stepping toward Marina. She backed away from him toward the stairs. Just then a door creaked open behind her on the second floor. She swung around in time to see two people begin to descend with a massive dog straining at its leash. The dog bared its teeth and growled as the deathly-pale woman flashed a macabre grin.

"So you're back," the man observed.

Marina's terror escalated. Her legs inexplicably went numb and her vision blurred. She clung to the banister to fight the gravitational pull drawing her into oblivion. The stairs abruptly fell from under her feet into a precipitous abyss. The ceiling simultaneously descended as the walls tilted and all semblance of reality gave way to impenetrable darkness.

It was then that Aurelia stepped out into the hallway. At the sight of Marina reeling on the stairs, she nudged Papito into the living room and gestured for her son and daughter-in-law to return upstairs.

"Why?" Gabriel demanded.

"Just do as I say," Aurelia commanded.

Laurie, who understood Spanish but did not speak it, nevertheless continued down the stairs. Aurelia cast her a look that stopped her in her tracks. Gabriel took advantage of the moment to drag her and the dog back into their apartment. An argument ensued as the door slammed shut behind them.

Aurelia wisely moved no closer to her daughter. "You're home, mi'ja. Don't you remember we picked you up at the hospital? Don't you remember the car ride home?"

Marina suddenly grew still. Yet even with her eyes open, even with each of her senses wary and alert, she was unable to see past darkness or to make out the voice's source.

"I know it's hard to believe you're finally home. But you really are, mi'ja. You're home and no one here is going to hurt you. No one here will—"

That voice, hypnotic and barely louder than a whisper, filtered through Marina's fear. She listened as it droned on and fluttered soft as wings against her ears. Her muscles began to ease. The rhythm of her heart steadied even as the sensation of falling leveled and the stairs solidified under her feet.

"I can tell you're so tired you could just nod off right there on the stairs. But if you come inside I'll make your bed so you can rest. I'll make sure you're comfortable and safe."

Aurelia risked stepping closer to her daughter. When Marina remained as still, she climbed the stairs and delicately placed a hand on the one clinging to the guardrail. Marina felt that hand warm and soft against her own. Its heat traveled up her arm, thawing the last of her fear and dispersing the darkness before her eyes.

No one with such hands could possibly mean to do her any harm. No one with such a kind voice would purposefully deceive her.

She tentatively released the rail. Her hand was instantly grasped and steadied by one stronger than her own.

"Mami?" she asked, focusing on Aurelia. "Mami?"

CHAPTER

 33

The sun was barely up when Aurelia rose from bed. Body aching from a restless night, she entered the bathroom and, not bothering with an overhead light, turned on the faucets before climbing into the tub. Tepid water swirled around her feet. She waited until it heated before directing its stream into the showerhead. Water poured over and warmed her body. She lathered herself cursorily, then rinsed off, all the time mentally listing the many things she had left to do before her married children and their families arrived.

She'd already made bread pudding, yucca patties, and a tripe and garbanzo stew—each of which would need to be reheated. Zoraida had been left in charge of the turkey; Nereida had volunteered to bake a guava cake; Azucena had been asked to bring beverages; and Laurie had offered to make a salad as well as to bake several dozen cookies. But Aurelia still had to make pasteles; fried sweet plantains; a pot of white rice; another of rice and peas; the traditional abichuelas con dulce; and stewed chickens for those who disliked turkey meat. When Papito returned from the all-night Christmas Eve vigil at the church, she'd have to ask him to drive her to the livestock market regardless of how tired he might be. She'd also have to enlist Iliana, if not Rebecca, to help her clean the house.

Aurelia toweled herself dry and slipped on a crumpled night-gown she needn't worry about getting soiled. She then returned to her bedroom and searched through a drawer for a pair of the sweat socks she had salvaged from the trash after Tico had decided they'd gotten too ratty for him to wear. Pulling them on, she shuffled into the kitchen.

Any minute now her grandchildren would climb up the basement stairs. All it usually took to wake them was the sound of her steps and an anticipation of eating their first meal of the day. They'd enter the kitchen with sleep still in their eyes to disrupt the few hours she had been accustomed to having to herself. Allowing them no chance to argue, she'd send them back downstairs to wash. She would then take advantage of her few minutes alone to quietly sip a cup of cocoa. On this morning, however, she set no time aside for herself and instead began stirring up a batch of pancakes to mark the day as special for her grandchildren. She had fried fewer than a dozen when one of Rebecca's children traipsed into the room.

"What you making?" Soledad asked.

"Pancakes. Christmas pancakes."

Soledad darted to a window. "I forgot! You think it's gonna snow?"

Aurelia smiled and shook her head. "I don't think so. But maybe we'll be surprised."

"Something smells gooooood," Esperanza said, trailing in a moment later.

"Well, aren't you bright-eyed this morning," her grandmother observed.

Esperanza swiped a pancake from those stacked neatly on a platter. "When's the party? When's everyone gonna get here?"

"Not until this afternoon. But right after breakfast, I want all of you to shower. That way your aunt can comb your hair before I sweep."

Rubén was the last to straggle into the kitchen. Noticing his eldest sister munching on a pancake, he snatched the platter out of her reach. "You so greedy. You ain't the only one who's gotta eat!"

"There's more than enough for everyone. Just grab a plate and serve yourself. The syrup's on that shelf, and you know where to find a glass." Aurelia spooned batter into the skillet and watched as her grandchildren proceeded to raid the kitchen.

"Can we eat in the living room?" Esperanza asked.

"What? So you can watch TV?"

"What else we gonna do? No one's getting here till this afternoon."

"You could sit here and keep me company. That's what."

"We'd only be in your way. That's what you always telling us."

"Yeah, and you only remember when it suits you. But go on. You can watch TV until your eyes drop out. See if I care."

Plates in hand, the children departed from the room. Aurelia was relieved to see them go. She'd be able to fry the remaining batter and get on with her chores much quicker without the children engaging her in idle chatter.

She flipped the pancakes over. When they were done, she turned to add them to the dwindled stack. To her surprise, she found Soledad slumped at the kitchen table.

"You don't want to watch TV?"

The youngest of her grandchildren merely shrugged. Aurelia turned off the stove to sit beside her.

"Are the pancakes any good?"

Soledad nodded although she had barely touched her plate.

"You're eating mighty slow."

Soledad obliged her grandmother by placing a forkful in her mouth. "Are we gonna have to go back home?"

Aurelia frowned. "Why? Did someone tell you you'd be going back?"

Soledad swallowed without bothering to chew.

"Mi'ja?"

The child sullenly stabbed her pancakes. Sensing that pressuring her would do no good, her grandmother pushed back her chair and stood.

"No, but Mami always takes us back," Soledad mumbled.

"This time I won't let her," Aurelia answered fiercely. "And if she does, I'm going to make her bring you back to stay."

"Can you?" Soledad asked. "Can you really make her bring us back?"

"I'm sure going to do my—"

The word "best" caught in Aurelia's throat. She abruptly turned from her granddaughter watching her with the solemnity of an adult. As she proceeded to light the stove, it dawned on her that she had it in her to do much more than try. She actually had the resources to succeed. Shocked by the revelation, she dropped a slab of butter onto the skillet. Obstacles she had set up for herself, justifications born out of a hope that problems would right themselves on their own, and dread of the consequences of interfering, each toppled in one fell swoop as she confronted what she had hoped to keep secret even from herself. Yes. She could arrange for her daughter to leave Pasión once and for all. She could even vanquish him from their lives in such a way that no one else would be the wiser as to how it had been done. This was what her friend Rosita had hinted at the previous day, this what she herself had unconsciously known all along.

"Something's burning," her granddaughter announced.

Aurelia turned the flame off under the blackening skillet. Just then Rebecca, who usually stayed in bed until way past noon, sauntered into the room.

"Oh." She glanced from her youngest child to her mother who had stepped toward a window to let in a bit of air. "I was planning on making breakfast for the children. I didn't think you'd get to it so fast."

Aurelia slipped a hand out of the window to knock off the days-old snow that had accumulated on its ledge. "Uh-huh," she said, bypassing her eldest daughter and reaching into the refrigerator for a bowl of rice. "You were also planning on helping me clean the house."

"The house looks fine," Rebecca replied. "But anything you want me to do, I'll do."

Aurelia crumbled clumps of rice out of the window. She then watched as pigeons swooped down to seize the grains. Cold air nipped her fingers. The low-slung sky she glimpsed above neighboring rooftops and the snow blanketing the backyard both seemed to her an indifferent grey.

"And why is that?" she asked, pulling her hand back in and slamming the window shut.

"Why is what?"

"Why the sudden willingness to help?"

"You see how you are?" Rebecca asked. "One minute you're telling me I don't do shit, the next you're questioning why I would."

Aurelia heaped more pancakes onto Soledad's plate, then nudged her from the room.

"I see exactly how I am," she said when her granddaughter was safely out of hearing. "What I can't figure out is why you're offering to help when you've been here for days and have done little but lie in bed."

Rebecca's mouth fell open as if her mother's statement was news.

"I don't know what bug flew up your butt," she muttered, opening the refrigerator with a bandaged hand and slamming its door shut as if nothing inside it had appealed to her. "But for your information, I don't have to put up with your crap. I can pack my bags anytime I want."

"That's right," Aurelia said. "You can leave just as you tried to yesterday. What stopped you then, eh? Something having to do with rope?"

Rebecca swiveled around to face her. "I'm not going to let you work my nerves. You want an argument, go pick one with yourself."

She lifted the skillet off the stove and barely wiped it clean with a paper towel. She then took the bowl of leftover pancake batter and beat it with a spoon. As she concentrated on this task her mother noticed the makeup sloppily applied to her face in an attempt to conceal its bruises. Where wrinkles fanned out from the corners of her eyes the flesh stubbornly showed blue. Scabs remained visible on the lips whose lipstick had smeared onto her teeth.

Aurelia focused on that whorish and brutally crimson stain. "So you were again thinking of hightailing it back to Pasión."

Rebecca spooned batter into the skillet as if determined not to be provoked. Her indifference caused her mother to seize her by her wrist.

"I didn't raise you to ignore me after all my labor pains. When I speak to you, I expect to get an answer."

Rebecca snatched her wrist away. "Who the fuck do you think you are? You think I give a shit about your labor pains? What about my own damn pains? What about all I put up with for my children only to have you threaten to take them away like they were yours?"

"What you put up with for your children?" her mother asked. "What you put up with? Since we're naming things, why don't we call them exactly what they are? Why not come straight out and say you have yet to do a thing for them that didn't serve your purpose. Why not admit they're the ones who've had to put up with the unimaginable so you could continue with Pasión."

"This has nothing to do with him."

"This has everything to do with him and you know it! You think I didn't hear you late last night? What do you take me for, a fool? I have eyes and ears for anything that concerns my grandchildren! Don't think for a moment I'm going to let you haul them back into that hell! I'll see you or Pasión dead before I do!"

Rebecca turned away and made a show of flipping pancakes. Her mother stepped threateningly close. In a voice uncannily like Rebecca's, she mimicked her asking the children if they missed their father and then insisting, when she received no answer, that they had hurt him by leaving him all alone.

"I hate him," Rubén had said. "I don't care if he's alone. I don't want us going back."

The expression on his mother's face had instantly gone from manipulative to incensed. "You say that again and I'll beat you so bad you'll wish you'd never been brought into this world! What the hell do you mean by saying you hate your father? You think you'd be breathing if he hadn't wanted you alive?"

Rebecca grew apprehensively still as Aurelia spoke.

"Filling my grandchildren's heads with lies! You think they don't have eyes? You think they're about to believe their father's good just because you think they should? You're losing their respect and you don't even know it."

Rebecca edged away and calmly reached into a cabinet for a plate.

"I don't give a damn what kind of father you think Pasión has been. He's the only one they've got, and I'm not about to let them disrespect him. Next, they'll be trying to sauce me too."

"Oh, but you care lots about Marina hurting them—Marina, who's hurt no one but herself."

"I'm not taking any chances. Marina's crazy. She's—"

"And what do you call Pasión?"

Rebecca slid the pancakes onto her plate, then folded into a chair. "I call him my husband, and I have no intention of discussing him with you."

Aurelia nodded. "So you're saying he'll be your husband until the day he kills you or dies himself."

"If he'd wanted me dead, he'd have killed me long ago."

"And you don't think he's tried?"

"Listen!" Rebecca slammed her fork onto the table. "You've already dragged me here against my will! So I'm here, okay? That's all well and good for now! But don't think I intend to let you bury me alive! Don't think I'm going to let you turn my kids against me! They're mine, and I'll eventually take them back to where they belong! I don't give a shit if you disapprove or worry about what might become of me when we go back! If I lose my life at my husband's hands, it'll at least be better than letting you wear it out bit by bit!"

She picked up her fork and commenced to eat.

"There you have it. You can't bear to hear the truth, I'll make up lies and tell you anything you want. Just get off my fucking back."

"So that's how it is?" her mother asked, giving her a final opportunity to change her mind.

"Don't play the fool," Rebecca retorted with obvious disdain. "You heard every word I said."

Aurelia's stomach tightened with anticipation as she placed each of three chickens on the counter between the stove's burners. She'd had the butcher at the livestock market cut off their heads as well as drain their blood. She had then explained to him that she didn't want to have them plucked.

"You planning on working hoodoo with these birds?" the man had teased.

"That would probably be more fun," Aurelia had replied, chuckling in spite of herself. "But no. They're for my Christmas feast. I grew up in the country. If I can't raise chickens, I at least want the satisfaction of plucking them myself."

"I don't understand why you're giving yourself so much work to do," her husband had said when they'd climbed back into their car. "You should've just let the man do everything right there. It would've taken him five minutes instead of the hour it's going to take you to pluck the feathers out one by one."

"Ay, Papito, I just want to do it for old times' sake."

Like the butcher, Papito had looked at her as if she were planning on more than she was willing to admit.

"I don't know about you, but it used to turn my stomach to twist a chicken's neck and see it running around like it thought it was still alive."

Aurelia had laughed out loud. "I didn't say I liked it. I only said I wanted to pluck them for old times' sake."

She lifted the lid off a pot and inspected the water she had set to boil. When the water rolled violently, she took hold of one of the chickens and immersed it for a quick minute to open up its pores. She then did this with the others and, placing them on a platter, settled herself for her task.

It had been years since her fingers had felt the downy wet of feathers more difficult to extricate than their appearance might suggest. She grabbed a clump of them tightly enough to feel their quills. Holding the bird securely, she began plucking its feathers out.

With her hands busy, she was able to concentrate on the task for which plucking the chickens was a guise. Already her grandchildren had run squealing from the headless birds. Rebecca too had retreated into the basement. As for Papito, he had tucked himself into bed to catch up on his sleep; Iliana had been dispatched to make sure the children bathed; Tico had slipped out to visit a girlfriend; Marina sat listlessly watching TV. All in all, Aurelia had contrived the solitude and quiet she had anticipated would be difficult to achieve.

Her hands eased into a rhythm. This done, she focused all her thoughts on Pasión. Vaguely at first, then clearer as the seconds passed, she was able to make out the details of his face. She withdrew far enough to see the entirety of his giant's height and smiled with grim satisfaction when she recognized his surroundings as the third-floor coop of the house to which her daughter meant to return. By venturing there himself, Pasión had done just as she'd willed.

She watched him discard rotting carcasses into a burlap sack. As he did so, she decided that she wanted him to see her too. She wanted him to know that what was about to occur was not mere chance but had been purposefully willed by her. The strength of her desires jerked his head up as if it were attached to her hand by strings. As she'd intended, he saw her sitting on a window ledge at the far end of the very room in which he stood. He immediately blinked to banish the vision dismissed as dust billowed up by drafts seeping in through broken panes. Yet as he resumed his task, his head was again manipulated against his will. He saw her clearly then, saw her despite the improbability of her having materialized from air.

Aurelia remained still long enough for his conscience to terrorize his soul. When he backed away from her, she seized a handful of feathers and yanked them out. The feathers drifted up into the air as she released them. The chickens that had languished half dead throughout the coop simultaneously leapt up on their three-clawed feet. Their squawks shattered the silence. The dust disturbed by their wings swirled up in blinding clouds.

Pasión stumbled toward the door. Aurelia plucked and released more feathers. She did this again and then again, her hands moving at a dizzying speed, the air thickening with dust and feathers that choked Pasión. He fell to his knees and fumbled in a pocket for his inhaler. Aurelia instantly swung the largest of the birds through the air. The rooster whose wings her son-in-law had clipped followed her cue by defying gravity to knock the inhaler out of his reach. When Pasión lunged for it, Aurelia slammed the platter of freshly plucked birds onto her kitchen table. She then stood to shake her skirt free of the feathers that had drifted there. A flurry of birds scrambled forward, kicking the inhaler into the farthest corner of the coop. Aurelia stepped with the platter toward the sink. She turned on the taps full-force and began to scrub the birds. Dozens of them flew in a frenzy toward Pasión. Just as abruptly, Aurelia turned off the taps and rubbed salt into each bird. They lashed out at Pasión, pecking at his face, his hands, his wrists, and any other bits of skin exposed as he crawled from the room to collapse on the third-floor landing.

Even then, Aurelia felt no remorse. Even then, she persuaded herself that nothing short of his death would make up for his crimes.

She sailed toward him on the feathers depriving him of breath. His fear was palpable. It distorted his mouth and collapsed his lungs. It contorted his body as he struggled to retain what little life he possessed.

Having conjured death, Aurelia stood respectfully in its presence. Only when her son-in-law gave a final jolt did she tread on the feathers scattered throughout her kitchen floor and reach for a broom with which she wearily began to sweep. Bits of down fluttered up and adhered to her face, her hair, her hands. She stepped toward a window to sweep along its wall. To her surprise, she noticed that it had begun to snow. Pristine flakes descended lethargically to blanket the ash-hued snow covering her yard. She watched in wonder as they fell. Her grandchildren would be beside themselves with joy. She imagined the laughter that would ring from their lips like bells. Her pleasure extended to the prospect of having her married children reunited in her home. In honor of the occasion they would drop their grudges outside her door. They would submit to her embrace and to that of the siblings they often chose not to see. And, if luck would have it, the rest of the day would pass festively, if not without event.

CHAPTER

❖ 34 ❖

"Sit still."

"But you pulling!"

Iliana tried being gentler with the comb. "You see your sister? That's how pretty you're going to look too."

"You such a baby," Esperanza taunted Soledad. "You didn't hear me cry."

"Maybe not this time," Iliana replied, finishing the last of the cornrows and uncrossing the legs between which she'd been holding her niece still. "But you cried last time." She nudged the child to a stand and led her into the bathroom. "There. You see?"

"Yeah," Soledad mumbled.

"You're not even looking."

The child wiped her eyes and reluctantly gazed into the mirror. A grin broke across her face at the sight of her dozens of braids weighted by brightly colored beads.

"Are you through with the bathroom?" Rebecca asked, appearing at its door.

"You can come in," Iliana said.

Rebecca pushed in past her daughter. Iliana wrapped a protective arm around her niece and led her out of the bathroom.

"Why don't you go see if Abuela needs help. Tell her I'll be up soon."

Soledad and her sister immediately obeyed. Iliana returned to her room and searched through a closet for her clothes. Minutes later, Rebecca joined her there.

"So, aren't you nervous?"

"What? About the party?"

Rebecca dismissively sucked her teeth. "About Marina."

Iliana removed her party clothes from hangers. "Worried how?"

"You heard about how she attacked that nurse."

"I'd react the same way if I woke up to find some stranger poking needles in my arm."

"I don't know," Rebecca said, lowering her voice conspiratorially. "She makes me nervous, especially when I catch her around the children. She's already tried burning down the house. Who's to say what else she might take it into her head to do."

"Who's to say what *any* of us might do."

"And what is that supposed to mean?"

"Exactly what you think," Iliana said, heading back into the bathroom with her clothes.

"Fine," Rebecca said. "Don't say I didn't warn you."

Iliana shrugged. It annoyed her to think Rebecca might use Marina as an excuse to crawl back to Pasión. Whenever she was gearing herself to go, she paved the way by finding fault with others and by enlisting the support of anyone she managed to lure into her schemes. Worse, she habitually claimed that returning would be the best thing for her children.

Iliana slammed down the toilet's lid and flung her clothes on top. She'd had an urge to call Rebecca a hypocrite and to warn her that she'd notify the authorities as to the condition of Pasion's house. But past experience had taught her the threat would be idle unless her parents backed her up.

She undressed before a full-length mirror. Ed had been right when he'd said that she'd lost weight. The loss was significant enough to cause her bones to jab against her skin. She gazed disparagingly at her broad shoulders, meager breasts, narrow hips and excessively long arms. She then leaned forward to inspect her face. Her lips, with their tendency to curve down, seemed unkind. Her wide-set eyes and the arch of her unruly brows made her appear somewhat mad.

Years earlier, just after Papito purchased their current home, she, Marina and Beatriz had ventured into its basement. As her sisters inspected the debris-filled room which would eventually be theirs, she had entered the bathroom to aim her flashlight at where she had hoped to find a tub. Disappointed by the rust-stained shower stall, uprooted toilet and cracked tiles littering the floor, she had turned to leave the room. The beam of her flashlight revealed an intruder watching her from against a wall. This encounter paralyzed both and drew screams from their mouths. It was Marina who, dashing into the bathroom, had identified the stranger as Iliana's own reflection in a full-length mirror.

Remembering, Iliana tried to find in that same mirror the aspect of herself which she had failed to recognize years before. She tried as well to identify whatever it was Marina had glimpsed and been perturbed by early that morning when she'd pried open the bathroom door.

"Do you need to use the bathroom?" Iliana had asked.

Marina had only stared. Iliana had self-consciously brought her knees together and quickly peed before hiding her nudity behind a towel. Her sister had followed her into their bedroom to stare all the more intently as she dressed.

"I've been thinking," Iliana had said, hoping to divert attention from her body. "Tomorrow, if you're up to it, we could go out with one of my friends from school."

What seemed like suspicion appeared in Marina's eyes. "You—" Her tongue wormed out to lick her lips. "You never came to see me."

Bewildered, Iliana looked at her. "I went, Marina. I went almost every day."

"I would've remembered if you had."

Iliana tugged on the sweatshirt she had been holding to her breasts. "What—what about Mami? Do you remember her?"

"I remember everything and you never came."

Iliana sat down on her bed. She noticed that her sister's lips no longer trembled as they'd done the previous night and that her head no longer lolled as if it were too heavy for her neck.

"You were unconscious, Marina. You couldn't have known if—"

"I said you never came!"

Iliana held herself ever so still as Marina stepped threateningly near.

"I have the sight," she'd claimed. "There's nothing I don't know."

Iliana backed away from the mirror. She tried to shake off her lingering unease as she tucked her breasts into a bra, stepped into a pair of panties and a floor-length skirt, slipped on a billowing silk shirt. She had carefully selected these garments—keeping in mind that she needed to please her parents as well as her sisters who habitually accused her of dressing like a man.

"That's why you're single," Rebecca, of all people, often told her. "Men want to see legs. I thought you'd be smart enough to know as much by now."

Even Papito, who habitually scolded his daughters for wearing skirts above their knees, had once pulled his youngest aside to say she needn't wear hers so long that their hems brushed her ankles, if not the floor.

"You're a young woman and should dress like one," he'd said.

Iliana fully expected to be teased despite having opted for a skirt. It was sure to be judged as spinsterly, her shirt as much too loose, her boots as ugly in and of themselves.

Resigned, she untangled her hair, pulled it back and, as a compromise, clipped it with a bow. She then applied face powder and a lipstick she hoped was not too bright.

There, she thought, glancing into the mirror. *At least I can't be accused of looking like a man.*

CHAPTER

❖ 35 ❖

"Oh, good." Papito embraced Azucena and then her husband, Raúl. "That makes four of us." He turned to one of Nereida's sons. "Go upstairs and get your uncle. Tell him we're ready to begin."

Benny, Zoraida's soft-spoken husband who often found himself mediating the arguments that tended to result from domino games, raised a hand in protest.

"Count me out. I came only to stuff my mouth."

"Don't be silly," his father-in-law said. "We'll play a round or two, and Caleb or Vicente can take your place when they arrive."

Zoraida frowned in disapproval. "No way. I don't want him playing."

"For God's sake," Raúl said, taking off his coat and already heading toward the dining room where the dominoes were waiting on the table. "Loosen that noose around his neck. It's just a friendly game."

"A friendly game?" Zoraida asked. "A friendly game? There's no such thing as a friendly game in this group."

"Oh, come on, 'manita," Gabriel said, traipsing into the room behind Raúl. "Your husband's a grown man. He can take care of himself."

Benny glanced apologetically at his wife. "Just one game, then. Only one."

Zoraida rose from the couch to stop him as he headed into the dining room. Aurelia interceded by stepping in her path.

"Don't make a fuss," she advised. "The men rarely get to play."

"And we rarely get together as a group. You'd think this one time we could act like civilized people and just sit and talk in the same room. But no. The men get to take over the dining room and wait for us to serve them." Zoraida dropped back onto the couch and turned toward her sisters. "You know as well as me how ugly they get when they're playing dominoes. Sooner or later they'll be at each other's throats."

"Don't look at me," Nereida said. "That's why my husband no longer comes."

"Your husband just can't stand to lose," Gabriel called out.

In the dining room, all of the men laughed. Papito pulled out a chair at the head of the table and sat down. Thrilled with the prospect of the impending game, he reached for the box of dominoes, slid off its wooden lid, tilted the box so that all twenty-eight chips crashed onto the table.

"No pairing off. This round will be each man for himself."

He flipped each of the dominoes facedown. With dramatic flair and dizzying speed, he shuffled them until satisfied he wouldn't wind up with a handful of similarly numbered chips. He then chose seven and let the other men do the same.

"Who's keeping score?"

"I am." Gabriel waved a sheet of paper and proceeded to write each player's name.

"Double six, then," Papito said.

"I'm not ready yet." Benny fumbled with the rectangular chips and finally managed to position them in both hands.

"Holds them like a girl," Papito muttered, securing his own in one hand as did Raúl and Gabriel.

Raúl plucked the 6-6 from among his chips and slid it faceup onto the center of the table. Following the rules of the game which stipulated that it proceed counterclockwise, Gabriel slammed down a 6-3 and placed it perpendicular against Raúl's. Benny hesitated before playing a 3-5.

Gabriel smirked in obvious enjoyment of what the others had been as quick to notice.

"No 6's, huh?"

"Cut it out," Benny said. "You know talking about another player's hand is against the rules."

Papito palmed a domino, slid it across the table and turned it faceup to expose its 5-6 only when he had positioned it beside his son-in-law's 6-6, leaving Raúl with no choice but to play a 5 on either end of the forming line of dominoes or, if he had none, to wait until someone had set down a number he could play.

"You have another thing coming if you think you can block me this early on in the game," Raúl said, flashing a 5-5 before grandiosely adding it to the line.

"Don't get a hard-on yet," Papito warned. "You have no idea what other moves I have lined up."

"Sounds like you think you stand a chance to win," Gabriel said, slamming down a 5-4 beside Raúl's 5-5.

Papito distrustfully eyed his son. Gabriel was known to bluff his way through games and to play aggressively even when he held a losing hand. He also had a tendency to steal glimpses at other players' chips and to say out loud what he knew he had no business saying. As for Raúl, a dreamer and mediocre singer who claimed to have given up an illustrious career in the Dominican Republic, he was as unreliable as Gabriel for always believing he held a winning hand. Benny was inept and usually gave little thought to strategy, yet he sometimes managed to score by luck.

He now slid one of his remaining dominoes facedown across the table, changed his mind and played another.

"You can't do that," Raúl said, eyeing the freshly placed 4-4.

"Yes I can. I didn't expose the first one."

Papito followed Benny's move with a 4-6 and grinned broadly at Raúl. "Nervous about something?"

Raúl inspected his chips, then mumbled something under his breath.

"What was that?" Papito asked.

"You heard me. I said I pass."

Papito made no effort to hide his glee. "Like I told you earlier, you have no idea what other moves I have in store."

"You still have to contend with me," Gabriel boasted, setting down a 6-2.

"Yeah, right," his father said.

Benny, whose turn it was, played a 2-5.

"Help him win, why don't you," Raúl snapped.

Papito glanced at his own remaining dominoes. He prided himself on being an intelligent player able to estimate, from his chips as well as those lying faceup on the table, which sets of numbers each of the other players held. He already knew for a fact that Benny had no 6's and Raúl no 5's or 4's and probably no 6's. With a total of five 5's on the table and the last two of them in his own hand, he calculated that he'd be able to keep an end of the forming line of dominoes blocked to the other players. Yet with his son most likely in possession of the two remaining 6's, he'd also have to find a way to leave Raúl an opening to play a number Gabriel might lack so that he himself would not eventually be blocked by a 6.

"We don't have all day," Raúl muttered.

Papito ignored the comment. One of his primary pleasures during a game of dominoes was to fuel the anxiety of other players with his slow and calculated moves. He now calmly leaned back against his chair. The worries which had been haunting him of late dissipated as he shrugged off the conventions his life usually imposed. As a result, he felt free to capitalize on the weaknesses of the other players and to be as cruel and unyielding as the game demanded.

"There," he said, casting down a 5-0 as if to a dog, then contemptuously turning to face Raúl. "Let's see if you can use your wits for once and strategize a decent move."

Aurelia stepped past the men into the kitchen. She opened the refrigerator, took out the tripe and garbanzo stew, set it on the stove to simmer. She then checked the stewing chickens as well as a turkey heating in the oven. It was so rare an occasion to be cooking for the greater part of her family—all except for Mauricio and Chaco who now lived in Santo Domingo, Emanuel who had moved with his wife to Seattle, and Beatriz whom she hoped to track down soon—that she worried she had not prepared enough. She lifted the lids off the pots of white rice and of rice and peas. Confident there would be sufficient of each to go around, she wrapped dozens of yucca patties in aluminum foil and tucked them into the oven to warm beside the turkey. She then wiped her hands on a towel and returned to her daughters in the living room.

Watching them from the threshold and listening to her sons behind her, she felt her exhaustion ease into contentment and her anxiety of the previous days give way to pride. These were her children: ten of the fourteen whom she and Papito had reared into adulthood. That they had all ventured out of their own homes to spend Christmas Day with her and had set aside grudges to be reunited with their brothers and sisters seemed proof to her of the good parenting she had done.

Any worries she had harbored about her children's future, any ambivalence she had felt about intruding in their affairs or parental mistakes she had been conscious of making before that day were forgotten in the wake of her victory over Pasión. She was for the first time aware of the extent of her powers as well as firm in her decision to continue employing them in whatever ways might benefit her family. Euphoric with these newfound powers and surrounded by her many children and their offspring, she felt like a tree who had grown roots deep into the earth and could not be easily felled. This feeling of invincibility permeated her entire being, lending her a self-assurance she had previously not possessed and persuading her that she could from then on avert misfortune and keep her children safe.

Each of her senses was preternaturally tuned in to what was occurring throughout the house. She was aware of the harmless bickering of the men in the dining room; of Caleb and Vicente's impatience as they waited for the current round of dominoes to end so that they might join the game; of the conversations going on between her eldest daughters; of Marina's lethargy; of Iliana's fascination with a four-month-old nephew whom she'd just met; of the mischief of several of her grandchildren as they played; and of the delight of others in helping Laurie bake cookies up on the second floor or ruining their appetites with the sweets Nereida had placed in bowls.

All in all, the day was unfolding as Aurelia had hoped it would. She stepped into the living room. Avoiding a collision with a grandchild, she reached for the infant in her youngest daughter's arms. She then squeezed onto the couch beside her.

"Look at you," Iliana said. "I would've thought by now you'd have had your fill of babies."

"I'm still waiting for one from you," Aurelia teased.

"She'd better get herself a husband first," said Zoraida, the first of the fourteen siblings to have married and borne children.

"It's already too late for that." A wicked smile played on Iliana's lips as she raised her shirt and flashed her sisters a glimpse of her belly bloated with air. "Why do you think I came home from school to stay?"

"Hah!" Nereida, sitting on the arm of Zoraida's chair, snatched a peppermint from a bowl and pitched it into her mouth. "If that were true, you'd have been out on the streets in seconds flat."

"And what is that supposed to mean?" Aurelia asked.

Nereida sucked loudly on the mint. "Oh, please, Mami. You know full well Papi would've kicked her out for bringing shame into the house."

"Not only that," Zoraida added. "He probably would've whipped off his belt and tried to kill her first."

Aurelia frowned. "Your father might be a hard man, but I'm sure I would've brought him around to understand."

"Yeah, right," Iliana said, siding with her sisters. "Just like you brought him around to understand about Missy."

"And Missy was just a cat," Zoraida pointed out. "Imagine how much worse he would have acted had it been one of us."

"Your father threw her out because we couldn't afford to feed her and her entire brood."

"I see," Iliana said. "And that's why he used to call her 'whore' whenever she howled at a window or disappeared for days."

"The way he acted," Nereida asserted, "anyone would've thought poor Missy went out with the intention of getting herself knocked up."

"Actually," Aurelia said, forcing out a laugh, "that's exactly what she went out to do."

Rebecca, who had been silent until then, leaned forward in her seat. "Missy was a cat," she said with unexpected ire. "A damn cat. She couldn't have helped spreading her legs."

Aurelia's lips thinned in annoyance. "Maybe not. But my daughters aren't cats and better not go spreading their legs unless they first get themselves a ring."

"You see?" Nereida said. "You're as bad as Papi."

Aurelia was so taken aback by this comparison that she did not respond. She glanced at each of her daughters. As the conversation proceeded without her, alighting on other abuses her daughters perceived Papito as having committed, then lingering on the mechanisms each had employed to defend herself against his sporadic rage, she balked at the thought that they had been terrified of their father and had not only doubted her ability to protect them from him but had also interpreted her silence as proof of her complicity. This indictment was so painful to accept that she attempted to dispute it. Yet as her daughters waved off her excuses and laughed at the subterfuge with which they had found it necessary to survive their youth, the harshness of their tones and the brittleness of their laughter persuaded her that she had indeed failed all of them.

Shamed, Aurelia shifted the infant in her arms closer to her breasts. His dark eyes stared up at her, flickering with interest as conflicting emotions battled on her face. The past, she reluctantly conceded, was beyond her powers to alter or control. Yet the future was a clean slate on which she might somehow draw out her daughters' trust. It mattered little that she did not fully understand the workings of any of their minds or even of her husband's, and could only piece together the puzzle of their behavior. She told herself that, with her will resolved and her love for each as strong as it had ever been, she would find a way to avert future misunderstandings and curb misdirected rage. She would draw from each the camaraderie she needed to believe had merely been obscured by pettiness and discord.

Azucena chose that moment to huff into the living room. "That Laurie is a pig."

"Oh no. What did she do now?" one of her sisters asked.

Azucena placed her hands on her hips to emphasize her news. "I went upstairs to see how she was making out with the cookies and found her licking the mixing spoon and sticking it right back in the batter like we all want to eat her germs."

"Nah! She didn't!"

"She sure as hell did. She then had the nerve to offer me the spoon. 'Here,' she says, all calm and cool. 'Taste if the batter has enough butter.' I just looked at her like she was nuts and backed out of her kitchen. 'I don't like sweets,' I told her. 'But I'm sure the cookies will turn out fine.' "

"I better not catch my children munching on those cookies," Rebecca said.

Aurelia substituted the reprimand that had been on the verge of leaping off her tongue. "Now let's be nice," she said. "At least Laurie offered to make something. That's more than she's done any other time."

"She may as well not have bothered," Nereida said.

Zoraida's mouth remained pursed in obvious distaste. "That's white people for you. They offer you something nasty and expect you to be grateful." She shifted her over-two-hundred-and-fifty-pound body on the couch. "Don't you know just the other day the hussy whose brats I take care of came up to me all nice and sweet with a handful of her bloody underwear? 'Can you hand-wash these for me?' she asked, smiling all up in my face. 'They're delicates and I won't have a chance to wash them myself this week.' I smiled right back at her and told her to just put them in the washroom. As soon as she left for work I dumped those rags in the washing machine and set it to permanent press, hoping they would tear."

"All you had to do was tell her no," Aurelia said.

"And all she had to do was not ask me in the first place! What kind of nastiness was that, letting me see her menstrual blood? She thinks in this time and age I'd say 'Yes ma'am' and wear out my knuckles washing her undies when I was hired to watch her kids?"

Rebecca leaned forward in her chair. "You see," she said, her shifty eyes betraying the lie she was meant to tell, "that's why I'm grateful Pasión provides for me and my children so I don't have to go out and put up with such—"

"Oh, please. Don't get me started," Zoraida snapped.

"Nereida and I work too," Azucena informed her eldest sister. "You saying our husbands can't—"

"What she's saying," Nereida piped up with sarcasm, "is that pride is the reason she doesn't go out and find herself a job."

"Pride and self-respect," Rebecca had the nerve to claim. "You have something to say about that?"

"Yeah, I do," Zoraida said. "Instead of being grateful to Pasión, you should be thanking God for parents who take you in so you and your kids don't' starve."

"You lying bitch! My children have yet to go hungry a single day in their lives!"

"You think I can't see their bones? You think I haven't noticed the way they—"

"Just because you and yours are rolling around in fat doesn't mean—"

Aurelia rose to her feet. "That's enough! All of you!"

"No, I'm not through!" her eldest daughter yelled. "Every time we get together someone has to say something evil about Pasión."

Zoraida shrugged. "You're the one who brought him up. You don't want to hear what I have to say about him, don't bring his name up when I'm around."

"For God's sake," Aurelia said, glaring at her daughters. "It's Christmas!"

"That's just the point," Azucena retorted. "She should be opening up her eyes before the new year rolls around."

❖ ❖ ❖

Benny had long since joined the women in the living room, having lost the previous round to his father-in-law and willingly relinquished his chair to Caleb. Raúl, who had come in third and been made to give up his chair to Vicente, now sat at the far end of the dining-room table keeping score and watching the eleventh game of the round that had Gabriel leading with eighty-three of the required one hundred points; Papito gaining on him with a score of seventy-one; Caleb barely staying abreast at forty-nine; and Vicente, a nationally ranked chess player, trailing behind at thirty-two.

"So are you in or what?" Papito asked, impatient for Gabriel's next move although he would also have to wait for Caleb to play.

"In a hurry to lose, aren't you?" Gabriel taunted. He plucked the 0-0 from among his few remaining dominoes and slid it across the table. He then smirked at Caleb. "It's not much, but at least it'll give you a chance to unload a chip before you give me the rest as points."

Caleb silently set down a 0-4. His face was a still mask, yet the hand which held the last of his chips jerked as if with an impulse he could not control.

Papito again inspected the dominoes laid out on the table and then those in his own hand. Earlier in the round he had realized it was crucial that anyone other than Gabriel win. He had desperately wanted that person to be Caleb. But with that possibility growing fainter and with Vicente possessing no aptitude for the game, it would have to be up to him to thwart Gabriel himself.

"Now who's the one dragging his feet?" Gabriel asked.

Agitated, Papito ran a hand through his thinning hair. Any pleasure he'd felt during the previous round had quickly dissipated when Gabriel had begun to rack up points. He watched him roll up his sleeves and undo several of the buttons on his shirt. Gabriel's gestures were similar to those of a rooster—a rooster fully aware of the eyes of others on him as he preened.

"Well, what's it gonna be?" Vicente asked, his tone indifferent.

"You tell me," Papito muttered.

"He'd be wasting his breath," Gabriel said. "It's not like he's holding something that could possibly stop me now."

Having little choice, Papito threw down a 4-3 beside Caleb's 0-4. Vicente followed by playing a 5-2 on the opposite end of the line of dominoes. Gabriel slammed down a 2-3 for Caleb who clearly had no more 3's.

"Take that, you wuss," he said.

Papito watched Caleb's right hand curl into a fist and his left grip his remaining dominoes so tightly that his knuckles bleached. As this same son balefully eyed Gabriel, Papito recalled the gun that Caleb had turned over to him a few weeks after Christmas the previous year—a gun whose glinting steel cold against his own palm had lent truth to Caleb's admission that he had purchased it to wield against the brother who had seduced his wife. That Gabriel had actually stooped to this betrayal and Caleb had then considered killing him had been such disturbing facts for Papito to keep in mind that he had promptly buried the evidence of his sons' antagonism in the backyard. He had mentally buried as deep the details of all that had transpired and had prayed that his sons eventually forget too. Yet as he now witnessed the tension in Caleb's hands and the insolence Gabriel foolishly displayed, he realized that neither had forgotten a thing and that the emotions of both were all the more volatile for having festered for a year.

"He's speechless," Raúl commented about Caleb.

"He's stumped, is more like it," Gabriel said. "He was probably cocky enough to have imagined that he would beat me."

For the umpteenth time, Papito had an urge to do physical harm to this son. "You talk to your brother like that one more time," he warned Gabriel, who he suspected had no idea of how close he had come and might still be to death, "and I'll knock your teeth out like I never did when you were young!"

"Take it easy, all of you," Vicente, who had no chance of winning, leaned forward to advise. "It's only a game."

"Yeah, right," Gabriel retorted. "I'd like to hear you say that about chess."

"Chess is different. It involves strategy and—"

Caleb abruptly raised a hand to prevent Vicente from saying more. "Just can it, okay?"

"Well, look who finally spoke," Gabriel said. "I thought you'd go down without a word."

Caleb turned ever so slowly to meet this brother's gaze. "You flap that tongue of yours like a rag," he said in an eerily subdued voice. "Anyone ever tell you that?"

Gabriel appeared about to laugh off the insult, yet his features unexpectedly grew still. "No," he murmured, "but a woman once told me—"

These words had barely been uttered when Caleb leapt off his chair to haul Gabriel from his. "A woman once told you what, you fuck?" His body, lean and taller than his brother's, heaved with rage as he seized him by the collar and slammed his head against a wall. "Huh? You want to tell me now?"

Papito approached his sons and was instantly shoved back by Caleb. Alerted by the tone of their voices, Aurelia and her daughters rushed into the room.

"Don't," Aurelia begged, pushing toward Caleb.

Papito yanked her out of the way as Caleb aimed a fist at Gabriel's face.

"Go ahead and hit me," Gabriel said. "You think I don't know you've been dying to for a year?"

Caleb responded by smashing the fist into his brother's mouth. Benny simultaneously maneuvered past the others and with Raúl's and Vicente's help managed to draw the men apart.

"Didn't I tell you?" Zoraida shrieked, shoving back the children who were attempting to get a glimpse into the room. "We should never have let them play!"

Gabriel drew himself upright and made a show of wiping the blood off his busted lips. "You feel better now?" he asked his brother. " 'Cause if you don't, I'll turn the other cheek and let you—"

"Why, you arrogant son-of-a-bitch!"

Caleb broke free just as Aurelia did the same to land a resounding slap on Gabriel's cheek.

"How dare you!" she said. "How dare you play the martyr now!"

In the astounded silence that ensued, Caleb snatched his coat from where it had fallen off his chair. Aurelia turned to him as he flung the garment on.

"Mi'jo, please," she began. But her son was already heading out.

CHAPTER

❖ 36 ❖

"A glass of wine," Marina said, employing the British accent she hoped conveyed to others just how sophisticated and sane she was.

"Wine?" Iliana asked.

Ed glanced from one sister to the other. "Aren't you Adventist? I thought no one in your family drank."

"What kind of wine?" the waitress asked.

Marina thought about it for a moment. She wanted something appropriate for one who had risen from the dead, something tasting of life itself and able to suggest Christ's sacrifice.

"Red wine," she answered firmly.

"Merlot, Pinot Noir, Cabernet Sauvignon?"

"Red wine. Very red like blood."

A series of expressions pulled at her sister's face. "You can have anything you want, Marina. A glass of juice, soda, even coffee—"

"I want wine."

"I'll have a Coke," Ed mumbled.

"Marina, please. You're on medication."

"I said I want red wine!"

"How about the house red?" the waitress asked.

"That's fine," Iliana muttered, attempting to feign calm. "She'll have a glass of that."

Satisfied, Marina eased back against her chair. She was conscious of Iliana and Ed looking anywhere but at her. All morning, as they'd trekked through Manhattan streets, they had glanced at her sideways and fractioned her with their eyes: focusing on her lips, her nose, her chin or an ear, as if the sum of her were too much to encompass and rarely her eyes, as if they alone reflected what neither could bear to see.

Not that their behavior surprised her. In fact, it made perfect sense. She was certain that she radiated power and that her eyes glowed as had Moses's when he descended from the mountaintop. She was also wise enough to know that the unworthy, having never looked upon God, could not look directly at one who had. Moreover, sin-stained, they were inevitably made uncomfortable by those who, like her, had passed through fire to emerge redeemed.

She leaned forward for her glass. Careful to avoid swallowing ice, she sipped the water, clear as the thoughts flowing through her brain.

"Is the food here any good?" she asked.

"I don't know," Iliana replied. "We've never been here."

Her anxiety was palpable. Marina felt it as acutely as she did the blue-grey smoke filtering from Ed's cigarette into her lungs. She suspected this anxiety was what prompted her sister to start chattering about the restaurant's decor. As Iliana spoke she avoided facing her as if to will her to disappear. But Marina would do no such thing. Instead, she intended to reveal to others what her sister did not wish for them to see. She had already taken measures to regain her strength so as to be able to carry out this plan. Ever since her first night at home she had been tucking inside her cheeks and later spitting out the pills her mother placed directly on her tongue. Her body, which she continued to move slowly in order to deceive, no longer felt submerged. Her narcotic haze had dispersed.

Marina watched her sister fumble with a menu. Iliana's hands were as wide as Ed's, her fingers just as long. It was those hands which had first hinted at her secret. Those hands were too large for a girl. Veins and bones showed through their skin. Their nails were bare of polish and trimmed short to detract attention from them. Because those hands nonetheless moved gracefully, Marina had briefly doubted her suspicions. Yet having spent the morning observing Ed's, she had confirmed that gestures did not necessarily reflect a person's sex. Ed, although conspicuously male, moved his hands as gracefully as did Iliana.

Other details coalesced with the theory forming in Marina's mind. She noticed the width of her sister's shoulders, the prominence of her forehead, the impudent curve of her full lips. She noticed too the hair pulled austerely into a ponytail like Ed's and the baggy sweater more appropriate for a man. She added to this list of evidence the fact that her sister disliked skirts and usually opted for pants loose enough to conceal her hips narrow as a boy's.

That something was strangely wrong was further evidenced by the lack of sexual tension between Ed and Iliana. They interacted as boys would have and teased each other as Marina had seen her brothers tease among themselves. Iliana also addressed her friend with ease. Not once had she deferred to him as women were supposed to do with men, nor had she expended any energy flirting or attempting to look pretty for his sake. This despite the fact that he was eligible, appeared to have genuine regard for her and was far more handsome than the men Marina herself had the opportunity to meet.

The longer she examined her sister's behavior the more unnatural it seemed. Even her voice, as she turned to ask what Ed would order, sounded inordinately deep.

Marina tallied up the mounting evidence, including what she had uncovered earlier that day. Feigning sleep, she had watched her sister move naked through their room. Iliana's body—with its meager breasts, long arms and massive hands, thin legs and knobby knees—had appeared as lean as a prepubescent girl's and more so like a boy's. Her gait, when she'd headed into the bathroom, had been the exaggerated walk of a man imitating a woman.

That walk had confirmed Marina's suspicions and lent truth to her parent's jesting assertion that their thirteenth child had defied fate by being born a girl. It had also persuaded her that, as such, her sister had usurped the position of seventh daughter and had hexed the preordained order intended for the eight boys and six girls their mother had been meant to bear. Equally paired, the fourteen children might have escaped the influence of selfishness and greed. They might have learned compassion and remained steadfast in their faith instead of attending church without any genuine belief in God.

Marina had then hit upon another alarming fact. The numbers seven and thirteen could only be divided by themselves and the number one. As such they were complete unto themselves and took into account no others. Following closely on the heels of this discovery was the realization that her youngest sister thought only of herself. She was as self-seeking as a man and, like Vicente, had abandoned home when she'd been needed most. Since her return, she had rarely concerned herself with the problems of her siblings. She was as indifferent as Tico, as confident about her opinions as Gabriel, as volatile as Caleb. Overall, she behaved more like her brothers and shared few of the personality traits of her sisters.

Seated across from her in the restaurant, Marina recalled having heard of children born in the Dominican Republic with both male and female organs. In such cases the penis had been snipped off to render the child a girl. However, it was obvious to her that other sexually confounding and harder-to-detect birth defects could occur. Of those she had considered, the most insidious was the possibility that a child could be born with male organs tucked inside. If such were the case with Iliana, it would be the reason why she'd never had a boyfriend, expressed no interest in marrying or bearing children, and appeared at moments like a woman but at others like a man. It would also account for why her parents, sensing that she was different, allowed her more freedom than they had granted their other girls.

"You should let your nails grow," Marina remarked, wanting to hear what her sister's excuse would be.

"Long nails would only get in my way."

"But they'd make your hands look pretty."

"I keep telling her the same thing," teased Ed. "But she won't listen."

"Next thing, you'll be saying I should've curled my hair."

Marina leaned forward with intent. "You should've. You'd look a lot more like a girl."

"It's not like I need to be wasting time trying to look girly every single day."

"It's not like you have anything better to do either," Ed said.

"He's right. I've seen you spend hours—"

"Who the hell are you?" Iliana snapped at Ed. "My guardian?"

Barbs of pain shot through Marina's head at the utterance of those words. Her ears simultaneously began to ring. It was as if a malevolent force had clapped its palms around them, as if another had jammed a fist into her mouth to prevent her from saying more. She slumped against her chair. Vise-like fingers clamped around her temples and strove, with devilish resolve, to obliterate her thoughts and hurl her back into the oblivion from which she had only recently emerged.

"I won't let you!" she shrieked, causing heads to turn throughout the restaurant. "I won't let you take me back!"

"What the hell—"

The ringing grew painfully shrill inside Marina's head. "Just stop!"

Ed tried to reach across the table for her hand.

"I know full well what the two of you are up to! Don't think for a moment that I don't!"

"What the hell did I do now?" her sister demanded.

"You don't fool me! I've seen the way you look at me! I've seen you passing signs! But God will cast you down instead!"

"Marina, please," Iliana begged. "People are—"

Marina barely heard her speak. She resisted the pull of gravity on her lids, resisted too the vise tightening around her skull.

God could not have summoned her back to life just to let her be cast back into hell. God could not mean for her to have suffered so in vain.

She called on Him for strength. Instantly, the chandeliers above her head began to swing. Beams of light sparked off them, dispersing the shadows that had threatened to encroach and allaying her fears. She watched in awe God's display of power on her behalf. It was then that she heard the rustling of His robes and felt the familiar ecstasy alerting her to His approach. She reverently bowed her head. His voice murmured in her ear, reassuring her of His love and leaving her with no doubt as to what it was He would have her do.

"I know you," she informed her sister as the waitress belatedly brought their drinks. "I know exactly what you are."

She raised her glass to chug back the wine whose crimson color and bitter taste reminded her of the blood shed on Calvary. Her sister watched her, bewildered, as she set down the empty glass.

"I'll take another," Marina told the waitress.

When Iliana leaned forward to object, Marina pegged her with a look that caused her to slump back against her chair.

Ed edged closer to his friend and surreptitiously sent her a look that conveyed: *I know now what you meant.*

"I know too," Marina murmured. "I know too."

CHAPTER

❖ 37 ❖

Iliana lay in bed. It was so dark in the basement room she shared with Marina that she was unable to detect even her own hands when she raised them to her eyes. Such darkness unnerved her. As a child she used to imagine that were her limbs to dangle over the bed's edge they would be devoured by darkness or by the evil lurking in its midst. She used to lie beside her sisters with her arms stiff against her sides and with her body pressed as close to theirs as they allowed. Well versed in the Bible from which she had early on taught herself to read, she had learned that Lucifer existed as surely as did God. She had also heard enough tales of ghosts and worse sighted by her parents in the Dominican Republic to know beyond a doubt that phantoms were real. Quick-witted, she had deduced from these accounts and those she read herself that evil arrived at dusk and left with dawn. She understood too that the devil had grown astute over aeons of observing mankind and could infer the thoughts of humans from their gestures; the minutest changes in their body temperature, pulse and breath; the slightest contraction of their pupils. He was also able to appear to them in the shape of their deepest fears and to possess their souls should they relax their guard. Tormented by this knowledge, she had deprived herself of sleep. She had also labored to regulate her breaths. Yet the more steadily she had tried to breathe the more spasmodic had been its rhythm. Certain that Satan and his hosts feasted on her fears, she had resorted to pulling blankets over her head and to leaving only her nose and mouth exposed. This continued to be one of the few ways in which she was able to drift cautiously into sleep.

Tonight, however, even this method failed her. She lay clutching the edges of the blankets she had tucked under her chin. Eyes staring into darkness, ears attuned to the merest whisper of a sound, she grappled with guilt and with the forebodings that had accompanied her to bed.

"We had a great day," she had told Aurelia, unwilling to admit she'd made a mistake by taking Marina out. "She and Ed got along well, and they both enjoyed the restaurant."

She had mentioned nothing about her sister's creating a scene, running the tab to over a hundred dollars Ed had reluctantly paid for with a credit card or imbibing several glasses too many of red wine.

"Don't worry. She's just tired," she had claimed, rushing her inebriated sister past their mother, down the basement stairs and directly into their bathroom where Marina had promptly agreed to brush her teeth. Iliana had been relieved and at the same time somewhat disconcerted. Based on her sister's behavior throughout that day, she had expected at least an argument. She had not anticipated that Marina would willingly disguise her liquor-smelling breath or keep from blurting out that she had partaken of the Holy Ghost.

Iliana could not shake off the certainty that her sister equated her with the devil and had some wicked plan in store. Already Marina had risen furtively from bed as if to ascertain that Iliana lay fast asleep. When Iliana had called her name, she had lain back down without bothering to reply.

Each of Iliana's senses was preternaturally alert. She could hear her sister's breaths, the shifting of dust in air, the sigh of darkness as if it were a living thing. Yet she no longer knew if her senses could be trusted. Several times during the night she had glimpsed a denser darkness moving toward her only to then hear Marina tossing in her bed. She had also felt breaths lightly brush her face and had caught whiffs of scents which, though not unpleasant, were nevertheless different from her own.

❖ ❖ ❖

Iliana seized the hand tugging at her blankets. She simultaneously shot up to pull the string of a bulb hanging directly above her bed.

"What—what's wrong?"

"I'm cold," Marina said. "Can I sleep with you?"

Were it not for the abruptness with which Marina's teeth began to chatter and the contrived manner in which she then wrapped her arms around herself, Iliana might've been persuaded that her sister was genuinely cold. Yet both her claim and question had been too direct for someone in her mental state. Marina no longer conversed clearly. She spoke in tangents and ellipses, her motives hidden, her words circling her thoughts. Her request would have been just as alarming had she been sane. Theirs was a family in which it was taboo to express intimacy or to expose their bodies. Even as children, when she and her sisters had slept several to a bed, they had shared blankets under which each lay separated by her own sheet. Moreover, eventually getting to sleep in individual beds had been for each the equivalent of sleeping in separate rooms. They did not willingly share theirs unless driven by circumstances they could not avoid in any other way.

Iliana racked her brain in search of an excuse. There was no way she could allow her sister to share her bed. Ever since her nights at school, lonely nights when her mother's voice had lulled her to sleep with tales of the Dominican Republic evocative enough to make her sweat under an imaginary sun, she had taken to sleeping nude.

"Can I sleep with you?" Marina asked again.

Against all logic, Iliana was pervaded by fears similar to those she had experienced at school seconds before a student who'd stalked her had drunkenly forced himself on her late one night. On that occasion the source of her danger had been conspicuous. But it was no stranger standing before her now. It was her sister, whom she was meant to trust, her sister, with whom she had shared the greater part of her life.

"I—I don't think that's a good idea. My bed's too small. You'd be—you'd be better off in yours."

"But I'm cold."

Anxiety dampened Iliana's palms. "Here." She peeled off one of her blankets and held it out. "If you want, I can go find you more. They'll keep you warm for sure."

Marina snatched the blanket and flung it back. Iliana was assailed by a memory of this sister barging into the bathroom to see between her thighs. What this memory suggested was so horrifying that she instantly dismissed it.

"Marina, please," she said, attempting to feign calm. "I'm tired. You must be too. You should get back into bed."

Her sister startled her by actually stepping back.

"If you—if you need anything, just wake me. I'll—I'll be right here," Iliana added.

She tucked the edges of the blankets under her body and meticulously arranged her pillow. She did all this in the hope that by the time she'd finished Marina would have returned to bed. As a last resort she sat up and reluctantly turned off the light.

"Do you want me to—to go upstairs and heat you up some milk?" she offered, when her sister started pacing.

The only response was Marina's footsteps.

"Why don't you go to bed?"

Still, Marina said nothing.

"Marina?"

Silence followed, and then what could only have been the creaking of springs on Marina's bed. Relief flooded Iliana as she leaned back against the headboard of her own. It was then that her sister leapt through darkness to hurl herself onto her bed. Iliana felt the cold rush of air and the burn of friction as the blankets were stripped from her. She felt the pressure of her sister's body on her own.

"What the fuck!"

Her head was knocked against the headboard, her body dragged until it lay flat.

"Marina, no!"

Pubic hairs pricked Iliana's shins, her knees, her thighs as her sister humped up along them to seize her arms. These were forced together at the wrists with one hand as the other clawed at and pried her thighs apart.

Every cell in Iliana's body rebelled. Every circuit in her brain shrieked no. Yet her sister's strength, fueled by madness, was far greater than her own.

"Wake up, Tico! Please!"

Iliana freed her hands to claw at her sister, but her nails were short and Marina's skin rubbery and thick. She clenched her fingers into fists and aimed, but it was as if Marina had merged with darkness and could see clearly enough to avoid the blows.

"Tico!"

Her sister's hand tore into her. The pain, when it shot through her, was incisive as a blade.

"Ticohhhhhhhhh—"

Back arched against the raging pain, hands clawing futilely at the fitted sheet, Iliana thrashed and writhed. The world, as she had known it, crashed irrevocably around her head as her sister's hand curled into a fist. Her thoughts screeched mercifully to a halt as that fist crashed against her womb.

"What's going on?" Tico muttered, his voice pebbled with the remains of sleep as he flicked on a light in his sisters' room.

Two hundred pounds shifted on Iliana.

"Nothing!" Marina yelled. "Just get back to your room!"

Iliana's eyes opened.

"Tico—"

She did not know if she continued in the throes of a nightmare or was just then waking. She was not sure if she had conjured her brother or if he was really standing at the bedroom door.

"I almost had it!" Marina shrieked, yanking her hand out from between her sister's thighs. "I almost had it in my hand!"

Tico leapt toward the bed. With wondrous agility and strength, he hoisted Marina off Iliana.

Iliana shut her eyes and did not move. She suspected that if she stirred her head would roll off her neck as it often had in dreams. She suspected that her limbs would forsake her body and drop lifelessly to the floor.

"I was right!" her sister shrieked again. "I knew it all along!"

Should Iliana open her eyes slowly, slowly; should she move with the utmost care; should she concede that waking too was part of the dream she dreamed, she might succeed in summoning the willpower which on occasion had enabled her to alter the course of dreams. She might succeed in keeping herself intact regardless of what else transpired in the expanding realm of what she now feared.

Anything was possible. Anything. The truth of this had finally been driven home. Therefore, the same had to apply to her. For good or bad, she needed to accept this truth as well.

A determination to defy fear lent her the courage to shift toward the bed's edge and to look at her sister's face. To her surprise, what she saw evoked no emotional response. It was as if her brain had short-circuited and was unable to process the information it received, as if she had detached from her surroundings and nothing but her own will had the power to affect her now.

"You fucking bitch!" her brother yelled, kicking their sister where she lay. "I should have killed you the night you snuck into my room!"

Marina gaped up at Tico from the floor. She seemed unable to believe that she lay prostrate or that he, inches shorter and not much more than half her weight, had overpowered her alone.

Iliana drew her legs together and sat up on her bed. Blood stained the sheet and oozed from the claw marks on her thighs. She wiped some off and covered herself with a blanket. She then eased her legs off the bed and teetered to a stand.

"Oh, Iliana," her brother moaned.

"I'm fine," she mumbled.

Tico placed a hand on her bare shoulder. Iliana immediately brushed it off.

"I'm so sorry," he said, his voice splintering as if from the bur-

den of what he'd seen. "I'm so sorry. I thought you were screaming in my dreams. I thought—"

"I'm fine," Iliana repeated, unwilling to have him confirm
what had occurred.

"Do you want me to wake Mom up? Do you want me to—"

"No!"

"But she—" A sob erupted from Tico's throat. "She might—"

"She didn't do anything to me."

Marina chose that moment to rise off the floor and pull her
crumpled nightgown down over her naked hips.

"I saw," Tico murmured. "I saw—"

His voice affected Iliana as a mere buzzing in her ears. Trans-
fixed, she watched him look anywhere but at her. She became
convinced that she was vanishing bit by bit and that he was losing
his ability to see her. She confirmed this by stepping close and staring boldly at the heart-shaped mole pulsing erratically on his neck.
That mole had started out at his nape and, over the years, had traveled to the cleft below his Adam's apple. As a child she had begged
him to trade it for the stationary mole at the corner of her left eye.
She had coveted his mole so badly that he would willingly have
traded it if he could.

"Nothing happened," she repeated when his gaze remained
averted. "I'm fine."

Her brother's muscular shoulders sagged. It struck her than that
he was almost an adult. She hadn't noticed this before. She hadn't
noticed that the baby brother who had once led her through darkened rooms she had been afraid of entering on her own had grown
up while she'd been gone.

"You can't sleep here, Iliana. I won't let you. I won't—"

Iliana stepped past him into the bathroom and deliberately
locked its door behind her. The blanket she had wrapped around
herself fell to her feet. Cloaked in darkness, she groped for the toilet's lid and soundlessly lowered it over the seat. Drafts seeped in
through the room's chinked walls as she sat down. The concrete
floor oozed cold. Yet she was insensitive to these discomforts and
aware of her body only as part of the darkness that concealed it
from her eyes.

She told herself there was no need to make a fuss, no need to wake her parents, no need to wipe the blood off her thighs or to consider in other ways the body that had been violated for what amounted to a mere fraction of her existence. She was far more than the sum of her spilled blood and her flesh that had been pierced. She was the breaths seeping from her lips, the heart resounding in her chest, the anima enabling her to perceive.

This was the litany that buoyed her thoughts. Bodies recovered. Wounds healed. Scars faded and left no mark.

It was her sister who needed to be pitied, her sister who'd lost her mind and had no sway over the tenets of her own soul. Emotionally, Iliana was the stronger of the two. She knew this now. Besides, her sister had not meant her any harm. It was her madness which had lashed out—a destructive madness incapable of making distinctions and as likely to be turned on Marina herself.

As their mother had once said, Marina impulsively gathered stones. She flung them at whoever was around and shortly forgot they had escaped her hands. Compassion made it necessary for those who loved her to dodge out of harm's way. If struck, it was best that they themselves forget. Forgetting required no effort on Iliana's part. Nor did forgiving. Already the anger she'd harbored throughout most of her nineteen years had been consumed in the wake of her sister's hand. What remained of rage cooled like ash beneath her tongue.

She had no use for emotions now. To rail against what had been done to her would be to credit her sister's madness with having affected her. It would be to confer on the fleeting a permanence able to haunt her for the remainder of her years.

In order to stay sane she needed to proceed as if nothing significant had occurred. She needed to leave the bathroom and climb fearlessly back into her bed. Were she to flee upstairs, she would forever glance over her shoulder to see if danger followed close behind. Her soul would constrict with paranoia. Her will would become as impotent as the fists she had tried to wield in self-defense.

Dizziness made a vortex of darkness as Iliana leaned forward to retrieve the blanket. She shut her eyes and waited for the floor to level, for the plummeting ceiling to rise again. Heartbeats later, she shrouded her nakedness and eased herself to a stand.

Several feet forward and she would open the bathroom door and step out into her room. A few feet more and she would reach her bed.

Considering nothing beyond the motion of her limbs, Iliana dragged her feet along the basement's concrete floor. Her sister lay inert under a sheet. Oddly enough, her arms were folded across her chest as if she would never again wake.

Iliana stepped past Marina into the walk-in closet. She turned on its light and left its door ajar. She then flicked off the light her brother had left on and apprehensively climbed back into her bed.

Faulty wiring caused the closet light to flicker, lending the bedroom's furniture spectral shapes and making them appear to heave. The walls themselves seemed to tilt, the floor to ripple as if it were liquid reflecting concrete.

Iliana lay wide-awake. Minutes later she saw her sister rise and turn off the closet light. She instantly pulled the string of the brighter bulb above her bed.

"We can't afford to waste electricity," Marina scolded.

There was no trace of sleep or madness in her voice. Yet there was malice in her eyes as she reached to turn off the bedroom light.

Iliana feebly pushed her sister's hand aside.

Marina watched her with intent. "You afraid of me?"

"Either the closet light stays on or this one does."

"You don't have to be," Marina murmured.

"I'm not—"

Marina smiled. "You want the closet light on, turn it on yourself." She returned to her queen-sized bed and climbed under its sheet. "You better turn off that light, Iliana."

"I need—"

"It's too bright. If you're afraid, just turn the one in the closet on."

Iliana remained in bed, unsure as to what to do.

"You heard me, Iliana. I don't want to have to tell you one more time."

Iliana reluctantly slid one leg, then the other off the bed. Wrapped in blankets, she edged along a wall into the closet. It was then she thought she heard a mattress creaking followed by what might've been muffled steps.

"Marina?"

The silence from the bedroom was oppressive. Iliana turned on the closet light and warily stepped out. A razor-blade scream sliced from her throat as her sister leapt from behind the closet door to knock her back onto her bed.

Hatred was visible in Marina's eyes: raw, unadulterated hatred that confirmed those times Iliana had detected glimmers of it but had dismissed it, times when her sister had said, "You're so beautiful, so smart, so cool." Hatred that now conveyed: *You think you're so special, so goddamn smart and cute! Let's see what you think of yourself after I'm through!* This hatred paralyzed Iliana as the blankets were again stripped from her body, her legs violently pried apart. This hatred pierced her infinitely deeper than the hand thrust between her thighs.

Tico rushed like a madman into the room and flung himself onto his sister's bed. Marina yanked her hand free to fight him off.

Scream upon scream surged from Iliana's throat, spilling out of her mouth like blood, flooding in waves throughout the house.

"What's going on here?" her father demanded from the stairs.

Rebecca stumbled into the room only to recoil and retreat in horror. Papito darted in with Aurelia following close behind.

"Carajo!" Papito sprinted forward. Tico scrambled out of the way as Marina was lifted bodily and hurled back onto her bed.

"No, Papito!" Aurelia threw herself against him as he aimed a fist at Marina's face.

"Let go of me! This is all your fault! Had it been up to me I would've had her locked up long ago!"

"Do you plan to strike me too?"

"I told you to let me go!"

Aurelia crushed herself against him all the more. "Look at us, Papito! For God's sake!"

Her husband attempted to shove her off only to succumb to tears.

"Just go," Aurelia told him. "Just go. I'll take care of things down here. You go too," she said to Tico standing in shock beside the door. "Just go on back into your room."

Iliana watched her mother nudge them out. Not once had any of them focused eyes on her. Their failure to have done so convinced her that her sister had effectively thrust her to the extremes of their peripheral sight where she was glimpsed, if at all, as no more than an abstraction.

She rose unsteadily from bed. Certain of her invisibility, she made no effort to hide her nudity or shame.

Aurelia turned back into the room. Either by sound or gifted sight, she located her youngest daughter as she stumbled toward the door. Her gaze was so penetrating that Iliana instinctively covered her breasts and pubes.

"She couldn't have known what she was doing," Aurelia murmured. "She couldn't have."

Iliana concentrated on holding herself erect, concentrated too on keeping her limbs from severing and her head from rolling off.

"You see?" Marina said. "Your baby girl is fine."

The equilibrium with which Iliana had managed to endure her mother's gaze was instantly displaced by her sister's voice. Her body shuddered, jerked forward, shook spasmodically and did not still.

Her sister knew. Her sister knew precisely what it was she'd done. She knew and was pleased that no one else would ever detect what it was she had destroyed. She knew and depended on shame to silence Iliana and to efface whatever self she'd been.

Iliana reeled toward the bedroom door. When her mother reached for her, she tore away and hurled herself up the basement stairs. Waves of nausea bent her body as she reached the first-floor landing. She pushed past the kitchen door and staggered toward the sink. Clutching its edge, she yielded to convulsions that sent bile and partially digested food heaving from her mouth. Her primary thought was that she wanted to go home.

Every spasm of her body, every tremor and heave only reminded her that she was already there.

CHAPTER
❖ 38 ❖

Aurelia sprang from the hard-backed chair on which she had spent the night. Here it was a new day and she had ushered it in by breaking the first of many promises she'd made. This thought tormented her as she rushed into the living room to find Iliana curled on the couch with blankets tangled around legs that must have thrashed in sleep. Alarmed by what Iliana's hand shielding her private parts had acutely conveyed, she had posted herself by the kitchen door leading from the hallway and had vowed to stay alert should Iliana cry out from nightmares or Marina creep up the basement stairs. All this task had required of her was that she keep her eyes open and her ears attuned. Yet her resolve to protect her youngest daughter had been insufficient even to help her ward off sleep.

Each of Aurelia's justifications for bringing Marina home now served only to accuse her. She was unable to deny that it was foolishness which had led her to believe this daughter would fare better in the care of family rather than in the custody of doctors. Heady from her victory over Pasión, she had assumed that everything pertaining to her family could be brought under her direct control. She had purposefully forgotten the many times she had been unable to curb Marina's violence. Worse, she had relied on the caprice of preternatural senses to inform her of impending danger when common sense alone should have alerted her to the risk inherent in keeping under her wing a daughter whose delusions enabled her to justify the most atrocious acts.

Faced with the aftermath of Marina's violence, Aurelia was

confronted with her own and hounded by the notion that the previous night's events had been fate's perverse retribution for her
crime. Plainly and simply, she had committed murder. She had
perfidiously convinced herself that Pasión deserved to die and had
thought little of the consequences.

Tears of remorse and grief spilled from her eyes. She had no
faith left with which to face the day. Throughout everything she'd
done, she had believed that love for her children justified any act.
Not once had she considered that she might wreak havoc in their
lives.

She drew the blankets over Iliana. Stepping from the couch, she
noticed that one of the floor's marble tiles had cracked. She then
imagined that the slightest disturbance might topple furniture,
collapse shelves, detach the chandelier. That she and her husband
had managed to purchase all these things as well as their own home
had often been offered as proof to their children of the stability in
their lives. Only now did she concede that nothing was stable—
nothing. The earth itself might give out under their feet, their
house burn down, madness take root, evil unfold into their lives.

Aurelia trudged back into the kitchen. From her bedroom
came the sound of Papito readying himself for work. She reached
into the refrigerator for eggs and above it for a bag of bread. She
then mechanically cracked the eggs into a greased skillet and
popped the bread slices into a toaster. She was about to reach back
into the fridge when her brain rebelled against the prospect of
pouring milk, flipping eggs, buttering the toast. The very banality
of these acts thrust her into a chair from which she doubted she
would ever rise again.

"For God's sake, Aurelia!"

Her husband entered the room and quickly switched the flame
off under the burning eggs, unplugged the toaster, extracted the
blackened toast.

"That's all we need! A fire!"

He dumped the bread into the trash and slammed the skillet
into the sink.

"Didn't you smell the smoke?"

Aurelia stared indifferently past her husband. He turned from her in frustration and was about to run water into the skillet when he noticed the vomit congealing in the sink.

"And what the hell is this?"

Aurelia did not reply.

"Marina did this?"

Ever so slowly, his wife directed her eyes toward his.

"Oh," he sighed, his anger instantly deflating. "Oh."

He turned on the taps full force and wearily scrubbed the sink. When he finished, he sat down beside Aurelia.

"We can't go on like this," he said. "We just can't. I have to go to work today, but tonight or first thing tomorrow morning we have to take Marina in."

A flock of pigeons flew into view through the kitchen window. Several of them perched on the sill and pecked hungrily at the glass.

"It's for her own good, Aurelia. You know that. She'd have an eye on her all the time. And the hospital isn't far. We could visit her every day."

The pecking at the window grew insistent. Aurelia rose from her chair and slammed her hand on the glass to shoo the birds.

"Believe me," Papito muttered, "you're not the only one who's upset by all of this. It means we failed and couldn't take care of her ourselves."

Aurelia's hand shook visibly against the glass.

"Fine. We don't have to talk about this now. But we're going to have to when I get home. I refuse to make this decision on my own."

Papito departed from the room. Minutes later he returned wearing his coat. Only then did Aurelia turn to face him.

"I—I can't help you," she blurted out. "You have to—to make that decision on your own."

Papito sighed. "I know this is all too much to take in at one time, but we both need to be strong."

Aurelia's tongue went dry in the cavity of her mouth. "It's not that. It's not that at all."

"Sssssssh," Papito murmured. "We don't have to talk about this or make a decision until tonight."

"You don't understand. Everything last night. It was all my fault. If I hadn't—"

Her husband drew her into his arms. "There was nothing either of us could do, Aurelia. We were—"

"Yes there was! I—"

"We were sleeping, Aurelia. Sleeping. We ran down as soon as we—"

"But Iliana, Papito! Iliana—"

"Iliana will be okay, she's the smartest of our girls and knows Marina has done worse things. She'll—"

"No!" Aurelia jerked out of Papito's arms. "No! Iliana won't be okay! Don't you understand what Marina—"

"Ya, Aurelia, please. We're going to get Marina help. Tonight we'll—"

Aurelia backed out of his reach. "Just go," she gasped, realizing then that he did not know. "Just go. I need to get some rest. I'll see things clearer then."

Aurelia paced the kitchen floor. Each time she took notice of her high-strung movements she tried to sit only to again leap onto her feet. Every nerve in her body felt on edge. Every thought contradicted those that followed. Irrationally, she longed for the counsel of one who had been long dead. Surely her mother, who had wielded powers similar to those she had disastrously employed, would have been able to tell her how to proceed.

A legacy of woe: this was what she now concluded Bienvenida had cursed her with. Yet even as she thought so, she recalled other gifts her mother had bestowed—gifts intended to guide her in the use of those only she and a brother had inherited.

"Because I want you never to forget," Bienvenida had said, handing her the quilt pieced with reminders of family deaths that had resulted from old age, malnutrition, disease but as often from sorrow, madness, deceit and guilt. "Because the future will hurt you worse if you deny the past."

Aurelia again saw the faded colors of that quilt. In her mind's eye she also saw the burlap sack containing dirt, an earthen jug, a piece of glass, a stone, a bone, a feather, a bit of bark. She recalled her mother's pronouncements as pertained to each, but she was unable to attribute meaning to the words.

Frustrated, she opened the refrigerator with the intention of preparing breakfast for her grandchildren. Her attention was immediately diverted to the filth inside. A cracked egg had leaked its stench, spilled milk had curdled, produce she bought in bulk lay rotting, bottles were gummy with rancid condiments. She impetuously loaded her arms with the first things her hands could reach. After dumping the items on the kitchen table, she returned to the refrigerator and zealously threw out overripe tomatoes, wilted lettuce, spawning onions and potatoes she would have tried to salvage prior to that day. She then discarded any leftovers into the trash, filled a pot with scalding water, located a box of Brillo pads, fell to her knees and remained there until she had scrubbed the fridge. Still not satisfied, she rose to battle the freezer too.

Boxes of food were frozen in mounds of ice. She pried loose those she could. Unwilling to admit defeat, she employed a knife to chip off ice she heedlessly flung onto the floor. It then dawned on her that a hammer would better serve her purpose. She left the kitchen in a mess and darted into her room to search through her husband's tools.

Their bed was a rumple of linen. She fluffed its pillows, folded blankets, smoothed sheets, and spread a bedspread over the mattress. This done, she employed brute strength to haul the tool box from under the bed. She was about to reach inside it when she realized that she had forgotten to give Marina her medication. All thoughts of defrosting the freezer were chased from her mind as she searched through a drawer for the vials she kept hidden from her daughter. She had found the ones she needed when her eyes were drawn in the direction of a clock. Only then did she register the silence throughout the house—a silence all the more alarming for resounding as loudly as her grandchildren's voices usually had by that time of the day.

Disheartened, Aurelia rose to her feet. There was no need for her to hurry now. Regardless of whether she rushed downstairs to give Marina her pills or out into the streets to locate Rebecca who she assumed had returned with her children to Pasión, misfortune would continue to precede her.

She left the bedroom and made her way through the kitchen she had wrecked with her good intent. She then proceeded out into the hallway and down the wooden stairs which moaned under her feet.

"Mami?" a child called out from the rear of the basement.

Aurelia gripped the banister to absorb the shock of hearing her grandson's voice.

"Can we get up now? Please?"

Steadying her racing heart, she rounded the stairs and stepped toward the makeshift bedroom lit by shafts filtering in through dusty panes.

"She's gone, isn't she?" her eldest grandchild blurted out.

Aurelia could think of no reply.

"I told you," Esperanza hissed, turning on Rubén.

"But she said—"

"You so stupid! You think she'd keep us in bed just so she could go talk to Abuela?"

"Then why didn't you go upstairs and check?"

"Because—"

"Because why?"

"Just shut your face!" Esperanza shrieked, leaping into her brother's cot and pummeling him with the force of her unexpected rage. "Just shut your stupid face!"

Aurelia darted forward to pry the two of them apart.

"It's not my fault she went back!" Rubén sobbed.

"I told you to shut your face!"

Soledad peered wide-eyed from under blankets as Esperanza struggled to break free from their grandmother, then unexpectedly gave in to tears.

"She said sheshe'd—we'd be in trouble if we got out of bed. She said she—we—we're always being bad and that's why Papapi hits her."

"Listen to me," Aurelia instructed. "Listen to me." She sat on a cot so as to be level with the child. "Sometimes adults say things they don't really mean. It's what happens when they feel bad."

Esperanza shook her head in vehement dispute. The other children remained still, their solemn expressions conveying that they too rejected their grandmother's glib excuse.

Aurelia released Esperanza and hid her trembling hands between her thighs. Again, she found herself thinking of all she had failed to say to her husband before he left for work. She also thought of the many more things she had never revealed to her children or her grandchildren: details of their own and of their family's past which might have helped them better understand themselves as well as the world through which they moved. The silence enveloping these legacies, the half-truths meant to gloss over and protect, the falsehoods uttered for fear of causing pain, and the inability or unwillingness to speak, now seemed to her to have inflicted greater harm.

Look at her grandchildren whose fragmented views of their lives led them to blame themselves for circumstances over which they had no control; at their mother who continued to believe herself unworthy because of misunderstandings originating as far back as her childhood; at Iliana, perplexed by traits she had inherited from her grandmother and been told nothing at all about.

By uttering one of many truths now, Aurelia might undo the lie her eldest daughter had told her grandchildren. She might absolve them of their guilt, if not reduce the impact they were sure to suffer upon learning of their father's death.

"There's something you need to know," she told them. "Your father—your father has been beating your mother since before any of you were born."

Her grandchildren's shock was obvious.

"That means that your father hitting your mother has nothing to do with you. It doesn't even have to do with her." Aurelia groped for words with which to explain what she was not sure that she herself understood. "The truth is that none of us know why he does. All we know is that he's been doing it for a long time. That's why your mother is so unhappy. That's why she's scared enough to be mean." Her gaze settled on Esperanza. "How she feels is sort of like how you felt a few minutes ago when you hit your brother. It's also like how he felt the other day when we were skinning beans."

"Yeah, but she went back," Rubén pointed out. "She doesn't— she doesn't care about—"

"Go on," Aurelia prompted.

"She just doesn't care. That's all. She doesn't care."

Something merciless radiated from Esperanza's eyes as she withdrew from Aurelia to sit beside Rubén. "If someone hit me, you wouldn't find *me* going back."

A sigh escaped from Aurelia's lips. She averted her eyes and watched as specks of dust drifted toward windows where they appeared to be held aloft by light.

As much as she wanted to dispute her grandchildren's words, as much as she wanted to tell them they had no right to judge their mother, no right to say what they would or would not do if in her place, she found that she could not.

Defeated, she fingered the vials of medication she had placed in the pockets of her housecoat—the same pockets which, days earlier, had held the food her grandchildren had hidden throughout the house as well as the scissors she had employed to snip off their mother's hair. Less than a week had elapsed since then and she felt as if months had gone by instead, felt too as if she could not possibly withstand another day.

She released the vials and dropped her forehead onto her palms. Soledad, the youngest of Rebecca's children, slid from bed and, twining arms around her grandmother, began to rock her. Aurelia submitted to the tenderness of those arms, to their lulling motion, to their unexpected strength.

To remind you that in our blood we carry the power of the sea, she heard Bienvenida say. *To quell your fear of darkness and teach your spirit that it can soar.*

Aurelia again gazed at the faces of her grandchildren who had experienced far more than children their age—or anyone, for that matter—should have experienced. Their existence was proof that life was a deviant path. Yet the miracle was that, despite misery, her grandchildren's will endured. The miracle was that, young as they were, they were making her understand what her mother had tried to convey to her so many years before: that genuine power originated from a soul resilient enough to persevere against all odds.

"It's true your mother went back," she admitted, valiantly rising above her own despair. "But this time will be different. This time she'll be changed when she returns. . . ."

CHAPTER
❖ 39 ❖

Rebecca gulped cold air, exhilarated by its sting on her face and by the sunlight filtering through her half closed lids. She felt as giddy as a child and as carefree as when she used to sneak out to the countryside in the Dominican Republic to experience the thrill of grass and the warmth of rays on her naked skin. Desire unfurled along her limbs, rejuvenating her cells and sensitizing them to the rub of clothes and to the fierce caress of wind. She wanted nothing less than to submit again to the possessive passion that usually overtook her husband after she'd been gone. She longed, with an urgency that kept her legs moving quickly, to lose herself in his embrace, to experience the familiar rush of blood and loss of breath, to feel the laying on of his long-fingered hands and the demanding weight of his body on her own. Her lust was ravenous enough to make her swallow her shame at slinking back but disconcerting enough to have her concocting alternate reasons for why she had chosen to return.

One more day of her mother's undermining her authority as a parent and she would have torn out the little hair she had left. At least by returning home her time would be her own, her children hers to raise as she saw fit. The previous night's events had also established that her children were at risk living in the same house as their aunt. Out of necessity, she had left them there while she went to mend things with Pasión. But first chance she got, she planned to return them to their rightful home.

She rounded a corner onto her block. Inserting first one key, then another into locks, she pushed open her front door. A stench of decay wafted out. She had forgotten the vigor of that smell, had forgotten too the chickens by now rotting in the third-floor coop. She hesitated outside the door. In an abrupt deviation of her thoughts she blamed her mother for the revenge Pasión would inflict on her for the death of his beloved birds. The perverse gratification of being able to hold someone else responsible for her predicament lent her the courage to step inside. She had just flicked on a light and slammed the door shut when she was astonished to see a hen scurrying through the corridor. Her first thought was that someone had broken into the house and set the chickens loose. Yet she as quickly recalled that in her eight years of living there the stench alone had been enough to keep intruders out.

Every one of her senses went on alert. She heard a rooster crow, then a rustling of wings throughout the house. A sense of foreboding electrified the short hairs on her nape. Stepping forward, she apprehensively climbed the stairs heaped with pornographic magazines, rusting coils, dismembered mannequins and toys. She reached the second-floor landing and maneuvered through a corridor cluttered with auto parts, bicycle frames, warped mirrors and other refuse her husband haphazardly collected. Shafts of light straining in through a skylight's dusty panes revealed hens roosting along the balustrade as well as on the third-floor landing. Feathers were everywhere. Bird droppings coated almost everything in sight.

Rebecca cupped a hand over her mouth and nose and steeled herself against the stench. A hen swooped at her from above. She dodged out of its way and proceeded up the stairs. Other birds leapt toward her in a pandemonium of dust and wings. She gripped the banister and clumsily fought them off. Compelling her forward was a determination to lock up the birds gone wild. Gathering at her core was a fear compounded by her inability to replace any of the dead birds with live ones from the market and by the fact that her husband would know exactly how many had expired as a result of her neglect.

Her feet tripped on the carcasses of birds as she continued

toward the third floor. It was then that she glimpsed Pasión. Hens nested on his body. His face lay partially hidden under feathers and debris.

Rebecca flung herself up the remaining stairs and recklessly lashed out at the birds. Their squawks were deafening, their strength alarming as they retaliated in an onslaught of beaks and wings.

"Damn it, Pasión!" She dropped to her knees beside him. Heedless of the birds pecking at her hands, she seized him by his lapels and attempted to make him sit. "I've had it with your games!" she shrieked, denying the evidence before her eyes. "This time you've gone too far!" She released him to pound him with her fists. Just as abruptly, she fell back against a wall.

Her husband remained unearthly still. Feathers had been sucked into his mouth. Bits of flesh had been plucked from his face flaking in places with dried blood. As for his eyes—eyes whose brown had been delicately flecked with gold—all that remained of them were orbs of congealed red.

A wail surged from Rebecca's lips. There had been so many times she had dismissed her husband's asthma as an excuse not to remain with her in the house. So many times she had pitied herself as she had watched him gasp for air and stumble out of bed to spend his night with someone else.

She reached her left hand toward her right and deliberately worried the flesh the hens had clawed. Insensitive to the pain, she pressed down on frail bones, dug nails into fresh wounds, picked at the cast under which her broken fingers had not yet set.

Every aspect of her husband's appearance suggested that his had not been a mercifully quick death. Claw marks at his throat revealed that he had tried to dig an alternate route through which to breathe. His legs hanging over the first few stairs indicated that he had attempted to escape only to be hindered by the trash he himself had hauled into the house.

Rebecca continued to stare at her husband's lifeless body. Despite her own stillness, despite her unblinking eyes and suspended breath, she found her thoughts hurtling forward as each of her justifications for coming home toppled to expose the subterfuge of her existence. Only now that Pasión lay dead did she recognize that he alone had been the reason for her return. Only now that he would never again tower over her or raise a hand to strike her did she concede that she had depended on his abuse to be the ongoing and conspicuous reason for her despair, the catchall for her failures and disappointments, the attribute of their marriage which was to have exonerated her of both blame and responsibility for her own and her children's lives. Not once had she considered that he might actually be ill. In her imagination, stoked by his abuse, she had rendered him invincible. As such, she had taken it for granted that he'd outlive her.

Tears streamed from Rebecca's eyes. Eight years of believing herself misunderstood and it was she who'd understood little, she who had misjudged her husband and abandoned him to a solitary death.

Her body heaved with sobs. Choking on remorse and grief, she remembered the egotism and passivity with which she had held Pasión accountable for the misery in her life while discounting the tenderness he had sporadically displayed—a tenderness which had been her only source of joy. She also recalled his laying his giant's body beside hers on their bed and for the first time acknowledged that, unlike Samuel who had rejected her after learning she was unable to provide him with a green card, Pasión had desired her solely for herself and had not once asked for anything she wouldn't have been able to provide. Yet even what she could have dutifully offered him as a wife—unconditional love, a well-kept house, nourishing and homemade meals—she had given grudgingly or not at all.

Rebecca inched closer to her husband. In his blood-encrusted eyes she saw proof of his vulnerability. In his feather-stuffed, gaping mouth she found evidence of the love he must have borne for her and their children to have repeatedly returned to them regardless of the risk posed by entering the house.

She reached out a hand to touch his face. It briefly appeared to her that his eyes were again whole, that his nostrils had inflated, that his lips had moved as if to speak. She slipped her thumb and forefinger into his mouth. Needing to absorb into her affection-starved soul the love that fate had allowed her to perceive only by means of her husband's death, she withdrew a wad of feathers and planted a tender kiss on his lips.

With the audacity of one who had everything to gain and little but her soul at stake, she then vowed that death would not rob her of Pasión. Before she notified anyone of his demise, before she allowed others to share in her grief or to express relief, she would bathe him and return to him the dignity that death had robbed him of. She would trace with her fingers and commit to memory the contours of his body which would finally be hers alone. Only when its details had been etched indelibly into her brain, only when she knew she'd be able to resuscitate his flesh and lend him breath with thoughts, only when she could conjure him at will and love him with an intensity which she had failed to offer him in life, would she allow his body to be interred.

CHAPTER

❖ 40 ❖

Iliana slowly, methodically, buttoned up her coat. She would be all right as long as she did not glance at her reflection in the hallway mirror. Were she to look and find that her face bore scars or that her eyes conveyed how she'd been marked, her remaining self-control would thaw and she'd be unable to bring herself to set foot back inside her parents' house once she ventured outside their door.

Tense, she stepped out onto the stoop and past the gate. Although she had made no plans with Ed, she hoped to persuade him to accompany her to Central Park. She wanted to leave Brooklyn's filth behind, needed desperately to exchange concrete and brick for earth and trees. It mattered little that the park would be sheathed in ice-packed mud or that the limbs of trees would be weighted down by snow. Her eyes would be satisfied with any bit of green they might chance upon; her ears would welcome the wind whistling as if across great distances.

She turned off Bradford at Atlantic and headed toward Van Siclen. There, she waited for the traffic light to change. She sincerely believed—if only because she felt trapped inside her skin as well as in the city where she was able to see no further than to the next block—that were she to walk aimlessly in the park she would eventually stumble on the one justification able to reconcile her to all that had occurred. It was only a matter of finding the time and space to think. It had to be. Somewhere in her thoughts was sure to be the key which would enable her to proceed from that day on.

Three men watched her as she stepped off the curb and crossed the street. A "Give me a smile, won't you, babe?" and she feared that she would fly apart. She quickened her steps to pass them by. Seconds later she heard one of the men behind her.

"Meeeeeeeeooooow."

The sound was an appeal, like that of a cat wanting to be stroked.

"Meeeoooooooow! Meeeeeeeeeeooooooooow!"

A pause followed, then a shriek like that of a female cat in heat.

Iliana imagined that her hips swayed inside her coat at a wider arc than they had spanned the previous day.

"Woof, wooofff wooooooooooooooooofffff!"

She made an effort to contain the movements of her body.

"Grrrrrrrrrrrooooooooowwwl!"

Steadily, ever so steadily, she maneuvered her legs forward and tried her damnedest not to panic. She told herself that if ignored the man would go away. Yet she could not help but recall her brothers' notion that a woman's walk conveyed her sexual status and availability. If she had been penetrated, and recently at that, her hips would thrust forward and sway as if unhinged. If she remained intact, she would walk as if protecting what she foolishly deemed a treasure.

"Damn, girl! What does a man have to do to get a play?"

The voice was now to Iliana's left and level with her ear. She raised her head and gazed directly at the sun, wanting it to obliterate the man from sight or to render her a shadow invisible to his eyes.

"Oh, come on. Just tell me your name. Your name, that's all."

The man's voice was a slippery caress, insinuating itself under Iliana's clothes to slither along her flesh. Its intimate tone made her feel vulnerable and exposed, made her feel drawn into complicity although she had not said a word. Surely her walk had convinced him that she was loose. Otherwise he would not have followed her halfway down the block, would not have risked being spurned within clear sight of his friends.

"I can give you what you want," he murmured. "I can do it the way you like."

Whorish. That was how Iliana's sisters habitually described her walk. Wanton and inviting, conveying that she wanted to be fucked.

"Oh, I see. So you think you're such hot shit you can't even say a word?"

Iliana did not turn to face the man. Whatever he might take it into his head to do to her would occur whether she willed it to or not. His treatment of her had been preordained by fate, molded into her flesh, solicited by the provocative movement of her hips.

"Fucking cunt," he spit out, abruptly turning on his heel. "That's why bitches like you get raped!"

The cold, harsh glare of sun seared Iliana's sight, momentarily blinding her as the man's words echoed in her ears. Half a block more and she would reach the train station. Her thoughts remained as suspended as they'd been that morning when she entered her parents' bathroom to find, despite the fact that it was winter, hundreds of ants crawling from between the tiles. Spellbound by what logic denounced as an illusion, she had watched the ants invade. She had been sure that blinking would make them disappear. Yet each time she had, her eyes had opened to find more ants teeming from the floor. Ants which could not possibly have been there. Ants whose appearance suggested that her sister had succeeded in pushing her over the same edge past which she herself had tripped.

Iliana climbed the stairs to the elevated station. Her hands shook as she slipped a ten-dollar bill to the woman in the token booth, then gestured that she wanted only two. Having pushed herself through a turnstile, she went up a second flight of stairs to wait outside. She was oblivious to the cold, to the wind whipping her coat around her legs, to a youth mouthing kisses to her from across the tracks.

She walked to the far end of the platform and listlessly peered over the rail at an abandoned lot. The shantytown she had seen there the previous week was gone, leaving behind no trace of the lives she'd glimpsed or of the woman whose resentful stare had sent tremors of self-doubt coursing through her brain. That incident now seemed to her to have occurred to the someone she had once been, ages back. Thrust since then into a state where time was measured by the lapses between her heartbeats, a week and a half was an eternity during which she had learned to recognize reality as an ever-shifting and precarious realm where her sister could transform into the terror of nightmares; her mother could shape-shift right before her eyes; her own body could be violated and nonetheless survive; ants could surface by the hundreds in the midst of winter.

Iliana moved back from the rail. Reluctantly, she recalled how she had tried to summon the courage to step past the ants toward the tub only to then wonder if she were going mad by accepting as real what could not possibly be there or by doubting what she perceived. According to her mother, her sister saw things too. It was seeing spiders which had made Marina set fire to the kitchen. It was a certainty that her body sprouted mold which had made her take Brillo pads to her arms and legs.

The possibility that she too had lost her mind sent Iliana out of the bathroom in search of corroboration for what her eyes conveyed.

She found her mother at the kitchen sink. Unable to form the words to ask for help, she stood silently behind her.

"What? What was that?" Aurelia asked, turning as if she had heard her speak.

Iliana managed to gesture in the direction of her parents' room.

Lines of concern fanned out across her mother's brow. "Yes?"

"I—I think— There are—I saw—"

Aurelia headed into the bathroom without waiting to hear more. Only on hearing her shriek had Iliana resigned herself to the freakishness of life.

A J train pulled into the station. Iliana stepped inside and remained on board until Delancey where she transferred to the F. One stop later she emerged in Manhattan and made her way toward the building on Second Street where Ed was staying. She rang the buzzer to his apartment, then did so again to no avail. The extraordinary willpower with which she had risen from the couch

that morning, had kept from bolting out of any room her sister occupied, had bravely stepped out of her parents' house and remained calm despite a stranger's harassing her halfway to the
station, dissipated as she tried the building's front door to find it
locked. Suddenly, she felt too weary to attempt going to Central
Park alone, to get herself back home, to do anything at all.

Her body folded onto the stoop. Her thoughts turned in from
the cold stealing under her clothes, turned in from curious passersby staring at her as they walked by, turned in and retreated from
consciousness to the lethargy she had struggled against since the
previous night.

Seconds slipped into minutes, then into hours. Iliana's gaze settled on a centuries-old cemetery across the street. Its few tombs
stood forlorn, their white stark above the brown brittleness of
grass. Indifferent, she watched the sky above the cemetery darken
and descend over the graves as if it could not continue holding itself aloft. Its somber shade seeped into concrete, stone and brick,
tingeing them grey and lending them a mournful appearance that
prevailed even after lights flickered on along the street.

"Excuse me." A stranger's hand tapped Iliana's shoulder. "Are
you waiting to get into this building?"

Iliana glanced up to find a woman drawing keys out of her
purse.

"It's cold as a motherfucker out. If you want, I'll let you in so
you can wait inside."

Iliana teetered to a stand.

"You okay?" the woman asked, peering at her face.

Iliana managed a slight nod.

"You sure?"

She forced herself to meet the woman's gaze. "Yeah, I'm fine."

Inside the building, a corridor appearing not to have been
painted since the turn of the century led to marble stairs caked
with dirt. Iliana gripped its ornate metal rail and struggled up five
flights. She then turned left and walked past a series of doors in the
direction of her friend's apartment.

"Ed?" she murmured, pressing her lips against the sliver of a gap between the door of his apartment and a wall. "Ed?" She rapped her knuckles on the door, then listened for sounds coming from inside. "Ed, please. I need to talk to you. I need—"

She hit the door with the flat of both her palms. Although she knew full well that her friend was not at home, she could not help striking the door again, could not help shattering the silence threatening to corrode her tongue.

"Ed, I was— Last night I was—"

Iliana was barely able to draw breath. Fighting dizziness, she leaned her forehead against the door. Her head grew unbearably light; her muscles went powerless and slack.

"Ed, I was—I was attacked, Ed. Last night I was a—attacked."

Her brain tried to absorb the impact of that single word. Attacked. Was that what she'd endured? Was that the term for her pinned body, for the fist jammed in between her thighs, for the pain that had ripped through to her very core? Could any of it be labeled such considering that she had stopped fighting midway through and had remained in her basement room, causing the onslaught to begin again? Could her sister—her sister? Sister. That was the word that stuck in her craw, the word that prevented her from speaking to anyone about what had occurred. Sister. The mere definition of the word chilled her blood and made her heart murmur, with each apprehensive beat: *no no I will not have this life I will not have this blood which also flows through my sister's veins I will not have it daily reminding me of the feel of her intrusive hand of its fingers tinged with red of her weight upon my own.*

Iliana crumpled to the floor. Had she possessed the courage, she would have cut herself open to witness the spilling of her own blood. She would have hurried home, thrust her slit wrists before her parents, told them: "This here is the problem, this blood in my veins which my sister has made me despise just as she has despised her own." She would have severed the cord connecting her to her sister and enabling her to understand, even in the midst of her own despair, why it was that Marina hated her so. She was the prodigal daughter who had returned, the one her parents now proudly offered up as an example although in leaving she had broken most of the rules by which she had been raised, rules her sister had abided by and had received no recognition for.

The tears, when they fell, streamed so fast that Iliana did not bother to wipe them dry. Each of her reasons for returning home was shadowed by the knowledge that her sister would have preferred for her to stay away and by the sudden realization that she had returned not so much to help as to be embraced. She had wanted, more than anything, to belong. Having spent years plotting how to leave only to discover, when she finally did, that she felt as displaced out in the world as in her parents' house, she had made the decision to return and to re-establish a connection with her family so that, regardless of where she went thereafter, she would have comforting memories of home propping her up and lending her the courage to confront the prejudices she had encountered during eighteen months away. Yet she could not now conceive of being able to interact with the members of her family or even of making her own way through the world should she again leave the only home she knew.

A light in the living room had been left on. Iliana noticed it as she stepped toward the house. She inserted her keys into the front door. She was conscious not only of having disrespected her parents by staying out unescorted after dark, but also of having committed an unpardonable sin by seeing to her own needs on the one day God had set aside for Himself.

Quietly as she could, she stepped inside the house. She was in the process of locking the door when she heard someone entering the hallway. She immediately swung around. Her father stood before her, his eyes shot through with what appeared to be either rage or the last traces of sleep.

"Bendicíon, papá," Iliana murmured, greeting him with a request for blessings as she had done throughout her life.

His arm swung up so fast that she had no opportunity to move out of its reach.

"Shameless hussy! Whore!"

Iliana heard the sharp sound of his palm as it landed on her face. Yet she felt no pain, only rage. Rage potent enough to swell her veins and cause one of them to throb rebelliously on her forehead.

"It's not bad enough one of your sisters has gone and lost her mind and another has crawled back to her husband. No! You have to stay out till all hours of the night like you too have no sense!"

Papito again lashed out with the strength of his accumulated anger and frustration. Iliana remained where the force of his hand had knocked her against a wall. The words "hussy" and "whore" resounded in her ears, overriding pain and searing a path along her brain.

"I don't care what you did while away at school! But as long as you live under this roof you will abide by my rules and by God's!"

Iliana stood ever so still in front of the father whom she suddenly despised. Her blood coursed vehemently through her veins. Her soul reclaimed every inch of her body as her thoughts coalesced into a stream of silent vows.

NoNo. I will not fall or flinch. I will not let you or anyone else ever knock me down again. I may have been molded from your flesh but this body is mine and mine alone. You will not make me be ashamed of it as my sister did. You will not make me recoil from it or renounce my life as I thought I would do. I will survive all this. I will walk out of this house erect. I will amount to more than you can ever hope to be and you will rue the day you saw me leave.

Her resentment surged like sap, lending her the strength to withstand each blow of her father's palm.

"Oh my God! You have gone mad!"

Papito's arm froze midair at the sound of Aurelia's voice.

"How could you, Papito? How could you?" she asked, flinging arms around their daughter to shield her should he decide to strike again.

Papito turned to Iliana who had still not moved. He turned to her with wide and startled eyes. Just turned to her as if he'd only then emerged from sleep and was surprised to find her there.

"I—" His arm dropped to his side.

Iliana gazed at him with insolent and unforgiving eyes. As a child in the Dominican Republic she had shouted, "Papi! Papi!" and had run outside each time a plane had flown over their house. She had then cried inconsolably when informed that her father was not coming back, at least not then. Looking at him now, she silently denied that she had ever loved him as her memory claimed or had once cried tears of longing for his sake. No. The man standing before her was as much of a brute and stranger as the man who had followed her earlier that day. Like him, Papito knew nothing of who she was. If he'd had any inkling, he would not have called her "whore," would not have struck her, would not have treated her as if she'd actually been found in a latrine and was not his progeny as her siblings often teased for the sheer pleasure of witnessing her grief.

"Are you through?" she asked, her tone venomous enough to convey to her father that she meant more than was he through with her and meant as well was he through with life, with pride, with the righteous man he had believed himself to be.

Papito's lips parted, flapped, hung open like a wound. Satisfied that he'd been utterly defeated, Iliana drew away from Aurelia to pass him by.

She left the hallway and made her way through her parents' bedroom into the adjoining bathroom. Standing before a mirror, she inspected her face as she had not dared to do since the previous night. Already bruises were swelling where her father's hand had struck; blood was coagulating on her lips knocked against her teeth.

Iliana spit blood out into the sink. Resolve directed her movements as she collected her toiletries from a cabinet and carried them into the living room.

"Forgive him, Iliana María. He didn't know what he was doing."

Iliana dumped her things on the couch before turning to face her mother.

"That's what you said last night. Marina didn't know, now Papi didn't either. But I'm supposed to know, right? I'm supposed to understand and be able to take in everything they do."

She lifted onto the couch a suitcase she had lugged up the basement stairs that morning. She then stormed past her mother to snatch her clothes out of a closet in the dining room.

"Well, I've got news for you. I'm sick and tired of trying to understand and of waiting for others to consider me. You think I never get angry enough to want to hit everyone in sight? But no, that privilege is not for me, I'm supposed to exercise self-control."

"What about me?" Aurelia asked. "Don't you think I get tired too? Me, who has to be here for everyone every single day?"

Iliana shrugged.

"Mi'ja, please."

"He called me 'whore.' "

"If you leave now, pride will prevent him from letting you back inside this house."

" 'Whore.' Like I was some floozy who'd walked in from the street."

"He didn't mean it, Iliana. You know that deep down in your heart."

Iliana stuffed her clothes into the suitcase. "I went away for a year and a half and came back a virgin only to—only to—"

"Mi'ja, please. We're going to get help. Your father and I already discussed it. First thing tomorrow morning we plan to—"

Iliana shook her head. "It doesn't matter. I can't live here anymore."

She and her mother held each other's gaze. The space between them resonated with what neither could bring herself to say.

"Where will you go?" Aurelia finally asked.

Fatigue settled on Iliana. She watched her mother struggling to appear calm. It dawned on her then that should Aurelia die she would have to refer to a photograph to remember the details of her face.

"I'll go to Ed's in the morning. Afterward, I'll probably go back to school."

Aurelia's lips thinned with the weight of the sorrow she was attempting to swallow whole. "We tried our best, mi'ja," she murmured. "Don't hold it against us if we didn't always manage to do right."

Iliana dropped her gaze from her mother's face. Yet even Aurelia's legs, roped with varicose veins, revealed a vulnerability she had not wished to see.

"I know," she said, although she actually had her doubts. "I know you did your best."

The sun was barely up when Iliana woke to a sensation that someone watched her. She immediately clutched the blankets and searched the room. Her father leaned forward in a chair he had dragged to inches from the couch on which she'd slept.

"I was—" His voice broke off when she sat up rigidly on the couch.

"You—you scared me."

In the dim, grey light of dawn it appeared to Iliana that her father winced. She watched him slump against his chair. Half-moons of perspiration showed on his sleeves. His heavy-lidded eyes indicated he'd gotten little sleep.

"How long have—have you been up?"

Papito did not reply. Although he sat so close that Iliana could have reached out a hand to touch him, she had the distinct impression that his spirit had traveled far away.

"You . . . were . . . three," he murmured, his voice so gravelly that it sounded as if each word had been strenuously unearthed. "Three . . . and . . . barely . . . higher . . . than . . . my . . . knees."

Iliana glanced at a clock at the far end of the room.

"Three and already getting into trouble with a curiosity that—that nothing scared you out of."

"Papi, please. It's not even—"

"You—you used to drive your mother half out of her mind. I remember how one time you ran into the house with a tarantula you were so pleased to have caught that you plopped it onto her lap. At your age, any of your sisters would've run screaming from anything that crawled or hopped. But not you." Papito paused as if in wonder. "You used to chase anything that moved. It didn't matter if it stung or bit. You were so hardheaded that you rarely thought about the consequences."

Iliana rubbed the last traces of sleep out of her eyes. She was indignant that her father had disturbed her sleep to tell her accusatory tales on the morning after he had tried to knock the sense out of her head.

"I remember how you cried when I killed the spider. Just cried and cried, not understanding it could've been poisonous and might've hurt you."

Agitated, Iliana glanced toward the kitchen in the hope that her mother, usually the first to wake, would rise and persuade her father to return to bed.

"That night your mother and I didn't sleep. We were so worried that we kept going into your room to see if you showed signs of being sick. But luck was on your side. Despite your foolishness, you slept peacefully and woke up the next morning as good as new."

The hand that had rested on an arm of Papito's chair slid to his lap. For a moment, he gazed listlessly out of a window.

"You would've thought that seeing us so afraid would've taught you something. But no more than a week had passed when you slipped out of the yard where we thought you were playing with your sisters. We found you hours later. You were more than a mile away throwing twigs into the river and giggling as you watched them tumble downstream. You could've drowned out there by yourself. Yet there you were, laughing and having yourself a good old time, laughing and showing no fear of being out there all alone. I was so relieved to find you and so angry that you'd put yourself in danger that I pulled your dress up right then and there and whacked your butt. You didn't even cry. You were three years old and you didn't even cry. What you did do was shut your eyes real tight until a vein showed on your forehead from the effort you were making not to cry. You only opened them when I pulled your dress back down. The look you gave me then made my blood run cold. It was like—like an adult was looking at me out of your eyes. An adult who knew exactly what she'd been doing and judged me as if I were the one who had done wrong. I'd noticed that look before, but never as clearly as on that day. Never as—"

Papito appeared to grope for words.

"I mean—you—you didn't even know half of what I knew. You didn't know about all the things that could hurt you bad. Yet you had the nerve to look at me like you knew all there was to know about the world. You—you had the nerve to look at me like I was the one who had no sense and had gone out of my way to hurt you."

Papito choked out a mirthless laugh. Iliana's blood simmered in her veins.

"But I hadn't set foot into the river."

Her father turned to face her.

"What?"

"You beat me, and I hadn't set foot into the river."

Papito looked at her as if she had entirely missed the point.

"You didn't that time, but you could've next."

"I was gone for hours and you found me throwing twigs. Just throwing twigs. Nothing more."

"You were three," Papito said in a tone that begged her to understand. "Anything could've attracted your attention and had you tumbling in to grab it as you usually liked to do. You couldn't have known the river was strong enough to pull you under and smash you against rocks."

"I must've known or—"

"You were headstrong even then. I had to teach you a lesson so that you'd learn to be afraid. Without fear, anything could've happened to you. It was my responsibility to teach you about danger and keep you safe."

"But I—"

"It was just like with the spider. I had to teach you that not everything was for you to play with. I had to—"

"The spider wasn't poisonous!"

"You didn't know that."

"Didn't I?" Iliana retorted. "Tell me, did I ever pick up anything that actually hurt me or someone else?"

"No, but—"

"Couldn't that mean I somehow knew instinctively what was dangerous and not?"

Papito averted his gaze from Iliana's. "You were three years old. Only three."

Silence descended between them, leaving Iliana more resentful than she had been at the outset of her father's tale. She watched him with unforgiving eyes. With his profile turned toward her, she appraised him as she would otherwise not have dared to do. She took a long, hard look at the deeply etched wrinkles on his brow, at his corneas yellow as the yolks of eggs, at his sagging cheeks and lips sunk into the cavity of his mouth because he had neglected to insert the false teeth he nightly stored in a glass of water beside his bed. To her surprise, she also observed that he'd lost weight. She had been accustomed to thinking of him as a sturdy man. Yet the flesh on his arms hung loosely, and his collarbones, glimpsed above the neckline of his T-shirt, appeared frail enough to snap. He had also gradually shrunk with age so that it now became apparent to her that she was in fact taller than the man she had held in awe for the greater part of her life.

Papito ran a vein-mapped hand through the dyed black hair that had deceived Iliana into believing he was younger than sixty-five.

"I wanted——" he began. "I wanted so much for my children. I never imagined that . . ."

Iliana barely paid attention to his words. She found herself recalling how, as a child whose father had flown away to a New York as distant and reputedly glorious as the heaven he had taught her to believe in, she had prayed not to a white-bearded God but to a Papa God whose face she had imagined as that of the father whose return she had waited for every day. This father, she'd been told, had gone on to prepare a better way. This father, her mother had repeatedly assured her as a means of comforting her, would someday make all of their dreams come true by sending for them to join him in that distant land to which most people longed to go. As a consequence of this information, Iliana had endowed him with powers no human could possibly possess. The longer he'd stayed away the more magnificent she had made him out to be. It was to this imaginary father that she had compared Papito upon her arrival in the United States. It was out of his failure to measure up that her resentment toward him had eventually been born.

Looking at him now, Iliana for the first time recognized him as no more than an old and very tired man. Irrationally, she had persisted in seeing him through the eyes of a child who had believed herself to be at the mercy of a father both as daunting and almighty as the God she had long ceased believing in. She had also continued to judge him by standards higher than those by which she judged others and herself. As her father Papito was supposed to have been the paradigm of perfection. He was supposed to have borne her aloft if she grew weak, braced her with a steadfast love, watched over and encouraged her when she stepped out into the world and again when she returned. If necessary, he was supposed to have shed his blood to deliver her from harm. He was supposed to have been free of the base emotions to which humans were all prey as well as impervious to the effects of the world in which they lived.

". . . no English and not even a dime to spare. You don't know how difficult it was. There were times when . . ."

Papito's posture remained that of a man conscious of having failed his children and fostering no hopes of being redeemed before their eyes. His tone was one of disillusionment, not with any of them but with himself. Listening to him, Iliana suddenly understood that it was himself he'd been blaming all along. She understood as well that he was more afraid of the world than she herself had ever been.

"I would've done anything had I thought . . ."

The resentment Iliana had been nurturing as if it was what would give her strength to live dissipated in the face of her father's fear. She dropped her gaze to his hands lying palm-up and empty on his lap. Those hands were actually no larger than her own. Those hands which had struck her with so much force were no more powerful than her own. Recognizing this gave her an indication of her own strength and opened her up to the possibility of forgiving him. Yet it also presented her with full responsibility for her life. If she could neither depend on him to save her nor blame him for her existence, any difficulties she encountered from then on would have to be hers to work out on her own.

"You see, I couldn't—"

Iliana reached for her father's hand. Any additional words he'd meant to speak caught in his throat as she silently weighed his sporadic violence against the devotion with which he had grown frail working to support a family of fourteen. That each of his children had made it into adulthood without falling prey to the lure of the streets he feared; that, with the exception of one whose madness he could have done nothing to avert, each continued to carve out a life in the best way each knew how, was proof to her of the good example he had tried to set.

Papito tenderly clasped her hand. Drawing her to him, he embraced her with the force of a love all the more powerful for its flaws. Although Iliana knew that she still had to leave, she did not pull away. Like her mother's and father's too, her soul had transformed into a complex and resilient thing able to accommodate the best and worst. Everything she had experienced; everything she continued to feel for those whose lives would be inextricably bound with hers; everything she had inherited from her parents and had gleaned from her siblings would aid her in her passage through the world. She would leave no memories behind. All of them were her self. All of them were home.

Acknowledgments

For their support, I thank The New York Foundation for the Arts; Ragdale Foundation and the U.S. Africa Writer's Project; Djer-rassi Art Colony and Henry Louis Gates, Jr.; Cottages at Hedge-brook; The MacDowell Colony; Yaddo; and The Millay Colony for the Arts, Inc. For encouragement and much more, I thank my agent, Susan Bergholz. For her patience and absolute belief in me, I thank Kathryn Court.

For friendship in its truest form, I thank Bruce McNally, Jandy Nelson, Teresa Stack, David Ehrich and Steven Greenstein.